DOUBLE PLAY

AN EXTRA INNINGS NOVEL

AK LANDOW

Published by Author AK Landow, LLC

ISBN: 978-1-962575-11-9

Edited and Proofread By: Chrisandra's Corrections

Cover Design & Illustration By: K.B. Designs

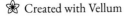 Created with Vellum

DEDICATION

For my father and husband who support women's athletics wholeheartedly. Both of you have spent countless hours teaching and coaching women's sports. You've left an indelible impression on hundreds of girls and women who have felt seen, supported, and empowered by you, one that continues to have positive impacts on all their lives, mine included.

"Confidence is a superpower. Confident little girls grow up to be empowered women."
~Unknown

BASEBALL/ SOFTBALL GLOSSARY

WORD/PHRASE	DEFINITION
Can of Corn	An easy to catch fly ball to the outfield
Gun Them Down	Throw out a baserunner with a strong throw
A Dime	Incredibly straight, accurate throw
Talk Turkey	No-nonsense talk about a topic
Ejected	Thrown out of game for violating rules
World Series	Annual Major League Baseball championship
Squib Ball	Ball hit with very little force
Pop Time	The time from when the ball hits the catcher's glove to when it hits a fielder's
Beaning	Ball purposefully thrown at batter
Free Agent	When a player's contract is over and they're free to sign with another team

AK'S BASEBALL/ SOFTBALL GLOSSARY

WORD/PHRASE	DEFINITION
Third Base Coach	Dirty Talk
The Bull Pen	Self pleasure
Pitcher's Mound	Anal sex
Backdoor Slider	Accidental anal
Switch Hitter	Bisexual
Home Dugout	Your bedroom
Away Dugout	Their bedroom
Helmet Buffing	A blow job

PROLOGUE

LAYTON

I punch the back of the seat in front of me and shout into my Bluetooth earpiece, "Are you fucking kidding me, Tanner?"

The Uber driver turns around and gives me a dirty, disapproving glare. I hold up my hands in surrender and mouth, "Sorry."

In my ear, I hear my longtime agent respond, "I'm sorry, Layton. It came directly from the Greene family. Barring some miracle, they're not planning to renew your contract after this season."

"How can they treat me like this? The Greenes are like family to me. I used to spend holidays with them. I've dedicated fifteen years to the Philly Cougars and they're not going to let me finish my career here?"

He's silent.

"What is it, Tanner?"

"Well...umm...maybe you should finally consider

retiring. I know we've briefly discussed it in the past, but perhaps it's time to formulate a legitimate exit strategy. You'll finish your career as a Cougar. I'm sure they'll be on board to make it seem as though it's your decision to walk away from the game. They wouldn't deny you that dignity. We can focus on the next chapter for you. You're wildly popular in Philadelphia. We can probably get you a lucrative deal in the broadcasting booth or coaching. And you know I'm always fielding offers for you to promote products and brands."

I blow out a breath. "I'm only thirty-four. There's more gas left in this tank; I know there is."

He sighs. "I love you like a brother, but it's a fact that you're the oldest player on the team, Layton. You're not performing like you once did. You should be happy they haven't benched your ass yet. In reality, if the rookie catcher hadn't hurt his shoulder, you probably wouldn't be starting right now."

I know he's right about that, and I appreciate that he always shoots straight with me. "Is there anything I can do to change their minds?"

"I don't know, man. They seem pretty set on this. When the team owner tells the General Manager that he refuses to re-sign you, there's not much the GM can do. His hands are tied. I suppose if you start playing like you did a few years ago, that might help. But they said they won't be having any more conversations about it with me in the near future. It means you've got the second half of the season to prove yourself. It's the all-star break right now. You have a few days off to think about things before the rest of the season kicks into gear. Give the final three months everything you've got. Leave nothing on the table."

"I hear you. I'll do my best. Thanks."

"Sure thing. What are you up to tonight?"

I probably shouldn't tell him that I plan to drink excessively and find a hottie to take home. "I'm meeting a few guys from the team for a beer."

"I see. Well, whoever you take home, make sure she looks good on camera. We wouldn't want your reputation as Philly's favorite bad boy to take a hit. The hashtag *laidbylayton* is trending. It's good for your brand."

I let out a laugh. "Will do. I certainly don't want to let down my fans."

"Seriously, you get a lot of money to make appearances at clubs because of the type of women you attract. Stay on brand."

I cringe. I hate the club appearances, but it's easy money and I know my playing days are numbered. I need to capitalize while I can.

"I'll try not to disappoint you. What are you doing tonight?"

"I have Harper this weekend. She wants to hit the batting cages tonight."

I chuckle. "I love that she's a little tomboy. Tell her hello from Uncle Layton."

"I will. Thanks. Have fun."

"Later."

We hang up just as the Uber driver pulls up to Screwballs, a longtime favorite watering hole for Cougars players. The owners keep it relatively lowkey and ensure we're not bombarded by fans. We have a standard table roped off from the rest of the crowd.

Screwballs is by no means a club, but they always have a local band playing cover music. The younger guys on the team usually gravitate to the more traditional clubs, with us older guys hitting this place. By older, I mean over the age of thirty. Not exactly real-world old but, unfortunately, professional baseball old. I only go to the clubs when I'm being paid to do so. It's not my scene anymore.

I walk in and see my boys already at our table. I pull down my hat so I'm not recognized and bombarded as I make my way over to them. They all smile and nod in acknowledgment when they notice me approaching. My eyes find Ezra Decker, Quincy Abbott, and Cheetah, our nickname for speedy Cruz Gonzales.

I sit next to Quincy at the end of the circular booth. "How are things looking tonight, Q?"

He wiggles his eyebrows. "I love this place. There's a lot of talent here."

I turn my head and look around. He's not wrong. There are several attractive women. Nearly all are wearing form-fitting jeans and cropped, midriff-bearing, tight tops. That seems to be the uniform of the women that come here. Several are already on the makeshift dance floor, swaying their hips, facing our direction. A table of professional baseball players usually garners a lot of attention.

Even though Quincy is new to the team this season, he's fast become my closest friend. After me, he's the oldest on the team. We have a lot in common and immediately clicked. When he moved here in the off-season, Harold Greene asked me to spend time in the gym with him. It naturally led to forming a friendship well before the season even started. Now we're like old friends who have known each other for years.

I look around. "Did Trey make it out tonight?"

Ezra shakes his head. "He texted earlier that they're

unlikely to come." He smiles. "You know what that means."

I sigh. "Shit." We have a self-imposed team rule. Whoever arrives last to anything has to give everyone a random fact. Quincy brought it to the team as a bonding thing and an incentive to be on time. It's become a fun tradition and I've honestly learned a lot.

Cheetah nods his head. "Let's hear it."

I smile. I've been holding back on this one for a week, dying to share. "Sitting on a sea turtle is a third-degree felony in the US."

They all start laughing. Quincy shakes his head. "I have so many questions about the logistics of doing that."

For the next thirty minutes, we crack several sea turtle jokes, but I notice Q constantly looking at the door. I ask, "Are you waiting for someone?"

He shrugs. "I thought my sister was coming by tonight. I guess she didn't make it. I suppose it's not her scene anyway." He mumbles, "At least not anymore."

"Your sister? I didn't know your sister was visiting. She lives in Southern California, right?"

"She did until this week. She just moved here a few days ago. Because of our travel schedule, I haven't even seen her yet." We had road games all week, just arriving back in Philly late last night.

He looks like he's going to say more when he points to a woman who's been staring at him since I walked in. "She looks good to go. I'm going after that. I'll catch you guys later."

Quincy is known for bailing early and leaving with women. I may be known for *Laid by Layton*, but *Hit It and Quit It Quincy* is worse than me. He's just newer to town so he's not as well known. The girls love his West

Coast blond, messy surfer look. He likes them *very* curvy. He has a clear type.

He slides out of the booth and makes his way to the woman. I see him whisper in her ear while she giggles the whole time. He grabs her hand, and they make their way out of the bar. I can't help but internally laugh at how quickly he makes it happen.

While I'll end my evening leaving with a woman, I prefer to enjoy a few hours with my friends before I do so. I also like to have more than two minutes of conversation with them before we make a night of it.

Just after he leaves, Trey and Gemma walk in. Trey is our teammate and Gemma is his wife of a few years. He's tall, with light brown hair like mine, while hers is dark brown and very long. They're an attractive couple and may have the healthiest relationship I've ever witnessed in my life.

They smile when they see us. I stand to greet Gemma. After kissing her cheek, I say, "Wow. You look amazing. I can't believe you had a baby a few months ago."

Her face lights up at the genuine compliment. "Ooh. Keep talking."

Trey wraps his arms protectively around her waist. "Stop hitting on my wife."

I smile. "Can't blame a guy. You've got the best one out there." I'm not kidding. Gemma is incredible. She's beautiful, smart, sweet, and treats us all like brothers. She likes to dress a little fancy at times, though appearances can be deceiving. A lot of our teammates make fun of Trey for always bringing her out with us, but she's like one of the guys. She can hang.

"Dude, you're still hitting on her."

I wink at them while they slide into the booth. Trey

immediately throws his arm around her, letting everyone know who she's with. He's always done this with her, even when they were dating.

I shake my head. "You're such a caveman."

"One day you'll get it. I'm going to fucking rip you apart when that day gets here."

"Unlikely. I'm the oldest unmarried man in the entire league." I straighten my collar. "I have a rep to protect."

Gemma laughs as she nuzzles her body into his. "His possessive side is such a turn-on. Women love that. Me in particular."

He bends his head and kisses her neck. "*Everything* about you turns me on."

She swivels her head, and they kiss. Not a peck. An open mouth, deep kiss.

Oh boy. Here we go. I thought having a baby might simmer things down for the two of them. If anything, it's getting worse.

Cheetah shouts, "Gemma, you're giving me a chub. Tone it down."

She and Trey smile into each other's mouths as they break apart.

She raises her eyebrow. "With all the romance novels you read and the porn you watch, it's Trey and me kissing that does it for you?"

We all burst out laughing. It's well known among the team that Cheetah loves to read romance novels and watches a ton of porn. We often draw names out of a hat as to who's forced to share a hotel room with him on the road. He watches porn all night long. It's disturbing.

He rubs his hands together. "You would love the book I'm reading right now. It's sexy and sassy. The banter is chef's kiss. The main characters just had sex in the bucket of an excavator."

Gemma scrunches her nose. "Eww. That sounds dirty."

He wiggles his eyebrows up and down. "It was. In the best way possible."

She giggles as we change subjects and chat about nothing in particular for about an hour. I always have fun with this group. I truly love my teammates. I can't imagine playing anywhere else. I'm suddenly hit with a moment of sadness. This could be my last three months with them. My family. The only true family I have left.

At some point, I excuse myself and go to the bathroom. As I turn the corner, I notice a table of women laughing. They're tucked away, completely removed from the action of the bar. While women laughing isn't unusual, what stands out is that they're all in sweatpants and hoodies. Their hair is in messy ponytails, and they don't have on any makeup. It looks like they just came from soccer practice or are coming from the gym. I don't think I've ever seen women in here dressed like that. It's always women dressing like they're on the prowl for professional baseball players, wanting to put their best foot forward. These women don't give a shit.

After using the bathroom, I walk out and notice a blonde at that same table whose back was to me earlier, but I can see her face now. She's effortlessly gorgeous. Stunning.

Something her red-headed friend sitting next to her just said made her laugh. Too bad Quincy left. The redhead is exactly the type of woman he likes, curvy and outgoing.

Blondie snorts in laughter. So fucking cute. I find a

genuine laugh to be incredibly attractive in a woman. I hate it when they fake laugh. And her smile. It's breathtaking. *She's* breathtaking.

I decide to head over to their table. As I approach, I give them a smirk. Admittedly, one that often works in my favor. "You ladies look like you're having the best time of anyone here. Will one of you tell me what's so funny?"

The redhead's blue eyes widen. "Holy shit. Layton Lancaster. You're even hotter in person."

I shrug. "I suppose that's better than the alternative."

She giggles as she holds out her hand. "I'm Ripley. It's nice to meet you, Layton Lancaster."

"You don't have to say my full name. It's just Layton." I take her hand and kiss it. "It's nice to meet you, Ripley." I stare at the blonde next to her. "In all honesty, your friend's beautiful smile and *distinguishable* laugh caught my attention. I had to come over here to meet this stunning person."

While Ripley seems impressed, blondie does not. She rolls her eyes. I hold my hand out to her. "And you are?"

She practically snarls at me. "Not interested. This isn't the Layton Lancaster groupie section. You have no chance of hitting a home run at this table. Move along to the skanks who are no doubt fighting with each other to dance within eyesight of your booth, praying to get a whole three minutes of your *undivided* time and attention."

I let out a laugh. That's kind of true. The women here do often jockey for position so they can be within our sight.

I lean over and whisper in her ear, "I promise it lasts way longer than three minutes." I stand back to my full six-feet-four-inch height. "And I guess you noticed me too?"

She pinches her eyebrows together in confusion.

"You knew I was in a booth."

She grimaces, knowing she's busted.

Ripley elbows blondie. "Excuse my friend." She points to the women on the other side of the table. "Let me introduce you to the gang. These gorgeous ladies are Bailey and Kamryn. Before you ask, yes, they're twins."

Oh shit, she's right. They're identical, with stick-straight, jet-black hair and big brown eyes.

The one that she indicated was Kamryn gives me a sexy smile. "To be clear, I might be offering a home run later."

She's beautiful, but it's blondie that caught my eye. Before I can reply, Ripley continues, "And Ms. Mannerless next to me is Arizona."

"Arizona? Do you have the kind of parents who name their kids after the place they were conceived?"

Arizona quirks an eyebrow as she sarcastically replies, "Wow, I've never heard that one before. I've never even thought about it. Perhaps I should ask my brother, Tex, and my sister, Georgia. Maybe they have the answers."

I can't help but chuckle at that.

I hold my hand out to her again. "How about a dance, Arizona?"

She shakes her head. "I'm going to pass. We just arrived and ordered our drinks. I'm here to hang out with my friends. Run along. Find someone else to play with."

I'm not known for pushing. Frankly, I never have to. "I hear you loud and clear." I nod at them. "You ladies have a good night." I wink at Arizona. "If you change your mind, I *know* you know where to find me."

With an unexpected flare of sadness, I walk over and rejoin my friends in our booth. We have a few rounds of drinks and enjoy ourselves, as always. I, admittedly, have a bunch of women making it clear that they're interested, but there's only one woman here piquing my interest tonight.

About an hour later, the song "Shivers" by Ed Sheeran starts playing. The dance floor quickly fills, including Arizona and gang. The four of them are laughing and having a great time, clearly having had several drinks since I last saw them. They're all a bit wobbly and giggly.

I can't keep my eyes off Arizona. Even dressed down, she's the most beautiful woman in this bar. The fact that she doesn't even try makes her all the more attractive to me.

There's something about that smile of hers. It's got me in a trance. She's looking a little more carefree than she did earlier. Maybe she's lightened up now and will dance with me.

Gemma follows my line of sight. "She's not your usual type."

"What do you mean? She's gorgeous."

"She's not wearing a *come fuck me* sign. In fact, just the opposite. That's a girl who's here to have fun with her friends, not prowl for ballplayers."

I give her my panty-melting grin. "The chase is half the fun."

I start to stand but she grabs my arm. "She's not a one-night-stand girl. Even I can tell that. Stay in your lane."

11

Is that all people think of me? I've been friends with Gemma for over four years. She probably knows me better than any woman in my life, and this is what she thinks? I suppose I've never given her a reason to think otherwise, but it still stings.

I pull away. "I'm capable of more. I just haven't found the right one yet." I hope.

"She's clearly had a lot to drink. Don't push it."

I look at her feeling a bit hurt. "I *never* do."

Her face softens. "I know. I'm sorry."

I walk away, annoyed, and head to the dance floor. I place my hands on Arizona's hips from behind. She starts to turn around, but I hold her tight to keep her in place. I bring my front to her back and whisper in her ear, "Just give me one dance, sunshine."

I see the little hairs on her neck stand at full attention. She takes a deep breath. "One dance, superstar, then buzz off."

It's hot when she calls me superstar.

I'm only now realizing that she's tall. I didn't appreciate it when she was sitting. I usually tower over women, but I don't with her. She's only six or seven inches shorter than me. I don't often meet women this tall.

We move in unison to the fun beat of the song. She gradually lets loose. We're having a good time, both smiling as we dance the unofficial "Shivers" swing.

I love her smell. It's not some fancy perfume. It's natural. It's almost like the ocean. There's something else to it that I can't put my finger on, but it's unique, and I'm into it. *Very* into it.

When the song is over, she turns around. I can see that her eyes are greenish blue like mine. I bet they change color depending on what she's wearing or when she's in the throes of ecstasy. I know mine do.

She smiles shyly. "Thanks for the dance. It was fun. Have a good night."

I gently grab her arm before she can walk away. "Can we go somewhere and talk?"

She shakes her head. "No. I don't date baseball players."

"Why not? We're not all bad."

"A lifetime of intel suggests otherwise." She appears sad when she says it. "And cheesy pickup lines don't really do it for me."

"Cheesy? I said you have a beautiful smile and laugh. That was honest. If you want cheesy, I'll give you cheesy."

The corner of her mouth raises. It's adorable. "Give me your worst, superstar. What's the cheesiest line you've ever used?"

"Hmm. Let me think." I scratch my chin. "I've got one. *Well, here I am. What are your other two wishes?*"

She snort-laughs again. "Oh my god. That's terrible. Women don't fall for that, do they?"

I grin. "You'd be surprised how often it works. God, I love your laugh. It's so genuine."

Something in her face softens. I think I'm making headway.

A slower song begins to play. It's "Until I Found You" by Stephen Sanchez. I hold out my arms. "One more dance? I promise I won't bite...unless you want me to."

She rolls her eyes. "I told you, I'm not into baseball players."

"Why is that?"

"You're all inherently selfish. Career and libido above all else. I know your reputation. You're the worst of them all, love them and leave them Layton. Or wait, what's the hashtag?" She smiles. "*Laidbylayton*. I have no interest in being one of your many hashtags. I'm not a one-night-stand person. You are. Go find someone who's interested."

"How about one more dance to prove you wrong? If I fail, I won't bother you again. I promise I'll leave you alone after that unless you ask me to stay."

She sighs. "One last dance and then you promise to leave me alone? For real?"

"If that's what you want, yes."

She nods and I pull her into my arms. It's hard to hear over the music, but I think she sighs. I can definitely feel her relax into me.

I'm enjoying the sensation of her body on mine. I'm usually staring at the top of a woman's head when dancing, but not with her. She's not even wearing heels, but I can still sink my nose into her neck and take her in.

She tilts her head ever so slightly, giving me more access. I don't think it was a conscious move, but it happens. All hope is not lost. She's attracted to me; she just doesn't like my reputation. I can work with that.

Our bodies are pressed together, her arms around my neck. I whisper in her ear, "You're so beautiful."

She squeezes me a bit tighter. I can feel her breasts pushing against my body. I can't truly see her body in the oversized clothes she's wearing, but I'm dying to explore every inch of her.

The song ends and a fast one starts playing, but we don't stop moving as we were. We continue to sway to the slow beat of the previous song, lost in our own world.

She looks up at me. "I shouldn't admit this, but I think I'll blame it on the three drinks I've had tonight.

When I was a teenager, I had a poster of you above my bed. You were my favorite ballplayer."

I can't help but feel good about that revelation. "*Were*, as in past tense?"

She hiccups at the same time she says, "Yep," and then snort-laughs again. She's definitely had a few drinks.

"I'm determined to win you back as a fan."

She smiles. It's so damn perfect. We stare at each other. We're having a moment. I know she feels it too.

My nose moves along her cheek until I reach her lips. I give her a soft kiss and she allows it. I'm about to push the kiss further when the music comes to an abrupt stop.

The owner takes the microphone and looks straight at me. "Boys, check out the televisions."

He motions for the bartender to turn up the volume. The televisions in this bar only play sports channels. They're all tuned to ESPN, which has something scrolling about breaking news from the Cougars organization.

I pull away from Arizona and look at the screen. Before I know it, Harold Greene, the elderly owner of the team, takes the podium.

"Good evening, everyone. What I'm about to say may come as a shock to most of you, but after careful consideration of both my failing health and my family's wishes, we have decided to sell the Cougars."

Holy. Shit. I turn and look at my teammates. They appear as stunned as I am right now.

He continues,

"I didn't take this decision lightly. I want to make sure the team is in good hands. The right hands. The Cougars have been sold to a group consisting of three families, two of which are lifetime Cougars fans, and the third family are longtime trusted friends of mine. Without any further delay, please allow me to introduce the new owners. The Daulton, Windsor, and Bouvier families have purchased the Cougars organization. Effective immediately, they are the new owners of the team. The deal was finalized this evening. I know they will take care of my baby.

"Thank you all for over fifty years of loyalty. No fans are better than Philly fans."

He holds up his hand like a paw, the traditional Cougar salute.

"Claws up, Cougars."

He steps off stage. I see an attractive blonde woman in a business suit take the stage and walk toward the podium, but I can't hear a word she says. My head is spinning, and my ears are ringing.

I feel my phone vibrate in my pocket. Taking it out, I see that it's Tanner. I immediately answer as I walk toward the front door and outside so I can hear him better.

I answer, "Holy fuck."

"Did you see it?"

"Yes, everyone in Screwballs saw it. What does this mean for me?"

"I don't know, Layton, but the new owners want to

see you first thing tomorrow morning. They've already contacted me."

"Did they say why?"

"No clue, but it can't be good. I hope they're not releasing you. You need to prepare yourself for the worst. They don't ask for meetings like this to offer good news. Get your ass home and get a good night's sleep."

I hold my hand up for a cab and get in. "Already on my way."

"Be at the stadium at nine sharp. No fucking around. You need to be on your best behavior."

"I got it. I'll see you then."

As I ride in the cab on the way home, it hits me that I just abandoned Arizona. I played right into the dialogue of what she thinks about baseball players, me in particular. I'm such an asshole. I guess it doesn't matter. I won't see her again. I don't even know her last name.

Damn. I was attracted to her. There's something different about her.

THE NEXT MORNING, I arrive at the stadium fifteen minutes early. Tanner is waiting for me by the front door to the executive offices. He's in his mid-forties, with salt and pepper hair. He had aspirations of playing professional baseball at some point, even playing at a local college. When he realized that wasn't happening, he went to law school so he could become an agent. I was one of his first clients. I was eighteen when I met him. Even though he's only nine years older than me, he's become like a father figure to me. The only one I've ever known.

We walk inside together, and he rubs my back. "Are you okay?"

"I'm just in shock."

"I think the entire baseball world is in shock. No one saw this coming. Let's head to the conference room. They said to meet them there. Whatever they say, we'll manage our way through it." He places his hand on my shoulder. "You have options, Layton. I'm here for you. No matter what goes down today."

"Thanks, bro. I appreciate you always supporting me."

I look around, suddenly feeling nostalgic knowing this might be the last time I'm in the stadium I've called home for over fifteen years. What will I do with my life? The Cougars are all I've ever known. I can't imagine living anywhere but Philly. I don't want to.

We walk into the conference room and see six people waiting for me. I immediately recognize the attractive blonde woman from the television last night. In person, she looks like a model, not a businesswoman, though she's dressed in a nice pantsuit. She's probably close to my age. Maybe even younger. Wow.

She looks at Tanner. "We want to speak to him alone. Can you wait in the hallway?"

Tanner looks to me for approval and I nod. I walk in and she closes the door behind me before holding out her hand. "Hi, Layton. I'm Reagan Daulton. This is my husband, Carter." She points to a mountain of a man who looks like a football player in a business suit. He must be a former professional athlete that I've just never heard of. "This is Beckett Windsor and his fiancée, Amanda Tremaine." I recognize Beckett. I think he's known as the richest man in America. I've seen him in gossip rags. He's a little older than everyone else. His fiancée is a good-looking brunette who appears to be pregnant. "And this is Auburn and Gianna Bouvier. They're from New York. Gianna will handle the accounting for the Cougars moving forward, but they'll otherwise be a bit more hands-off, as they live in New York City." I recognize Auburn too. He looks a few years older than me, but his wife is *way* younger. There must be some daddy issues there.

I shake everyone's hands. "It's nice to meet you all."

I have no idea why I'm their first order of business, but I'm nervous as hell. My hands are shaking. I sit down in a chair at the table and am about to ask what I'm doing here when the conference room door opens. Everyone turns to it.

My eyes just about pop out of my head. "Arizona?"

She looks equally shocked to see me, but then she gives me that scowl I remember from last night when I met her at the table. If looks could kill, I'd be fish food right now.

Reagan says, "Oh good. You know Arizona Abbott. I guess that makes sense with her brother being on the team."

Her brother? Her brother is on the team? Abbott. Oh shit. She's Quincy's sister. I suddenly remember him mentioning her last night. A sister that just moved to the area. A sister that was supposed to come to Screwballs.

Reagan continues, "Well, I'm thrilled you know each other because we've got a very unconventional proposal for you. One that will require you two to spend a lot of time together. Intimately."

CHAPTER ONE

ARIZONA

My cell phone begins ringing and it feels like a hammer to my head. Too much tequila last night. I slowly peel my eyes open and glance at the clock. Ugh. It's seven in the morning. Who the hell would dare call at this hour? I reach over and lift my phone, noticing a familiar name. Why is my coach calling me on our one day off? That's odd.

In a groggy voice, I answer, "What's up, Coach Billie?"

In her slight southern drawl, she says, "Hey, Arizona. I apologize for the early call. I know you girls were hoping to finish unpacking your new apartments today, but I just got the strangest call that required me to reach out to you."

"No problem. What do you need?"

"I need you to head down to the Cougars stadium for a meeting at nine."

I sit up, a bit startled. "The Cougars? The baseball team? Why? Who will I be meeting there?"

"Yes. I don't know why, but I do know that it's with the new owners. Did you hear that the team was sold last night?"

Did I hear? Hell yes, I heard. Layton fucking Lancaster bailed on me without a single word the second he heard. What a dick. I should have known better. Damn three drinks loosened my senses. Ugh, and I let him kiss me. What was I thinking? Tequila brain. I'm blaming it on that.

"I heard. Why do they want to meet with *me*?"

"I don't know, but I need you to go. It came directly from management."

I blow out a breath. There go my plans for the morning. "No problem, Coach."

"Thank you. They said to go in the executive entrance and ask for the main conference room. Call me afterward and let me know what they wanted."

"Will do."

We hang up and I sigh. What in the world could they want with me? The Cougars are a billion-dollar franchise that's been around for nearly a century. The Anacondas are a brand-new softball team barely worth the cost of our new uniforms.

I hear a creaking noise and turn my head to see my bedroom door open. Ripley walks in wearing a long T-shirt, the same one she's worn since college. It was her college boyfriend's shirt. She doesn't care about him, but the shirt reads *I Love to Eat Out* and it has a stick figure woman sitting on the face of a stick figure man. She stole it from him on the way out the door and has worn it to bed most nights since.

She looks around. "Damn, you're alone."

"Um, why wouldn't I be?"

"I heard you talking. I was hoping it was to a man."

I moan, "Argh. I barely remember what it's like to have a man in my bed. I think I'm a virgin again."

She giggles as she crawls into bed with me and lays her head on a pillow. Her face turns serious as she tucks my hair behind my ear. "You've got to let the past go, babe. We're in a new city. It's a fresh start for you."

My eyes fill with tears. I whisper, "I wish it didn't still hurt so much."

"It's been over a year since the breakup and...everything else. It's time to move on. It's time to get yourself out there. It's time for my real best friend to come back to us."

"It was more than a simple breakup, Rip."

"I know. But it's still time to put it behind you. Onward and upward." She smiles and her face looks hopeful. "Layton Lancaster seemed *extremely* into you."

"Layton Lancaster is a manwhore. He's the exact opposite of the kind of man I want. No baseball players." I make a slash through the air with my hand to reiterate my point.

"But he's so hot and I know you used to dream about him. I'm not asking you to marry the guy. Just fuck him." She bites her lip and mock shivers. "I bet he's amazing in bed. He could fuck the re-virgin right out of you."

"He's certainly had plenty of practice." I mumble, "Fucking *#laidbylayton* is practically trending all the damn time. It's pathetic."

"Who *were* you talking to just now? If it was your vibrator, I'm staging an intervention."

I let out a laugh. "It wasn't Captain America."

She scrunches her nose in disgust. "It's weird that you named your vibrator Captain America."

"Why? He's the sexiest superhero ever."

"Debatable. I'm more of a Thor fan. I love his hair. Actually, come to think of it, Layton Lancaster sort of looks like Captain America. Is he the reason for the name?"

In a high-pitched voice, I squeal, "What? No he doesn't

look like the Captain." He totally does, but I'm not admitting that there may be a correlation between the two.

She gives me a look suggesting she doesn't believe me. "Do you dream about getting railed by Captain America? The real one."

"Hmm. Maybe a little bit."

She laughs. "Who was it on the phone this early in the morning?"

"Coach Billie. She said that management wants me to go to the Cougars' stadium this morning for a meeting with the new owners."

"The Cougars? Holy shit. What for?"

"I have no clue." I look around at all the boxes in my room. I know there are plenty more all over our apartment. "I'm sorry I have to bail for a few hours. I'll help unpack when I get home."

She waves her hand dismissively. "It's fine. I don't mind. You're pretty useless anyway."

I smile. Ripley is a clean freak. She hates that I'm not. "You'd probably prefer I not be here so you can put things where you want them."

"Very true. Have you...umm...talked to your brother? I thought we were going to see him last night."

I swear she's always had a thing for him, but he's five years older than us and has never given her the time of day. He sees her as a little sister. "He was *supposed* to meet us. That's why we went to Screwballs after practice. I guess he never made it, or he left before we got there. I suppose we were running late. I'll catch up with him this week. Maybe tonight for dinner or tomorrow for breakfast."

"Gotcha. Sounds good."

All of a sudden there's a loud pounding at our front door.

We hear Bailey's voice. "You guys need to come see this. Hurry up!"

We exchange baffled looks before jumping out of bed, running to our apartment door, and opening it. Bailey is standing there shaking her head. "Kam has officially gone off the deep end. Literally." She motions for us to follow her to the apartment next door that she and Kamryn share.

We walk through to Kam's bedroom. As we enter, we see her spread out on her bed with her hands behind her head. The bed is rippling, as is her body on top of it.

I gasp. "Is that a freaking waterbed?"

Kam smiles. "It sure is. I've always wanted one. Now I can afford it."

She presses a few buttons on a remote control, and it lights up in a variety of neon colors.

Ripley shakes her head. "Is it the eighties? Are we in a time warp? Do adults actually still own waterbeds?"

I laugh. "I'm just glad we're not in the apartment below them. With the amount of sex she has, that bed will definitely pop. I hope you bought bed insurance."

Kamryn is very sexually open to say the least. She doesn't care if it's men or women. She freely moves around from person to person without a second thought or regret. I wish I had a sliver of her courage. I suppose I used to, though I never quite reached her level of uninhibition.

Bailey scoffs. "It's going to sound like *Finding Nemo* in here every night."

Kam giggles. "I'm hoping for *Point Break*, with hot guys surfing on top of me. Or maybe *Blue Crush*, with hot girls surfing on top of me."

Ripley pushes on it a few times and it ripples. "How do you get into a rhythm on this? Or worse, what if you're out of rhythm?"

Kam shrugs. "I don't know. I'll be sure to do a lot of research so I can let you know." She taps her lip for a moment. "Maybe I should indulge in some *solo research* before I bring in another person." She air quotes *solo research*.

She begins to pull down her pants.

I grab Ripley. "Ugh. Let's go. We don't need to see this."

Ripley shrugs. "I kind of want to see how it goes down on the waterbed. I'm fascinated by the logistics of it all."

I start toward the bedroom door. "I'm getting dressed and heading out. I'll see you guys later. Enjoy watching Kam get herself off on her fish tank."

Bailey and Ripley giggle as they follow me out the bedroom door and close it behind them.

A FEW MINUTES BEFORE NINE, I make my way into the stadium's executive entrance. A guard shows me to the conference room. When I open the door, my eyes look around at a few familiar faces from the television last night until they land on *him*. Layton *fucking* Lancaster. Asshole extraordinaire, sitting in a chair, with a *cat got your tongue* look on his face, while blurting, "Arizona?"

A blonde woman who I recognize from the press conference last night smiles at me before looking back at Layton. "Oh good. You know Arizona Abbott. I guess that makes sense with her brother being on the team."

The look on Layton's face tells me he had no idea that Quincy was my brother. I know they're close friends. Q talks about it all the time. Layton is so self-absorbed that he didn't even know the name of his best friend's sister. It's not like it's a run-of-the-mill kind of name.

The blonde woman rubs her hands in excitement. "Well, I'm thrilled you know each other because we've got a very unconventional proposal for you. One that will require you two to spend a lot of time together. Intimately."

Intimately? What the hell does that mean? What is going on here?

I'm about to ask these questions when the blonde woman approaches me and holds out her hand. "Arizona, I'm Reagan Daulton. Thank you for coming in on such short notice. It's nice to finally meet you. I'm a huge fan. I've followed your career."

I tentatively shake her hand in return. "I honestly have no clue what I'm doing at this stadium in this conference room. My coach told me I needed to come here at nine this morning but didn't tell me why."

"I promise to clear up all confusion. Come meet everyone, and then I'll explain."

After introducing me to everyone in the room, which consists of six billionaires, I'm asked to sit in a chair next to the president of the douchebag club, Layton Lancaster.

He smiles as I sit. He's got some nerve smiling after his disappearing act last night. I almost fell for his charm. Those fucking eyes and that chiseled, square, sexy jawline almost got me. *Never* again.

Layton's eyes toggle among all the owners. "Can someone explain what's happening here?"

Reagan nods. "Allow me. Layton, are you familiar with the Philadelphia Anacondas?"

"Umm, it sounds familiar. I think I've heard it mentioned a few times. Is that the name of the new professional women's softball team?"

"It is. We quietly started a new team here this season."

I pinch my eyebrows in confusion. "We? You're the silent

owners?" So far, we haven't been given the name of the owners. We were told it was forthcoming before the season officially starts, which is next week.

She nods. "Yes. The same three families who now own the Cougars also own the Anacondas. We didn't want that to go public until the Cougars purchase was finalized. We'll issue a press release about it later today."

I'm confused. "Why did you want to start a pro softball team in Philly? Especially if you were already buying the baseball team."

She smiles. "I like thinking women." She steeples her fingers. "The women's professional league is struggling financially. Right, Arizona?"

Unfortunately, that's a true statement. I nod in agreement. "It is. We're not sure whether or not the league will remain in business after this season. That's why we were surprised at the expansion team being created. None of this makes any sense."

"I understand your trepidation. Know that softball is near and dear to me. My mother played in college. We have a grand plan that ties into our purchase of the Anacondas. The Cougars are beloved. We're going to turn this town into *both* a baseball *and* softball city. It's going to start with cross-promotion and synergy between the Cougars and Anacondas. We're going to use the Cougars to help the Anacondas gain a dedicated fanbase. One we hope will eventually become equally devoted. Layton, do you know much about softball?"

He shrugs. "Not really."

Of course he doesn't. Dickhead.

"The balls are bigger, right?"

I smirk. "Yes, our *balls* are *way* bigger than yours."

Reagan lets out a laugh before continuing. "Arizona is well known in the softball world. She may be the most popular player in the sport. That's why we did everything we could to get her on our team."

The truth is, I was offered a lot of money to come here, about double what I would have made this season with my California-based team. Getting a fresh start away from everything that happened this past year was beyond appealing to me. And they promised to sign Ripley, who was playing for a team out of Texas. She and I haven't played together since college nearly six years ago. I was dying to play with my best friend again. Playing in the same town as my brother was another incentive. All of that combined made coming to Philly a no-brainer for me.

Reagan continues, "While the fanbase for professional softball is significantly smaller than that of professional baseball, it's loyal and diehard. She's one of the best players in the league. Layton, you're the baseball darling of this city. You're practically a Philly treasure. You're not only a ballplayer, but you're also a celebrity."

She pauses as if Layton and I should understand where she's heading with this. It's clear that neither of us do.

"Layton, we want you to use your celebrity to help the Anacondas gain attention. Arizona is going to be the face of the Anacondas franchise. Imagine the excitement and press that would surround you two as an item."

My chin drops in astonishment. What does she mean? She can't be suggesting that we date. "I'm not dating this asshole. I might be getting a sexually transmitted disease from simply sitting this close to him."

Layton winces. "While I can assure you that I'm disease free, I have to otherwise agree with Arizona. I'm not into forced relationships. I'm not even into relationships."

I hate that his words sting. Dickwad was singing a different tune last night. Though I suppose I should have known he just wanted to get into my pants to add to his *#laidbylayton* count.

Carter Daulton cocks his head to the side. "To be clear, we don't care if you actually date. In fact, we prefer you don't. It only complicates things. We simply need you to *act* like it. Publicly. This is purely a PR relationship. They happen all the time. Way more than you know about."

I smack my hand on the arm of my chair in frustration and astonishment. "This is absurd. I'm a professional athlete. I've worked my ass off my whole life to get where I am. I'm not someone you can whore around. I don't care who you are or how much money you have. Go to hell."

Reagan lets out a laugh. "I fucking love you, Arizona. I dig strong women. That's one of the many reasons I want the team and the league to succeed. Young girls need women like you to look up to. I understand your concerns about a fake relationship. More than you know."

She looks at Carter and something passes between them before she turns back to me. "I don't control the simple fact that women's professional softball is struggling. I don't control the fact that it might not exist in a year from now. I'm trying to fix it. I'm trying to get Cougars fans interested in softball. Imagine what it would be like if we could get even a small fraction of Cougars fans to attend Anacondas games. By my math, the Anacondas would be considered wildly successful if we were to convert roughly fifteen percent of Cougars fans into Anacondas fans too. I'm sorry to be blunt, but sex sells. I'm not asking you to have sex, just look like you are. With the way you two appear, you'll be Philadelphia's sweethearts. With any luck, maybe even America's sweethearts. Mark my words."

I'm speechless, having no words for this insanity.

After a few moments of awkward silence, she sighs. "Why don't you sleep on it? I'm not forcing you into this. I'm hoping you'll come to realize that it's for the best. The only thing I ask is that you keep it among the people in this room. As soon as even one other person knows, it will spread like wildfire."

I shake my head. "Not that I'm agreeing to this, but if I do, my brother will have to be in on it. He knows I would never date someone like Layton. It's not the kind of woman I am."

She nods her head in agreement while Layton shuffles in his seat before asking, "Not to be an asshole, but what's in it for me? Why would I care about the Anacondas' success?"

Beckett Windsor clears his throat to gather our attention. He's the oldest person in the room. I'm guessing he's in his upper forties. He's insanely attractive. If I had a daddy kink, I'd be very into him, though he's been pouring his pregnant fiancée a glass of water every two minutes and encouraging her to drink it. She keeps rolling her eyes at his hovering. Honestly, the way he dotes on her is kind of endearing.

"Layton, we're well aware that the team was planning to release you at the end of the season." What? "We're prepared to offer you a three-year contract extension if you help us with this side project. You'll get to finish your career as a Cougar. Your salary won't be quite as much as you're earning now, but it will be in keeping with what you'd get anywhere else. The paperwork is being sent to Tanner Montgomery's office now. Our expectations are laid out clearly in the document. Arizona, we don't have an agent of record for you." Because I don't have one. "A copy of the pertinent terms in Layton's contract was sent to you as well so you're clear on our expectations for both of you."

I turn to Layton in a bit of shock. He appears embarrassed. I almost feel bad for him. Layton Lancaster has been the face of the Philly Cougars for well over a dozen years. I remember when he first came into the league, making a huge splash. A baseball prodigy with all-American good looks and a tragic backstory. His face was everywhere. I was thirteen and, like every teenage girl, especially softball players, Layton Lancaster was my dream guy. Not that I'd ever admit it to him.

He nods in understanding. "I'll take a look at the contract, discuss it with Tanner, and get back to you."

Beckett turns to me, his face softening. "We have a seven-year-old daughter. Her name is Andie. She has your poster in her room. You're her idol. Andie, and girls just like her, are the reason we're doing this. It would be a crime for the women's professional softball league to fold. When Reagan brought this plan to us, we were immediately interested. I not only wholeheartedly believe in Reagan's business prowess, but also want to do my part to see to it that you ladies get to continue doing what you love and inspire the next generation of women, like my daughter, to do the same."

I nod. "I understand. I hope your daughter will be at our games this year. I'd love to meet her."

He smiles. "Nothing could keep her away, and I appreciate the sentiment. She'd most definitely like that."

Reagan stands. "We're all on the same team, working toward the same goal. I think we've given both of you some things to consider, but we need this to be quick. The Anacondas' season starts next week."

I want some more clarification before I consider doing something this absurd. "I know I'll be sent his terms, but can you explain exactly what would be expected of us in day-to-day layman's terms?"

"I can. When you don't have your own games, you need to attend each other's games. Layton appearing at Anacondas games will draw a crowd. You attending Cougars games feeds the dialogue of your relationship, which I have a feeling people will be excited about. Your schedules are tight, but any nights off, we'll need you to appear out and about like a normal couple. Maybe even a few lunches since you have a lot of night games. You basically need to appear like a normal couple spending time together. Oh, and I'm in negotiations with *Sports Illustrated*. They're doing a couple's body image issue, similar to what they did a few years ago. I'm pitching them on another dual-sport couple, like they did with Zach and Julie Ertz in that first issue."

My eyes widen. "I might be in *Sports Illustrated*?" It's the most well-known sports magazine in the world. Being in it is basically the dream of every athlete.

"Possibly, but they need to think you're a couple. The body image issue is only for couples."

This could be huge for the sport of softball. Everything she's saying will help my team and my league. As much as I don't want to do this, I know I probably need to.

I'm more concerned about being around Layton. He's my childhood crush, but he's a womanizer and no good for me. He was flirtatious last night, and I fell for it. I need to be strong and put an end to that. Whatever it takes.

LAYTON

My mind is reeling. This is the craziest thing I've ever heard. I was obviously attracted to Arizona last night, but she's venomous toward me today. How am I supposed to pretend to be in a relationship with her? Is this what my all-star career has come down to? What a joke.

Auburn Bouvier looks between Arizona and me a few

times. "Just to be clear, neither of you can see anyone else during this time period. In any capacity."

I spit out, "What? How long is this expected to go on?"

He answers, "Through the season. The softball season ends around the same time as yours, so approximately three months, give or take a few weeks depending on playoffs and the like. It's all spelled out in your contract."

I haven't gone three days without sex since I was fifteen. Three months is impossible.

Reagan interrupts my thoughts. "The all-star game is in New York City tomorrow. Tonight is the formal cocktail party. I've arranged for us all to go. Why don't you two test the waters? It can be your coming out party as a couple. We'll see how the press reacts. But I need you both to play your part. Even if you ultimately decide against this, for tonight, you need to make it seem as though you're a new, happy couple. Arizona, I have a hair and makeup crew coming to your apartment at three. Carter's assistant, LeRond, will stop by with an appropriate dress for you. The limo will pick Layton up at six and then you after that. Layton, please take a look at the terms of the contract this afternoon. We have a very specific part we need you to play, which includes a lot of Anacondas promotion."

I should probably keep my mouth shut until I read the contract and talk to Tanner, so I simply agree to go to New York tonight and walk out of the room.

Tanner stands as soon as I exit. "A contract just came through. What the hell is this shit?"

I sigh. "It's complete and total insanity. Let's go somewhere else and talk about it."

Twenty minutes later, we're sitting in his office. He's

scanning the terms of the contract on his computer. "Fuck, Layton, I've never seen anything like this."

"They want to trade on my name and my notoriety to generate interest in the Anacondas. It's plain and simple. They're admittedly using me, but they know they've got me by the balls. The money is way less than I'm making now, but probably about the same as I would get on the open market as a free agent. This way I get to finish my career here in Philly, like I wanted. Either I uproot my life and try to earn a few more pennies elsewhere, or I accept this offer and know I get to finish my career where I want to. You're the lawyer. Tell me if I'm missing something. I personally don't see any way around it."

He nods in agreement as he continues reading the fine print. "If you fuck up in the slightest, they can void this contract and release you."

"Tanner, you've known me for fifteen years. Tell me if there's any other option that doesn't include me leaving Philly."

He blows out a long breath. He knows I'm right. "Is this Arizona chick the same blonde that walked into the conference room right after you?"

"Yes.

"She's smokin' hot."

"She's also Quincy's sister. I met her last night. I hit on her. Full court press. I didn't know she was his sister at the time. I didn't know anything about her other than she's gorgeous and sassy. She fucking hates me though. Was a total bitch to me today. She said she doesn't date ballplayers."

He lets out a laugh. "I like her already." He scratches his short beard. "Is it that big of a deal to parade around town with a hot chick for a few months? You'll get what you want if you do."

I stare out the window. "Something doesn't sit right with me, but my hands are tied. Philly is my home. I don't want to leave. Even when I retire, I plan to stay here." In a solemn voice, I admit, "I have nowhere else to go."

He nods. I know he understands. "Layton, you can't sleep with her. You know that will screw up everything. If things go south, they *will* void this contract. They have no reason not to. They've given themselves an out if you make any missteps. You're their puppet for the next few months."

I sigh. "I don't think I'm at risk of sleeping with her. She legit hates me." She was practically staring daggers at me throughout the entire meeting.

"That's good. Make sure it stays that way. They're basically paying you as an investment in the Anacondas. That's what they care about. Carefully read Paragraph Eleven. You need to promote the shit out of Arizona, the Anacondas, and softball in general. Do a little research on softball this afternoon. It's similar, but not the exact same as baseball."

"You would know better than I would." Tanner's seven-year-old daughter plays softball and is obsessed with it.

"I would." He places his hand on my shoulder. "You can avoid all these shenanigans and simply retire. I know your knee hurts more than you're letting on."

"My knee is fine." It's not fine, but if I start voicing knee issues, I know that will be the end of my career. "I'm not ready to retire. I'm doing this. Let the insanity begin."

CHAPTER TWO

ARIZONA

On the way back to my apartment, I think about what just happened. It's crazy but, on some level, I honestly get why they're doing it. I want professional softball to take off as much as anyone. As irritating as he is, Layton Lancaster's endorsement and promotion could truly help our sport. I hate being dependent on him, but I can't argue the fact that he's a famous star. Philadelphia fans worship the ground he walks on.

I decide that I absolutely can't keep this from Ripley. She's been my best friend for over twenty years. She'll smell the bullshit immediately. I trust her to keep the secret. I'm going to need to lean on her when things get tough, and I know they will.

I get home and explain everything that went down in the meeting. She sits there completely dumbfounded. "Wow. That's one of the craziest stories I've ever heard."

"I know. Please don't tell the twins. They can't keep a

secret, especially Kam. Just let them think we met last night and are now dating."

"No worries. Thanks for telling me." She gives me a compassionate half-smile. "It's not so bad to have to parade around town with that hottie. Maybe you'll finally get some action."

"I don't want a guy like Layton Lancaster, Rip. He's nothing but trouble. This is a business arrangement, that's all. I need to give him that message loud and clear."

"What do you have in mind?"

I smile. "I have a few ideas."

AFTER BEING PLUCKED and pampered for hours, I'm ready for our first public outing. Ripley smiles at me as I examine myself in the mirror in disbelief. "You look beautiful. Wow. Just, wow."

The most eccentric man I've ever met, LeRond, brought over a very low-cut, turquoise, sequined dress that hits me above the knees. *Well* above the knees. Apparently, one of the owners, Auburn Bouvier, is a famous designer, and he designed this dress specifically for me. LeRond said that movie stars clamor for his creations and that I should feel honored to be wearing it.

LeRond had Ripley and me in stitches while he managed to touch me more intimately than any man has in over a year as he poured me into this dress. I don't think he meant anything by it. His husband, Avery, was with him, helping.

My makeup has never looked this good in my life. My long, blonde hair is wavy and styled. I usually wear it up, but it's down and looking its glowing best now.

I adjust the bustline. "I feel very exposed, like my nipple could pop out at any moment. You know I would never normally wear something like this."

She claps her hands together in excitement. "I know. That's why I love it. Stop fidgeting. Your tits look amazing, and they're glued in. They're not going anywhere. If I had your body, I'd walk around naked all the time."

I give her an incredulous look. "What are you talking about? You *do* walk around naked all the time. I've seen your naked body more than my own this week. I know firsthand that you're a natural redhead."

We both giggle at the truth of my statement. Ripley often walks around naked, without bothering to cover up. I love her confidence. She wasn't like that until after high school. Ripley is curvier and bigger boned than me. She always has been. Her being extremely self-conscious about her size and weight when we were growing up was a constant topic of conversation. I always reassured her, but she was uncomfortable in her own skin and would never reveal her body to anyone. That changed dramatically during and after college. She's objectively beautiful, with curly red hair, and I think she must have garnered a lot of attention when she lived in Texas. It's made her blossom, and I love to see it. She's attractive and perfect just as she is, and she's finally embracing that fact.

I can see her face light up in the mirror. "Admit you're at least a little excited that you're going out with the man whose posters you used to kiss when we were kids. I remember one of them being on the ceiling above your bed. You probably diddled Miss Daisy to him every night."

I can't stop the corners of my mouth raising just a bit. It's true. I was undoubtedly looking at his face the first time I came. The first hundred times.

She places her hands on her hips and raises an eyebrow. "I thought so."

I shake my head. "That's in the past. Unfortunately, the personality doesn't match the looks. This is a business arrangement to help our league. That's it." I'll be saying that over and over in my head.

She pats my back in a condescending manner. "You keep telling yourself that, sweetie."

Before I can respond, the doorbell rings. I run past her to answer it, as best as I can in these heels, and open the door to see Layton standing there in a traditional tuxedo fitted perfectly to his big body. Holy shit, he's hot. He's just so classically handsome.

His eyes move up and down my body. "Wow. You're stunning."

I raise an eyebrow. "Ripley knows we're a bullshit couple, Layton. No need for fake compliments in front of her."

He smirks. "Oh, well, then you're ugly as fuck. Does that make you happy, sunshine?"

Ripley starts laughing hysterically. "I like him. You two have fun." She kisses my cheek and whispers in my ear, "I'd fuck him in the limo if I were you. At least let him dally Miss Daisy."

I roll my eyes at her antics.

Layton holds out his arm for me, but I shake my head. "No touching unless someone is watching."

"Okay, but I find that someone is *always* watching."

I poke my head out and scan the hallway. No one is here.

Without grabbing his arm, I begin walking down the hallway mumbling, "Let's get this shitshow on the road."

We make our way out of my building and see a huge, black stretch limousine. We get in, and as the driver pulls out, Layton says, "We've got a ninety-minute ride. Maybe we should get to know each other a little bit. We're supposed to be a couple. There are certain things we should probably know about one another."

"You're right. As you learned only this morning, my name is Arizona Abbott. I suppose despite being good friends with Quincy for most of the past year, you never bothered to ask his sister's name."

He does appear a little embarrassed for not knowing. "I'm sorry about that. He never mentioned a name. I don't like talking about my past, so I tend not to ask people about theirs. I'll work on being better. How much older is he?"

"Five years. I'm twenty-eight, in case you don't know how old your *bestie* is."

He sighs in annoyance and then nods for me to continue.

"We grew up in a small Northern California town where our parents still live. We were a modest, middle-class family. We both played ball at UCLA but obviously not at the same time. Quincy was drafted after his junior year. I graduated and then played professional softball in Southern California until last week when I signed with the Anacondas."

"Why did you agree to come to a new, unproven team?"

"I guess, in part, I wanted to be closer to Quincy. We haven't lived in the same town since he first left for college. The other part is that my roommate, Ripley, is my childhood best friend. She moved from Canada when we were in elementary school, and we've been tight ever since. We played softball together through college. I was drafted to the Anaheim, California team, and she was drafted to the Houston, Texas team. Coming here was an opportunity for us to play and live together again. We can't play softball forever. This was a shot to finish our careers on the same team, just as we started them."

And I needed to get away from the nightmare of the past year.

"Houston? That's where your brother played his whole career until this year, right?"

I nod. "It is. I'm sure they saw each other around. They've always been on friendly terms. Kind of a brother and sister relationship."

"What position do you play, Arizona?"

"Catcher."

"Like me."

"I'm way better than you. I can gun them down from my knees."

He smirks. "I have no doubt you're good on your knees."

I narrow my eyes at him, but he simply keeps smiling. "What number are you?"

He gives me a look that suggests he knows the answer. He must have Googled me today.

"Same as yours. Eight."

"Did you pick it because of me? I know you had a poster of me above your bed. You looked at me every night before you went to sleep."

My big fucking mouth. I'm never drinking again. At least I didn't tell him that I did choose my number because of him. "No, I chose it because Yogi Berra was number eight, and he's the greatest catcher of all time."

His face lights up. "That's why I chose it too."

"What about you? What's your story? Other than the obvious things people know about you."

He briefly looks out the window. "I grew up in a run-down, small town in Oklahoma. As you may know, my parents were in a fatal car crash when I was a baby. I somehow survived it without a single scratch, but they didn't. I was raised by my grandmother, who was kind of quirky and spread thin but had a heart of gold. Things were a bit of a struggle, but we persevered."

I know this story. Most people do. It's been highlighted on ESPN many times throughout the years. How he overcame tragedy and poverty to become an all-star baseball player. A true rags-to-riches story.

He continues, "She ran a group home for kids without parents until she died when I was twenty. There were always little ones in and out of our house, waiting to be fostered or adopted. I keep in touch with a few of them. I was drafted out of high school, and I've been in Philly ever since." He looks down. "I know I'm headed toward the end of my career, but I think I still have a few years left in me. Philly and the Cougars are the only family I have. I'm not ready to give it up just yet."

"How come you never got married?" I've never even read about him having a girlfriend. I've known him for less than a day, and I can already tell he aches for a family and a sense of belonging.

"It's not a conscious decision. There's never been anyone special enough in my life to make me consider it."

"That's kind of sad."

"Your brother is a year younger than me and hasn't gotten married yet."

"Much to my parents' chagrin, I assure you. It's a constant topic of conversation in our house."

"What about you? You're not married either."

I look away, trying to keep the tears at bay that always threaten when this topic comes up. It's still so hard for me to talk about. "I was engaged once. It didn't work out."

He nods in understanding, mercifully not prying any further.

We continue to talk until we arrive at our destination. He's surprisingly easy to talk to and seems genuinely interested in what I have to say. I can't tell whether or not it's an act. I'm skeptical.

As we arrive at the party, I can see photographers roped off on a huge red carpet. There are several people dressed nicely, getting their pictures taken.

Layton asks, "Have you ever been to anything like this before?"

I shake my head. "No."

"It can be intense. Just stay close and smile. They're vultures. They capture every little misstep. Play it straight. Are you okay with me touching you? We're supposed to look like a couple."

"Is this just an excuse to touch me?"

He smiles. "A little, but I'm not wrong."

"I suppose. Don't abuse the privilege. I won't hesitate to throw an elbow your way or kick you in the balls."

He chuckles. "I'll do my best. I'll keep it to your back and hand, if that works for you."

I nod as I reach into my purse, grab what I brought with me, and shove it into my mouth.

He pinches his eyebrows. "What was that? It can't be what I think it was."

I smile. "If you thought it was a clove of garlic, you'd be right."

"Why would you do that?"

"Just making sure you don't kiss me again tonight."

"If I really want to kiss you, do you honestly think a little unsavory garnish will stop me? I spend my days with sweaty men in locker rooms. Not much gets to me." He places his hand on the door handle. "I'll get out first and help you out of the car. I wouldn't want you pulling a Britney."

I let out a laugh at his Britney Spears reference from years ago when she was exiting a car commando, and her dress rode up. The paparazzi caught it *all* on camera. Every exposed inch. "You mean flashing everyone?"

His unique blue-green eyes sparkle with mischief. "Exactly."

I sarcastically quip, "Wow, you're quite the gentleman. I bet you even catch the names of at least half the women you sleep with."

"You're way off. It's at least seventy-five percent. Maybe as high as eighty." He winks as he exits the car to a sea of female screams.

He stands there for a few minutes, smiling as he waves to the crowd. Flashes are blaring. It's insanity, but he looks right at home, like he's done this a million times before. He poses for multiple pictures from multiple angles, taking his sweet time. Not remotely caring that I'm sitting here waiting.

Eventually he turns back around and holds his hand out for me. I take it as he carefully helps me out of the limo, very cognizant of not showing my Britney.

I'm immediately blinded by flashes of cameras. They're shouting for Layton. "Layton! Who's the blonde beauty? What's her name? Are you dating? Is this your girlfriend?" They repeat the same questions over and over again.

Layton places his warm hand on the exposed small of my back. I can feel the callouses of a man who takes hundreds of swings with a bat each day. I'd be lying if I said it didn't make my body temperature rise a few degrees.

He looks straight at the reporters and photographers. "Shame on all of you for not knowing this talented woman. This is Arizona Abbott of the Philadelphia Anacondas. She's the best professional softball player in the whole country. You'll likely see her in the Olympics in four years." He flashes his huge, all-American, perfect smile. "I'm lucky she agreed to slum it with me tonight."

He leans over and whispers, "Smile for the cameras, sunshine. Our pictures will be all over social media within the hour. It's a good thing they can't smell your rank breath."

As if on autopilot, I immediately smile, holding my breath. I'm severely regretting the garlic decision. It feels like something died in my mouth.

They all start firing questions at me about softball. I can't make them out. My head is spinning at all the attention. This is nuts. I know for a fact that my brother doesn't garner this type of attention.

Layton gently guides me down the red carpet, stopping every few seconds for us to pose for the cameras. At some point, a reporter asks him if he's a softball fan.

He smiles down at me. "I am now. Whenever it doesn't interfere with my Cougars obligations, you'll find me cheering on Arizona at all the Anacondas games this season. Be sure to come out. We've got the best pitching and catching in the league. My girl can hit too. It's going to be quite a show."

I look up at him. Without losing my smile for the cameras, I manage to channel my inner ventriloquist and ask, "Did you do a little softball homework this afternoon, superstar?"

He looks down at me. "I studied up on softball. I know *everything* now. And I know you're the best catcher in the league and Ripley is the best pitcher. I know the twins play shortstop and second base. Reagan Daulton knew what she was doing when she created this team. You guys are immediate contenders. I also know that the distance to the pitcher's mound and between the bases is shorter than in baseball. I know that pitchers throw underhand from a flat mound, not overhand from a raised mound like in baseball. I know a full game is seven innings, not nine like ours. And your fences aren't as deep as ours."

I stare at him in shock. I wonder what his contract had in it that made him study so hard. That he suddenly seems all in. I know it's a facade, but I'm still impressed. They sent me a copy; I didn't have time to read it yet. I need to do that right away.

He moves his lips to my ear, whispering, "Be careful about calling me superstar. I know you think you're pushing my buttons, but it really just makes my dick dance in delight."

I'm speechless as he smiles innocently, intertwines his fingers with mine, and walks us through the door of the venue.

As if he didn't just mention his dancing dick, which I'm now staring at, he asks, "Did you study me too? I mean things on the internet, not what's happening below my belt."

My eyes snap back up to his, which are twinkling with amusement at having caught me staring. I take a moment to compose myself before answering, "I already know everything, Layton Eugene Lancaster."

He scrunches his face. "Ugh. No amount of money can scrub my middle name from search engines."

I giggle. "Your middle name suits you." I squeeze his hand. "I know you're a natural lefty, which is why you bat left-handed, but baseball isn't as forgiving of us lefties as in softball, so you learned to catch right-handed."

"You're a lefty too?"

I hold up my right arm so he can see my watch on my wrist. "I am."

He nods. "Us both being lefties could create a logistical problem for us in bed, but don't worry, we'll overcome it."

I'm about to kick him in the balls when I realize he's just messing with me. "I hope you remember what Auburn said. You can't date for the next three months. That left hand of yours is going to be getting a workout." I make a jerking motion with my left hand. I then do the same with my right, as I say, "You can switch it up sometimes and go righty. Maybe it will feel like you're with a new person. I suppose if you can handle one ball right-handed, you should be able to handle two. You do have two balls, right, Layton?"

He lets out a deep laugh. "You're funny. I like you. How about we become friends? I think the next three months will be a lot easier if we get along. You've made it clear that you don't want anything physical with me. Message received. I'm admittedly attracted to you, but I know deep down that it would be a mistake to start things with you given what we're supposed to be doing."

He looks down for a moment before looking me in the eyes. "I imagine you were a bit surprised today when they mentioned that I was going to be released after the season if the Greenes held onto the team. I only learned that fact yesterday. This is a second chance for me. I don't want to leave Philadelphia. I'm willing to do whatever it takes to hold up my end of the bargain. I'm only asking you to do the same." He holds out his left hand for me to shake. "How about a lefty shake on friendship?"

I pretend to think about his seemingly sincere statement. "Umm. I don't have any lefty friends. I suppose I could use one. To be clear, I'm only using you for your *leftiness*. Nothing else about you is appealing."

He smiles. "I understand completely. Thank you for your honesty." He intertwines his fingers through mine again. "Let's find the bar, friend. What do you like to drink?"

"I drink beer, like every other ballplayer." I scrunch my face. "Sometimes tequila shots like last night, but usually beer."

"I think I'm in love with you."

I shake my head. "You're already breaking the rules of our budding friendship. You took a lefty oath. I take that shit seriously."

"I've just never met a woman who drinks beer. Oh wait, I know one. Gemma DePaul. She likes fancy drinks *and* beer."

48

"Is that Trey DePaul's wife?" Trey is the Cougars' third baseman. I remember seeing something about them in the news a few years ago.

He nods. "It is. She's the best. You would like her. She's down to earth and normal. They're the most in love married couple I've ever been around in my life. They just had their first baby, so I don't know if she'll be at many games. Maybe we can go out with them on one of our fake dates."

"Let's see how tonight goes. You might not get a second date, superst...Layton."

He winks as he turns to order our drinks.

We enjoy our beers while I get to meet some of the most famous baseball players in the world, both past and present. I'm trying to remain calm while seeing so many of the idols I've had over the years.

At some point I see the Daultons walking over toward us. They're a ridiculously attractive couple. They look like Barbie and Ken. Well, if Ken swallowed another Ken doll. Carter is huge. He's built like Nick Bosa. He's got a beard, and his tux looks like it was painted on. They're holding hands, smiling at each other, obviously in love. How nice that must be.

Reagan smiles as they approach. "You look stunning, Arizona."

"Thank you. So do you."

"Thank you." Her eyes toggle between Layton and me and our close proximity. "Everything...okay between you two?"

Layton places his hand on my back. "My *girlfriend* and I are having a great time. She sucked on a clove of garlic just before we got out of the limo to remind me of our loving status."

Reagan and Carter smile at each other in amusement before turning back to us. "Are we good to move forward with our plan?"

Layton and I look at each other in silent agreement and then I turn back and nod. "I think we're both settled on it being right for everyone involved. We'll do our best to make it look real without compromising our own integrity."

Layton echoes, "I agree with Arizona. Tanner should have everything over to you tomorrow. He just wanted to make sure I returned home from this evening intact before finalizing the contract." He pinches his lips together, looking a bit choked up. "I know this isn't conventional, but I appreciate that you're giving me the opportunity to finish my career in Philly. It's important to me to do so. I promise to do my best to hold up my end of the bargain, and I also promise to give it my all on the field. I hope to truly help the team. It's a good group of guys. The best I've ever played with."

I have moments where I think Layton Lancaster is shallow, and then he says something like this, which makes me believe there's a bit more depth to him. Maybe I misjudged him. Maybe he's not such a bad guy.

I wonder why he feels so tied to this city. He's not from here. He has no family. Interesting.

Carter nods. "We're contenders this year. Your experience and leadership will go a long way. We're counting on you."

Reagan says, "I agree. I think the situation will be advantageous for everyone. In the happy news department, it looks like we're good to go with *Sports Illustrated*. Your shoot will be in six weeks. I'll have LeRond get you all the details. He's handling it from here."

I let out a laugh. "That guy is a riot. I don't like getting dressed up, but he made it fun today."

I see Carter's shoulders shake a bit in silent laughter. "He's been my assistant for fifteen years. He's a character."

"He is. Thank you. I'm excited about the opportunity with *Sports Illustrated*. It's a dream come true for me."

Reagan smiles. "You're very welcome. You two are going to look amazing in it."

Carter takes Reagan's hand and kisses it. "We're going to head out. It's rare we get a night away from our son. I want to fully take advantage of my wife." He says that with no shame and with fire in his eyes. And he didn't say *take advantage of the situation.* It seems he purposefully said *take advantage of my wife.*

Fucking hell, it just got hot in here. The look the two of them are sharing could burn a town to the ground. I'm looking at real, live, storybook passion playing out in front of my eyes. Proof it exists.

We say our goodbyes to them. When they leave, Layton shakes his head in disbelief. "That's how Trey and Gemma are. I've honestly never seen marriages like those two couples."

I fan my face, which must be bright red right now. "Me neither. I can't imagine that kind of passion."

He looks at me with surprise. "Your fiancé?"

I shake my head. "If I'm being honest, no."

"Do you want to talk about it?"

"If I'm being honest, no."

"Want to get out of here?"

"If I'm being honest, yes."

He chuckles as he takes my hand, and we make our way back to the limo to begin our long drive back to Philly.

CHAPTER THREE

ARIZONA

"Hey, Mom."

"How's my beautiful girl?"

"I'm good."

"You're more than good, sweetie. I saw pictures of you online this morning in a fancy dress, out with Layton Lancaster. You looked stunning, and he's *very* handsome."

Shit. I don't want to lie to her, but I also don't think she'd care for the truth. I think I'll be purposefully vague.

"Yes, we went to a party together last night. The group who bought the Cougars also owns the Anacondas. They set it up for us to attend together as *friends*."

"I see. Did I mention that he's handsome?"

I let out a laugh. "You did, and he is. But like I said, we're just friends."

"Hmm. Maybe that will change in due time. How's life in Philly?"

"So far, so good. I honestly haven't done much. Besides last night, I've mostly just had practice. And we're still unpacking, though Ripley got a lot done yesterday."

She giggles. "I guess Ripley is still a clean freak?"

"Most definitely. She practically picks up my clothes as soon as I drop them on the floor."

"Some things never change. How is that wonderful girl? I haven't seen her in ages."

"She's great. I'm so happy to be with her again. It feels very full circle."

"It is. I love that you two are together again. The dynamic duo reunited. I ran into her mother at the market last week."

"How is she?"

"Single and ready to mingle, like always." Ripley's mom raised her alone and constantly had an active dating life. Ripley used to be embarrassed about it but then it became the source of many laughs.

"I hope she makes it out for a game or two."

"She plans to. Have you seen your brother? I know the team was traveling this week."

"Not yet. We're having brunch this morning though. Do you guys think you'll make it out for any of our games? Now that we're playing in the same city, it should be easier for you."

"We'd really like to. We're aiming for later in the season. It's so hot and sticky in Philly in the summer. We'll come in the fall when the weather turns."

I try to mask my disappointment. "I understand. How's Dad?"

"In his woodshop, building God knows what now." I smile. My dad lives for carpentry. He's made custom furniture since he was a boy, taking over the business from his father after a short stint playing professional baseball. They run a small boutique in our hometown that is always overflowing with inventory. Not because they don't make sales, but because my father works twenty-four hours a day creating things. Neither of them, particularly my father, ever made it to many games because they're open seven days a week and don't trust anyone else to run things.

"Tell him I said hello. I hope to see you soon. I miss you."

"I miss you too."

"I need to head out. I'll talk to you in a few days?"

"Okay, sweetie." She's quiet for a brief moment. "Arizona?"

"Yes."

"Find your smile again, sweet girl. Nothing that happened is your fault and everything happens for a reason."

I bite back the tears. "I'm trying, Mom. I really am. I hope that one day I can view it that way."

"You will. I promise."

I'M HEADED to brunch with Quincy. I need to talk to him before he sees anything online about Layton and me.

He arrives at the diner just a few minutes after me. I'm already seated in a booth toward the back.

I'll never admit it to him, but Quincy Abbott's presence is known anytime he walks into a room. He's tall, with overgrown blond hair, curled in the back, that's always a bit messy and always looks like he needs a haircut. His eyes are sky blue, way bluer than mine, but the family resemblance is there.

Admittedly, he attracts the attention of women, though he's always so secretive about his relationships with women. He's never brought one home for us to meet. Not once.

Despite our age difference of five years, we've always been close and have fun joking around with each other. He's severely protective of me, more so in the past year than ever before. We might have a little sibling rivalry at times, both being athletic, but when everything went down, he was there for me, and when he had to leave, he called every day to check in on me for those first few months.

A few patrons hold out their hands to high-five him. He's the ace of the Cougars' pitching staff and seems to have already ingratiated himself with the often-fickle Philly fans by having a great first half of the season. One of the best of his career. I'm so happy for him.

He smiles at everyone in the restaurant, but his face drops when his eyes meet mine. That's very unlike him. He's always happy to see me. In a low voice, he says, "We need to talk."

I give a big, fake smile. "Good to see you too, big bro. Thanks for the nice welcome to Philly. I'm feeling very loved."

His face immediately softens as he slides into the seat across from me in our booth. "I'm sorry. I woke up to a million texts about you and Layton Lancaster. And then I saw pictures of you two online at the all-star party last night. What the fuck is going on?"

"Relax. It's not what it looks like. I'll explain everything."

The waitress walks over and takes our orders. After she leaves, I explain to him the whole fake relationship proposal from the owners.

He shakes his head. "This is fucked. They're using you for your good looks. I won't let them treat you like this. Why in the world would you agree to it?"

"I'm trying to save my sport. The league is in dire straits. This could legitimately help. Q, you get to play the sport you love for a living, every single day. If our league can't turn things around, I won't be able to do the same. Think about Layton's star power. As crazy as it seems, it actually makes a lot of sense."

"Why the hell would he do this? What's in it for him?"

"That's his private business. If he wants to share it with you, he can. I'm not going there."

He momentarily lifts his backward hat and runs his fingers through his messy hair. "He's a womanizer, Z. He bounces around from faceless woman to faceless woman. I don't want you to be one of them. One of many."

"I totally agree. I'm not stupid. I've been clear with him that this is a business arrangement. It's nothing more. Layton understands and agrees it's for the best. He was a perfect gentleman last night." Sort of. His dancing dick has been playing on a loop in my mind.

He takes my hand. "You've been through a lot. He's no good for you. Keep that in mind."

"I know. That's why I insisted on you being in the loop. I knew you'd never believe that I'd date someone like him because I genuinely wouldn't."

His face relaxes in relief. "Z, I just want my sister back. The happy, confident, carefree sister I had before that fucking jackass broke you."

My eyes fill with tears as I squeeze his hand in return. "I want that too. It was one of the many reasons I decided to move here. I needed the fresh start. Away from *him*. Away from the constant reminders."

He smirks. "It wasn't to be near me?"

I let out a laugh. "Of course it was to be near you. All of it. The new start, living in the same city as you, and the chance to live and play with Ripley again."

I see his jaw tic slightly. "How's Ripley acclimating to Philly?"

"You know Ripley. She'd be fine anywhere. It's so nice to live with her again. Having someone I trust and love wholeheartedly is priceless. You don't appreciate it as much until it's gone."

"And what about crazy and her twin sister, slightly less crazy?"

I smile. "Kam and Bailey are fine. They live next door to us. It's just like the good old days."

He rolls his eyes. "Oh god, I feel bad for everyone in your building. That's going to be one loud floor."

I giggle. "True."

"I do think being back with all your girls will help you break out of your funk." Ripley and I played with the twins in college. We all lived together for those four years but not since.

My shoulders fall. "I do too. I want that more than anything." It's been a long year for me. "What about you? Catch me up on things."

Our food arrives, and we're quiet as the waitress places it on the table.

Once she leaves, he garbles, "Nothing to report. Same ole stuff," around a mouth full of bacon.

"You're having an awesome season."

He smiles as he swallows his food. "I know. I'm psyched. I like this team. A lot. My arm feels better than it has in years. I think we have a chance of going far in the playoffs."

"For sure. I can see it in your body language. You're happier here. It seems like you've made good friends."

"Honestly, Layton is my best friend. He was so good to me when I first arrived in Philly. I love the guy; I just don't love him for my sister. I've seen too much."

It's not like I haven't come to the same conclusion. "I know."

"There's a good crew of us *oldies* that hang out together. It's hard to believe that I'm now the gray hairs of the team. How did that happen?"

I pretend to examine his locks and joke, "You've got at least one or two years before the gray hairs fully set in. I only see a small handful."

He twirls a few of his curls on the back of his head. "East Coast girls fucking love my hair. It's like there are no blond men out here. They're obsessed with it. It's like shooting fish in a barrel."

I scrunch my face. "Eww. I don't need to hear that."

He smirks as he gobbles up the last of his breakfast sandwich in one giant bite. "What about your team? How are they looking?"

"Really good. Ripley's throwing heat right now. We can hit through the lineup. We're immediate contenders."

"Cool. Are you going to think about entering the dating pool again? The thought makes me sick to my stomach, but the thought of you alone and as miserable as you've been the past year makes me sicker."

"I can't date while I'm in my business relationship with Layton. That's one of the rules."

He lets out a laugh. "Does Layton have the same rules?"

"Yep."

"That will *never* happen. He's the biggest player I've ever met. He doesn't even have to try. Women legitimately fall at his feet. Even more so than for me."

I scrunch my face in disgust. "You're so conceited. Just wait until you lose your hair. Then no one will want you."

He gasps. "Never."

"You should lock someone down. I think I see a receding hairline starting to take shape."

His eyes widen and he pulls out his phone, carefully examining his hair in the camera. "No way. It's thick and perfect. It's not going anywhere anytime soon."

I laugh. I love messing with him about it.

He pinches my arm like he used to when we were kids. I smack his hand. "Ouch. That hurts."

He chuckles. "Are you going to be able to come to any of my games?"

I nod. "Anytime Layton and I don't have our own team obligations, we're supposed to show up at each other's games, so I'll be there. I would have come anyway to see you play, but now I'll get VIP treatment."

"Sweet. I can't wait to come watch you play. It's been years since I've seen your games in person."

"You can sit with my boyfriend."

His face falls. "Not funny."

LAYTON

I'm putting the finishing touches on sanding the latest bat I made when I notice there's a call coming through from the front desk. I answer. "Hey, Frederick."

"Good afternoon, Master Lancaster. There's a Quincy Abbott who wishes to see you. I asked him the purpose for the visit, but he insists that it's a private matter."

Yep, I was expecting this. Arizona mentioned that she was going to tell him about everything over breakfast.

"Does he look mad?"

Frederick, who definitely watches too many episodes of *Downton Abbey* and thinks he's on the staff there, responds, "I would have to answer in the affirmative to your inquiry, sir."

I let out a laugh at his response. "Send him up, Frederick. Thank you."

A few minutes later, there's a loud pounding at my door. I open it to see a scowling Quincy. In a sarcastic tone, I ask, "What brings you by, Q?"

He narrows his eyes as he walks through the door. "You know exactly why I'm here."

I hold up my hands. "It wasn't my idea. It's a business arrangement. That's it."

"That's what she said. What's in it for you? Why do you give a shit about her or women's softball? Arizona said your business wasn't hers to discuss but I want to know."

I like that she wouldn't tell him my reasoning. It says a lot about her character.

"If I give them what they want for the next three months, I get a three-year contract extension. I get to finish my career here. Otherwise they're releasing me after the season."

His face falls in sympathy as he nods in understanding. "I'm sorry it's come to this. I really am. I suppose I get why you're doing it, but you can't touch her. She's off-limits. Indefinitely."

"I get it."

"I'm not fucking around."

I make a show of placing my hands deep into my pockets. "Hands off. She's also made that clear. It's best for the arrangement anyway. I don't need anything complicating my extension."

He blows out a breath as he plops down on my couch. "You need to understand, she's been through hell and back."

"She briefly mentioned a failed engagement. She wouldn't say much more than that."

"I'm not getting into details, but he dicked her over big time, and it damaged her. She hasn't been the same since."

"What do you mean she hasn't been the same?"

"Until a year ago, my sister was carefree and happy. *All* the time. She had sass and fire that we only get glimpses of now. She's always been extremely popular..."

"I'm sure. She's gorgeous."

He growls. "Don't even fucking look at her that way. And I know exactly what my sister is and isn't. It was more than her looks though. It was her confidence and personality. She was magnetic. It's like having a broken heart fractured her spirit too. She's different. She used to be totally uninhibited, even wild at times. Adventurous too. But since then, she's clammed up. She's fucking timid and fragile in a way I've never seen from her. Coming here is her fresh start. I can't have you fucking with her. I will straight up kill you. I'm not messing around, Lancaster."

"What did he do to her?"

"Not my story to tell, but I'm warning you. Teammate to teammate. Friend to friend. Man to man. She's. Off. Limits."

I nod. "I get it. I promise." And I mean it.

"Thank you."

"I don't know what she shared with you about the specifics of our deal but know that we're under strict instructions to hang out like a normal couple. You're going to have to be cool with that."

He sighs. "I'll try."

"We thought it might be more fun to do so as a group tonight. Her gang is coming to Screwballs. You in?"

"Anytime I can be there when you have to be with her, consider it a yes."

WE'RE all squeezed into the booth at Screwballs. I introduce Ezra and Cheetah to Arizona's three friends. The two of them are practically drooling over the girls, especially the twins. It's unspoken guy code that we all want to have sex with hot twins. I've done it a handful of times, but I don't think this is the time to bring it up. These twins are crazy hot, so my boys are going nuts for them.

The girls are in sweatpants. Arizona, Ripley, and Bailey are in normal T-shirts. Kamryn is in a cropped one, showing her toned abs. I can't help but inwardly laugh at their clothes. All the women in the bar are dressed to kill, but not these four. I love their confidence. I love that they're not here to score baseball players.

I'm learning quickly that Ripley and Kamryn are very outgoing, while Bailey is more introverted. Arizona lies somewhere in between, always laughing at her friends' antics and chiming in now and then. I think about what Quincy said earlier today. About the shift in her since her breakup. I wonder what she was like before. She seems pretty fucking sassy to me now.

Quincy arrives last. Ezra smiles at him. "You're last, Q."

He mumbles, "Shit."

Arizona's jaw drops. "Oh my god, Quincy. Did you bring the random fact thing to this team?"

He nods.

She smiles. "Our mom was always afraid that Q and I would be as absentminded as our father, so she started this game at family dinners. It then spread to our friends and teams. It caused practically everyone in our community to be an hour early to everything." She proceeds to explain it to Kamryn and Bailey. Ripley already knew.

Ezra nods at Quincy. "Well?"

He scratches his head. "Umm. Mona Lisa has no eyebrows."

Everyone immediately pulls out their phones to Google the Mona Lisa. Sure enough, no eyebrows.

Cheetah feels his. "I've got plenty for her and me." Cheetah is of Latino descent and, despite his blue eyes, is often mistaken for a younger Mario Lopez, with his larger-than-life smile. He's got thick, dark eyebrows.

Kamryn looks him up and down. "Why do they call you Cheetah? I'd think everyone would call you AC Slater."

I smile because Mario Lopez played AC Slater in the ninety's television show, *Saved By the Bell*.

He gives her a cocky smirk. "Because I'm fast. *Very* fast."

She raises an eyebrow in challenge. "No one likes a man who's fast, *Cheetah*."

"I'm fast on the field, sweetheart. In bed, I'm more of a tiger than a cheetah. A different feline but an animal nonetheless."

Kamryn gives him a playful smile. "You look like more of a kitten to me, preppie. Speaking of felines, do you think that attractive woman over there is looking at me or you, *kitten?*"

His eyes widen as he looks at the girl in question and then back at Kam. "Is that what you're into? Explains why you're busting my balls instead of gargling with them."

After taking a sip of her beer, she smoothly explains, "Sometimes I like a banana in my fruit salad, and sometimes I like to dip my toes in the kitty pool. It depends on my mood. I'm a mood fucker. How about a little wager, *kitten?*"

"What do you have in mind, *Kam bam?*"

She smirks at the nickname. "If she wants you, I'll let you come home with me tonight to break in my new waterbed. If she wants me..."

Cheetah leans forward in wide-eyed anticipation.

"...you need to come to our first game next week, topless, with my name written across your chest in thick Sharpie. It has to read, *Kam's Kitten.*"

Cheetah smiles and eagerly holds out his hand. "Deal. You and I will be riding that wave within the hour."

She shakes it with a devious smile as they both quickly leave the table and race toward the unsuspecting cute brunette.

The rest of us watch on in amusement as they both bombard her. Her head is toggling between the two of them.

Bailey sighs. "I'm the real loser in this bet. Whichever way it goes, she's going to be loud in her room tonight. All. Night. Long."

Ezra sidles up to her and then wraps his arm around her. "You're welcome to stay with me tonight."

She shifts out of his embrace. "I'm good, thanks."

I lean over to Arizona and quietly say, "It's amazing that they're twins. They're so different."

She nods. "Yep. Night and day, though Bailey goes out with her fair share of men. She's just not as overtly sexual or obvious about it as Kam. She's also a bit of an old soul. Guys our age don't do it for her. She likes them old, like you."

I mumble, "I'm not old."

She simply smiles. She's messing with me.

"Only men for her?"

"For Bailey, yes. Kam is a switch hitter. She'll go any which way she pleases in a given moment. She's attracted to the person, nothing else."

"I've gathered." I turn to Ripley. "Did you and Q hang out in Houston?"

She looks at Q and then back at me. "I guess we crossed paths a few times, right?"

Quincy nods. "We went to the same clubs. One of her teammates was dating one of mine for a while."

Ripley nods. "Oh right. He was such a dick to her."

"He *is* a dick. I told you back then to warn her."

I look at a handful of curvier women in the crowd and nod their way. "Q, have you checked out the action tonight? I think there are a few ladies for you."

"Nah. I think I'll make sure Arizona and Ripley get home safely."

"I can take care of that. Do your thing."

He leans forward so only Arizona, Ripley, and I can hear him. "You will not step foot in their apartment. *Ever.* I've got them."

Arizona rolls her eyes.

Ripley crosses her arms. "What if I want to go home with someone tonight?"

His eyes widen. "You'll do no such thing. I will make sure that you and Arizona are tucked into bed safely and *alone*."

Arizona musses his hair. "Aww, I love it when you get brotherly with Ripley too."

He fixes his hair. "Stop messing with my perfect hair."

Just then, Delta, a woman I've hung out with a few times, approaches the table. She's attractive, with dark hair, dark eyes, and a hot body. She's wearing the unofficial Screwballs women's uniform. "You want to dance, Layton?"

All eyes at the table are on me.

"Not tonight, Delta. I'm hanging with my friends."

Her shoulders drop. "Okay. Let me know when you're heading out. I'll come with you."

"Oh...well...I'm seeing someone."

Her eyes widen in shock. "You are? Who?"

I put my arm around Arizona's shoulders. I feel her stiffen but squeeze her close and hold her in place. "Delta, this is my girlfriend, Arizona."

Delta gives her a fake smile. "It's nice to meet you."

An equally awkward Arizona responds, "You too."

She looks Arizona's casual wardrobe up and down, clearly judging her. That seems to piss off Arizona. With a bit of sexy edge, she stands and takes my hand in hers. "Why don't *we* dance, superstar? I've been dying to get *my* boyfriend out on the dance floor."

I can't help but smile as I stand. "I'd love to, sunshine."

Despite Quincy audibly growling at us, we make our way to the dance floor.

I twirl her around and she easily falls back into my

waiting arms. We admittedly look like a real couple having a good time. I see a few people taking pictures. I suppose that's what we want. We were all over the news this morning, smiling at the event last night. This feeds into the dialogue.

I have to admit, I don't mind being here with her and not going home with Delta or anyone else. I just wish Arizona would relax a bit. We're having fun but she keeps me at arm's length. I need to make sure things remain friendly between us.

I joke, "I almost ate a can of tuna fish before we came tonight to get you back for the garlic." I scrunch my face. "It was tough being so close to you all night with that potent garlic breath."

She gives me a huge smile. There's something so special about her smile. Her whole face lights up. "I would have deserved it. I'm sorry. It was kind of immature."

"Yes, you would have, and yes, it was. But I forgive you." I twirl her again before asking, "What sightseeing have you done since you got to town?"

"Unfortunately, none. We've been unpacking and having two practices a day. We've been too exhausted to do much more."

"Have you eaten a cheesesteak?"

"No."

"Have you been to Reading Terminal Market?"

"No."

"Have you at least run up the Rocky steps?"

"Nope. Nothing."

"Well, since we have to spend time together anyway, maybe we can do stuff like that. I have all night games this week. I usually need to get to the ballpark by midafternoon. How about we meet earlier in the day? Kill two birds with one stone."

"You don't mind?"

"Not at all."

I feel her relax in my arms. "Thanks, Layton. That's really nice of you."

We make our way back to the table in time to see Cheetah return, looking defeated. I'm in shock. He rarely strikes out. "Did you lose the bet?"

Nodding toward the entrance, he sighs. "I did."

We see Kam heading out of the bar with the girl. She turns back and smiles at the table. She makes the notorious Cougars claw with her fingers and mouths *Kam's Kitten* and then laughs to herself as they exit the bar.

Cheetah has his head in his hands. "What does she have that I don't?"

Arizona smirks. "A vagina."

CHAPTER FOUR

ARIZONA

We're huddled on the field with Coach Billie. She's a former Olympian, now in her early forties, with light hair, blue eyes, and an adorably dimpled smile. She was a speedy outfielder, so she's a little smaller than most of us, but she's a ball of fire with an endless amount of energy.

In her always enthusiastic tone, she yells, "Great practice this morning, girls. You ladies already look like a team, and it's only been a little over a week. We need to come up with a special cheer for the Anacondas."

Kam mumbles in my ear, "I could use an anaconda in me right about now. How's that for a cheer?"

I put my hand in front of my mouth to hide my smile.

Ripley raises her hand. "I've got one, Coach. One-eyed snakes, coming to get you!"

The team collectively boos her.

Kam jumps up and down. "I've got one. How about, *my*

anaconda DOES want some?" She shakes her ass and sings it like the Sir Mix-A-Lot song. Everyone starts laughing.

Coach Billie's eyes widen. "Maybe we'll work on this. Let's...sleep on it."

Kam starts to open her mouth, but Coach holds up her hand. "Enough. Let's find something...family friendly."

Poor woman. She doesn't know who she's dealing with.

She turns her attention to me. "Arizona, can I have a word with you?"

"Sure, Coach."

Everyone heads to the locker room. Once they're gone, she asks, "What did the Cougars want the other day? I never heard back from you, and then, all of a sudden, I learn that the owners of the Cougars own this team too, and then I see pictures of you and Layton Lancaster up in New York at the all-star pre-party event."

Just another person I have to lie to. I need something realistic and believable. I try to keep it ambiguous. "They asked me to make a few public appearances with Layton. Just to promote the team."

She nods. "I see. Well, I can't imagine it's too terrible to have to spend time with him. He's a dreamboat."

I let out a laugh. "He's a nice guy. We're friends. He and my brother are close. I'll have to hang out with him around town, and we're doing a *Sports Illustrated* shoot."

"Wow. *Sports Illustrated*? How exciting."

"It is. I'm a little nervous; it's a body image issue, but I know it will be good for our team and league. And it's great for younger girls to see women in magazines who aren't a size two."

"You're absolutely right. Well, as long as it doesn't take you away from your team obligations..."

"Never. You know I'm committed."

"I do. You're the clear leader of this team. I need to know I can rely on you."

"Of course, Coach. I'll do anything that's needed." I literally am doing anything that's needed by entering into a fake relationship with fuckboy, Layton Lancaster.

"Wonderful."

"Is there anything else? I have some plans today." I have a fake date and then I'm going to watch my fake boyfriend play baseball and act like the doting girlfriend.

"No. Have fun."

"I will."

WHEN WE GET BACK from our early morning practice, LeRond is standing by our apartment door. He breathes a sigh of relief as we approach. "Oh good, I was just about to leave." He hands me a bag. "Here are some things for you to wear to Cougars games."

"Thanks, but I don't need anything. I have one of my brother's jerseys."

He smiles. "You're Layton Lancaster's girl now. You need to wear *his* jersey."

With a tremendous amount of attitude, I ask, "Does he have to wear Arizona Abbott clothing to my games?"

"Yes. I'm on my way to his place next."

"Fine. I'll wear it, but only if he does too."

"Sounds good. There are items for your friends too. Oh, and there are passes for you ladies. You get to go in a private friends and family entrance and then sit in their allotted section behind the Cougars dugout. They're good for every home game the rest of the season." He winks. "I put a little something extra into your jersey."

"Oh god. What did you do?"

He cackles as he makes his way to the elevator.

Ripley and I go inside and look through everything. I hold up the tiny jerseys. "Are these youth sizes? Do we really have to wear these?"

She holds up a number eight jersey and turns it around so I can read the back. "I guess *Layton's Lady* does." That's the name on the back of the jersey. *Layton's Lady.*

"Ugh. Is that jersey bedazzled? Who would wear crap like this to games? His better be bedazzled too."

Ripley giggles. "I doubt it."

"It barely covers one of my boobs."

"That's what you get for having a big rack."

Much to Ripley's clean freak disapproval, I toss the jersey onto the sofa and head toward my bedroom. "I need to shower. I'm meeting Layton for lunch."

"Have fun being *Layton's Lady.*"

Two hours later, Layton and I are sitting in a park known as LOVE Park for the famous statue of the letters spelling out the word, *LOVE.* He has three bags of food and is wearing a huge grin on his face as we sit on a bench. He looks like a kid on Christmas morning.

"Why are you stupidly happy right now?"

"I'm popping your cheesesteak cherry. It's so exciting."

I roll my eyes. "How much food did you get? It looks like enough to feed ten people."

"You can't live in Philly and not know which cheesesteak is your favorite. I got one from each of the three most famous cheesesteak stands. Pat's, Jim's, and Geno's. We'll do a taste test."

"Which one is your favorite?"

"I can't tell you yet. I don't want to sway you. Cheesesteak preference is very personal."

I can't help my laugh over how seriously he's taking this.

As he's slicing them like a trained surgeon with the knife he conveniently brought, I ask, "Why are you so set on staying in Philly?"

He's quiet for a moment before answering. "It's the only family I have left."

"The team?"

"Yes and no. Obviously the team. I was always close to Harold Greene. But not just that. My grandmother took care of a lot of kids when I grew up. They were mostly in and out, but there was one boy who became sort of a little brother to me. His name is Henry. He's twenty-four now but was only ten when my grandmother died. I was so caught up in my life and career, I didn't think about what would happen to him without my grandmother. She died about two years after I moved away. He bounced around from home to home, dealt with all kinds of terrible shit, and got into drugs and alcohol. By the time he was eighteen, he was a mess. I reconnected with him and immediately got him into a good rehab. After that, I moved him here and helped him get a job. He still struggles a lot, but I do what I can for him. Things would definitely go south if I moved away from him, and I don't think he'd be willing to move again."

"You feel guilty that you left him behind?"

He nods. "I do. If I had taken him with me, maybe things wouldn't have been so bad for him."

"You were practically a kid yourself."

He shrugs. "Maybe. But I still should have looked out for him. It's my biggest regret. I'm trying to make up for it both with him and by spending time with kids in similar situations. I volunteer when I can."

"What kind of volunteer work?"

"I coach a youth baseball team."

"That's awesome. Does Henry coach with you?"

"No. He doesn't like being around kids in those circumstances. I think it triggers him."

"What does he do?"

"I bought a condo for him in the city." He drops his head down in what looks like a bit of shame. "He's in and out of odd jobs. He can't seem to hold one down, often teetering on the edge of sobriety. I wish I could do more."

"You can only help someone who's willing to help themselves."

"I suppose. He had it rough. I feel bad for him."

"So it's all because of Henry? The reason you want to stay here?"

"Not just that. I love the kids I coach, I love my teammates, and I love this city. It's everything. It's home. I don't want to move. It's that simple." He pushes my plate in front of me. "Enough chit-chat. It's time for your taste test."

He has my cheesesteaks cut up for me on a paper plate. I've got three different selections. He points to them. "Geno's is the one with the longer strips of steak, while the others are chopped. The one with the steak chopped up most finely is Jim's. Pat's has the Cheez Wiz wit onions."

"*With* onions?"

He smiles. "When you go to Pat's, you've got to say *wit*, or they won't give it to you. It's on the menu that way, and they honestly won't give it to you if you say it in proper English."

I let out a laugh. "This town is weird."

He chuckles. "You have no idea. Oh, and they'll have Tony Luke's cheesesteaks at the stadium if you want to try a fourth option. That one is good too."

"A fourth? I'm going to need to run ten miles this week just to exercise all this off as it is."

"Be happy that I narrowed it down for you. There are dozens of great places to get a cheesesteak."

He takes a big bite of his, looking incredibly satisfied as he chews it.

He smiles and mumbles, "I'm a runner too—when my knee doesn't act up. I'll go with you. I'll show you the good running spots."

"You have a bum knee?"

"I've been catching for over twenty years. Of course I have knee issues. It's part of the job description."

"If you're in pain, why don't you retire? I assume you don't need the money."

He shrugs. "I'd miss the guys."

"Not because you love the game and would miss it?"

"I've been playing a long time. I'm sure on some level I'd miss it if I were to retire. Stop distracting me. You need to eat them while they're fresh. The bread being fresh is important. Eat up, sunshine!"

"You're very bossy."

He winks. "You have no idea."

My face flushes at the insinuation. Why is he so damn hot? And now I'm learning he's nice too. It's almost unfair.

I distract myself from his sexiness by diving into the cheesesteaks, taking bites of all three. With a mouthful, I manage, "Oh my god, they're all so good. I can't possibly choose."

"You have to pick one. It's an unwritten Philly rule."

I giggle. "I'll wait until I try Tony Luke's to make a final decision."

"Fair enough." We sit in comfortable silence for a bit as we continue to eat. At some point, he asks, "Will you tell me about what happened with your fiancé? Q wouldn't tell me anything."

"I don't like to talk about it. It wasn't exactly a happy time in my life."

"A brief summary?"

I sigh. "Fine. To make a long story short, I was left at the altar. Literally. It was our wedding day. I was dressed and ready. I received a simple text from him reading, *I'm not ready to settle down. I don't think you're the one for me. Sorry.*"

"Holy shit. That's terrible. What did he say when you spoke?"

"I haven't spoken to him since. That text was our last communication. I had to go, by myself, in front of our friends and family to tell them the wedding was off. It was as horrific as it sounds. Even worse."

His eyes widen. "He called off your wedding, made you tell everyone, and then never was man enough to sit down with you and have a real conversation about it?"

I sigh. "That's exactly right."

"What a dick."

"Yep. It's made me wary. I...umm...haven't dated since. Back home, I was always afraid of running into him. I didn't think I could handle that, so I barely went out. It was just one of the many reasons for me to move out here. I needed this fresh start. Somewhere that I'm...unafraid."

"Did...did he hurt you? I don't understand why you're afraid."

"Not physically like you're thinking. Honestly, I'd rather not talk about it anymore. It's depressing, and I'm making an effort to look to the future, not the past."

He nods. "Okay." He gently tucks my hair behind my ear and then catches himself and pulls his hand back. "Sorry. I didn't want it to get into the food."

Layton Lancaster is different from what I expected. He's sensitive and engaging. I thought he'd be conceited and aloof. He's confident, but not in an asshole way.

He's incredibly humble and sweet with fans. Every few minutes, both kids and adults approach him to get autographs and their pictures taken with him. He's very kind and accommodating to them, never saying no, even when it's disruptive to our conversation and our meal.

As we're finishing the cheesesteaks, a woman approaches and asks him to sign the top of her breasts. His eyes toggle between me and her. "I'm here with my girlfriend. I'm happy to sign something else if you'd like."

The woman looks me up and down. I'm suddenly very conscious of my athletic shorts, tank top, ponytail, and makeup-free face. This is like that woman at the bar last night. I might need to up my wardrobe if I'm going to be on Layton's arm for the next three months.

Layton and the woman eventually agree on him signing her arm, which he does.

When she leaves, I smile. "Does that happen a lot?"

He smirks. "Every damn day."

So much for not being conceited.

BY THE TIME I arrive home, there are a bunch of photos online of Layton and me eating our cheesesteaks in LOVE Park. Headlines with puns about Layton in LOVE are abundant. I didn't even notice any cameras. I suppose I need to be on alert when I'm out with him.

I'm going to my first Cougars game tonight. I squeeze my body into the jersey that's about four sizes too small. This shirt is definitely not made for someone with boobs, especially my bigger size. Is it really necessary for it to be so damn tight and revealing? LeRond absolutely did this on purpose.

Kam and Bailey walk in wearing equally tight jerseys with Lancaster on the back. Ripley walks out of her bedroom in a bigger jersey with my brother's name. I look at her in question.

"Layton has enough fans in this group. I'm giving Quincy some love too."

"I don't remember seeing that jersey in LeRond's bag," I note accusatorially.

She gives a guilty look. "I had already purchased it. I owned one in Houston too. Us pitchers have to stick together. Just because we don't play every day doesn't mean we don't need fans in the stands."

Kam places her hands on her hips. "Are you fucking Quincy Abbott?"

I make a look of disgust. "Ugh, no. She would never do that. He's like a brother to her too."

Ripley nods. "I grew up with him. I'm supporting my friend, just like I would do for you."

Kam shrugs. "He's hot. He looks like Jax from *Sons of Anarchy*. I'd fuck him if I were you."

I stare at her in astonishment. "Can you please not talk about my brother like that? It's gross."

"Your brother has to deal with you dating Layton. I'm sure he's disgusted too. He didn't seem very happy about it last night."

I hate keeping this from them, but I can't let the business arrangement leak.

"Quincy will get over it."

"No brother wants to know that his sister is getting laid."

I shake my head. "I'm not sleeping with Layton. He and I are taking things slowly. We're getting to know each other."

"Why? Just fuck him. He's so hot. Honestly, he could fuck anyone he wanted, anytime he wants it."

Ripley intervenes on my behalf. "You know exactly why she's not jumping into bed with him. Leave her alone. All in her own time. Her hanging out with him is a big step. Let's be supportive of her doing this in her own way."

"Fine, but I wouldn't wait too long. A guy like Layton Lancaster doesn't go more than a day or two without sex."

I hope he can keep it in his pants. We're both screwed if he doesn't.

LAYTON

I look up in the stands and see Arizona with her friends. It's nice to have someone here for me. Because of not wanting to leave all the kids, my grandmother never made it to a Cougars game before she died. She kept putting it off until it was too late.

Lots of women wear my jersey, but no one that I care about. Certainly no one in the friends and family section.

She sees me looking at her and smiles, holding up a wrapped Tony Luke cheesesteak. I can't help but let out a laugh. She then turns around and points to the back of her Cougars jersey. It reads *Layton's Lady* and it's got some kind of jewels all around it. It's also very tight and more than shows her curves. Fuck, she's sexy.

Quincy follows my line of sight. "That's bullshit. She used to wear my jersey to games."

I give him a friendly elbow. With a huge grin on my face, I say, "Not anymore."

He narrows his eyes at me. "It's not real, Lancaster. Three months. You only get this fake treatment for three months. Then she'll be back in my jersey."

My smile quickly fades as that reality hits me like a ton of bricks.

CHAPTER FIVE

LAYTON

Tonight is Arizona's first game. Luckily, we have an off day, so I'll be there, and I'm throwing out the ceremonial first pitch. I'm looking forward to seeing my first real softball game in person. I've admittedly watched a few online so I can learn the subtle differences between the two sports. There are more than I thought.

Carter's assistant dropped off an Anacondas jersey for me. It's Arizona's number and reads *Abbott's Admirer* on the back. I can't help but laugh at it. At least it doesn't have rhinestones on it like Arizona's did.

I had planned to send her flowers for opening day, but instead, I decided to send her a poster of me. I smile at our post-delivery text exchange.

> Arizona: What am I supposed to do with this poster?

Me: Put it above your bed. Just like when you were a teen. I thought it might inspire you like it did then.

Arizona: OMG. Why did I tell you that?

Me: I love it. One day you'll admit that you chose your number because of me.

Arizona: You were much cuter when you were younger. I have a poster of Butch McVey above my bed these days.

Butch McVey is currently the most popular baseball player in the league and the face of professional baseball. He's probably about Arizona's age. Women definitely swoon for him. He's also a catcher, so she knows this will sting a bit.

Me: But I was your first crush. That's the most important one. You never forget your first.

Arizona: That was a long time ago. Now you're just old. TBH, it's kind of gross. This poster should be an AARP ad.

I laugh. That's funny.

Me: Older than a week ago when we met, and you were totally into me?

Arizona: Can't talk. Heading to the ballpark. Bad reception. Got to go.

Me: LOL. Good luck, sunshine. I'll be
cheering for you.

Arizona: Thx.

The Anacondas publicized the hell out of the fact
that I'd be there and that I'm throwing out the first
pitch. Several of the local news shows have mentioned my
relationship with Arizona. There was a good amount of
coverage of her cheering at our game. It's given the
Anacondas a lot of buzz around town. I hate to admit it,
but Reagan Daulton knew what she was doing. Our
relationship is good publicity. Even though it's fake, I'm
kind of happy that it's potentially helping the girls. I
genuinely like all of them.

Reagan asked me to ride with them to the game to
talk. Of course, I agreed.

At the allocated time, I get a call from Frederick in
the lobby. "Master Lancaster?"

"Hi, Frederick."

"There's a rather immense vehicle of transportation
that has arrived. After a brief inquiry by me, the driver
has informed me that Mr. and Mrs. Carter Daulton are in
the back and that you were anticipating their appearance
at your abode. Shall we wait for you, or shall I send them
away?"

Why is he so bizarrely formal? Yes, this is a nice
building, but no one in Philly, nor in the twenty-first
century, talks like him.

"I *shall* be down in a minute. Thank you."

I walk out the front door to a black Suburban and
climb in. There's a driver in the front. Reagan, Carter,

and a toddler are in the back of the car. Reagan smiles. "Hey, Layton. This is our son, George."

I wiggle my fingers at him and he giggles. "Hi, George. How old is he?"

"Nearly eighteen months."

"He's so cute." He looks a lot like Carter.

"Thank you."

Carter then grabs a toy to distract George while Reagan and I chat. "How is it going with Arizona?"

"Fine. We get along. I think I've been doing everything that's been asked of me."

"You have. Thank you. Your dates have garnered a lot of attention. And people are completely eating up her being at your games. It's like they're seeing a love story unfold before their eyes. The meal in LOVE Park was a nice touch."

"I'm glad it's working."

She takes a deep breath. Clearly she has something else to say. "You two were a little snippy with each other when you were in my office, but you seem to be getting along well now."

"It's easier to be friends. Our goals are aligned. When I reminded her of that, she agreed."

"Sorry to be blunt, but I have to ask. Is that all it is?"

I nod. "Yes."

"Great. I need it to stay that way. Too much is at stake. I can't have you two getting involved and then have it go south. I need to get through the next few months with everyone adoring you two. There's a lot riding on the success of the Anacondas."

"That's fine. She's not into me that way. She's made it clear."

"Are you into her?"

"Look at her. How could I not be? I was into her before I ever met you and this situation came to be. But we're just friends. That's how it's going to stay."

"Good. I don't want to be a dick, but you know your contract and your status with the Cougars all depends on this. I need it to remain platonic. It's a business relationship. A PR relationship. That's it. Are we clear?"

"Crystal."

We arrive at the stadium. Reagan has some sort of owner's suite, and she invites me to sit with them, but I want to sit behind the dugout like Arizona did for me. It's more fun to watch games up close.

I look around the ballpark, which is roughly a quarter the size of ours. It's about half full. I have no idea if that's good or bad for women's softball.

I'm announced and then throw out the ceremonial first pitch to a sea of cheers. Catching Arizona's eye, I turn and point to the back of my jersey. I see her laugh as that beautiful smile of hers takes shape.

I'm trying to learn the differences between softball and baseball, besides what I already mentioned to her. I notice the women wear way tighter pants. I don't think I could play in pants that tight. And all the pants end just below the knee, with the socks pulled all the way up. Almost all baseball players wear pants to their ankles, though there are a small handful that wear them shorter like the girls.

You can see all their curves with the way they wear their pants. I can't believe more men don't realize this. They should publicize that. I don't think there's a man in America who wouldn't want to see Arizona Abbott in tight clothing.

I knew in theory that the field was smaller, but seeing

it in person makes it come to life. They don't have any grass in the infield. The balls must come at them crazy fast.

I hear commotion in the stands and look up. I see Quincy, Cheetah, and Ezra walking down the steps toward me. Fans continuously stop them for selfies and autographs, which they happily oblige.

They eventually make their way to me. We all say our hellos, and I smirk at Cheetah.

He gives me his self-satisfied smile. "Dude, I would never go back on a bet. Where's Kam bam?"

"They're about to take the field. She's the shortstop."

"Ooh. My future wife is a star."

I notice that Quincy is wearing Ripley's jersey, not Arizona's. I give him a questioning look.

"I knew you'd be wearing my sister's jersey. I'm simply supporting all the girls."

They eventually take the field, and we all cheer for them. My eyes immediately find Arizona. She looks so badass yet adorable in her catching gear.

I see Kam is looking our way, as does Cheetah. He immediately tears off his shirt. Sure enough, he has written across his chest, in thick Sharpie, *Kam's Kitten.* He even has an anaconda drawn under it, leading into his pants. It's professional-level artwork. He must have hired someone to draw it.

He stands on his chair so everyone can see him. He starts screaming for Kam. "Kam bam is the bomb! Go Anacondas! I love softball!" And then he takes it a step further and does a little *Magic Mike* dance routine, rolling his body and hips.

The whole crowd starts cheering for him. The

cameras find him, and he's shown on the big screen. This will undoubtedly be on SportsCenter later.

I see all the girls on the field laughing at his antics. None of it deters him. He keeps dancing and smiling the whole time.

The game finally begins. The four of us sit in awe at the level of play. They're amazing. I had no idea.

ARIZONA

After a lopsided victory in the debut game of the Philly Anacondas, we head to Screwballs with Layton and the boys to celebrate. They were incredible today. They cheered like lunatics the whole game. All the fans were getting a kick out of them, and the cameras were on them the whole time. I have no doubt the team will get a lot of press from it and more fans will come out.

As we walk down the street, laughing at some crazy thing Kamryn said, I feel my face with my hand. It almost hurts from smiling so much. I look around, suddenly realizing I'm happier than I've been in a long time. I get to play with my friends again, we're making new friends with the guys, and I'm really liking my new city. And, if I'm being honest, hanging out with Layton isn't as bad as I thought it would be. I'm enjoying his company.

When we walk into Screwballs, the whole crowd cheers for us. The owner asks to take a few pictures for us to sign so he can hang them on the walls. Of course we oblige. My friends are all on cloud nine too. I notice that a lot of the televisions at the bar have coverage of our game. Half the coverage is of Cheetah dancing, but the rest is of the real game. Kam and Bailey hit back-to-back home runs. They're already being dubbed the slugger sisters. I love it. It's good to see softball getting so much attention.

We sit in our booth, yes, *our* booth, and order a round of beers. Layton is next to me with Quincy watching us like an angry hawk. He's ridiculous.

Kam lifts Cheetah's shirt. "I need a picture with this." She hands her phone to Bailey who gets the picture of Kam with a happily grinning Cheetah. Naturally, Kam takes it a step further and poses for a few shots of her clawing him and biting his nipple. It doesn't seem to bother him though. In fact, he clearly seems to be enjoying the attention from her.

He has himself positioned between Kamryn and Bailey. His head toggles between the two of them. "Have you two ever done a guy at the same time?"

Bailey rolls her eyes. "I'm not into incest. Sister threesomes are a made up thing for porn. No one does that in real life."

"Have you guys ever hooked up with the same guy?"

She bites her lip and scrunches her nose at that one. I know they have.

Cheetah smiles. "So you *are* spit sisters too."

She sighs. "No wonder my sister won't have sex with you."

He feigns shock. "She will. Eventually. Maybe tonight."

Kam shakes her head. "Nope. Not happening."

His shoulders drop. "Ugh. Come on. I was your number one cheerleader tonight. Did you find another girl you like?"

She shakes her head. "No. That guy has been eye-fucking me." She points to some random guy at the bar who is, in fact, staring at her. "He's cute. I might take him to my deep-sea abyss tonight."

Cheetah sucks in a breath. "That guy? He's like six inches shorter than you."

She shrugs her shoulders. "Hooking up with a short guy doesn't matter when you're lying down. I'm not reproducing with him."

"If you're a man under five foot, six inches, you were probably the precum."

Kam gives him a small smile but simply shakes her head letting him know it's not happening tonight.

Cheetah starts mumbling in Spanish.

I know Kam enough to know that she's going to mess with him for as long as she can and then eventually have sex with him. I miss being playful and confident like her. I'm trying to find that part of my personality again.

Layton turns to me. "I understand that you're a lefty slapper. Explain it to me. We don't have slappers in baseball."

It's cute how much he's trying to learn softball.

"You saw that the distance between home and first base is sixty feet instead of ninety like in baseball, right?"

"Yes."

"I have a home-to-first speed of under two-point-four seconds."

His eyes widen. "Holy shit. Cheetah is the fastest baseball player I know, and he's about four-point-one."

"The theory is that I put the ball in play and use my speed. If the defense is back, I either bunt or lightly place the ball in play. If they're playing up on me, I pound it over their heads. It's hard to defend."

"That explains why you were on base every time you came to the plate tonight."

I try to give a modest smile. "That won't happen in every game, but I'm definitely on base a lot. That's why I'm the leadoff batter."

He smiles. "I think you're amazing. I had the best time watching you play. You have a cannon of an arm. I've never seen a woman throw as hard as you. Hell, I know a few guys in our league who don't throw as hard as you."

I rub his arm. "Thank you." Jeez, there are a lot of muscles in that arm.

My phone buzzes again and I look at it. Another message about a sponsorship opportunity. I look up at Layton. "I've had a bunch of emails and voicemails from companies about me being a spokesperson. I've had two or three over the years, but they were small and simple. I was able to manage them. These are bigger. Do you think I need an agent?"

He nods. "Definitely. Do you want me to connect you with Tanner Montgomery? He's been with me since I was in high school. I trust him implicitly. He's like family to me. His daughter plays softball, and I bet she'd love to meet you."

Tanner Montgomery is like the Jerry Maguire of the baseball world. Everyone knows him. He's a top sports agent. "That would be great. Thank you."

Just then, the song "Bye Bye Bye" by *NSYNC starts playing. Quincy looks at me and smiles. Ripley looks at both of us and starts laughing. "I'm in."

The three of us stand and go to the dance floor. Before we know it, our entire table is out there doing the official "Bye Bye Bye" dance. We're all laughing and having a great time. I can't believe how long it's been since I let loose and had fun like this. I don't look at the door worrying that my ex will walk in. I don't even have the pressure of men hitting on me. It seems to be understood here that I'm with Layton. I'm finally feeling free to just be me.

Layton joins in and is adorably terrible, but it doesn't stop him from trying.

THE NEXT MORNING, we're having coffee with Bailey in our kitchen when Kam walks in like she just woke up. Stretching, she groans, "Damn, that girl was a stage-five clinger. I hate women like that."

I look at her in question. "Woman? I thought you had your eye on a man last night?"

She gives her best evil grin. "I did but then Cheetah wanted to bet again, so we found some random woman and made her the subject of our bet." She blows on her nails. "I won, yet again."

"What does he have to do this time?"

She giggles. "He has to shave my name on his head before our next home game."

Ripley looks unimpressed. "You should have made him do a full striptease. The mini one he did at our game was hot."

Kam's eyes light up. "Ooh, good idea. Next time."

I look behind her. "Where's the girl? Still battling the evil sea witch, Ursula, in your bed?"

"Nah. She black-bottom-hoed it out of here."

I can't for the life of me figure out that one. "What does that mean? Though I'm afraid of the answer."

Kam looks appalled that I don't know. "Black-bottom hoes are women who go out for the night in high heels and then go home with someone. When they leave in the morning, they don't want to put their heels back on, so they have to walk barefoot. Theoretically they're walking on pavement and their feet get dirty, hence black-bottom ho."

The three of us burst out laughing. I shake my head. "I don't know where you come up with this shit."

She shrugs. "I think that's, like, a common dictionary term."

I shake my head. "It's definitely not. I don't think Webster has thought of that one quite yet."

CHAPTER SIX

LAYTON

I t's Saturday morning. Arizona and I didn't see each other at all the past few days because both of us have been out of town for road games. I have a game tonight and need to be at the ballpark in a few hours. I have something to do this morning that I like to keep private, but I trust she'll keep it between us.

We meet at the address I gave her at the allocated time. We're in front of a row home in West Philly. She tugs on her baseball cap. "I've got my hat on, per your instructions. What's with all the cloak and dagger? Where are we? Are you kidnapping me?"

I let out a laugh as I fiddle with my own hat. "Nope. This is a group home for kids without anywhere else to live. Most are hoping to be fostered by amazing people like my grandmother, but even if they aren't, the director, Linda, treats them all like her own."

"Like an orphanage?

"No one calls it that anymore, but yes. It's named Linda's House." I point to the sign indicating as much. "Remember I mentioned that I coach a baseball team? This is that team. We have a game today, and I thought you might like to help out."

She gives one of her big smiles. "I'd love to, but you're doing a wonderful thing. Why do you hide yourself?"

"I don't do it for the notoriety. When I coached at a different home, it was publicized. They started getting all kinds of weird people hanging out in front of the home hoping to see me. I had to stop coaching them to avoid causing a scene or potentially putting anyone in danger."

"If we're trying to hide, why did you bring me? We're not getting any publicity for it."

I guess I didn't need to bring her here, but I wanted to. "Because I think the girls could use a positive female role model."

She smiles again. "Good answer, superstar."

When we walk in, Linda, the director, embraces me. She's probably in her early seventies, with graying dark hair and blue eyes. She's dressed in jeans and a T-shirt, per usual. "The kids have been looking forward to this all week."

"Me too." I turn to Arizona. "I had to miss their last two games because of the Cougars' schedule. Linda, meet Arizona. She's going to assist me today."

Linda's face lights up, likely because I've never brought a woman with me before. "Arizona, it's so nice to meet one of Layton's *friends*. Do you know much about baseball?"

"I think I can probably manage."

I let out a laugh at her humility. "She's a professional

softball player. She knows *everything*. Probably better than I do."

Linda practically bursts with enthusiasm. "Wonderful. The girls on the team will be thrilled."

Arizona gives me a curious look. "There are girls on the baseball team? I assumed you meant girls in the home."

I nod. "Yep, they're on the team."

"Why isn't there a softball team too?"

"There are only a total of eleven kids on the team. There aren't enough. Besides, all the local homes only have baseball teams, not softball."

"Then why don't they participate in local Little Leagues? That way the boys can join baseball teams and the girls can join softball teams."

"Linda is only one person. She can't have them all on different teams. It's a transportation and adult supervision issue."

She mumbles, "That's bullshit. We should..."

Before she can finish the sentence, a bunch of kids come running into the room in uniforms, screaming my name. I crouch down and they all pile on and hug me.

They range in age from seven to nine years old. Their uniforms are an exact replica of the Cougars' uniforms, except instead of Cougars, theirs read Cubs.

Arizona raises her eyebrows. "Baby Cougars?"

I wink and nod. "You bet." I turn to the kids. "You guys look great. Best uniforms in the league. Right, Perry?"

I hold up my hand for him and he gives me a high five. Perry is the smallest kid on the team and probably struggles more than most. I don't know his background, it's confidential, but I think he has some sort of nerve damage in his throwing arm. It's weak and lacks mobility. And he's extremely shy. I relate to him, having been shy myself until I started playing ball.

I introduce Arizona to all the players on the team. One of the girls recognizes her. "You're the famous softball player, right?"

Arizona nods. "I sure am." She crouches down and holds out her hand. "I'm Arizona. What's your name?"

The little girl appears a bit starstruck. "I'm...I'm Lucinda. I'm a catcher too. I want to learn to throw from my knees just like you."

"Awesome. It's all in the follow-through. Maybe I can show you a few tricks before the game starts."

Lucinda's eyes widen. "Really?"

"You bet."

Lucinda pumps her fist. "Yes!" She looks Arizona up and down. "You're even prettier in person."

"Thank you. You're all so cute." She looks around at all the kids. "Who's our competition today?"

Randy, the most precocious kid in the group, answers, "The Lil Marlins. They beat us last time. By a lot." He pounds the center of his baseball mitt. "They're going to take the big L today, right, Coach Layton?"

I chuckle. "They sure are. But let's make sure we learn something and have fun. Win or lose, ice cream is on me after the game."

Linda moans. "Ugh. Layton, we've discussed this. You can't pump them full of sugar in the middle of the day and then be on your merry way."

I smile. "I sure can. Ice cream is the best part, right kids?"

They all enthusiastically agree. Linda shakes her head in exasperation.

We pile the kids into the new van I recently purchased for the home. As we're driving, Arizona takes in the new van smell. "Did you buy this for them?"

I shrug. "The old one was in bad shape. They needed it." I lean over and whisper, "Just so you know, we haven't won any games this season. The league is for ten years old and younger. We're way young and very small."

"Again, they could play in other leagues, maybe with kids their own age. Isn't there something we can do about that?"

"It's about the resources, transportation, and the adult-to-child ratio. It's just easier if they're all on the same team and in the same league. Linda is spread thin as it is. When I take them, I think it's one of her few breaks. Even then, she comes and watches the games more times than not."

She sighs in frustration. I get it. I often feel the same about the things they can and can't do.

"Does Linda get *any* time off?"

"Rarely. There's a woman who comes in once a week to give Linda a little breather. Like my grandmother, this is a lifestyle choice for her. Unfortunately, it doesn't leave much time for a personal life. My grandmother certainly never had one."

"We should offer to hang with the kids one night so she can go out. Maybe a date."

"She's, like, seventy-five."

"So? I'm sure she'd like to meet someone."

"It's nice of you to offer. I'll talk to her about it."

We arrive at the field well ahead of gametime to get warmed up. Arizona is working with Lucinda. She's teaching her how to throw down to second base from her

knees. Lucinda is one of the best athletes on the team, so she's picking it up quickly.

ARIZONA

Okay, this is officially fun. These kids are so eager to learn. I don't even need the actual game. I would have been happy simply practicing with them.

When I was a teen, I helped our local Little League run clinics, but I don't think I appreciated then how excited little kids are to learn or how rewarding it is to teach them. They're sponges.

Layton is a mild-mannered coach. That's not really my style, so I'm shouting instructions to everyone on the field.

He whispers, "Relax, sunshine. It's Little League."

My eyes widen, part in jest and part serious. "What kind of competitor are you, superstar? Now I know why you guys haven't won any games this season. If you're gonna play, play hard. Play to win."

He chuckles. "Oh boy. I've unleashed the beast."

I yell out, "Let's see the heat, Randy!"

Randy enthusiastically nods and shouts back. "You got it, Coach Z."

All the kids except Perry have hit well. I think he's got some muscle mass issue. Or maybe his bat is too heavy. I walk over to the bats to check them out. Each kid has their own wooden bat with their names burned into it.

I hold one up and ask Layton, "Where did you get these? They're awesome." I run my hands along them, appreciating the quality craftsmanship. I know from growing up with a carpenter father that these aren't regular bats available in stores.

"Oh...umm...I made them."

"You're into carpentry?"

"Just bats. I couldn't afford them growing up and I kept breaking them, so I learned how to make them. It's a hobby now. I still make my own bats. I make them for a few guys on the team too."

"Did you know that my father is a carpenter? He makes furniture, not bats, but he has his own shop."

"Quincy mentioned that once. Does he have a big shop?"

"Huge. He's in there all day, every day."

"I get the appeal. It's addicting. I lose time when I'm working on a project."

"Yep, my dad lost a lot of time in there. My mother calls it the other woman."

He smiles. "I can see that happening."

The game progresses, and we're up by one run with two outs in the last inning. There's a runner on first and the batter hits a routine flyball to right field. Perry is out there.

I shout, "Can of corn," which means it's a routine, easy-to-catch flyball.

Layton mumbles, "Not a can of corn for him. He's going to miss it."

Sure enough, he does. Shit. These poor kids were one out away from victory. Now there are runners on first and third, potentially the game-tying and winning runs.

Randy sighs and appears defeated as his chin drops to his chest. I turn to Layton. "I think he needs to come out of the game. Who's the reliever?"

"They're eight. We don't have a full bullpen. If you want to find someone to throw strikes, take your pick. None of the kids throw as hard as Randy, with the exception of Lucinda, and we need her catching."

I call a timeout and both of us walk out to the mound to strategize with Randy and Lucinda. Layton asks, "How are you feeling, Randy?"

He lifts his head and enthusiastically responds, "I can finish the game, Coach Layton. I'm no quitter." I love his competitive spirit.

I look over toward first base. The baserunner is small. I bet he's fast. "They're probably going to try to steal second base to get the winning run in scoring position. Randy, throw the ball hard and a little outside. Let Lucinda throw him out."

They both widen their eyes. Lucinda toes the dirt nervously with her shoe. "He's really fast, Coach Z. None of the catchers in our league are ever able to throw anyone out, let alone a fast runner like him. If I miss, the runner from third will score, tying the game. I don't want to let the team down."

I place my hand on her little shoulder. Her face is dirty, and her hair is a mess. She reminds me so much of myself when I was younger. "I have faith in you. You've got this." I nod in further reassurance.

She smiles. "Okay. I'll try my best."

"Toss your left knee out and throw with your whole body, just like I taught you before the game." She was throwing well in warm-ups. She has it in her.

"Yes, Coach Z."

Layton shows Randy a way to grip the ball across the seams to get a little extra speed on it. "Throw one more hard pitch. The faster you throw it, the more time Lucinda will have to throw it down to second base."

"Don't worry. I'll give him the gas. No Uncle Charlies from me."

I can't help but let out a laugh at his use of baseball slang.

Gas is a fast pitch and Uncle Charlies are curveballs, which are slower than fastballs.

Layton and I head back to the dugout. Randy winds up and does a decent job throwing a hard outside pitch. I see the runner take off from first base, just as I suspected he would. Lucinda does everything I told her to do and puts every ounce of her little body into the throw.

I can't help but grab and squeeze Layton's hand. I'm more nervous about this than my own damn games. Xavier, the shortstop, covers the throw to second. Lucinda throws a dime, and the runner is out by a mile. Game over. Cubs win.

The kids go crazy. Layton and I go even crazier, jumping up and down, hugging each other.

He holds me close a few seconds longer than is reasonable. He buries his nose into my neck and inhales. I should pull away, but I don't. I inhale his masculine scent too. It's already become familiar and comforting to me. Our bodies touching feels like something more. Want. Need.

In order to break the weirdness of the moment, I whisper, "I'm a better coach than you."

We pull apart and he laughs. "I can't argue with math. You have a perfect record."

I giggle. "I do." I motion my head toward the kids piling on each other on the field. "Let's celebrate with them."

Twenty minutes later, we're eating ice cream for lunch, per Layton's promise. The kids are having a blast, still on cloud nine from their first victory.

He and I sit on a bench outside the ice cream shop, licking our own cones. "Tell me more about the kids. Why aren't they being adopted?"

"I don't know much, their records are sealed, but I know that the older they get, the less likely it is that they'll get adopted. Some will get fostered, but people want to adopt newborn babies, not kids they assume come with baggage. It's sad."

"I think it's fantastic that you coach. I'm happy to help you anytime. I genuinely enjoyed today."

"That would be great. I truly love these kids. I'd do anything for them."

"How many group homes are there in Philly?"

"I'm not sure of the exact number. A few dozen."

"Are there *any* softball leagues for the girls or do they just tag along in baseball?"

"I don't know of any."

"Maybe we can help change things. Get them access to age-appropriate leagues, the boys playing baseball and the girls playing softball."

He seems happy with my interest in it. "I'll do whatever it takes. I don't know how it will work, but I'm willing to try."

I swear I wanted desperately to dislike Layton Lancaster when this arrangement first started, but he's making it impossible.

CHAPTER SEVEN

LAYTON

I wake in the morning and look at the clock. I have a few hours before Arizona's game.

I look down at my impossibly hard cock and blow out a long breath. He's never gone this long without being inside a woman. He's looking at me like he's pissed off. I fist him to a near-painful level and then sigh. He won't go down if he doesn't get a little bit of relief.

I grab my phone and pull up photos of Arizona from her game the other night. Seeing her in her uniform, in her catching gear, managing the game, was so damn sexy. There's one picture of her with her mask off. She's smiling. I run my thumb over her face, wishing I was able to touch the real thing.

That's the money shot for me as my hand begins to stroke my cock. I think of the way she smells. It's beachy and natural. I could probably smell her from a mile away. I'm dying to know what she tastes like. And her body. It's a dream. She's not dainty like many other women. She's strong and athletic. Toned. Perfectly toned. And her tits. I was watching them bounce while she danced at Screwballs. So damn full and perfect. I can almost feel them in my hands.

She never tries to look sexy. She just is. That's what makes her so appealing to me. She's incredibly different from other women, in the best way possible.

I've noticed that she's getting more relaxed around me. She's starting to smile more and more. It's my goal to see that smile as often as possible, whatever it takes.

When I hugged her at the game, I could feel her relax into me. She trusts me. I love that.

Now I'm thinking of the *Sports Illustrated* body image photo shoot we have coming up. She's going to be nearly naked, with her body pressed against mine for hours. I'm going to have to jerk off five times that morning to manage my way through the day. Just thinking about it sends me over the edge.

When it's over, I take a few deep breaths. Fuck, I'm totally into her. I can't deny it.

After cleaning up and getting dressed, I make myself breakfast. While I'm eating, I pick up my phone to make my weekly call. He answers on the first ring. "Layton! How's it hanging?"

"Long and low, Henry. How about you?"

"Longer and lower."

I let out a laugh. "How's work?"

"My job sucks. I hate it. My boss is a dickless ballbreaker, but I'm managing."

I have to bite my tongue. Henry having an issue with a boss is nothing new. I wish he could find something he's passionate about.

Then I have to quickly think about where he's working these days. It changes constantly. I suddenly remember that it's at a coffee shop. "I bet you make a mean cup of coffee. Are you keeping your nose clean?"

"Yes, sir," he says in a mocking tone. "I've seen a lot of pictures of you online lately. Does the famous Layton Lancaster actually have a girlfriend? I never thought I'd see the day. Gammie is dancing in her grave right now."

I chuckle. "She's pretty cool. We're just hanging out."

"She's fucking hot."

"Yep, she is. Have you been going to meetings?" He's an alcoholic.

"Every Friday night. I swear. I love shitty coffee and stale donuts. I live for that shit." He's quiet for a moment. "I'm...I'm...seeing someone. Maybe you could meet her sometime. I'd like to meet your girl too."

I'm not sure him dating is a great idea. His highs and lows are extreme, with the latter often pushing him off the wagon.

"How did you meet her?"

"She came into the coffee shop. We started flirting. That's why my boss is annoyed with me. I may have ignored the other customers to talk to her."

"Take it slowly. Relationships are better that way."

"Because you have so much relationship experience?"

"I just want to protect you."

"I'm good. I need to run. Come by sometime. I'd love to see you."

"Will do."

I'M WALKING out of my dugout onto the field. We're in a tight game in the eighth inning. I turn back and see Arizona and her friends laughing together in the stands. Several fans are watching them. A group of gorgeous women tends to draw a lot of attention. Add to that the amount of press the Anacondas are getting lately, and as many fans watch them interact as watch us play. At least it feels that way.

I notice that Arizona is eating a hot dog. Holy fuck, the way she's eating it is so damn erotic. It feels like it's happening in slow motion with some slow, sexy song playing in the background, as though it's porn hotdog eating. She's not doing it on purpose, but I can't peel my eyes from the obscene scene unfolding before me. She then licks some of the dripping ketchup off the end and I start to harden.

Oh god. I haven't gotten hard in the middle of a game in years. It fucking hurts in a jockstrap and cup. I try to adjust myself, but it's jammed in there. There's no way I can free it without being obvious. There's *definitely* no way I can play in this condition.

Cheetah walks by me and stops, giving me a skeptical look. "What's wrong with you? You look like you're in pain. Are you injured?"

I nod toward the stands while leaning over to hide the evidence. "I just saw Arizona licking a hot dog. I've got a pocket rocket situation."

He starts laughing. "Oh my god. That's classic." He turns and looks at her. As if on cue, she stuffs half the hotdog into her mouth and then licks her fingers. He begins to roll his hips a bit. "Oh shit. Now I've got a purple homewrecker too."

I whisper-yell, "You can't get hard looking at my girl!"

"She's hot. And they're all eating hot dogs. It's like weird food porn. Have you ever seen those food fetish videos on Instagram? My ex-girlfriend, Lakshmi, was totally into them. I never understood the appeal until now."

We're awkwardly holding up the game. The ump walks over. "Are you ladies done gossiping? We're in the middle of a game, in case you haven't noticed."

I grimace. "Give me a timeout. I've...umm...got a cramp. I need to stretch."

He barks, "You have two minutes, Snow White."

I squeeze my eyes shut. "Dead puppies, dead puppies, dead puppies."

Cheetah mutters, "Margaret Thatcher, Margaret Thatcher, Margaret Thatcher."

I narrow my eyes at him. "What? That's stupid."

"No, it's not. It's worked in the past."

Just then, Trey walks over. "What are you two fuckwits doing? It looks like you're swinging a hula hoop around your waists."

As we both squirm, Cheetah grits, "The girls were eating hot dogs. It was sexy as hell. Now we've both got a diamond cutter situation happening south of the border."

Trey looks at us with disgust. "How old are you? You're pathetic."

I plead, "Help us. We can't get rid of them."

He thinks for a moment. "Run through the all-time worst television series finales. That never fails to keep things at bay. I do that when I'm having sex to make sure I last longer. For me it's *Dexter*. The whole lumberjack thing sucked. And I still don't believe it's possible to survive a hurricane on a small boat in the ocean. It was a bullshit ending to a great series."

I shake my head. "No way. It was *Lost*. That ending was such a buzzkill. They were dead the whole time? I don't understand it. It's like they didn't care about the viewers."

Cheetah sighs. "You two are missing the worst series finale in existence. *Gossip Girl*. There's no way Dan was gossip girl the whole time. It doesn't even make sense. He was the vicious target of gossip girl half the time."

I stare at him with my mouth wide open. "That show is for fourteen-year-old girls. What grown man watches that teen soap opera trash?"

We both smile. I turn to Trey. "You're a genius. That worked."

I'M at another of Arizona's games today. The boys are here too. They love tagging along. Softball is a slightly different and faster game than baseball. We genuinely enjoy ourselves and we're happy to give the girls more publicity.

I look around. I think the stands are about seventy-five percent full tonight. That's progress.

At some point in the game, there's a runner on first. The batter rockets a ball to right-centerfield. The girl that was on first is motoring around the bases. The outfielder throws the ball in to Bailey, who's the cutoff person. She quickly turns and throws the ball home to

Arizona. Arizona fields the ball and then positions her body perfectly to block the runner from home plate.

I see that the runner isn't slowing down; she's about to collide with her. I feel so powerless at this moment. My heart skips a beat.

She dives headfirst into Arizona. There's a loud thump as we all witness a brutally hard collision. Arizona falls back, lifelessly laid out on her back on the ground.

In theory, I know that it's part of being a catcher. Collisions with baserunners happen all the time. But something primal takes over. It's like I'm having an out-of-body experience. I don't think, I simply react.

Before I know it, I'm hopping over the dugout and onto the field. My friends' voices screaming for me are nothing but white noise as I'm solely focused on Arizona.

She's still on her back on the ground. I run so fast that I beat the trainer to her, and I fall to my knees in front of her. She blinks her eyes open and immediately looks down at the ball still safely in her glove, which means the runner is out. All true catchers would do the same. They value getting the out over their own well-being.

She then scrunches her face and grumbles, "Layton? What are you doing here?"

I run my fingers through her hair. "Are you okay?"

She gives me a look of disgust as she sits up. "Are you nuts? Get off the field."

The trainer attempts to check her pupils with a small flashlight. Arizona brushes her away as she stands to a sea of applause from the fans.

She's a little wobbly, so I reach out to steady her.

I can't help but grab her face and look her over to

make sure she's okay. Without another thought, I kiss her forehead, thankful that she seems no worse for the wear.

At the same time, it feels like thousands and thousands of flashes go off. That's the precise moment we go from the darlings of the city of Philly to full-fledged America's sweethearts.

CHAPTER EIGHT

ARIZONA

I'm meeting with Tanner Montgomery today. After Layton's insane behavior last week, all hell has broken loose.

The video of him charging the field like a madman and then kissing my forehead has been viewed over fifteen million times on social media. It has practically played on a loop on every sports broadcasting channel. *Lovedbylayton* is the number one trending hashtag right now.

Our relationship is being splashed all over various magazines. We're on every sports and entertainment website. My phone is ringing off the hook with all kinds of offers. All of our games are sellouts. My jersey is now the top-selling jersey in all of women's sports. It's a cultural phenomenon.

Whatever the owners were possibly hoping to get out of our fake relationship has come to fruition. The Anacondas are all over the place. Everyone stops us on the street for pictures and autographs. All the girls on the team are reaping the benefits. Kam secured a big endorsement for a skincare line. Ripley is modeling plus-sized lingerie. Bailey has offers but said she isn't interested.

Reagan Daulton insisted on arranging security for me. I have a driver who doubles as a guard when I go in and out of larger, public places.

I've had over a thousand calls about endorsements, which is why I'm finally meeting with Tanner. We decided to meet at his office considering I can no longer eat in a public place without being bombarded by fans.

A woman behind a reception desk greets me with a smile and points toward an office door. "He's expecting you, Ms. Abbott. Please head right in."

I walk into his office where I see a little girl sitting on his lap.

He stands and holds out his hand. As I shake it, he says, "Sorry. My nanny quit this morning, so my angel is working with her daddy today. Right, angel?"

The adorable brunette, little girl seems to be starstruck. Speechless. I smile at her. "Hi, I'm Arizona."

She stands, frozen, with her mouth wide open. Tanner chuckles. "You're her favorite player. We've been to a few games. She has your posters all over her room. This is Harper." He looks down. "Harper, can you say hello to Ms. Abbott?"

I correct him, "Arizona. You can call me Arizona. I love your name, Harper. I heard that you're a really good softball player. Is that true?"

Her eyes widen. "You've heard about me?"

"Yep. Layton Lancaster is a big fan of yours."

She sucks in a breath. "Wow."

"Maybe we can throw a ball sometime."

Now both her eyes and mouth are wide open. "Can my best friend, Andie, come too? She loves watching you play."

"Of course."

Tanner nods. "Andie is the daughter of one of the owners, Beckett Windsor."

"Oh, I met her once. She comes to games with her mom and dad all the time."

He nods before looking back down at Harper. "Angel, can you hang out with Shannon and read a book or something?"

"Sure, Daddy."

He calls the woman who was sitting at the desk out front, who I'm guessing is his assistant, and she walks into his office to gather Harper.

Once they leave, he motions for me to sit, which I do. "Sorry about that. I have shared custody with my ex-wife. My nanny unexpectedly quit, and my ex is out of town. It's been a little crazy. I won't leave her with just anyone. It's not like hiring a temp to work in an office."

"It's really not a big deal. You know, one of my teammates usually nannies in the off-season. She's great with kids. If you can work with our softball schedule for the remaining weeks of the season, she'll be wide open after that. Maybe that could work for both of you."

His eyes light up. "Harper would love it if a professional softball player was her nanny. Which player? I'm familiar with the team at this point."

"Bailey Hart."

"She plays second base, right?"

"That's the one."

"If you could leave me her contact info, I'll call her immediately."

"No problem."

"Great. Let's talk turkey. Obviously, your face and name are everywhere right now. I know softball players don't make a fraction of the amount baseball players do. This is a huge financial opportunity for you."

"I know. I'm overwhelmed. I'm not totally comfortable with all this attention, but I also know I'll probably never have another opportunity like it, and I'd be crazy not to capitalize."

"I totally agree. I've reviewed all the offers you sent and narrowed it down to the ones I think will best benefit your brand and pad your bank account."

"I have a brand?"

He lets out a laugh. "You do. You're not just a pretty face holding up a product. There's substance to you. You're about strength, health, fueling the body, hard work, perseverance, clean living, work ethic…"

I hold up my hands. "Okay, okay. I get it. You'll give me as big of a head as Layton."

He chuckles. "No one has a bigger head than Layton Lancaster." We both smile at that. "In all seriousness, little girls all over the country want to be you. And unlike many other so-called role models out there, parents like me are happy to have someone like you as the role model for our little girls. I don't want my daughter to be a Kardashian. I want her to be an Abbott."

"I never thought of it that way."

"Think about it. If you were a parent, would you want your daughter to look up to overprivileged women famous for sex tapes, who star on reality shows and look like they've never enjoyed a burger, or would you rather they look up to someone like you who has worked hard, remained disciplined, and sacrificed to be at the pinnacle of her sport?"

I nod. "I understand what you're saying."

We spend the next hour going through all the offers. We focus on a few that promote what I'm learning is my *brand*, are easiest for me to commit to, and those he thinks he'll be able to negotiate a good amount of money for on my behalf. I can't believe how much money I'm going to make this year. Way more than the entire rest of my life combined. I'm going to make Quincy-like dollars, something unheard of for softball players.

We get to the final one on the list. It's a huge, international bathing suit company that wants both Layton and me. Tanner already knew about this one because it was offered to Layton too. When the season is over, they want us to spend two months traveling the world. They want to hit multiple exotic beaches with us in their products. It's the trip of a lifetime.

He leans back in his chair. "Let's discuss Fantasy Suits and their offer. It's technically a conflict for me to represent you in this because of Layton, so you're going to need to have someone else represent you on this deal. They should discuss the details of the contract with you more thoroughly than I'm permitted to. Layton waived the conflict for me to give you one small piece of advice. After that, my professional ethics rules dictate that I have to step aside, despite Layton agreeing to waive all conflict."

"I understand. What detail?"

"They're offering you a fraction of what they're offering Layton. I have his permission to share that with you. He's upset on your behalf and implored me to tell you about it so that you can rectify the situation."

I shrug. "He's a huge star. I'm not."

"I hate to break it to you, but you're now a huge star too. Again, I have Layton's permission to say this. He's a fading star in a sea of stars. There are a lot bigger names in baseball right now than Layton Lancaster. He's replaceable. You're not. You are *the* star of women's softball. You're the face of the sport. You're the one every little girl like mine wants to imitate. They want to look like you. They want to play like you. They want to wear the same clothes as you. Fantasy Suits is well aware of this."

He briefly pauses. "I know you two have that *Sports Illustrated* photo shoot coming up. Can I be straight without it coming across as sleazy? I promise I'm just trying to help."

I let out a laugh. "Please do."

"You're stunning. That's not opinion. That's fact. You have a gorgeous, healthy figure. You practically ooze sex appeal in everything you say and do."

I can't help but cringe at the last one.

He smiles. "The fact that you're so unaware of it makes you that much more appealing. You don't post provocative pictures of yourself on social media. You've unwittingly made those pictures *more* valuable because none currently exist."

"What exactly are you getting at?"

He clears his throat. "Once the photos from *Sports Illustrated* hit the stands, you're going to be catapulted into the stratosphere. Even more so than you are now. I know it. Layton knows it. Fantasy Suits *definitely* knows it. You should prepare for it. Fantasy Suits is trying to book you in today's dollars when, in a few weeks, you're going to be pulling A-List dollars. That's really all I can say without the conflict being too much. Find a lawyer. Have them push for the dollars you should be getting. Have them explain all the terms of the contract."

"I hear what you're saying. I'm less worried about the money than I am about Layton and me. You know we're not in a real relationship. Our little PR arrangement is supposed to end when the season is over. Are we now supposed to continue the facade? Through the Fantasy Suits shoot? Through the release of the campaign? When does this end? Both of our personal lives are on hold until it does."

"I understand your concerns. It would most definitely mean extending your relationship with him for the duration of that contract too. It's clearly included in the terms. You and Layton are the only ones who can figure out if that works. But please pay attention to the language about your relationship in the contract. They have a lot of control."

I leave his office feeling good about everything except Fantasy Suits. Layton and I may need to discuss it further.

LAYTON

Okay, I may have overreacted when I charged the field last week. I saw her hurt and had this innate need to get to her. I've never in my life felt more protective than I did at that moment.

Arizona is off today, and I don't need to be at the ballpark until later this afternoon. We decided to go for a jog around the river. We move in slightly awkward silence for a bit until she admits, "I met with Tanner this morning."

"Yes, I knew you were meeting. How did it go?"

"It went really well. He's so smart and helpful. Thanks for advocating for me on the bathing suit deal. I appreciate that you were looking out for me."

"You deserve to make real money on it. Their offer was bullshit."

She nods nervously. "Do...do you want to do it?"

I was anticipating this question from her. "There are worse ways to spend two months than traveling the world to exotic beaches on someone else's dime. Have you done much traveling?"

"None. I've never left the country. It's not that though. The traveling sounds incredible. It's more about us continuing to have to fake a relationship. There's a lot of language in the contract about the status of our relationship. From what I can tell, we basically have to continue to fake things not just through the shoot, but through the three-month campaign afterward."

"I know. Tanner said they won't budge on the issue, and I understand why. They're selling the same thing Reagan Daulton is trying to sell. There's already proof it works."

She silently nods.

"I understand that this is life-changing money for you. That's why I'm willing to consider it." And I wouldn't mind extending our time together because my crush is reaching feverish heights. "Why don't we see how the *Sports Illustrated* shoot goes for us and then make a decision? It's kind of an intimate shoot. Let's make sure we're comfortable and that it runs smoothly before we commit to months of doing that every day."

"I hear you. That makes sense. We'll shelve it for a week or so."

"Great. That's settled. Tell me what your life was like in Southern California after you graduated college."

She gives me a sad smile. "For a few years, it was amazing. I missed Ripley, but I made new friends. I liked my teammates. I started seeing Marc about two years after college. I know you don't see it now, but I was fun back then."

I let out a laugh. "I think you're fun."

She rolls her eyes. "I'm not. Anyway, we had a good time for a long time. After the wedding that never was, I clammed up. I did a lot of thinking. There were several red flags with him that I missed. Ignored."

"Like what?"

"I'm pretty sure he cheated on me. He was always so secretive and territorial about his phone. He never made real attempts to get to know my family. Quincy hated him and was never shy about it."

I let out a laugh. "I have no doubt. Quincy would hate anyone you dated."

She nods. "True. Marc never came to my games. I know he was busy with his own career, but I think it's weird that he never cared enough to come cheer for me. I'm not sure I realized it until you and the gang started coming to our games. I know you're contractually obligated to come, but..."

"I'd come to your games even if I wasn't obligated. I love watching you play."

She blows out a breath. "I know you do. That's what made me realize how strange it was that he didn't. After the breakup, I stopped going out. I spent a lot of time on the beach. Alone. If there's one thing I miss about Southern California, it's the beaches."

"The Jersey shore is only like an hour away. It's not as pretty as Southern California beaches, but it gets the job done."

"Maybe I'll check it out after the season."

I smile. "Remember, we have seasons here."

She lets out a laugh. "Right. I need to prepare myself for my first Philly winter."

"It gets cold. *Very* cold."

She stops running. "Can we sit for a minute?"

I immediately stop with her. "Of course."

We find a nearby bench and sit. Her eyes fill up with tears. It physically hurts my heart to see her in pain.

"What's wrong?"

"It's a really emotional thing for me to talk about."

"You don't have to tell me if you don't want to."

"I want you to know. It will help you understand me a bit better. My family and Ripley are the only people in the world that know the full story. Can I trust you to keep it between us?"

"Of course."

I take her hand in mine, knowing she needs it. I'm relieved that she lets me.

"Marc and I fought a lot. I kept telling myself it was passion, but I know now it wasn't. A week before our wedding, I found out I was pregnant. I was honestly over-the-moon excited. I've always wanted to grow my family and didn't think it was a big deal to start a little earlier than expected. Marc didn't feel the same. He said he wasn't ready for kids. He also mentioned possibly not being ready for marriage. I foolishly thought it was run-of-the-mill, average nerves and stayed the course. I thought once we were married, he'd feel differently. I loved him...or I thought I did. Sometimes I'm not so sure. Nonetheless, I moved forward as if he didn't express his concerns to me."

The tears are freefalling now. I can't help but wipe them with my thumb and then taste her tears with my tongue. I don't know why I did that. I wanted to take away her pain. She watches on, her eyes darkening. We stare at each other in silence. My eyes must mirror the longing I see in hers.

A little girl softly saying, "Excuse me," breaks whatever just happened between us.

I turn and smile at her. She's holding a piece of paper and a pen. "Do you want my autograph, sweetie?"

She shakes her head and points to Arizona.

"You want Arizona's?"

She nods. Arizona discreetly wipes the remaining tears and smiles as she gives the little girl her autograph and poses for a picture.

Once the little girl is gone, I wrap my arm around Arizona, sensing she needs it. "Continue. Please." For some reason, I need to know.

"You know the callous way he broke things off, via text. I was in shock and hysterical for days. Inconsolable. Three days after the non-wedding, I suffered a miscarriage." I squeeze her close to me. "You never know the real reasons for these things happening, but I imagine being emotionally distraught was a contributing factor."

"Maybe it just wasn't meant to be."

She nods. "That's what my family and Ripley always say. I know they're right. It wasn't the ideal circumstances to bring a child into the world. It doesn't make it hurt less. I can't explain it. I was prepared to spend my life with him, yet he ended things via text. Then the fact that he didn't care enough to at least contact me regarding our baby cut me even deeper. It's not something you easily move past. The whole situation robbed me of the joy I once had."

She looks down. "I...umm...haven't been able to be intimate with a man since. I haven't been touched by a man since him. I'm terrified of it. I haven't gone on a single date. Our fake relationship is the most intimate thing I've had since it all went down."

I tuck her hair behind her ear and rub my thumb along her cheek. "Thank you for sharing it with me. I'm sorry for what you've been through. I hope you know that you can trust me. I care about you."

She gives me a small smile. "I know you do. You charged on the field like a psycho the other night because of a collision at the plate. You know more than most that collisions are standard operating procedure for us catchers, yet you acted like a deranged lunatic."

I can't help but let out a laugh. "Yeah, I may have been a little crazy. I saw you go down and I lost my marbles for a minute. I needed to make sure you were okay."

"Reagan Daulton couldn't have scripted it any better."

"It wasn't scripted. My concern wasn't fake."

She nods. "I know."

"For what it's worth, I personally think you're different in just the few weeks I've known you. Maybe you're coming out of your hibernation. You're definitely smiling more often. I love your smile. It's contagious."

As if on cue, she smiles. I'm so filled with pride that I put it on her face. "I think you're right. Even though our relationship is fake, it's made me realize how much I miss..." she moves her hand between me and her, "being with someone. Being spontaneous. You might not believe it, Layton Lancaster, but I was a little nutty when I was still a functional human being."

"Nuttier than dancing publicly to *NSYNC?"

She giggles. "*Way* more."

I stand and help her do the same. "Follow me."

"Where are we going?"

I wink at her. "You'll see."

About twenty minutes of jogging later, we're at the foot of the steps of the Philadelphia Art Museum. The steps which were made famous in the movie *Rocky* when he ran up them and then jumped up and down in celebration at the top. There's even a statue of Rocky next to the steps.

Arizona smiles. "The *Rocky* steps?"

"Are you ready to do the most touristy thing you can do in Philadelphia and run up them?"

Her eyes widen. "People will see us. It will probably be on SportsCenter tonight."

I shrug. "Who fucking cares? It's fun. A little... *spontaneous*. A little...*nutty*."

Placing my foot on the first of many steps, I challenge, "I'll race you. I'll give a Cheetah-type striptease at your next game if you beat me."

She grins from ear to ear. "What if you win?"

"Hmm. You have to dance wildly at my game tonight."

Her face immediately drops. "I'm not coming tonight."

"What? Why not?"

"I...umm...can't. I have something."

I'm trying to mask my disappointment. We're home for the next week, but then we're on the road for the following two. I want to see her whenever I get the chance. But I know she's sad today, and I want to keep things light, so I bite my tongue.

"Okay. Well, at the next game you come to."

As she sneakily gives herself a head start, she shouts back at me, "Deal!"

I yell, "Cheater," as I begin my own climb.

We race as fast as we can to the top of the steps. I'm not sure why I agreed to race the fastest player in softball, but I did. And I lost. It was totally worth it to watch her celebrate at the top. Like Rocky in the movie, she lifts her hands in the air in triumph and jumps around in glee. I can't help but join her silliness. We even mock shadow box like Rocky did.

A few people start taking videos of us, but who cares? I'm frankly happy that we'll have this moment memorialized. The moment when I think I see Arizona begin to truly break free of her demons.

After taking a few photos with fans at the *Rocky* statue back at the bottom of the steps, her more than me, we part ways knowing we'll see each other at the big photo shoot tomorrow.

CHAPTER NINE

LAYTON

I don't know why it's bothering me so much that Arizona isn't coming to our game tonight against Anaheim. Maybe I'm just annoyed that she has no legitimate reason for not coming. I've grown accustomed to seeing her in the stands. Her games are mostly in the afternoons, so she's been to nearly all our home games. And her brother is pitching tonight. The whole thing makes no sense to me.

We're on the field. It's the second inning and there are two outs. Quincy is throwing heat. He's mowed down the first five batters of the game. Marc Whitaker steps into the box.

I can see Quincy's face tighten all the way from the pitcher's mound. He starts mumbling to himself. I wonder if he has an issue with Whitaker.

I remove my mask and turn back to the umpire. "I need a timeout."

He nods, holds up his hands, and yells, "Time."

I slowly jog out to the mound. "What's up, Q? Do you have beef with this guy?"

He gives me a look of shock. "You don't know?"

I shake my head. "Obviously not."

"Whitaker is her former fiancé."

"Whose former fiancé?"

He gives me a *duh* look.

My eyes widen as things fall into place. "*He's* the one? That's *the* Marc?"

Quincy nods.

"Holy shit."

"I don't know how much you know..."

"I know everything. I just didn't know it was *him*." I can feel my jaw ticking. My stomach is in knots. I want to pound his face in.

"I've beaned him every time I've faced him over the past year. The league says if I do it again, I'll be suspended. I don't know what to do." Beaning is when a pitcher intentionally hits an opposing batter with a pitch.

I squeeze his shoulder. "I've got you, brother."

He subtly nods at me, knowing I'll have his back.

"Walk him."

"What? Are you crazy? I'm not giving him a free pass."

"He's speedy, right?"

"Yes."

"Walk him, and then throw three straight balls to the next batter. Trust me."

Without any more hesitation, he says, "Will do."

I head back to home plate and crouch down. Whitaker

steps into the batter's box. He's a big guy in that he's muscular. I'm much taller than him, but he's built like a brick house. He's been in the league for years, but I've never had any real interaction with him. I'm about to now.

He spits in front of me and then grunts, "If that fucker hits me again, we're going to rumble."

I smack my glove and hold it up for Quincy. After the third ball in a row, Whitaker mumbles, "What a pussy." He side-eyes me and smirks. "Say hi to Arizona for me. I hope you're enjoying my sloppy seconds."

I have to bite the inside of my cheek not to kill this guy. It's tempting to take him down right now, but what I have in mind will be much more satisfying.

After Quincy throws ball four, Whitaker takes first base. The douchebag flips his damn bat in triumph, like he hit a home run.

Through gritted teeth, I allow him to steal both second and third on the next two pitches, feigning fumbling with the ball. On the third pitch, I pretend like the ball got by me and run back to search for it. Whitaker takes the bait and sprints toward home.

With the ball in my glove, I run back toward home plate. We're on a collision course. It's like two trains about to meet on the same track. One is about to get derailed. It's a matter of who will get there first and who will stand strong.

With my free hand, I squeeze my glove closed so the ball doesn't fall out and lower my shoulders. We collide like two Mack trucks. You can hear a collective, "Ooh," from the forty-five thousand fans in attendance.

Whitaker goes down. Hard. I don't. I stand over him as he gasps for air, drop the ball on his chest like a microphone, and calmly say, "Keep my girl's name out of your mouth."

I see Quincy smiling as he runs my way and practically jumps on my back. "Fuck yeah, brother."

We start walking off the field toward our dugout with big, shit-eating grins on our faces. Whitaker is now sitting up with a trainer giving him attention. He shouts, "She sucks a great cock though, doesn't she?"

My world stops in that moment. I can't hear anything. All I see is red. Without another thought, I throw my glove to the ground and run toward him at full speed. I dive at his body like a linebacker tackling a running back, taking him back down to the ground. Quincy and I both get in several punches before our teammates and his pull us apart. Then insanity breaks loose with everyone on both teams trading punches. Our team against theirs.

That's the thing about teammates. They don't know what provoked the altercation with Whitaker, they just know we're pissed at him and that's enough reason to swing away at anyone wearing the opposing uniform.

The fans are going nuts. Bench-clearing brawls don't happen often anymore, but when they do, the fans love it.

The officials and coaches eventually break us all apart. Fifteen minutes later, Whitaker, Quincy, and I are all ejected from the game.

ARIZONA

I'm sitting on my couch with my three best friends watching the funniest softball movie ever created. *All-Stars* is a mockumentary that came out about twelve years ago. It follows the families of an all-star softball team. The girls are ten years old, and they have crazy, overzealous helicopter parents. It's dead-on accurate, and, despite having seen it at least fifty times, the four of us are hysterically laughing. My eyes are completely watering in laughter.

I shake my head. "This is the most underrated comedy of all time."

Ripley smiles. "Totally. My mom made me sleep with my ball and glove like the father in the movie made his daughter sleep with the bat."

Kam nods. "Our dad was like the stat-keeper, lunatic character. He knew every girl on the team's exact stats at all times. He'd go nuts if the coach didn't play them where he thought they should according to the precise stats."

We've got piles of ice cream, popcorn, beer, and candy on the coffee table. I'm thankful to my friends for tonight. I couldn't go to the game and see Marc. I'm okay, more than okay, with not being married to him. But it just reminds me of the fact that I know he never truly cared about me and, of course, about the baby I lost. A baby he never once cared enough to ask about. He probably assumes I had an abortion. Or maybe he doesn't think about it at all. How could I have been so wrong about him?

Even though Ripley is the only one here that knows about the baby, Kam and Bailey know I don't want to see Marc, and that's enough reason for them to be here with me.

I can't even watch the game, which is why Ripley suggested

this movie. It never fails to make us belly laugh and forget anything weighing on us.

I saw the sadness in Layton today because I wasn't coming. I felt terrible, but he doesn't know it's Marc Whitaker, and I see no reason to tell him. Hopefully Quincy will behave himself. I told him to stop beaning Marc every time he faces him.

Bailey turns to me. "Thanks for recommending me for the nanny job. I'm interviewing with the man and his daughter tomorrow. He said she loves softball. It could be fun. I need something to do in the off-season, and it's only part-time since he has shared custody. It gives me the opportunity to work out and hang out with you guys. This could be perfect for me."

"I thought of you as soon as he said his nanny quit. I met Harper. She's adorable."

Suddenly, all of our phones ping at the same time. We see a sports app notification that there was a big brawl at the Cougars game tonight. I breathe, "Oh shit. My brother probably beaned Marc and then the teams fought. He can't afford to get suspended. I begged him not to. Turn on the game. Let's see what happened."

Ripley fiddles with the remote until she finds the right channel. There's coverage of the fight at the Cougars game, but it's not of my brother and Marc. It's Layton. He cleaned Marc's clock during a collision at home plate. Marc is a solid wall of muscle, but Layton put him right to the ground and then taunted him by dropping the ball on his chest. I think he spit on him too. I can't make out what he said, but he definitely said something nasty to Marc. I guess Layton figured out who he was.

We see my brother practically skipping over to Layton in glee before they embrace. I get choked up with emotion for Layton. He did it for Quincy. So Quincy wouldn't get suspended. *And I know in the back of my mind he did it for me too.*

We see them then walking off the field. I shrug. "That's not so bad. I wouldn't call that a brawl. More like a one-sided beat down."

That thought is short-lived because suddenly we see both Quincy and Layton sprint toward Marc and take turns punching him before it does, in fact, turn into a full-on brawl. Both teams are going at it, trading punches. It's mayhem.

I gasp. "Oh my god."

The ticker under the video footage reads, *Arizona Abbott's brother and boyfriend fight with her former fiancé as the teams turn a baseball game into a heavyweight fight.*

In the end, it looks like Quincy, Marc, and Layton were all tossed from the game. Quincy and Layton walked off shoulder to shoulder with huge smiles on their faces. Marc had to leave the field with the assistance of two trainers.

Kam smiles. "Holy shit. There was a brawl in your honor. You're my idol."

"I need to get down there. Thanks for tonight. I'll see you guys later."

All three of them stand. Ripley grabs my hand. "We'll go with you."

We head down to the stadium and enter through the friends and family entrance. The game is still going on, but the personnel recognize us, so we manage to get to the locker room area. I turn to my friends. "Let me go in alone."

Bailey nods. "We'll be waiting right out here." She rubs my arm. "We love you."

Kam rubs my other arm. "If any of the guys are naked, come get us."

Despite the heavy moment, I let out a laugh. Only Kam.

I carefully walk into the locker room. I see Layton sitting

alone on a bench, still in his uniform and catching gear. His legs are spread wide, and his head is down while he runs his fingers through his hair over and over again.

"Are you okay?"

His head snaps up. I see a small bruise forming on his cheekbone. "I'm fine. I thought you weren't coming tonight."

"I came when I heard what happened. Where's my brother?"

"He's in the training room having his hand iced."

I walk toward him and stand between his legs. I run my fingertips over his injury. He looks up at me with sad eyes. "Why didn't you tell me who it was?"

"I told you the night I met you that I don't trust baseball players. Now you know why."

He grabs the arm of my hand that's on his face, turns his head, and softly kisses the inside of my wrist. He looks me in the eyes and whispers, "I hate that he hurt you. I hate how much you've suffered."

His eyes are full of nothing but sincerity and pain. Pain for me. My mind is swimming with emotions for this man.

His hands move up the bare backs of my thighs and pull me an inch or two closer to him. My body reacts to the intimate contact in a way it hasn't for a long time. I take a moment to enjoy the fact that the touch of a man still feels good. Perhaps it's just this particular man.

He sinks his face into my body, just above my stomach. I run my hands through his hair over and over as we're otherwise silent.

At some point, he tilts his head up so his chin rests on me. I've now got my hands on his scruffy face, caressing it. Running my fingers lightly over his injury again, I whisper, "I hate seeing you hurt too."

I can feel my heart pounding a million beats per minute.

He stares at my lips as he licks his own. Bending as we move our faces closer to each other, I breathe, "Layton."

He stretches his face toward mine and breathes back, "Arizona."

Just as our lips first meet, we hear the locker room door open. I jump back several feet from him and turn in time to see Quincy round the corner.

He gives me a huge smile. "Hey, Z. Did you see Layton take out dickhead? It was epic. That guy is going to be pissing blood for a week. Let's hope the fucker loses a kidney. Serves him right."

I nod. "It was pretty incredible." I notice his black eye, split lip, and ice-wrapped hand. "Are you in pain?"

He instinctively touches his injuries. "Nah. They're superficial. Dickwad is in way worse condition. He looks like he was in a boxing match. His eye is swollen shut. They had to carry him off the field." He turns to Layton with a big grin. "Lancaster, I think I'm in love with you."

Yeah, brother, me too.

CHAPTER TEN

ARIZONA

The headlines this morning all read *Laid Out by Layton*. I can't deny taking a little pleasure in that. Marc is probably humiliated. He had his ass kicked on national television and it's being replayed over and over again. There are hundreds of funny memes of him going down. The ones of Layton dropping the ball on his chest are my favorite. The intensity on Layton's face almost brings me to my knees.

Today is our *Sports Illustrated* shoot. I'm a mixed bag of emotions over Layton Lancaster. He's not what I thought he'd be. He's attentive and caring. Sweet and sincere. Kind and even humble most of the time. A few weeks ago, I would have used none of those words to describe him.

I'm in my dressing room, looking at myself in the mirror. I'm wearing dark-blue lace panties and a matching bra that practically has my boobs pouring out of it. I've never wished for smaller boobs more than I do right now. The only other article of clothing I have on is a Cougars button-down white-and-blue pinstripe jersey.

How did I get here? I'm in a fake relationship with the famous Layton Lancaster, and we're about to do a half-naked photoshoot. Our faces are plastered on every website and gossip magazine, but now we're about to be featured in the number one sports magazine in the world as a couple. The craziest part? I think I have feelings for him, and I think he has feelings for me too. What they are, I don't know. What does it mean? I haven't got a clue.

What I *do* know is that I'm going to have his hands all over my half-naked body all day long. This is going to be an exercise in restraint.

I take several deep breaths. I'm doing this for my team, for my league, for young girls aspiring to be softball players. I keep repeating all this over and over in my head, hoping to keep the nerves at bay. It's not working.

As I'm finishing the buttons on the jersey, I hear a knock on my dressing room door. I shout, "Come in."

Much to my relief, it's LeRond. He gasps as he clutches his chest. "Oh my lawd, you look beautiful. I brought you a little something to help."

He holds up and wiggles two mini bottles of tequila in my face.

"Oh god, thank you." I reach out my hands and wiggle my fingers. "Gimme, gimme."

He chuckles as he hands them to me. I quickly open one and down it immediately. As it makes its way through my body, I let out a deep breath, finally feeling my body relax a bit.

"Do you feel better, foxy lady?"

"Much better. Thank you."

I hand him the second bottle. "Can you hold this in case I need it later? I don't have...umm...any pockets in this." I run my hands down my body. "Quite the outfit selection. I assume I have you to thank."

He smiles. "That's what they want you wearing. I see you went with the dark-blue undies."

I nod. There were two sets for me to choose from. One in the Cougars darker blue and one in the Anacondas lighter blue. I figured I should match Layton's uniform top that I'm wearing. "I did. Does it look okay?"

"Okay? Way more than okay. You might be the first woman to turn me on in...well...ever."

I giggle. "I'll take that as a compliment."

"You should. Try to stay calm. There are worse things than being half naked with one of the hottest men on earth."

Please just let me make it through this unscathed.

LeRond offers me his arm. "Are you ready?"

"As I'll ever be."

We walk out of the dressing room and into the studio. There must be ten people working on all the equipment. I didn't realize so many people would be here. That makes it more embarrassing. All these people looking at me, nearly naked, while Layton's hands are all over my body.

LeRond whispers, "Relax. Pretend you're at a pool in a bathing suit."

"Millions of people don't see me in a bathing suit."

He mumbles, "They will soon."

Before I can respond, a man with a camera around his neck makes his way over to me and holds out his hand. In heavily French-accented English, he says, "You must be Arizona." He pronounces it *Air-eee-zo-nah*. "I'm Francois."

I shake his hand. "It's nice to meet you, Francois."

A younger, small man who already looks exhausted, is trailing behind him with five more cameras around his neck.

Francois motions toward him. "This is my assistant, Raphael. If you need anything, ask him."

"Thank you."

He points to the green flooring in front of a green screen. "We'll work here. I will transform the green floor and backdrop into various parts of a ball field in my studio after we take the pictures."

I nod. "I understand. Is Layton here yet?" I haven't seen him this morning.

Before he can answer, a door on the other side of the room opens and Layton walks out. He's wearing an Anacondas jersey, but it's unbuttoned. Shit. I don't need to see his chest and abs, which, incidentally, are chiseled like they were carved by an artist. He's got a drop of chest hair that matches the hair on his head and a sexy trail from his belly button into his pants. He's broad, muscular, and gorgeous. Perfection. I hope my battery-operated version of Captain America is charged. He will most definitely be getting a workout tonight.

When I'm done staring at his top half, I move down to his bottom half. It occurs to me that he's in baseball pants. I cross my arms as I turn to LeRond. With an extreme amount of edge, I say, "They must have forgotten *my* pants."

LeRond has a guilty look. "Sorry. It came from above."

Layton realizes why I'm pissed. He nods his head. "She's right. Either we both wear pants or neither of us wears pants."

LeRond places his thumb up to his ear and pinkie by his mouth like it's a pretend telephone and starts bobbing his head. "Aha. Yes. I see. No problem." He pretends to hang up the imaginary phone. "It's just come down from management that neither of you should be wearing pants."

Layton and I can't help but laugh at LeRond, easing the tension a bit. Layton unbuttons and removes his pants.

For the love of God. Why did I open my big mouth? I

should have voted for him to keep them on. He's wearing navy-blue boxer briefs that leave very little to the imagination. His legs are even more muscular than one would expect from a catcher. The fact that he squats all day certainly shows. His thick quads are bigger than my entire body.

LeRond starts fanning himself and breathes, "Holy hell." I can't disagree with that.

He eventually composes himself. "You two remember that this is for a positive body image issue. All different types of athletes will be represented. You two were chosen for baseball and softball. Show off your sport as best you can. Unfortunately, I have to go. You have my cell if you need anything."

I give him a small smile. "Thanks, LeRond."

He leaves and Francois motions for us to stand on the green mat, which we do. I run my fingertips over Layton's cheek. "Wow, you can't see any bruising."

"Raphael put something on my face to hide it."

I giggle. "Layton Lancaster, are you wearing makeup?"

He smiles. "I thought it would have been badass to show it, but Raphael said no."

Francois manipulates our bodies a bit as he gets what seem to be test shots. We then take a large grouping of pictures, posing with our bats and gloves. A few with our arms crossed. We haven't had to touch much. A few back-to-back poses, but nothing too intimate. Maybe this won't be so bad.

Eventually, Francois says, "Arizona, turn your back to Layton." Gladly. I don't think I can look at his perfect body anymore. "Layton, wrap your arms around her and pull her into your body. Then slowly explore her body with your hands."

The moment I feel his front on my back, I can feel my eyes flutter. When his hands touch my thighs, I have to contain the moan. Would it be awkward to spontaneously orgasm in front of a dozen people from a simple hug?

"Arizona, tilt your head to the side. Layton, run your lips up her neck, but don't actually kiss her. It will create creases in your face. We want the illusion of kissing, but *never* an actual kiss. It's better for the camera."

As his hands move up and down my waist and hips, his soft lips gently move up and down my neck. My whole body erupts in goosebumps. I'm powerless against it.

"Good job, Arizona. You relaxing your mouth like that looks authentic. Like you're genuinely enjoying it."

I can feel Layton silently laughing, so I throw him a solid elbow to the stomach on the side facing away from the camera.

He gives me a mock grunt of pain in a way only I can hear, though it's like my elbow hit a brick wall. Does he have any fat on his body?

After several photos in this position, Francois says, "Arizona, now turn around and face him." I do, but I can't look Layton in the eyes. Those blue-green eyes of his will be my official undoing. "Layton, slowly unbutton her shirt."

I snap my head to the photographer. "What?"

"Mon chéri, you agreed to a boudoir photo shoot. It's about body image. We need to actually *see* your body. You know you're wearing a thousand-dollar pair of undergarments. It's art showing your love, your sport, and your athletic body. Pretend we're not here."

If they weren't here, he wouldn't have his hands all over my body. At least that's what I'm telling myself.

Layton begins to unbutton my shirt. I notice a slight tremble to his fingers as he works his way down. Him being nervous puts me at ease.

"Layton, open her shirt so we can see her body."

He spreads it open while his eyes take me in. Slowly.

Sensually. Seductively. He sucks in a breath. I think his eyes are turning a deeper shade of blue. Is he turned on right now?

Francois's scoffing breaks Layton's obvious stare down. "If I didn't know better, Layton, I'd think it's the first time you're seeing her body. You're an excellent actor. She does have a beautiful figure. Now move your hands all over that work of art. You'll be the envy of every man in America. In the world."

His hands don't move from my shirt. He first looks me in the eyes, seeking permission.

I give him a small nod.

His big hands wrap around my bare waist before slowly moving over my stomach. They then move up and down my sides, tracing the same path over and over. Our eyes maintain contact. Once again, I have goosebumps everywhere. There's no way he's not noticing them, but at least he's not being a dick about it.

Our mouths are so close together. I can smell his breath. It's minty and something else. I realize it's tequila. He needed a shot of liquid courage too.

"Good, now over her breasts."

Layton turns his head to Francois. "That's not necessary. This isn't porn. It's about body image. You can get your shot without me fully groping her on camera. I think she deserves more respect than that."

Maybe he doesn't want to touch me, or maybe he's just being chivalrous. I'm confident it's the latter.

Francois sighs. "Very well. Place your hands on her hips." He does. "Now, Arizona, rub your hands on his chest and stomach."

Fucking hell. I start to move my hands over his mountainous pecs and rippled abs. His body is ridiculous. I hate how much it's turning me on to both touch him and have him touch me. I can feel the wetness between my legs.

I've never been so grateful to not be a man. At least I can hide it.

That causes me to look down where I learn that Layton's boxer briefs are getting stretched and tighter by the second. He notices my line of sight and whispers, "Sorry, I can't help it. You're so sexy."

For some reason, I feel the need to protect him like he did for me. I whisper back, "Lift my front leg. It will hide it from the camera."

He nods as his hand moves to the back of my thigh, which is making me feel all kinds of things. He lifts it around his body. My leg now shields his hard-as-a-rock cock from everyone but me. I can't seem to take my eyes off it. It's massive. I'm not sure how long we'll be able to hide it. It's like having a third person between us.

I hear Francois. "Very nice. Good idea, Layton." He continues clicking away while Layton's lips move all around my face and neck, leaving a scorching hot trail in their wake.

My fingertips slowly travel up his chest, over his broad shoulders, and then to the back of his neck. I run them through his hair. It's soft. Softer than I imagined. *Yes, I've imagined it.*

"Layton, lift her other leg too." Francois then looks at me. "I know they're long, but wrap them around him, Arizona. Lock your ankles."

Layton looks down at me with concern written all over his handsome face. I'm realizing that he's thinking of the words I said to him yesterday. About my intimacy issues.

I whisper, "I'm okay. It's fine." In fact, I feel totally comfortable in his warm embrace. At ease.

I tighten my hold on his neck as I prepare to be lifted. I'm not one of those tiny women that can be tossed around. I'm tall and muscular. I have real body mass. But Layton lifts me like I am one of those small women. It's easy and effortless for a man like him.

I wrap my legs tightly around him. His hard cock is immediately pressed to my center. Oh dear god. *Throb throb throb.*

He thrusts his hips just a bit. I can't help but let out a small moan. I think if he rubs or pushes anymore, I'll have an orgasm.

He whispers in my ear, "You're turned on."

I swallow and then whimper, "Nope. I'm cool as a cucumber."

I feel him silently laugh. He knows I'm full of shit.

With his hot breath on my neck, he says, "I can feel how wet you are. It's leaking onto my boxers."

I pull my head back and look down. Oh my god. He's right. It's all over his cock. Even with the dark-blue boxers, I can see the wet spot I've left behind.

I should be humiliated, but I'm not. I have no brain capacity left for anything other than the size of that cock and how much I suddenly want it inside me. It's been so long since a man has been inside my body. And it's Layton *fucking* Lancaster. I spent all of my hormonal, formative years fantasizing about something like this. The teenaged me is in the corner with pompoms, doing cartwheels and back handsprings.

And now that I've gotten to know him, the real thing might be even better than the fantasy.

With him holding me, we're close to eye level and staring at each other. I recognize the same need written all over his face. He wants me too. It's oozing from every pore in his body.

Our mouths are only an inch apart. He smiles. "You don't smell like garlic today."

I giggle. "You don't smell like tuna fish."

His smile widens. It's perfect. He's perfect, and so damn hot. The man I spent my teen years staring at posters of on my ceiling as I drifted off to sleep at night is holding me, practically naked, and I'm pretty sure his hands just drifted down to my ass. Yep, they definitely did. And now I think they just slipped under my panties. And I like it. *Really* like it.

I can't seem to help myself, I'm losing the battle of wills. I lean forward, tighten my grip on his head, and join my lips to his.

His hands grip my ass hard as we both open our mouths, and our tongues meet for the first time. I think I hear Francois complain, but I'm not focused on him. I'm focused on Layton as his tongue begins to explore my mouth.

My chest is flush to his. My entire body is tingling, head to toes. I roll my hips, grinding onto him. He lets out a low grumble from deep in his chest.

Someone yells, "Take five."

Without breaking our lips, Layton turns and heads us straight in the direction of his dressing room. The kiss immediately turns frantic and needy. His lips. His tongue. His teeth. They're consuming me. I know it's weeks of tension finally breaking free.

He pushes us through his dressing room door and then slams me back against it, causing the whole room to shake as it closes. He begins hard, wet kisses down my neck. "Please tell me I can have you. I've wanted you for so long. Since the moment we met."

I breathe, "Get inside me. Now." I can't wait any longer.

He pulls down the cups of my flimsy bra and grabs my breasts. Squeezing them together, he alternates licking and biting my nipples, all while pressing his cock against my center.

I buck my hips as I practically claw at him. "Layton, I need you." I've never felt so mad with desire for a man. Not even Marc.

He lifts his head. "I want to take my time with you, making you feel good. I want to explore every inch of your gorgeous body."

"He said take *five*. I'm pretty sure he didn't mean five hours."

He smiles as he moves me over to the table and lays me down. My breasts are out, and my legs are spread wide. My core is physically throbbing, practically crying at the loss of contact with him.

He looks down at my panties and slides them to the side, slipping a finger through me and then sinking it inside me. I feel myself flutter as he moves deeper and deeper to the spot that's begging for him. "Fuck, you're tight and wet."

You bet I am. No one has been in there for over a year, and I'm looking up at the nearly naked sexiest man alive. Literally, he won that title like ten years ago.

He pulls his finger out and then runs it under his nose, inhaling deeply. "I love the way you smell." He then takes it into his mouth and seals his lips around it. "Hmm," he moans. "You taste better than I imagined. I need more of it."

He grabs my thousand-dollar panties and rips them off my body without a second thought. I suppose I should care, but I don't. I have one thing on my mind right now, and it's not the cost of my fucking panties.

He falls to his knees and sinks his face into me, mumbling, "So fucking good."

His fingers part me as his tongue begins to move through my slippery flesh. Skillfully. Perfectly. I can feel my wetness oozing out of me. How have I gone twenty-eight years without this man's mouth on me?

My hips start moving of their own volition. I have no control over my body right now. It's all his.

I've been worked up for the past hour. I nearly came when we were covered, I'm most definitely coming like this.

His tongue leaves no inch untouched as he slides two fingers inside me. They curl and he feels around until he finds the spot that makes my eyes roll to the back of my head.

"Oh god, Layton. Right there." As if he didn't somehow already know.

I know I'm getting louder. Everyone can probably hear me, but I don't give a crap right now. My body is about to explode in a way I haven't in a long time. Maybe ever. My brain isn't registering anything else but this. I can't remember a time when I've been this turned on.

His tongue is moving faster and faster. I grip the back of the table, arch my back, and moan, "I'm coming."

I swear the whole room goes dark as my entire body spasms. It feels like a dam breaking as fluids pour out of me. Did I just gush? Did I squirt? My vision hasn't come back but I think I did both. I can feel it dripping down my legs and ass.

Suddenly there's a knock at the door. I hear Raphael's voice. "One more minute, lovebirds."

My vision starts to return. Layton is now standing in front of me. His face is covered in my juices and his cock is now out. It's bigger than I could have ever possibly imagined and is oozing from the tip. It's not just big, his head is enormous. Is there a helmet on there? That will never fit inside me. He's standing there jerking it ferociously.

I start to sit up. "Let me do it."

He pushes me back and manages, "No time. I'm almost there."

With his free hand, he grabs my torn panties and brings them to his nose. He inhales deeply, grunts loudly, and then comes all over my stomach. It's no ordinary load. Long, hot, white streaks cover me, pooling in my belly button.

His motions gradually come to a stop. He's breathing heavily. He looks down at my exposed, come-covered body with heavily lidded eyes. "So fucking hot with my come all over you. They should take a picture of *that*."

I'm at a loss for words.

He runs his finger through his come and holds it out in offering. I open my mouth and he slides that finger in. Sealing my lips around it, I look him in the eyes and suck every last drop of the salty, manly essence he's offering.

He pulls his finger out. I assume he's going to grab something to clean me, but instead he rubs his come into my skin like it's lotion. And I let him because I want it all over me.

His eyes stay focused on the motions of his hand rubbing me. "You'll be covered in me all day. Marked by me. Mine."

As a feminist, I feel like I should be offended by that statement, but instead, I'm wildly turned on. No man has ever spoken to me like that and I'm here for it.

I can't help but sit up and run my fingers through my sensitive and fully saturated pussy. I then rub my come all over his stomach. Looking at him in challenge, I say, "And you'll be covered in me. Marked by me. Mine."

His lids are heavy as he smells his fingers, rubbing them just under his nose. "I wear it proudly."

We need to leave right now and have sex. I may have just had a monster orgasm, but I need more of him. *Much* more.

We hear movement outside and both of our shoulders drop realizing that we're not going anywhere right now. We have hours left of shooting.

He sighs and holds out his hand for me. "Shall we continue?"

I hold up my torn panties. "I can't go out there like this."

He gives a mischievous, guilty look, one that tells me he's not sorry at all. "Whoops."

There's another knock at the door. We hear Raphael's voice. "It sounds like you're done. It's showtime. The second act starts now."

I tell Layton, "There's another set of underwear in my dressing room."

He pulls up his boxers and walks over to the door. Opening it slightly so that Raphael can't see me, I hear him say, "Can you run to Arizona's dressing room and grab the other set of undergarments? We umm...misplaced hers."

I hear Raphael cackle. "I'll be back in a jiffy."

After a quick wardrobe change, we begrudgingly head back to the green carpet.

LAYTON

If I thought the sexual tension during the first half of the shoot was off the charts, I was mistaken. Now that each of the rabid beasts has received an appetizer, we're both that much more ravenous for the main course.

The first part of the shoot was timid, full of soft, tentative, and nervous touches. Now it's anything but that. Our hands are all over each other's bodies. We both seem to forget our audience at times. They keep yelling at us about kissing, but I can't help myself. All I can think about is getting out of here and getting better acquainted with her gorgeous body. I need to touch, kiss, and lick every square inch of her.

I lick around my own face and taste her. I run my fingers under my nose and inhale her scent every chance I get. Her eyes darken every time I do it.

I love that she's lathered in my come and I'm lathered in hers. It's our dirty little secret.

I've been hard as a rock throughout the entire shoot, but I don't care. They can edit it out if they need to. I can't imagine they'll put my hard dick in *Sports Illustrated*.

She's got her pussy practically plastered to it anyway, constantly rubbing herself against me. She's so fucking hot. All the tension of the past few weeks has officially snapped.

I've got her pinned to the green screen with her hands above her head. She's wearing catcher's leg gear and her legs are wrapped around my body. My face is buried in her breasts, nibbling and sucking her soft skin.

She moans, "I can't take much more of this. I want you. So badly." She gives me a sexy smile. "Slip it in. Maybe they won't notice."

I chuckle into her neck.

"Funny that you think I'm kidding. You've been hard for over an hour. I don't know how you're managing."

I look up. "It's the same for you. You've been wet that whole time. It's leaking out of you."

She narrows her eyes. "It's from earlier."

"No, it's not." I sniff. "It's fresh and it's telling me how hard you want me to fuck you."

I can see her nipples immediately stiffen at my words.

Without anything else being spoken, our lips meet again. It's not sweet and controlled. It's wet, wild, and perfect.

I hear Francois yell, "Stop kissing! Putains d'animaux." *Fucking animals.*

We smile into each other's mouths.

As we pull apart, I whisper, "Your place or mine?"

"I'm going to my place and you're going to yours."

My eyes widen but she simply giggles and kisses me again. She's fucking with me.

"Je n'en peux plus. Nous avons fini." *I can't take it anymore. We're done.* "Get out of here. Both of you!"

We continue kissing until she breathes, "Take me back to your dressing room. I want you. Now."

"Not here. Not like this."

"Where?"

"Follow me to my place."

We both dress in record time. I practically pull her arm out of the socket as we make our way to the parking lot. I planned to just walk her to her car, but I end up pinning her against it and kissing her. She bites my lip as she rubs the entire front of her body against mine.

I honestly can't remember a moment in my life where I've been as ravenous for a woman as I am for her. I'll do anything to have her right now. Anything.

She breathes into my mouth, "Either fuck me here or let's get going so you can fuck me at your place. Either way, I need you to fuck me."

I can feel the ejaculate seeping from my cock at the uncharacteristic way she's talking. The devil in me wants to just impale her here, but my heart tells me that she's special. I want to take her home where I can finally claim her as mine. Where I can stay buried in her for hours without any more interruptions.

In the end, my heart wins out and I tear myself away.

I see a flash of disappointment in her eyes. I'll make it up to her.

"Follow me."

Taking several deep breaths, she silently nods.

I'm driving, but my eyes continuously toggle between the road and my rearview mirror, making sure she's following behind, fearful that she'll change her mind. We're almost to my place when my phone rings. It's Henry. I accept the call.

"Hey, bud. I don't have much time right now. What's up?"

He croaks out, "Layton." He sounds terrible. "I'm in a bad way, man. I need you."

"What's going on?"

"My girl left me. I'm standing in front of O'Reilly's. I want to go in."

"Shit. Don't you dare." I squeeze my eyes shut and take a deep breath. With a mountain of regret, I say, "I'm on my way. Stay right where you are. I'll be there in twenty minutes." Fifteen if I take a few shortcuts.

I hang up the phone and punch my steering wheel. "Fuck! Fuck! Fuck!"

I need to cancel with Arizona.

CHAPTER ELEVEN

ARIZONA

> Layton: So sorry. Something important came up. I'll call you later.

Tears immediately fill my eyes. He changed his mind. Cooler heads prevailed and he changed his mind. I don't bother to respond as I pull off the highway and head toward my apartment.

By the time I walk in the door, my face is full of tears. Ripley is sitting on the sofa watching television. As soon as she notices my state of distress, her eyes widen. "Oh, sweetie, are you okay? Was today that bad?"

I shake my head. "No. Just the opposite."

I lay down with my head in her lap and proceed to tell her everything that happened. She sits there in complete shock.

"Wow. The mutual attraction has been obvious to everyone but the two of you." She bites her lip. "Have you seen any of the photos? I bet they're scorching hot."

I shake my head. "We didn't stick around. We were both anxious to get out of there and over to his place. At least I was."

"Maybe something important really did come up. Guys don't usually pass on sex with hot chicks unless it's something major. And I've seen the way he is with you. He wants you. Badly."

I sigh. "Maybe it's a sign that I shouldn't go there with him. We both know it's a mistake that will only end up in me getting hurt again. What if it impacts the team and the league? Maybe I'm being selfish."

She runs her fingers through my hair. "The last thing in the world you are is selfish. You did this whole thing for the team and league in the first place." She grabs my chin, forcing my eyes to meet her. "You can't continue to live in fear of getting hurt. It's always a risk, but your hibernation for the past year hasn't been healthy. It's not like you've been happy."

I pout. "I'm happy. Happier."

She smiles. "You're only happy because you get to live and play with me again."

"Being with you does make me happy."

"What about your concerns over being intimate with a man? You've been so trigger-shy. How did him touching you feel?"

I blow out a breath. "Honestly? It felt incredible. I didn't have any of the issues I thought I would the first time a man touched me after all this time. I hate to admit it, but I think it's him. He makes me feel safe. As foolish as it was, look how he behaved at the field when he thought I was hurt. Look what he did to Marc. He's always asking me questions about my life. Everything he says and does makes me think he cares."

She rubs my arm. "I know he cares. I'm convinced he wants you and has for a long time. And that's why I think something big must have really come up."

"Maybe you're right." I sigh. "What are you up to tonight?"

"I...umm...I have a date, but I can cancel."

That brings a smile to my face. "You do? With whom?"

Her face flushes. "No one you know. I'll cancel. You need me."

I shake my head. "Absolutely not. I'm going to grab some food then go for a long jog to clear my head. After that, I just want to take a nice, hot bath and go to bed early. You have fun. *A lot* of fun."

Her face flushes again. She likes this guy, but she'll tell me about him when she's ready. I don't want to push.

"What are you wearing?"

"I was deciding between three or four dresses. Will you help me pick one out?"

"Of course."

After we pick out a dress, I grab a quick bite and leave for my jog.

LAYTON

As soon as I pull up to O'Reilly's, I see Henry sitting on a bench out front, nervously running his fingers through his curly, dark hair.

I illegally park and practically hop out of my car, immediately sitting next to him. "I'm here. What's happening?"

His head is down but he's now tugging on his hair. His voice breaks. "She left me."

"This is the girl you met a few weeks ago?"

He nods. "Yes."

I need to get him away from the bar. I grab his arm. "Let's get some hot chocolate and you can tell me about it."

"Not coffee?"

"You serve coffee all day. Is that really what you want right now?"

He gives me a small, crooked smile. "No, it's not. I love hot chocolate. It reminds me of Gammie."

Gammie thought every problem could be solved by a cup of hot chocolate. I spent many nights watching her make it from scratch before sitting down with her to unload my problems.

"I remember. Me too. Let's go find the good stuff."

We head to a restaurant nearby that's famous for its hot chocolate, and I order two.

We're seated in a quiet booth in the back of the restaurant "Tell me what happened."

He shrugs. "She said I was getting too serious too fast."

"Were you?"

"Maybe a little. I really liked her."

"Tell me what you liked about her."

"The sex was amazing. Best of my life."

My shoulders fall. "What else?"

"She's pretty."

"Anything substantive?"

He appears baffled by the question. "Like what?"

"Her personality. Do your interests align? Your values? Did you talk about your future? Anything beyond the physical?"

He pinches the bridge of his nose. "I guess we never got that far."

"So you were about to throw away two years of sobriety over a good lay who you know nothing else about?"

He rubs his hands all over his face. "Fuck, when you say it like that, it sounds bad."

"It *is* bad."

He leans back in the booth and is quiet for a minute or two. "Have you ever truly gotten to know a woman before it got physical?"

I can't help but smile. For the first time in my life, I can answer yes to that question. "I have. The woman I'm seeing now." Sort of seeing.

His jaw drops. "You haven't banged the hot blonde I see in all those photos?"

I shake my head. "No, I haven't. We've been taking it slow, getting to know each other." I leave out the whole fake relationship thing. "And honestly, it's been nice. I already know her better than any other woman I've been with in the past. I've quickly realized that we have so much in common and I genuinely like it. I care about her. When it happens," hopefully when I leave here, "it will mean something because we've already connected and care about each other on a deeper level."

I see him considering my words and find myself considering them too. It's true. I genuinely care for her and feel a deep connection. While we haven't engaged in the ultimate act of intimacy yet, our relationship is more intimate than any other I've ever had in my entire life.

I take his hand in mine. "Henry, life isn't always easy. You know that more than anyone. You can't fall into a black hole of despair when it doesn't go exactly as you thought it would."

"You can say that because your life is perfect."

"My life isn't perfect. Just because you see it online doesn't make it the truth."

"What does that mean?

"Nothing."

"I'm sorry. I guess I'm just lonely. I had her in my life for only a few weeks, but it felt good to be needed by someone else."

I'm suddenly overcome with a large sense of guilt. I should be spending more time with him. "I need you, Henry. You're the only family I have. Why don't you come to a game?" He never comes to games, despite my constant invitations. I have no clue why, but he's always declined my invitations, and I suppose I stopped trying.

"Are you sure?"

"Of course."

He smiles. It's so genuine. "I'd like that."

Once I know that Henry is out of danger and not at risk of a slipup, I can't help but start driving toward Arizona's apartment. I won't go the night without seeing her. A phone call isn't enough. I know I should have given her more information when I bailed, but I was in a rush and panicked. I wasn't thinking straight.

I start pounding on her door until it opens. It finally does, but it's not Arizona. It's Ripley standing there in a nice dress, looking like she's about to go out.

She sighs when she sees me. "What are you doing here? I'm not sure it's such a good idea tonight."

"I need to see Arizona."

"Haven't you fucked with her enough for today? You

better have a good reason for abandoning her like you did."

"I had a family emergency. I'm here now."

"She's not here."

"Where is she?"

"She went for a long jog to clear her head. You upset her. She's questioning everything."

"I didn't mean to hurt her. There's nothing for her to question. I want to be with her."

"She's very sensitive. With reason."

"I know what happened. She's shared it with me. *All* of it."

Her eyes widen in shock.

I nod. "I know *everything*. Our time together these past few weeks has meant something. She means a lot to me."

"I appreciate you saying that. You have to understand that Arizona hasn't been herself in a long while. She was never insecure. She's been the wild one. Well, maybe not to Kam's level, but close. I've seen a gradual change in her since we got here. She's happy. She's coming back to us. I can't have you mess with her progress."

"Did it ever occur to you that I'm part of the progress?"

She's quiet, perhaps realizing I might be right.

"Can I wait for her? I want to talk to her. I need to clear the air. I want to tell her how I've been feeling."

She thinks for a few beats. "If I let you in, I need you to promise me you won't hurt her. She's been dicked around enough in the past year. She doesn't deserve any more of it."

"I'm not here to dick around with her. I care about her. I swear to you."

She blows out a breath and then widens the door in invitation. "Don't make me regret this, Layton Lancaster."

"I won't."

"Okay. I'm leaving. Respect her wishes, whatever they are. If she doesn't want you to stay, you need to go."

I nod. "I will."

"And stay away from Captain America."

"Who's Captain America?"

"Her vibrator."

"She named it Captain America?"

"Yes."

"Why?"

I see a small smile forming on her lips. "She says it's because he's the hottest superhero, but I think it's because he looks like you. Her fantasy is to get railed by the real Captain America one day." Her smile grows. "Maybe you could help her out with that."

I can't help but smile back at her. "Thank you for the insight." I scratch my chin. "I'm now definitely going to have to check out Captain America to...make sure the mold fits. I'm a lot to live up to."

She rolls her eyes at me before leaving for the evening.

Having never been past the doorway before, I look around. Their apartment is nice. It's comfortable, just like Arizona. I peek into both bedrooms and find the one that's clearly Arizona's. It's got my California sunshine written all over it.

She has family pictures scattered around her room. I can't help but smile at one of her and Quincy as kids, both in their respective team uniforms. She can't be more than five or six. So damn beautiful, even then.

There's another one of her and Ripley as teens in

what must have been Arizona's bedroom. I let out a laugh as I make out a poster of me on her ceiling in the background. I remember that one. It was one of my first. It feels like a hundred years ago.

I open the drawer in the small table next to her bed. Sure enough, a giant red and blue vibrator sits there. Like a psycho, I pick it up and smell it, hoping to get a whiff of her scent. It doesn't really smell like her, at least not the real thing. The real thing is so much better.

Realizing I've severely crossed a line, I place it back in the drawer and close it.

I lay down on her bed and inhale her pillow. That definitely smells like her. It's the beach and something else. Maybe lavender.

Turning my head, I see the poster of me that I sent her for her first game. It's rolled up in the corner of her room, but it's not in the plastic packaging and has clearly been opened. I love that she looked at it.

Remembering our conversation, I quickly look up at her ceiling. No poster of Butch McVey. I knew she was kidding when she said that, but I just wanted to make sure.

The sun is just starting to go down. I hate the idea of her jogging alone at night.

I must drift off to sleep because I'm awakened hearing and then seeing her walk into the now darkness of her room.

She doesn't notice me. She simply heads straight into her bathroom. I hear her turn on the water of the bathtub.

I assume she's going to come back out, but she doesn't. The subtle sounds of water sloshing around a few minutes later tell me she's gotten into the tub.

Standing, I quietly make my way to the open bathroom door, poking my head in. The aroma of lavender immediately hits my nose. It's so Arizona. My body reacts to it. Craving it.

She's settled in the tub. Her hair is up, she's laying back, and her hands are moving all over her body. The tops of her breasts are just visible above the sea of bubbles. The whole scene looks like a painting. It's almost too perfect to be real.

She examines the marks I left on her breasts today and I see the corners of her mouth slightly raise. I hope it's the memory of the things we did making her feel that way.

Her fingers slowly slide further down her body until they reach their final destination. Between her legs. I can't see her hand, but her arm starts to move. I'm officially a creepy peeping tom, but I don't care. Watching her touch herself is the hottest thing I've ever seen. I find myself praying that she's thinking of me.

She leans her head back as far as it can go and closes her eyes as she otherwise continues her movements. I can see her chest rising and falling at a gradually increasing pace. Her free hand slides along her body until it reaches one of her pink, rosy nipples, just visible over the bubble line now. She pinches it and moans.

All the blood in my body heads south. It's like I'm watching an erotic scene from a movie or book come to life. My dick is impossibly hard at this vision of perfection.

Her back arches and she breathes, "Layton." At first, I think she sees me, but she doesn't. Happiness fills me. She's thinking about me while she touches herself. She has no idea how many times I've touched myself thinking of her.

I watch for another minute or two until it's time to make my presence known. In my deepest voice, I say, "Would you prefer the real thing?"

She gasps as she jerks up and water splashes over the edges of the tub. "Layton, what are you doing here?"

"I was waiting for you. Ripley let me in when you were out."

Her eyes widen. "You've...you've been here the whole time I've been home?"

"Yes, and knowing you touch yourself to me is the sexiest thing I've ever imagined. You're so fucking beautiful."

Her cheeks turn red. She's embarrassed.

I don't want her to feel that way, so I redirect the conversation. "I'm sorry about today. I honestly had a family emergency. I came here as soon as it was done. I passed the Ripley inquisition. She let me in to wait for you."

She slowly nods her head.

"Can I join you? I haven't showered yet. I wanted your scent on me, but I wouldn't mind getting in, getting clean, and then refreshing your scent on me afterward." I nod toward her. "And maybe I can finish the job you started."

She's holding her knees to her chest, covering herself, but she nods again. I immediately remove my sweatshirt and then my shorts and boxer briefs in one go. My severely engorged cock springs free. I grab hold of it and give it a few long, slow pumps. She stares at my movements.

I smile. "Bigger and better than Captain America, right?"

Her mouth opens wide, but I can't help but smile. "Ripley has a big mouth. I checked him out. If he satisfies you, just wait until you see what I can do."

Her cheeks turn an even brighter shade of red. It's so fucking adorable.

I continue stroking myself. "I've been hard for most of the past twelve hours. I might set a world record."

She giggles. "I know you have. Believe me, I know." She scooches forward. "Get in."

I slide in behind her and extend my legs down the sides of the tub. I then pull her soft body into my arms.

She leans back, resting the back of her head on my chest. It's perfection.

I feel her hands on my legs. She breathes, "This is nice, but it's so...so...intimate."

"Are you okay with it? I don't want to push. If you want me to leave, I will."

She practically melts into me. "No, I don't want you to go. That's the weird thing. I'm okay. More than okay. I should be running the other way, but I don't want to. You make me feel good. You make me feel safe. You make me *feel* for the first time in a long time."

I run my fingertips up and down her arms, desperate to touch her but trying to take it slowly if that's what she needs. "For me, it feels good. It feels right." That's exactly how it feels. Like we fit together. Like it was meant to be.

She closes her eyes and mumbles, "Hmm," as her own fingertips start to move up and down my legs. I've never been so starved for the touch of a woman in my life. A simple, innocent touch from her does more for me than more purposeful touches from other women.

I lather her soap on my hands and rub it all over her body, leaving no inch untouched. She doesn't flinch. She seems to enjoy it. Her breathing gradually becomes more and more labored. I haven't even begun to really touch her, and I can already see her legs quivering as my hands explore her body.

I move my hands up and cup her gorgeous tits. For weeks, I've been imagining what they look like. In my wildest fantasies, they weren't this perfect. She's got the pinkest nipples I've ever seen. I wish I was in a position to suck them into my mouth right now. The dressing room earlier was so frantic. I need to take my time with her body. I'm dying for it.

I run my fingers over those nipples as they begin to harden, and she starts to squirm. I whisper in her ear, "Do you want me to finish what you started, sunshine?"

She doesn't say anything, but she spreads her legs as wide as they can in this space, so I take it as an invitation and move my hand down her body. I trickle my fingers down her stomach and the softness below her belly button until I reach her center, sliding my fingers through her wetness until they brush by her opening. After I run them through her a few times, I slip two fingers inside her.

I have to take a few breaths to calm myself. She's tight and soft and already squeezing me. Heaven.

She moans, "Oh god. That feels good. Go deep. I need it deep."

I know she does, having learned that earlier today. I push in as far as I can go, and she flutters around my fingers. "I can't wait for that to be my cock in there."

She squirms, and breathes, "Me too. Make me come, Layton. I've been on the edge for hours. Today drove me crazy with need. *You* drove me crazy with need. All day long. The dressing room wasn't enough. I need more."

"I feel the same." I continue pumping my fingers in and out of her. With my other hand, I begin to circle her clit. She's already sensitive and swollen, involuntarily jerking at first contact. She wasn't kidding that she's on the edge.

Her hips gyrate in rhythm with my fingers. She reaches her hand up to the back of my head, turns her face, and pulls my lips toward hers.

We kissed all day, but this somehow feels different. It's not in front of other people. It's not in front of the camera. It's just me and her doing exactly what we want to be doing without any sense of urgency. We can do this all night if she wants.

Her tongue practically wraps itself around mine. Her hips fuck my fingers as hard as she can in here. Her back is rubbing against my cock. I need more. So much more.

"Oh god, Layton. Don't stop. I'm coming."

She sucks on my tongue as her body shakes into her orgasm. I hold her down through it all until it eventually begins to recede.

As soon as she's done, she maneuvers her body around and straddles me. Her drenched pussy rubs all over my cock. Even in the water I can feel it. She mumbles into my mouth, "I want you. Don't make me wait any longer."

I need a condom, so I stand with her wrapped around me. Reaching for the big towel next to the tub, I dry us as best as I can in this position.

While kissing my neck, she points toward a drawer in her bathroom. "Condoms." I walk over and open it to find a box of condoms. As expected, and much to my relief, it's unopened.

I bring it with me as I walk us out to her bedroom. Her lips haven't left my body for a second, kissing, licking, and biting every inch she can reach.

I hate to pull her away, but I've got plans.

I toss her down to the bed on her back. "Spread your legs for me."

Her long, toned legs open wide. She looks like a goddess laying here naked, but I still need more of her.

"Wider. Let me see all of that pink pussy of yours." I lick around my face. "I've been tasting it all day and night, dreaming of it. Of you."

Her chest rises and falls rapidly as she spreads them as wide as they can go. I slowly run my index finger up her inner thigh until I meet her center. Her body is shaking in anticipation. I slowly dip it deep inside her before pulling it out and bringing it to my nose. Inhaling deeply, I say, "You smell so good. It does things to me."

I give that same finger a long lick. "You taste good too." Then I rub it all over my scruff.

She lets out a small moan as she starts to reach for me, but I quickly slap her pussy with the pads of my fingers. She gasps in shock as she sinks back down into the bed.

Shaking my head, I say, "I'm in control. You'll get it when I'm ready to give it to you. Tell me you understand."

Her eyes widen but she nods.

"Good girl."

I climb onto the bed and rub my cock through her dripping pussy over and over again, wanting her to feel every bit of my hardness for her. I don't enter her, but I run it through her needy lips until I'm certain she can't take it anymore.

She's writhing, attempting to manipulate her body so

I'll enter her, but I pull back and slap her pussy again. This time much harder.

Her back arches and she grips the sheets. "Oh god, Layton."

I can see her wetness pooling at her center.

Leaning over, I whisper in her ear, "You like when I slap your pussy, don't you?"

She nods.

"Has anyone slapped your pussy before?"

She shakes her head.

"That's very good. I'm going to give you levels of pleasure you've never known."

I stand back up and start to stroke my cock. She watches with her arms twitching, clearly wanting to touch me, but she's learning who's in control.

I tear open a condom and roll it down my length. Dipping my head, I give a long, slow lick through her pussy on my way up her body to her mouth. Finally, I fall between her legs and notch my tip at her opening.

I can feel her swallow. "Your head is so big. I don't know if it will fit."

"I'll make it fit. I promise to make you feel good."

"It's...it's been a really long time for me."

"I know. How long?"

"Fourteen months, three weeks, and five days."

We both smile at her precision.

She mumbles, "Give or take a day or two."

I rub my thumb over her bottom lip. "I've got you, sunshine."

My mouth meets hers. Her mile-long legs wrap around me. My tongue pushes into her mouth as my cock begins to enter her.

She moans into me, thrusting her hips forward. I

slowly push the tip in. I know my dick has an unusually large head. First entry needs a little finessing.

I take it slow and circle my tip, driving her crazy. Her juices are covering my dick already.

With a slight pop, I break through. She sucks in a breath and her body tenses. "Oh my fuck. So fucking good. Keep going."

I slowly surge forward, one inch at a time. Given how wet she is, it's not as difficult as I assumed it would be. She's tight as hell but is so damn turned on. She's shaking uncontrollably and dripping down onto my balls. I love it. I may never shower again.

I feel her nails scrape down my back. I think she's breaking skin. Fuck, she's hot.

She tilts her head back and squeezes her eyes shut. "Oh god, Layton. You're so big. So deep."

"I'm not all the way in yet."

She looks down to where our bodies join as if needing to confirm the veracity of my statement.

She squeezes her eyes shut again. I use it as an opportunity to push all the way in.

She winces, but once I rub her clit a few times, she seems to relax and takes all of me.

"Look at me."

She blinks open her eyes and does. Like me, her blue-green eyes turn dark blue when she's turned on.

I need to let her control the pace, at least at first as she acclimates to me. I flip us over so she's on top. Sitting up, I kiss my way up her neck. "Take what you need, how you need it." *I'm so fucking worked up that I'm afraid I might tear her in two.*

As I suck her nipple into my mouth, her hips begin to rock over me. She gets increasingly comfortable and starts to ride me hard, crashing down onto me with each pass. Her ass is smacking my thighs while her nails run over my chest. She's a scratcher. I love it. I love that I'll have her marks all over my body.

Sensing she's close, I take control and begin thrusting my hips up to meet hers. Her eyes roll to the back of her head, and she screams out as her pussy engulfs me in a vice grip. It takes everything I have not to let go myself. Her come squirts onto me. She did that a little bit today in the dressing room, but this time it's more. Much more.

She slows her motions and looks down wide-eyed. She seems embarrassed. "I'm..."

"Don't say another word. It's so fucking hot. You have no idea how much it turns me on. I wish it was on my tongue."

I run my fingers through it, bring it to my nose, and inhale deeply. "*Such* a turn on." I lick across the pads of my fingers. "Hmm. And so sweet."

Her eyelids are heavy, and her eyes are growing even darker. I see tears pooling in them. "What's wrong? Am I hurting you?"

She shakes her head. "Just the opposite. Don't stop. Take what you need."

Remaining inside her, I stand and walk us until I pin her to the closest wall. Restraining her arms over her head, I say, "I want to fuck you like we were positioned in the photoshoot. I was dreaming of being inside you the whole time. Wrap your legs tight and enjoy the ride."

She listens, and I begin my long, hard thrusts inside her. I gradually build my speed until I'm pounding deep into her body at a frantic, relentless pace as we both let go and come. Me into the condom and her all over me again.

I fall back onto the bed with her on top of me, still

buried inside her. We're both laboring for breaths, with sweat and fluids covering our bodies.

Her head is nestled in my neck. She mumbles into it, "Okay, I guess I now understand *#laidbylayton.*"

I chuckle.

She lifts her head and smiles. "That was amazing."

I give her a soft kiss. "We're just getting started."

CHAPTER TWELVE

ARIZONA

I wake to the sound of my door opening and Ripley's voice. "How did it go with loverb—"

She cuts her sentence short. I blink my eyes open to realize that my naked body is facing down, half draped over Layton's naked body. My head is on his chest, and we're tangled in the sheets, covered from my mid-back down.

She continues, "Oh man, it smells like sex in here. Hot damn! Yes!"

Even though Layton's eyes are still closed, I see the corners of his mouth rise. His hand moves down to my bare ass and squeezes it.

I turn my head toward Ripley to see her pick up the empty box of condoms on the floor. "Wow, I know for a fact that this was unopened yesterday. Good for you guys."

Layton's smile widens as he lets out a laugh. "I forgot what it was like to have a roommate. It's been a long time for me."

As if we're not naked and partially exposed in the bed,

Ripley sits on it. "I guess you two kissed and made up." She mumbles, "More than kissed."

I lift my head and look her body up and down before plopping it back down on Layton's chest. "Hmm. I seem to remember you wearing that same dress last night. Are you just getting home from your date?"

Her cheeks blush. "Maybe. You're not the only one who woke up naked in a room reeking of sex."

Layton grumbles, "What time is it?"

"Just after nine."

"Ugh. I need to get to the ballpark. You guys don't play today, right?"

I shake my head. "No. We'll be at your game."

His face lights up. I know how much he likes when we watch him play. "Great." He stares at me. "You'll be my inspiration. I'm hitting a home run for you today."

"Is that so? You can simply decide that and make it happen?"

He nods. "I can." Turning to Ripley, he says, "Bye, Ripley. I need to get dressed."

She scrunches her nose and stands. "Fine. I'll get the coffee going."

She leaves my room and closes the door behind her. He immediately flips us over so he's on top, grinding his erection against me.

I moan, "You're a machine. You don't have time and we don't have any condoms left."

"You better hit up Costco. You're going to need a lot."

I wiggle my hips. "I think you're right."

We're both grinning like lovesick puppies right now. I wrap my legs around him and run my fingers over his sexy, square chin. "I had a good time last night."

"I had the *best* time. Are...are we a thing now?"

I let out a laugh. "Are we *going steady*? I don't know what we are. What are *you* thinking?"

"That I want to be a thing. A real thing. I've honestly never uttered those words before, but I've completely fallen for you. I'm not playing childish games and pretending otherwise. I want to be with you. Do you feel the same?"

I run my hands through his hair. "You know I do. If I'm being honest, I think I fell for you a long time ago."

He smiles, but not a sexy smile. It's boyish, humble, and simply adorable. "Just know that this is new to me. I might make mistakes. Kick me in the ass when I do."

I pinch his butt. "It's a pretty good ass. No problem." I stretch my arms and let out a yawn. "Feel free to use the shower before you go. I know you don't have time to go back to your place."

He nibbles on my ear. "No way. I want your juices all over me. Your smell is my inspiration. In fact, I need a refresher before I go."

He runs his fingers down my body until they run through my severely sensitive and sore folds. He slides two fingers in deep.

As soon as I moan, he bites my nipple and I start giggling. "Ah, stop."

He pulls his fingers out and then abruptly stands, naked in all his glory. He sniffs his fingers and wiggles his eyebrows. "Yum. Thanks for the refresher."

I lay there, completely appalled. "You're kind of a freak."

He lets out a loud laugh as he begins to dress. "You have no idea."

I mutter, "I think I'm about to find out."

"You are." He leans over and kisses my cheek. "Now I'm your freak. See you at the ballpark, sunshine."

"Can't wait to see your home run, superstar."

As soon as he leaves, Ripley walks back in with a giant smile. "I'm guessing it went well?"

I grab an extra pillow and hold it to my chest. "Oh god, you have no idea. It was unequivocally the best sex of my life. I shouldn't even say that in the singular. It was *several* times. His hashtag is more than deserved. I've been fully *#laidbylayton*."

She laughs. "I guess your vagina still works?"

"Yes, thank you for your concern, though after last night, she may be out of commission for a while."

"Poor Captain America."

"Captain America is now on indefinite hiatus. He's the last thing I need. I have the real thing now. Can I ask you about something without you judging me?"

"No promises." She smiles. "Tell me. Does he have two dicks? I feel like if anyone does, it would be him. He's got a lot of big dick energy. Maybe it's two dick energy I'm reading."

I burst into laughter. "He doesn't have two dicks. He..."

She holds up her hand. "Wait! I feel like this is going to be big. Let's get Bailey and Kam over here." She starts typing away on their phone.

"I don't want them to know about us."

"Everyone already thinks you're together. You're just playing into that dialogue."

She does make a valid point. "Hmm. Fine, I'll take a shower. Let me know when they arrive."

"Don't. They're already on their way."

Less than a minute later, they walk through the bedroom door. Kam gives an overexaggerated sniff. "Holy shit, it smells like sex in here. Did you finally board Layton's beef bus?"

Her eyes widen when she notices my state of undress. "You *did* ride his beef bus. It's about time. I don't know what you two were waiting for."

Ripley practically bounces up and down. "She got *#laidbylayton.*"

The three of them start screaming in excitement. Who knew my love life could bring them so much joy?

Bailey asks, "How was it?"

Before I can answer, Ripley does. "It was the best sex of her life. And not just one time. It was several times. They blew through an entire box of condoms."

The screams start all over again. I bury my head in the pillow. Maybe I shouldn't bother to talk to them about this.

"But shhh. She wants to talk to us about something."

I turn around. I can feel my face flushing in embarrassment as they all stare at me in wide-eyed anticipation. "I umm... well...I think I squirted. Like every time I came, and it was in the double digits with him. He's very...skilled."

They're quiet for a moment before they all burst into hysterics. Bailey shakes her head. "I tell men I'm a squirter so they give me their best effort, but I've never actually done it. You should see how hard they work for it though."

I gasp. "That's horrible. Those poor guys probably feel inadequate."

She simply giggles. "But it's totally worth it."

Kam gives a knowing smirk. "Only women have been able to make me squirt. Trust me when I tell you they *understand* the female anatomy much better."

Ripley's head toggles between everyone. "Wait, squirting is a real thing? I thought it was a fake porn myth."

I shrug my shoulders. "I thought so too until yesterday. I was embarrassed at first, but he's so fucking into it. He loves it."

Kam nods. "It's legit. I can't say it happens with consistency, but now and then when I'm crazy turned on and my partner knows exactly what she's doing, it happens."

"Oh, well maybe it was because this was our first time together and we've had so much sexual tension. The photoshoot was like hours of foreplay. We were both more than good to go by the time we fell into bed."

Ripley holds up the empty condom box. "We can all see the evidence of that."

I can't help but smile. "He's very...energetic. I just kept coming over and over again all over the place."

As if it occurs to them all at once, they immediately pop up off my bed. Ripley scrunches her nose. "Eww, I'm never touching your bed again."

I can't help but laugh. "Good. Get out so I can shower. Let's eat before we go to the ballpark. I need something healthier than ballpark food and I most definitely need to hydrate." I may have lost half my body fluids last night.

Bailey and Kam leave. Ripley stays and mindlessly cleans my room, as she often does.

"What's on your mind, Rip?"

"I know sleeping with him was a big deal for you. This is your first time since Marc. I feel like my bestie has gradually been coming back to me. Just because he's famous, I don't want you to feel like the real Arizona can't continue her journey to the top of the mountain. Don't let him overshadow you. You're a star, and I don't mean just on the field."

I can't help but be filled with warmth for the love she has for me. "I love you too, Rip."

She blows me a kiss.

I sit up. "Tell me about your date. What's his name?"

She scrunches her nose. "It's nothing."

"You slept with him. It's not nothing."

"Drop it. I'm not like you. I don't need a relationship or feelings to have sex with someone."

"I think you're into this guy. I saw how excited you were to get ready for the date. Why won't you talk to me?"

"I'm not that into him. It's casual." She starts walking toward the door. "I'm taking a shower too. I'll see you in a bit."

She walks out of my room. What is going on with her? She normally tells me everything.

A FEW HOURS LATER, we're at the ballpark. We head down to our seats just as the game is about to begin. I remain in awe that we get to sit in the section right behind their dugout. In fact, they now put us in the front row. Because of my relationship with Layton, the cameras love to find me. My parents said they see me all the time on television in my *Layton's Lady* jersey. Today is a warm afternoon, so I'm wearing cutoff jeans shorts with it.

The Cougars take the field. Layton jogs out in his catching gear. I can't take my eyes off him. He's so hot. The backward hat, his ass in those pants, those thick, muscular quads. Yummy. Now that I know what's underneath, it makes him twice as hot. He's so solid and strong. And thick. *Everywhere.* The head of his penis is like nothing I've ever seen or experienced. It's a direct line to my g-spot. I should patent the mold of it and sell it. I'd make a fortune.

Since last night, things feel so different. I know deep down inside that my heart has always fluttered when I saw Layton Lancaster, but now it feels like it's twice as much. It's like my body involuntarily remembers the way he worshiped it all night long. I've never had a man give me the pleasure he gave me last night.

As if he can sense my thoughts, he turns his head and finds

me. Even with his mask on, I can see him wink at me. My heart starts beating rapidly.

Ripley leans over. "He looks like he wants to devour you."

I can't help but give a satisfied smile. "He *did* devour me. Over and over again."

She giggles, as do I.

The game progresses as normal until it's Layton's turn to bat. Just before he steps into the box, he looks at me and subtly runs his fingers under his nose. I can see his chest inflate as he inhales. I have to squeeze my legs together to tame the throb from what I know he's doing right now.

I quickly look around to see if anyone else notices the obscene move, but no one flinches. Ripley seems blissfully unaware. Kam and Bailey too.

I squirm in my seat. He notices and smirks just as he's about to step into the box. He sets his feet in the dirt. The pitch comes in, he swings, and *crunch*. It's a moonshot out of the stadium for a monster of a home run.

The crowd erupts in cheers, and Ripley throws her arms around me. "Holy shit, he actually hit a home run for you."

I can't help but smile. I suppose he did.

He winks at me again as he begins his slow trot around the bases.

Every time he comes up to bat in the game, he looks at me and smells his fingers. I have no idea why that's such a turn-on, but it is. It's our dirty secret and I'm about to combust from it.

He goes on to hit three home runs on the day, something he's only done two other times in his entire career, all when he was much younger. I watch him in awe. He's going to be in the hall of fame one day.

When the game is over, reporters rush to interview him about his big accomplishment and him helping the team to win an important game in the playoff hunt. Ripley and I are sitting on top of the dugout, waiting for the interviews to be over as the stadium begins to clear out.

At some point, I hear a reporter ask him his inspiration. He nods my way. "That beautiful woman right there."

The well-known, attractive reporter narrows her eyes at me and then turns back to him. "What do you have to say about unconfirmed reports that your relationship is nothing but a public relations stunt? An organization insider has informed me that you're not really dating, they're simply using your notoriety to get the Anacondas up and running. The whole thing is fabricated. That you and Arizona don't even like each other."

Oh shit. Who told her all that? I start to internally freak out.

He's quiet for a moment before he gives his signature Layton Lancaster smirk. The one that melts panties all over the world, including mine.

Without another word, he turns and walks straight over to me. Extending his arms, he lifts me off the dugout, but doesn't place me on the ground.

He grabs the back of my thighs, encouraging me to wrap my legs around him. He turns to the reporter and says, "Here's my reply to that." Moving his face back to me, his lips sweetly meet mine. As if we're not in a huge baseball stadium, his tongue traces my lips until it finds its way into my mouth. I meet his tongue with mine, powerless against my attraction to this man.

My eyes close and my fingernails scrape through his hair. My legs tighten around his big, sweaty, delicious body.

I have no idea how long we kiss. I just know that it's a long time and we're undoubtedly creating a spectacle. I'm sure this will be on the news later, but I don't care anymore.

At some point we hear Ripley clear her throat. "The reporter is gone, but you may want to talk to your brother."

We end the kiss and turn toward the dugout. Quincy is standing there with a murderous look on his face.

Layton presses his forehead to mine. "Maybe I should talk to him. I couldn't even change in front of the guys. I have scratch marks all over my body."

My chin drops. "No matter what, it will *never* be okay for my brother to see my scratch marks all over you."

He chuckles. "I wear them proudly. It's sexy as fuck when you do it. Clearly, they bring me luck, as does your scent. I'm happy to sit down with Q."

I sigh. "Layton, I don't know what we are. What would you even say to him?"

His face drops. "Is it not real for you too? I thought we discussed this."

"Of course it's real for me, but we're new and undefined. Can we please hold off on talking to my brother? Let's see how it goes. You said yourself, you're new at this. I just don't want issues between you and my brother if things don't work out for us. You're teammates and best friends. I don't want to come between you two."

"I guess you're right. We definitely can't let management know either."

"I thought they didn't care if we were real or not."

He pinches his lips together.

I narrow my eyes at him. "What aren't you telling me?"

He scrunches his face. "They specifically asked me not to touch you. They said it would jeopardize my contract extension."

My eyes widen as I quickly slide off his body. "Why didn't you tell me?"

"Because I don't give a fuck what they think."

"I do. I don't want to be the reason they cancel your contract. We absolutely need to keep our relationship a secret."

"Let me get this straight. We're in a real relationship, but we need to fake being in a fake relationship. So we're fake fake dating?"

I can't help but giggle at the absurdity. "Yes. We need to play the part."

"Ripley saw me in your bed."

"Ripley won't say anything to anyone. But my brother and management? We're fake in front of them."

He doesn't look happy, but he nods in agreement as he places me on the ground and silently heads toward the locker room.

CHAPTER THIRTEEN

LAYTON

The week after Arizona and I first had sex was crazy. Our schedules were the exact opposite, making quality time difficult. It was full of frantic stolen moments and late-night rendezvous for the first four days. Honestly, it was hot and dirty.

Having her smell on me for games has helped me to the best five-game hitting stretch of my career. And I think she gets off on the fact that it helps me. She goes out of her way to make sure I get my refreshers before each game, even if only for a few minutes in a closet in the stadium during warm-ups.

We finally have an evening where neither of us has games. It's our last night together before her team has a three-day road trip, and the Daultons asked us to show face at the season opening game for the Philly professional basketball team. They gave us four seats right on the floor, so we invited Quincy and Ripley to join us.

Just before the game starts, there's a man with a microphone on the stadium floor talking to the fans, getting them hyped. He looks over at us and points. Into the microphone, he announces, "Look who's in the house tonight." I sigh. This happens every damn time I come here. They always give me unwanted attention. "It's the best ballplayer this town has ever seen..." That's nice of him to say. "Arizona Abbott and some guy she's dating."

The whole crowd erupts in laughter, as do we. He continues, "And the best pitcher this town has ever seen..." Quincy smirks. "Ripley St. James." The whole crowd eats it up. "Oh, and I see Arizona's brother. I forgot his name." Again, nothing but raucous laughter from the fans.

Quincy and I look at each other and nod in a silent understanding. We both drop down to our knees and wave our arms up and down, worshiping the girls. The crowd overwhelmingly claps and hollers for us.

The game starts and we're having a great time drinking beer and laughing.

As is often the case during timeouts, the announcers play games and do giveaways with the fans. During one particular timeout, there's a Kiss Cam going around. The camera finds unsuspecting couples and they have to kiss. It appears on the big screen in the stadium. Sometimes it's cute and sometimes it makes you cringe.

After three couples are forced into kissing in front of twenty-five thousand fans, the cameraman sets up on the ground with his camera facing Arizona and me. Suddenly we appear on the big screen. The crowd cheers in encouragement of us kissing.

Quincy wags his finger in front of the camera letting them know it's not happening. The crowd laughs.

Arizona and I smile at each other as we move together until our lips meet. It's usually just a peck, but Arizona decides to take it a step further. She opens her mouth. When she does that, I'm powerless against her.

I cup her face as the kiss deepens. The tips of our tongues meet, and the crowd goes absolutely berserk. There's hooting, hollering, and catcalls.

Suddenly I'm torn away from her and in a headlock from Quincy. Though the crowd laughs thinking it's all in good fun, Quincy mumbles, "I told you to keep your hands off her."

We both grit out smiles though I manage to elbow him in the ribs. Everyone claps, clearly thinking it was a performance.

He and I glare at each other for the rest of the game. He's being a dick.

When the game is over, Quincy happily tells me he'll see to it that the girls get home and I should be on my way. Arizona whispers to me that I should wait outside and come in when he leaves.

Like the whipped man I'm quickly becoming, I'm waiting across the street from her apartment building. My phone buzzes and I see a text from her.

> Arizona: He should be leaving any minute. Come inside when you see him leave. I'll be in the shower waiting for you. I'm feeling extra dirty.

> Me: Shit. Now I've got to walk through your lobby with a boner.

Arizona: Save that boner for me. I'm going to need it extra deep to last the next few days.

She's so damn sexy. Her dirty texts have ramped up the past few days. It's like we opened a jar that can never again be closed. I have to adjust myself just thinking about her waiting naked for me in the shower and all the things I want to do to her.

I expected him to walk out right away, but he doesn't. At some point, I question whether I missed him. About ten minutes after her last text, he finally walks out of the building, looking pissed as hell. What is his problem?

I walk inside and take the elevator up to their apartment. After knocking on the door, Ripley answers. She has tears in her eyes. I touch her shoulder. "Are you okay?"

She nods. "I'm fine." She motions her head toward Arizona's room. "She's waiting for you."

I walk in and immediately hear her singing in the shower. She's so cute. It's some mangled version of a boyband song. I think it's supposed to be "This I Promise You" by *NSYNC. She really does like that band.

I quietly remove all my clothes and slide on a condom. I slip into the shower and run my hands up her body from behind. She yelps in surprise for a moment before relaxing her body into mine.

My hands cup her full tits. She lets out a soft moan. Turning her head back, she admits, "It's hard to be out with Quincy and not be able to touch you. It's been less than a week and I'm already spoiled. I don't know how I'm going to make it the next few days while I'm gone, and then you have your long road trip."

I rub and squeeze her nipples. "I know the feeling. Let's just focus on right now, not tomorrow." Running my lips up and down her neck, I ask, "How do you want it, sunshine? I'm so desperate for you right now. To fill you up. To feel your pussy milk me."

She runs her hands over mine and wiggles her ass onto my needy cock. "Do whatever you want to me, just do it hard. I want you to make me ache. I want to feel you inside me the whole three days I'm gone."

I shove her front onto the tile wall. I love that I can be a little rough with her. She's strong. She can handle it, and I'm learning she more than likes it.

After spreading her legs with my foot like a police officer, I brush my fingers over her pussy. "If I slip my fingers inside you, how wet would I find you?"

She breathes, "Why don't you find out for yourself?"

I reach my hand back and slap her pussy.

She gasps, "Oh god," and then nearly collapses. I have to hold her up.

"Answer my questions when I ask them."

"You...you'd find me ready for you."

I run my fingers through and then into her. "How long have you been wet? Tell me."

She breathes, "All night. Since the second I saw you." I push in as far as I can go. "Ah, Layton, keep going."

"You want my cock deep in there?"

"Yes. Now, please. Are you..."

"Yes, I'm wearing a condom." Understandably, she's always concerned about safe sex.

"Good. Please, Layton. Don't make me wait any longer."

I reach down and guide my tip to her entrance. I tease her a bit, running it through her and then only slightly into her. In and out only an inch or two. My thick head is stretching her.

She wiggles her hip and whines, "Get inside me. All the way in."

I immediately withdraw my cock and slap her pussy, this time with my dick. Her head falls back onto my shoulder. She breathes a long drawn out, "Oh fuuuuuck," as her body shakes uncontrollably, and she comes.

I know she likes when I slap her pussy, but coming from it is a new one for me. Now I'm frantic to get inside her and enjoy the aftershocks.

I run my tip through her drenched pussy as I immediately find her entrance and push in to the hilt. Her hands are still on the wall, but they're balled into fists. She screams out as her orgasm rolls on. Even with the shower water pouring down, I can feel that she squirted again. She's done that during almost every orgasm she's had with me. It's so damn hot.

As I take her hard and deep, I run my fingers through her come and bring my hand to my nose to inhale it. "I love the smell of your come. I want to bottle it. I'm going to fuck you all night until we fill that bottle."

She nearly collapses again, but I push in deep, pinning her to the tile wall. I love how much I affect her. I love her body's response to me.

I offer her my fingers. "Smell your come."

She inhales.

"Tell me what it smells like."

She breathes, "Like us."

"No, sunshine, it's you, but it smells like victory to me. Your pussy gives me my magic potion. I want to bathe in you."

She reaches back and scrapes her nails across my neck, breaking skin again. "Oh god, Layton."

"I love when you mark me."

I push into her over and over. Long, deep strokes. She's clawing everywhere. Moaning like there's no one else in the world.

Pushing two fingers into her mouth, I encourage her to suck them, which she does. The feel of her tongue on them almost makes me shoot my load.

I pull them out and bring them to her back entrance. She flinches and I whisper, "Relax. It will feel good. I promise."

I run them around her back opening a few times until I finally breach her entrance. She's tight. No one has ever been here before. I smile at the thought.

Pushing in further, she lets out a long moan. "Oh...oh my god. So...so good."

I work my fingers and cock in and out together while she swirls her hips in unison with my thrusts inside her. I move my other hand to her clit and begin to circle it with my fingers.

As soon as I do, I feel her pussy grip my cock so fucking hard that I'm not sure it will ever come out.

She screams out into another orgasm. I can't hold on as I explode into her for a mind-blowing orgasm of my own.

When it's over, she turns around and pulls me into the deepest, most meaningful kiss of my life. I feel like a million words are conveyed in that kiss. It's deep-seated want and need, coupled with care and affection. It's unlike anything I've ever experienced.

I'm totally fucking gone for this girl. That was fast.

CHAPTER FOURTEEN

LAYTON

My stats dipped during her absence. My current state of sadness isn't even about my lackluster performance on the field. I just fucking missed her. How did I get so used to having her in my life that I'm gutted by her absence?

When Arizona Abbott is in a room, it's full of color. But when she's gone, everything turns gray.

She got back into town exactly thirty minutes before we had to board a plane to go on our long, two-week road trip. I had to hire a car service with a front seat partition to be at the airport just so we could get that time alone in the back before I had to jump on a plane. The poor guy didn't even actually have to drive us anywhere. He just had to let us use the back of his car. I compensated him handsomely. I also made sure my body was covered in her before I left.

I marvel at the intense need I have for her. The feeling

seems mutual. She practically sprinted to the car at the airport and then lunged for me when she got inside. It's a passion and intimacy that I've never imagined possible.

This trip has been a time for me to reflect on how hard I've already fallen for her. It's the first long road trip of my career where I'm not out on the prowl for women after games. With the exception of Quincy, all the guys assume it's because I'm in a relationship with Arizona. Quincy thinks it's because I'm living up to my end of the bargain in the fake relationship. He keeps goading me into going out with the single guys. I don't understand why. It's like he's trying to get me to fuck up and break the terms of my contract.

I happily divert the attention of women to my teammates. I have no interest in them. Arizona is all I see. I now hang with the married players who we always made fun of for turning in early and never letting loose.

The good news is that the Anacondas play in the same city as us for our last three days on the road. I've genuinely been counting the seconds until I can see her again.

I've been trying to play it cool in front of Quincy, but Cheetah has been my roommate, and he notices how into Arizona I am. She and I spend hours on video calls every night as our schedules permit. I've never enjoyed simply talking to a woman the way I do her.

Tonight is our last night apart before they come to town. We had a twilight game but hers was later at night. As Trey and I sit at the hotel bar, I keep looking at my watch.

"You got a hot date, Lancaster?"

"Sorry. Arizona's game ended and she'll be back at her

hotel in fifteen minutes. I want to see her face before I go to bed."

His lips curl in amusement. "You're so whipped. I told you this day would eventually come."

"I'm not whipped." I am. I know I am. "I just haven't seen her in a while."

"So you didn't video chat with her last night? And every single night of this road trip?"

I mumble, "Fucking Cheetah and his big mouth."

He bursts into laughter. "This is epic." He places his hand on my shoulder as his face turns a bit more serious. "I'm happy for you. It's not so bad, right? One woman?"

"No, it's not. How did you know Gemma was *the one*?"

His face softens as if he's picturing her. "I knew the second I saw her. You know exactly what I went through to get Gemma. When it's the right one, the rest just fade away. Nothing and no one else matters anymore."

"Has it been hard all these years with long separations?"

"It's not easy, but I don't miss nights on the road at random bars, banging random chicks. Not even a little bit. I miss my wife, and I'm not ashamed to admit it." He wiggles his eyebrows up and down. "And, honestly, when you reunite after a little break, it's fucking hot."

"Still?"

"Every damn time."

"Your marriage is the only functional one I've ever witnessed. I thought it was an anomaly."

"But now you don't?"

"I'm just starting to see things differently. What you said about the others fading away perfectly describes how

190

I feel. I don't see anyone else, and, frankly, it's not hard at all. I simply don't want anyone else."

"Wow. You guys are progressing fast." He doesn't even know how fast it truly is. They think we've been dating for longer than we have, though I suppose in a way, we have been. We were spending time together before it turned physical. Most people would consider that dating.

Before I can respond, there's a loud commotion at the entrance of the bar. Ezra is holding Quincy up. Shit, he's trashed. We're not supposed to drink on the road. We all do, but in moderation. We can't be hungover for games. This is very unlike Quincy.

I hear Ezra trying to encourage him to go back to their room to sleep it off, but Quincy pushes toward us. He pokes my chest. "Look who it is, my sister's *boyfriend*. You completely broke bro-code."

What is he doing? As far as he knows, we're purely in a PR relationship. Why is he starting with me? Especially in front of everyone where we can't have a real conversation about it.

I push his hand away. "Sleep it off, Q. Maybe you'll be less of a dick in the morning."

He narrows his eyes at me. "You just keep your hands off her. You hear me, *brother*?"

Trey and Ezra rightfully have confused looks on their faces. I simply shrug like I have no idea what he's talking about.

I try to remain calm, but his overprotective shit is getting old. With a slight twitch to my lip, I say, "Your sister is an adult. Why don't you start treating her like one, *brother*."

His eyes widen and he looks like he's about to pounce

on me. Ezra and Trey immediately grab his arms and push him toward the elevator.

I take a breath. Does he know something? We did kiss at the game, but on some level, he must know we had to play to the cameras and pressure.

Forty-five minutes later, I'm in my hotel room, on the phone with my girl. It's about twenty minutes before curfew, so Cheetah isn't back yet and neither is Kam, who's rooming with Arizona while they're on the road.

We've been talking about our respective games for the past half an hour. I'm realizing how fun it is to have a woman to talk to about baseball. She loves to hear about and discuss every small detail of our games. She enjoys it as much as I do. We discuss her games too. Talking turkey with her is becoming one of my favorite things to do.

I called just as she was getting out of the shower, so she's in a robe. Without her realizing it, the robe falls open enough for me to see one of her nipples. I immediately harden. Her body, her smell, her taste, they all turn me on in an instant.

She looks down and notices my hard cock and me staring at her breast. She bites her lip as she rubs her nipple between her thumb and index finger. I touch my phone as if I can feel it too. "Tomorrow it will be my mouth around that, not your fingers."

She lets out a moan. "This has been the longest ten days of my life."

"You went fourteen months, three weeks, and five days, but these ten days are the longest?"

She giggles. "I can't believe you remember the exact amount of time. Not to give you an even bigger head than the two melons you're sporting, but now that I've had you, I'm addicted. It's on my brain all day, every day. It's a wonder I can focus on my games."

"Tell me what's most addicting about me."

A small, sexy smile takes form on her luscious lips. "I could tell you it's your intellect or searing wit, but..." Her eyes travel down to my lap.

I pull my hard cock out for her to see. "Is this the object of your addiction?"

"You know it is."

"He's been awfully dry without you coming all over him."

I see her neck flush with embarrassment. "Why does the squirting embarrass you? It's so fucking sexy. You have no idea how much I love it."

She shakes her head. "I just don't know where it came from."

"It's really never happened before?"

"Never. Not once."

I'm feeling about ten feet tall right now. I see her roll her eyes. "Oh god, I shouldn't have told you. Now your ego will be even bigger."

I smile. "It will remain big as long as I have you on my arm and in my bed. Now spread your legs wide, show me that pretty pussy, and touch yourself. I need to see you get off." I sniff. "I can almost smell your arousal."

Her eyes flutter at my words.

"You like when I talk dirty, don't you?"

"You're the best third base coach ever."

"Do you have a glossary of baseball-sex terms on hand at all times?"

She giggles. "I know them all. Now get back to coaching me through it. It's my favorite part of road trips."

We've done this every night since we've been apart. I love that she's so into it. "I want you to slide your fingers into your pussy and then smell them for me."

I see her visibly swallow. I truly love how much my words turn her on. She spreads her legs, slides her fingers in, and then brings them to her nose and audibly inhales.

I hear her hotel room door open, and her eyes move in that direction. She sighs as her legs snap shut. "Shit. Kam is back."

"Just tell me what I want to hear, sunshine."

She licks her lips. "I smell like I need to be #laidbylayton."

I lift my eyebrow. "I'm sure it smells like that too. But tell me what I want to hear."

She now slowly runs her bottom lip through her teeth, knowing it drives me crazy. It makes my cock ooze. "It's smells like victory. Your victory."

"That's right." I blow her a kiss. "Have a good night. I'll see you for a late dinner tomorrow, after which, I'll be getting two weeks' worth of refreshers."

She nods.

"Sunshine?"

"Yes, superstar?"

"I've missed you."

She runs her fingertips over the screen. "I've missed you too. Bye, Layton."

We both linger a few extra seconds, not wanting to end the call, but eventually we do.

ARIZONA WAS SUPPOSED to arrive in time for dinner tonight, but their plane got delayed and they're not arriving until the middle of the night. She told me to leave my room key for her at the front desk of our hotel.

I'm asleep in my boxer briefs when I feel a body climb on top of me. Before I even open my eyes, I taste Arizona's lips on mine. I smell her beachy, lavender aroma. There's nothing better. Relief fills every pore in my body at being reunited with her.

I immediately open my mouth as her tongue dives in. Her legs are straddling me, and she's already lined herself up perfectly.

I run my hands up her body and notice that she's topless. Breaking the kiss, I whisper, "Sunshine, I have a roommate."

I hear Cheetah mumble, "I've already seen her pink nipples. She's got a great rack. Congrats, man."

I feel Arizona shake in laughter. I pull her close, not wanting him to see anything. She seems undeterred by his presence, as she continues kissing along my neck and grinding herself onto me.

ARIZONA

Layton turns his head toward Cheetah. "Dude, take a walk."

"No fucking way. If I get busted out of the room after curfew, I'll get benched for a game. And, honestly, I want to watch you guys get it on."

"Not happening."

Layton needs to relax. I grind my hips harder. He sucks in a breath. "Shit. Oh shit. We need to stop."

I reach into his briefs and grab his engorged cock. "It's been eleven days and seven hours. I need you inside me."

I hear Cheetah chuckle. "That was bizarrely precise. Don't mind me. I'll just jerk off while you two go at it. Pretend I'm not here...unless you want me to join you."

Layton sighs. "Cheetah, please. Let me be alone with her."

"I love you, but I'm not breaking team rules so you can get laid. No way. You wouldn't do it either."

I honestly don't care if Cheetah watches. I've been starved for my man. My hands are moving all over his body. I breathe into his ear, "This is happening with or without him here. You can be on top, and we'll stay under the blankets if you'd prefer. I need you." I give his cock a squeeze. "I need this."

While still straddling his body, I lift my torso away from his, not remotely caring that I'm exposing my top half. I hear Cheetah gasp. "So fucking hot."

Layton's eyes widen, and he covers my breasts with his hands. Through gritted teeth, he says, "What are you doing, are you insane?"

"I have a condom in the pocket of my sweatshirt. I need to grab it." With his hands remaining on me wherever I move, I reach for my sweatshirt.

Cheetah laughs again. "I love that she came prepared with a condom. BYOC. Lancaster, you hit a grand slam with this one."

I giggle as I pull out the condom, tear it open, and roll it onto his length. I know he wants to stop me, but he also wants to cover my body so Cheetah can't see me.

Cheetah sighs. "Stop being such a little bitch. Your girl needs some amor. Give it to her."

I nod. "I do. You said Cheetah likes to watch. What's the big deal?"

"The big deal is that I don't want him to see your body and I don't want him to see us like that."

Cheetah shrugs. "I've seen you with women before."

"Not *this* woman."

As if my desire wasn't already on overload, that statement tips me over the edge.

Cheetah mutters, "Ugh, fine. I'll turn around and jerk off to the noises. Be loud for me, *sunshine*."

I slip off my shorts under the blankets. "That sounds like a fair compromise."

Layton looks at us both like we're crazy. "This isn't a negotiation or a group discussion."

Cheetah turns around, facing away from us. He shouts over his shoulder, "This is the most you're getting from me."

Layton is about to argue more when I lift, place his giant tip at my entrance, and wiggle my way down onto him. He breathes, "Holy fuck." I know I've got him now.

The head of Layton's penis is so fucking wide. Every time he enters me, the rest of the world around me disappears. I've never felt anything better. And he knows how to work it, how to rub it against the right spot. Each time with him gets better and better. I don't think it's possible, but then he outdoes himself.

I hear Cheetah snicker. Layton snaps his head toward him. "No noises from you, motherfucker."

"Don't worry. I just want to hear her noises."

I lean forward and take his face in my hands. With my forehead pressed to his, I say, "Pretend like it's just you and me. We're the only two who exist right now." That's the way it feels with him. Like no one else exists.

He looks at me with so much affection. I've known him for

only a few months and no man has ever looked at me the way Layton is right now. What is happening between us? It feels so strong. Too strong.

He seems like he wants to say something but doesn't because of our company. I whisper, "I feel it too."

Tracing his lips with my tongue, my hips begin to roll over him. He's a little stiff at first, but as soon as I get into a rhythm, I can feel his body relax. His hands begin to wander my body, worshiping every curve along the way.

We start off slow, happily getting reacquainted, but things build quickly. Our desire for each other, coupled with the long separation, pushes this to full-fledged fucking in no time. I'm giving him everything I have.

The room is filled with the sounds of our skin slapping, and our moans get louder and louder.

I can hear Cheetah mumbling in Spanish, but I'm trying to drown him out. My moans are nearly out of control. Layton tries to muffle them with his mouth, but I tilt my head back and completely give into the moment. I don't care about Cheetah. I care about what's happening between Layton and me as I feel him moving inside me.

In one swift move, he flips us over so he's on top and in complete control. He gives me long, deep strokes. That massive head of his rubs the right spot over and over. My world is spinning.

With his face buried in my neck, I hear a groan from across the room. I turn to see Cheetah watching us with heavy lids, stroking himself ferociously. Knowing what watching us having sex is doing to him is ramping up my own arousal. I don't think it's possible to be any more turned on than I am right now.

Layton brings me back to him by whispering in my ear,

"Mark me. I've missed it. I need reminders of you on my body. Reminders of what my cock does to you."

I scrape my nails down his chest and his eyes reach a shade of dark blue I haven't seen yet. The look of bliss on his face right now is everything. I want to commit it to memory.

My orgasm is building. I know it's going to be an explosive one, literally. A few weeks ago, I would have cared. Right now, I don't.

We're going at it hard. The bed is smacking against the wall. I almost feel bad for Cheetah, but not bad enough to stop. And he doesn't seem to mind in the least.

Layton is holding himself up on his big, muscular arms as we stare into each other's eyes knowing that we're both about to come. We're already familiar with each other's bodies. The connection we share is so powerful.

It builds and builds until I have no choice but to let go. My hips rise of their own volition as we both yell out. Our orgasms rush through our bodies at a magnitude I didn't know existed. Eleven days of longing, pouring out of us.

When it's over, he collapses on top of me. We're both breathless and sweaty.

Cheetah starts slow clapping. "That was honestly the best sex I've ever seen. Better than any porn. I came like ten minutes ago. You guys actually came together. I thought coming at the same time was fake romance-book shit."

Layton and I both laugh. He lifts his head and rubs his thumb over my lower lip. "I'm definitely feeling some romance-book shit."

Layton rolls his body off mine. I would have preferred he stayed on top of me. I've missed the feeling of my man's body on mine, between my legs.

After making sure I'm covered, I look at Cheetah. "Are you a closet romance reader?"

He smiles at me. "I'm not closeted. I'm proud of it. Gemma and I are in a book club together. Romance novels are practically a female instruction manual. The real question is, why don't more men read it? It's like *Romance for Dummies*. The shit Jade Dollston's characters do is hella hot. She's helped me add to my repertoire."

I turn my head back to Layton. "Do you read them too?"

He scrunches his face. "Not really, but sometimes Cheetah reads us scenes. He read me one the other night about a couple having sex on a horse. It was insane. And another with a couple on a motorcycle. I had to go on TikTok and watch videos to see if that was even feasible."

I run my fingers over his scruff. "I guess we'll have to get more creative."

He smiles. "More creative than a hotel room in front of Cheetah?"

I giggle. "I'll put some thought into it." I sigh, realizing the hour. "I should probably get going."

I start to sit up, but Layton grabs me and pulls me into his body. "I haven't seen you in eleven days and eight hours. Let me hold you for a little bit."

Cheetah groans in malcontent. "Dude, you sound like a girl."

Layton narrows his eyes at him. "If you had Arizona naked in your bed, would you be in a rush for her to leave?"

"Hmm. Fair point." He waves his hand dismissively. "Carry on."

I laugh as I nestle myself into Layton's warmth. I plan to stay for ten more minutes before I get into trouble for being out of my room, but I must drift off to sleep in the comfort of my man's arms because I wake in the daylight to a loud noise with my head buried in Layton's chest.

I inhale his yummy aftershave which never fails to stimulate my body. I'm like Pavlov's dog, drooling over him.

His hardness rubs through my wetness. I'm almost considering letting him slip it in without a condom when there's another bang. I lift my head and notice that it's coming from the door.

I hear Quincy's voice. "Dickless, wake up!"

Mine and Layton's eyes both pop wide open. I whisper, "Shit."

I turn and look at Cheetah who has a huge grin on his face. He rubs his hands together. "Q is going to kick your ass, Lancaster."

Layton quickly reaches for my clothes and hands them to me. I manage to get them on under the cover of the blanket. I then get out of Layton's bed and go sit on Cheetah's.

Layton slides on his boxers and answers the door. "Hey, Q. What's up?"

He pushes past Layton, saying, "I came to apolog..." He then sees me. "What the fuck is my sister doing in your room?"

I sigh. "Ugh, Quincy. Relax with the barbarian routine. It's getting old. You're not my father and I'm not a child. I had a book club meeting with Cheetah this morning. We like to read the same kinds of novels. Right, Cheetah?"

Cheetah grins widely. "Yep. We were discussing one of the best romance novels I've ever read. This hot chick with pink nipples rides her boyfriend like a rodeo star...and then does his roommate too. So hot. It was playing in my head all night."

I narrow my eyes at him. I see Layton's jaw ticking out of the corner of my eye.

Quincy looks at him with disgust. "You're such a chick reading that unrealistic shit."

Cheetah closes his eyes and has a dreamy look on his face. "Nope. Not unrealistic. It's playing over and over in my head.

Ooh. She just scraped her nails down his chest, leaving marks."
He rubs his bare chest. "I wish she was doing that to me."

My eyes shoot to Layton who is covered in my scratch
marks. He somehow manages to subtly put on a T-shirt while
Quincy is still looking in my direction.

I better get out of here. I stand. "I should get going. We
have to be on the bus in less than an hour." I wiggle my fingers
at them. "You boys have a good game."

I run out the door and get out of dodge quickly.

I head up to my floor and peek down the hallway of our
team rooms. The coast is clear. I quickly and quietly make my
way into my room. Kam is in her bed, smiling at me. "Ooh,
look who broke curfew. You're a black-bottom ho this
morning."

I show her my feet. "Nope. All clear."

"I guess you got *#laidbylayton*?"

I giggle. "Nope. He got *#attackedbyarizona*."

Her face lights up. "Look who's back. Arizona *fucking*
Abbott, ladies and gentlemen."

I take a bow. It feels good to be...me again.

CHAPTER FIFTEEN

LAYTON

A week later, we're lying in her bed, floating on the cloud of post-coital bliss. Her head is resting on my chest, and I'm aimlessly tracing my fingers over her back while she does the same to my chest and stomach. Even something as simple as this feels so damn good with her.

She lifts her head. "Tell me something about you as a little boy. I can't imagine you as a kid. Did you just have a smaller body with the same giant head?"

I tickle her and she giggles. "You seem to very much enjoy my giant head."

"I wasn't talking about *that* head."

"That's the only head you should be worried about."

"I'm being serious. Tell me something I don't know. Tell me about your time with your grandmother."

"After I went to live with her, I was quiet for a long time. I barely spoke at all. I've learned from the years at my grandmother's house that a lot of kids are like that when they suffer some sort of trauma and then move into a strange home."

"Like Perry?"

"Yep. At some point around eight years old, I went from quiet to angry. Angry at my parents for leaving me. Angry about having no money. We were incredibly poor, and my grandmother always had at least six or seven mouths to feed at a time. It wasn't easy, and I certainly didn't make it any easier."

"How did she get into running a home for kids in need?"

"She couldn't have kids of her own. Her jerk of an ex-husband left her for someone who could. My father was actually her nephew, but she raised him, and he called her *Mom*. I think she found her calling when he came to live with her, and she began to open her home to more and more kids. She was a teacher, so caring for children was second nature to her. I don't know how much I truly appreciated everything she did until she was gone. I wish I had been more helpful."

She kisses my chest. "You were a child. Children don't have perspective. Don't be so hard on yourself. You're more than making up for it now. How did you go from an angry kid to a baseball prodigy?"

I smile at the memory. "It's such a weird story. I was at a nearby lake one day. My form of both entertainment and anger management was throwing stones into the lake. There was a man in a canoe, fishing in the middle of that lake. He must have been nearly two hundred feet away. Some random kid bet me a bag of Skittles that I couldn't hit the guy. Like an asshole, I reared back and threw that rock as far as I could. Against all odds, I hit him square in the shoulder. He jerked in surprise and the canoe tipped over. I freaked out and ran as fast as I could, terrified of getting into trouble. Two hours later, the man showed up at my house. I thought he was going to rat me out to my grandmother. Instead, he told me that he coached the local Little League all-star team and wanted me to come try out. He said he'd never seen a kid my age throw anything that far. He promised not to tell my grandmother about the lake if I came to the tryout. I went and discovered a talent and passion I never knew I had. Until that tryout, I hadn't ever picked up a glove or a bat in my entire life."

"Wow. If you missed hitting him, your whole life could be different. That's an incredible story."

"I know. Lloyd, my coach, is the incredible one. He gave me my first glove and my first bat. He was a father figure to me at a time when I desperately needed one. That's a big part of why I don't want to leave Philly. Those kids at Linda's House need me. I try to spend a bit more time with them in the off-season. Even if only sporadically, I know how much a positive male influence can matter in their lives."

"How come your origin story isn't public? And your work with the group homes?"

I shrug. "I'm not a public figure by choice. It's just part of playing ball. It all kind of exploded when I started playing."

"Because you're a great player and unfathomably attractive."

I rub my chin and joke, "I do have a pretty good mug, don't I?"

She reaches up and caresses my face. "I think you're the sweetest, most sincere man I've ever met. That's more attractive to me than your sexy melon."

I smile down at her. "I'm just paying it forward. Lloyd's the sweet one. He's the one who taught me how to make my own bats. Linda said I can start teaching some of the older kids carpentry this off-season."

"What happened to Lloyd?"

"He still lives in my hometown and coaches in the Little League. I fly him out once a year to come to a game. I offer more, but he won't take it. I financially support the Little League as my way of thanking him. He won't let me do anything else."

She kisses my chest again. "I love it. You were fated to play ball and fated to be in the lives of those kids."

"Maybe. What about you? How did you get into softball?"

"Quincy played with the boys in the neighborhood, and all I wanted was to be like my big brother. Despite the age difference, he let me tag along. Despite getting shit from his friends about his little sister being there, Quincy never denied me. He's always looked out for me. At first, I was only allowed to be their runner when they worked on rundowns and things like that. Eventually, he started letting me do more. I swear at only three I could catch and throw with the much older boys."

I let out a laugh. "I bet. Your arm is insane. As good as his."

She giggles. "I'm telling him you said that. Obviously, he played Little League. I counted the minutes until I was old enough to join at five years old. I've been playing ever since. That's around the same time that Ripley moved to our area. Her mom was on the Canadian Olympic softball team. She was actually pregnant with Ripley during the ninety-six Olympics, which was the first time softball was a medal sport. She didn't know it at the time, she was only a few weeks along. She coached us from Little League until we got to college. My parents ran the store and couldn't take much time off, so I always traveled with Ripley and her mom. We were devastated when we learned that softball was going to be removed from the twenty-four Olympics. We dreamed of being on that team since we were little kids. Now we have our sights set on twenty-eight in Los Angeles. Softball will be back in the Olympics then, and it's likely our last chance to make the team."

I run my hands through her natural-blonde hair. "You're the best player in the country. I'm sure you'll make the team."

"I'll be thirty-two then. That's a little old."

I mock gasp. "Thirty-two is not old."

She laughs into my chest. "Whoops. Sorry, old man."

I smile. "Speaking of Quincy, he's been acting really weird toward me since the basketball game. I don't know if it's because we kissed in front of him, but he's kind of being a dick to me. I'm doing my best to let it slide, but it's bad. He was even trying to get me to go clubbing with the single guys on the road. All they do is pick up women. I'm not sure why he was pushing me. It's like he wanted me to get busted."

I feel her swallow. "Did...did you go?"

I lift her chin a bit so we're eye to eye. "Are you worried?"

"I just know how life on the road can be. Especially for you."

Rubbing her face, I say, "Not only would I never cheat on you, I can tell you with a straight face that I have no interest in other women. I only want you." I run my thumb over her bottom lip. "You're all I see."

I see her face relax. "I feel the same."

I squeeze her tightly. "Good, because I've fallen for you and I'm not letting you go." *Ever.*

She smiles softly. "I've fallen for you too."

I squirm a bit nervously, hoping this doesn't freak her out. "I've been thinking about Fantasy Suits. There's honestly nothing more appealing to me right now than traveling the world with you for two months and getting to see you in a bathing suit all day, while I'm basically being paid to grope you. We'll have off days where we can explore together. At night we'll be able to eat in local restaurants and then I can eat you up all night long in our private villa or maybe on the beaches. It sounds kind of perfect to me."

Her face lights up. "I was thinking the same. I see no reason not to move forward with them. They've been pressuring me to sign the contract. That Michael Longley guy calls me every day about it. I just wasn't sure how you felt. It's a five-month commitment to being...us."

"I feel great about it. Let's do it. You deal with your contract. I'll have Tanner deal with mine."

She agrees.

I've never in my life been more excited for a season to be over.

ARIZONA

I'm shopping with Ripley, Kam, and Bailey before I have to go to a photo shoot this afternoon. Next week is the *Sports*

Illustrated body image issue unveiling party. I'm with them, shopping for their new dresses. Auburn Bouvier designed another dress for me, so I'm wearing that, but I wanted to come with my friends and help them find something special to wear. They're all excited for the big night.

Bailey runs her fingers through the rack and subtly asks, "Will Tanner Montgomery be at the party?"

I shrug. "I'm not sure. Probably. Wouldn't you know? You're working for him." After I mentioned it, Tanner interviewed Bailey and hired her on the spot. She's been working there a few days a week ever since.

"I hang with Harper, not him."

Kam narrows her eyes at her sister and then widens them as if something has occurred to her. "Oh my god. You have a crush on him."

Bailey's entire face turns red, and she looks down. "No I don't. He's super old. Like forty-three, only a few years younger than Mom and Dad."

Kam places her hands on her hips, appearing unconvinced. She turns to me. "Is he hot?"

I nod. "So hot. He's got the whole salt-and-pepper, sexy older man thing going."

Kam smiles at Bailey. In a sultry voice, she teases, "Have you been a bad girl? Do you need a spanking?"

Bailey sighs. "Here we go."

"I bet you want to call him *Daddy*, don't you?"

Bailey rolls her eyes. "Drop it. He's my boss. I'm not interested in him like that. Age gaps that large are best left for fiction."

I shoot Ripley a knowing look and she gives me the same in return. Bailey is most definitely interested, but I don't want to further embarrass her. "Speaking of that kind of fiction, I learned recently that Cheetah reads romance novels. He said it's his female instruction manual."

They all burst out laughing. Cheetah is badass looking. Knowing he reads those books is comical.

I'VE GOT a photoshoot for a sports drink that I'm being paid a ridiculous amount of money to endorse. Layton insisted on coming with me, wanting to support my first big endorsement. Tanner is here too, making sure things run smoothly and that I'm being treated properly. They asked me to shoot in California, but he negotiated that it would take place here, which is great because I'd otherwise have to wait until after the season was over. With Layton and me leaving shortly after our seasons are over for the Fantasy Suits shoot, this would have been delayed for months. Once the executives realized my timeline, they agreed to do it here in Philly right away.

I'm now closely examining Tanner. He's a little old for my personal liking, but he's definitely an attractive man. His eyes are a unique shade of light brown. Almost golden. He's got a sexy beard, is tall, and is very well built. I wonder if anything is going on with Bailey and him beyond her obvious crush.

While I'm dressed in my Anacondas uniform, which is comfortable for me, I'm in full makeup, and my hair is blown out to styled perfection. I would certainly never look like this for an actual ballgame. It's kind of ridiculous.

Layton hasn't kept his hands or lips off me the entire time. The makeup crew yelled at him for making their work twice as hard, so the director forced him to stand in the back of the studio, where he's been taking about a thousand pictures of me from afar. He's completely annoying the photographer. At least it's making me smile. I think he's my number one fan. I love it so much.

While they're fixing one of the lighting angles, Tanner approaches, handing me a bottle of water. "How is everything going?"

"Thank you." I take a much-needed sip. "It's fine. This isn't natural for me, but hopefully they'll get a few good shots."

He lets out a laugh. "I think there will be more than a few. You look great."

"Thank you."

"So...what did you do to Layton?"

"What do you mean?"

"I've never seen him like this. So smitten."

I can't help but smile as I look toward the back of the room at him. He winks at me. He's just so...dreamy.

Tanner clears his throat, bringing me back to the present.

I let out a laugh. "I guess I'm smitten too. I think the whole thing is kind of unexpected for both of us. Especially given how things started."

He scratches his neck nervously. "On some level, I'm happy for him. On the other, I'm worried."

I nod in understanding. "You're worried about his contract extension?"

"Among other things, yes. He doesn't seem to want to retire, and he doesn't want to leave Philly. I'd hate to see this blow up in his face."

"I've been thinking a lot about it. We're just a few weeks away from the end of the regular season. Both teams will make the playoffs, so it will extend the timeframe a few more weeks. But they've gotten exactly what they hoped for. I don't think the owners are out to screw him over. They wanted this to last through the season and it has. They wanted it to help the Anacondas and it has. Our relationship has given them everything they wanted and more. At this point, it helps them that we're actually together because it will extend beyond the term of the contract. Frankly, us having a real relationship works in their favor."

He's quiet as he considers my words. "I hadn't thought of it that way. I think you might be right. I can't deny that you've obviously been good for his game. I haven't seen him play this well in a long time. You must have the magic potion." He doesn't say that in a way that I think he knows of my alleged *magic potion*, but it nonetheless makes me blush.

His eyes widen. "Sorry. I didn't mean to embarrass you. He's just playing loose and happy. It's been wonderful to see."

"I agree. I love watching him play. It's thrilling that he's on a hot streak. I hope it lasts."

"He loves watching you play too. And so does my daughter. We rarely miss a game at this point."

"You should bring her on the field to watch batting practice before our next game. I'll leave a pass for you."

"Thank you. Bailey suggested the same."

"How is it going with her?"

I try to get a read on him, but he's not giving anything away with his expressionless face.

"Amazing. Harper adores her. Can you imagine when you were younger getting to spend time with one of your idols? It's a dream come true for her."

I turn my head toward Layton and smile. "Spending time with your childhood idol sounds pretty amazing to me."

"Layton mentioned that you guys are moving forward with Fantasy Suits. He had me finalize everything on his behalf."

I nod. "Yep. I signed my contract this morning."

"You did? Did you find another lawyer to review it for you?"

"Oh, no. The terms all looked pretty standard. I spoke with

their representative, Michael Longley. He helped me understand everything and ended up giving me a lot more money than originally proposed. Thanks for the advice on that. Everything is signed and done."

His face drops. "You should have had an attorney look at it. Hopefully everything goes as planned."

I look at Layton again and can feel my heart thumping in my chest. I wonder if there will ever be a time when my heart rate doesn't increase from seeing him. It hasn't happened yet.

Two months of traveling the world together really does sound like a *fantasy* to me.

CHAPTER SIXTEEN

ARIZONA

Layton had another amazing game today. He's on the best tear of his career. I'm so proud of him.

Just before each time he steps into the batter's box, he turns to me and smells his fingers. It's a direct line to my libido, which has been on severe overdrive since Layton Lancaster came into my life.

I love that he considers me his muse. I love that we have our dirty little secret that no one else in the world knows about.

We're all walking into Screwballs to celebrate his big night when Quincy pulls me aside. "What's going on with you and Lancaster? I'm not blind, Z."

I hate lying but I suppose it's for the best right now. I mostly want to protect their friendship, but we're going to have to tell him at some point. Outside a bar late at night isn't the time or place though.

"Nothing is different. You know what's going on. We're playing a part. We're in a public relations relationship to help the Anacondas. You can't deny that it's working. Our stands are full for every single game. We're the first team in the league to turn a true profit. I've never made more money in my life. All the girls have endorsement deals on varying levels." That's all true.

"That's not what I mean. You two are suddenly different. You look like a real couple. I better be wrong."

"Then I guess we're doing our job." I playfully smile. "Maybe I'll win an Academy Award next year."

He doesn't bite on my attempt to lighten things. "I'm warning you again. He's bad news when it comes to women. I don't want to see you hurting all over again."

"I'm a big girl but thank you for looking out for me. I'm fine. Really. Don't worry about me, worry about your eyebrows. You look like Eugene Levy with those wild, bushy things."

He frantically feels his eyebrows. "What's wrong with them? I have good eyebrows, don't I?"

I smile. "You're too easy, Abbott."

He scowls. "You're a brat."

I straighten my shoulders. "Proud of it. What about you? What's going on in your love life? You've been different lately too."

He doesn't make eye contact with me. "Nothing. You know how it is for me. I'm not interested in anything long term. I'm *Hit It and Quit It Quincy*, right?"

I rub his arm, sensing that he's hiding something. "Are you sure? You don't seem yourself. I think there's something you're not telling me."

He pulls away. "Just drop it." Opening the door to Screwballs, he says, "Let's go celebrate your *fake* boyfriend."

"Fine." What's with the people close to me not telling me what's really going on with them? Ripley won't share anything.

I know something is going on with her. And Layton was right, Quincy is acting like a crazy man right now. We definitely need to sit down with him in the near future and tell him about us.

With Quincy unwilling to talk, I simply walk through the front door ahead of him and we make our way toward our regular booth, which is busting at the seams. Except for the spot next to Layton, which he motions that he saved for me. And I see my favorite beer sitting in front of the empty spot.

Quincy looks down at me and raises his eyebrows accusatorially.

I roll my eyes. "We're playing a role. Get a beer and relax."

He mumbles, "I wish someone got me a beer."

I giggle as I slide in next to Layton. He immediately pulls me close to him. He leans over and whispers, "I had to shower after the game. I'm going to need an Arizona refresher later. You saw what having your juices on me did for my game today. I need more of your magic potion." He runs his index finger up my leg. "You produced a lot of it last night. I want to find out how much more is in there."

I feel my face flushing thinking about everything we did last night and hoping for a repeat performance tonight. This man wreaks havoc on my body.

Gemma is seated next to me. We've only been able to hang out a few times, what with them having a baby at home, but I really like her. Despite the fact that she always dresses like she's going to a fashion show, she's very down to earth and definitely views Layton as a brother. I'm happy he has her in his life.

She briefly looks down at Layton's hand which is now aimlessly circling my inner thigh.

"I've never seen him like this."

"Like what?"

"So infatuated with a woman. He only has eyes for you. He's never been that way before."

"Really?"

"*Really*. He watches you. All. The. Time. When you're in a room together, his eyes rarely leave you. I've noticed it for weeks."

I try to contain my excitement. I can't deny that I feel the same.

"And in the stands at games. He always seeks you out."

That's true. He does. I doubt she notices that he also makes sure I always see him smell his fingers before he steps up to the plate. It's disturbing and hot all at the same time.

"The feeling is mutual."

"Good, because the world sees him one way, but I know who he is inside. He's viewed as a playboy, a well-deserved title, but he's much deeper than that. He's sensitive and caring. He goes above and beyond for the people he cares about."

I nod. "I know he does. I love that about him. There's so much more to him than anyone knows about."

Before we can continue, Cheetah chuckles loudly and then points at Quincy. "You were last to arrive, sucker."

"Ugh. Arizona was with me. Pick on her."

Cheetah shakes his head. "Nope, she was two steps ahead of you. Probably always has been. Let's hear one."

Quincy smiles. He usually has at least twenty random facts on hand at any time. "The tongue is the strongest muscle in the human body."

As if on cue, we all start to fiddle with our tongues.

Cheetah blows a kiss to Kam. "Speaking of strong tongues, I'd like to tongue-punch your tuna taco tonight." He flicks his tongue suggestively at her.

She smiles, wryly. "Did you learn that line in one of your romance novels?"

His eyes widen and he turns his head to me. I shrug. "Was

it supposed to be a secret? Doesn't everyone know you like romance novels and porn?"

Kam interrupts, "Porn? Now you're talking my language. By the way, *kitten*, women tongue-punch my tuna taco way better than any man ever has."

Cheetah shakes his head. "That's because you haven't had my tongue, Kam bam."

Trey sighs. "I wish you two would just do it and get it over with." He then raises his glass and shouts, "To Layton, for another career night. It's great to see you playing this way again, brother."

Layton smiles as we all raise our glasses to him. He turns his head to me and announces, "It's all thanks to my beautiful muse."

He rubs his thumb over my lower lip and looks at me with pure heat in his eyes. Before I know what's happening, he brings his lips to mine.

What happened to our fake fake relationship? Or is it regular fake? I'm so confused. All I know is that there's nothing fake about my feelings for him or the fact that his tongue just entered my mouth in front of all our friends.

He's so outwardly affectionate. I wasn't expecting this side of him, but I'd be lying if I said I didn't like it. I love it.

We're greeted by a sea of catcalls before a chair screeching breaks our kiss. I look up in time to see my brother's angry face turning and him stomping toward the front door.

I start to stand to go after him, but Ripley grabs my arm. "I've got it. I'll talk to him. You stay and have fun with your man."

"Fine by me. I'm sick of him treating me like a child when he's the *real* child. He just had a temper tantrum."

"I know, sweetie. He worries about you. I'll talk to him."

She stands and quickly walks out the door, hot on my brother's heels.

Layton squeezes my leg. "Sorry. I couldn't help it. Maybe I should go talk to him too."

"No. Let her deal with his immaturity. She was always better with him than me. I think you were right weeks ago. We should have told him we're not faking it anymore. I'm a goddamn adult, and I'm sick of him not treating me like one. He just made a spectacle of himself in front of our friends for no reason at all."

I'm getting mad. I know we're supposed to be fake, but so what if we're not? He can't act like this when I date someone.

Layton discreetly adjusts his pants.

I look at him in shock. "This turns you on?"

"I love when you're assertive. It's sexy as hell. It's like watching you play. When you take command behind the plate, I get hard. I have to bring a sweatshirt or a jacket to your games to hide the wood that inevitably comes when you're all badass."

I like that he's turned on by that side of me. *Really* like it. Fuck it. I decide to give him a not so discreet rub of encouragement.

He grabs my wrist. "Don't do that unless you're prepared to follow through."

"Who says I won't follow through? Don't you know me at all by now? I've already had sex in front of Cheetah. What's a few more people?" I stare at him in challenge.

He stares back, his eyes darkening. I love when he gets like this, looking like he's going to snap and bend me over the table. He's so hot.

Cheetah clears his throat, breaking us out of our mutual trance. "Hey, Kam, what's your story? Are you riding the pole or picking flowers in the lady garden tonight? I need to know where to spend my time."

She takes a long, slow sip of her drink. With her mischievous grin, she says, "I'm not sure what I'm in the mood for. Maybe both. What do you have in mind? You can't possibly want to lose another bet."

He nods toward an attractive blonde woman on the dance floor practically making googly eyes at Kamryn. "She's interested."

Kam shrugs. "Are you seriously looking to make another wager? Your hair just grew back. What's left? Tattoos?"

He smirks. "One of these days I'll win, and then I'm going to jam your clam so hard that you'll never be able to look at a fishing pole without thinking of me. It's worth the small sacrifices along the way." He looks at her with his ever-present mischievous blue eyes. "Same rules?"

Kam taps her chin for a moment in thought. "Meh. She doesn't do it for me."

He sighs in disappointment.

"I think my lady garden isn't feeling like a vegetarian tonight. She needs a little meat. Maybe some big Mexican salami. Know where I can find one?"

His chin drops. "Are you fucking with me right now? Is this for real?"

She slides out of the booth and stands before leaning her hands on the table. "Alright, guapo. Let's see if you can handle me. You better be the tiger I've been hearing about for months. Game on, motherfucker."

He stands in the back of the booth and leaps over the table. "I hope you've got vet insurance, Kam bam, cause I'm about to tear that pussy up. Let's go, momma."

He easily throws Kam over his shoulder like a fireman. She laughs as he sprints out of the bar with her in tow.

Layton grabs my hand. "Let's get out of here. I want to celebrate alone with you."

I stand and pull his hand. "Dance with me. Just give me one dance, superstar."

He smiles, knowing he said the same thing to me the night we met. "One dance, sunshine, then we buzz off." He licks his lips. "Together."

I giggle at him echoing my words from that night. "Deal."

He orders us an Uber on his phone before leading me to the dance floor as the music plays. He pulls me into his arms, his body flush against mine.

We're not kissing, but his lips are everywhere, as are his hands. He so easily makes me forget where I am, igniting my body with every touch. It's like we can't get close enough to one another.

I quickly glance around the bar. All eyes are on us. I whisper, "People are watching."

He whispers back, "I don't care."

I notice a few of them recording us. "I think they're taking videos."

"I don't care."

His hands move up the back of my shirt. He grinds his erection against me as his lips graze over mine.

"We should be careful. I don't want this causing issues for your contract."

"I don't care."

We need to leave before the videos become explicit and they're seen by management. I mumble into his mouth. "You win. Let's get out of here."

He smiles into my mouth before hurriedly pushing me toward the exit with the front of his body pressed to the back of mine. I can feel his erection on my back side. I imagine one like his is hard to hide.

As soon as we're out the door, he spins me and has me pinned to the brick wall of the building in less than a second.

He lifts my legs so they're wrapped around him, and then grinds himself into me.

I run my hands through his hair. "Are we going to my home dugout or your away dugout?"

"Sunshine, I'm going to make you scream so fucking loud tonight. We're going to my place. No roommates. I can fuck you anywhere and everywhere. All. Night. Long. There is one rule at my apartment though."

I smile. "What's that?"

"No clothes. Ever. It's a nudist colony."

I giggle. "Is that in your condo association bylaws?"

"Yep."

"I need to see them to verify. I'm a rule follower, so I need to be sure."

"I'll have my lawyer send you a copy tomorrow. In the meantime, you'll have to trust me."

"Hmm. Okay, I guess I'll have to trust you." I run my tongue along his upper lip. "But one small change. You fucked me last night. Tonight, I fuck you."

His eyes flutter and he thrusts his cock forward. "Oh shit, we need to get out of here before I take you right here."

I reach into my pocket and pull out my panties. "I'm way ahead of you, superstar. I haven't been wearing any panties since the game."

I've been waiting for the right time to tease him with this.

I run them under his nose, and he inhales deeply. "Fuuuck." He slides out his tongue and licks through them.

I'm about to throw caution to the wind and let him take me here when we hear a noise around the corner of the building. Both our heads snap in that direction.

We then hear the sounds of a car pulling up to the curb. We turn to see the Uber stopping in front of us. Placing my feet on the ground, he grabs my hand, and we quickly make our way to the waiting car.

As soon as we slide in and close the door, he grabs for my face to kiss me. The Uber driver smacks the seat in front of us. "None of that in here!"

Layton immediately pulls away from me. I look at him in amused surprise. "What happened to *I don't care*?" I say with a mock deep voice.

"I take Ubers everywhere. I can't risk having him trash my rating. I'm a four-point-nine. I take that shit seriously."

I burst out in laughter. "You don't care if people film us getting it on in Screwballs, but your Uber rating takes priority above all?"

He smiles, realizing how ridiculous this is, but remains steadfast. "Yes! One bad rating and no one will pick me up." He turns his head toward the driver. "Cal, isn't that true?"

The driver, whose name I guess is Cal, nods. He's a large man, likely in his sixties, with thinning gray hair. "Yes, sir, Mr. Lancaster. Hanky panky in an Uber is the second worst thing you can do to your rating."

I lean my head forward so he can hear me. "What's the worst, Cal?"

"Puking in the Uber. Not only does that kill your rating, but we all have a group chat. If you puke in an Uber, no one will ever pick you up at night again."

Layton looks amused. "I always suspected that there's a secret Uber driver chat where they discuss clients."

I start giggling uncontrollably. This is insane.

Cal eyes me skeptically from the rearview mirror. "Umm, how much have you had to drink, ma'am?"

"Half a beer, Cal." I sarcastically add, "I think I'll make it home before running to stick my head into a toilet."

I see him smile. "Thank you, ma'am."

Cal clearly recognizes Layton, and they begin chatting about baseball.

I'm wildly amused with what's gone on in this Uber, so I decide to have a little fun with Layton. I discreetly unbutton and unzip my jeans.

I see his eyes move that way and then widen. He subtly shakes his head.

I slump down a bit to make sure Cal can't see me before sliding my fingers into the front of my pants. Layton's breath catches.

Silently laughing, I toss my panties his way. He immediately balls them in his fist and brings them to his nose, sucking it in like a man who can't breathe and they are his oxygen mask.

His reaction to my scent never fails to deepen the throb between my legs.

While Cal chats away about the Cougars, I begin touching myself. Layton's eyes are glued to the just barely visible top of my pussy where my fingers slide through my wetness.

I momentarily pull them out, reach over, and run them along his lips. His jaw slackens as he slides his tongue around his Arizona-covered lips. I can hear his breathing becoming more labored.

I quickly slide my fingers back into my pants. My clit is pulsating at this point, begging my fingers for relief.

My own breathing picks up as my strokes become faster. He watches on with heavy lids and darkened eyes, my panties remaining under his nose, my scent taken in with every inhale. His jeans look like they might burst off him at any moment.

He's trying to stay present in his conversation with Cal but failing miserably. Fortunately for him, Cal is a talker and is carrying the conversation.

I work myself into a complete frenzy. At some point,

DOUBLE PLAY

Layton grabs his dick and squeezes it hard. I'm thoroughly enjoying driving him crazy.

I'm driving myself crazy too. I'm actually going to come in this Uber with Cal talking and Layton sitting three feet away from me teetering on the edge himself.

A few more strokes, and I squeeze my eyes shut as my body silently shakes into my orgasm.

The car begins to slow down. Layton practically growls, "Around the back, please. I have a private entrance."

I didn't know that. Anytime I've been here I've come through the front lobby, though I suppose I've never walked in with him. I have to deal with his eighteenth-century, weird doorman every time.

Cal drives to the back of the impressive looking building as I zip and button my jeans. I joke with Layton, "I'm exhausted. I might just head home."

He narrows his eyes at me and practically pulls my arm out of the socket as he drags me out of the car. I giggle as he pushes me toward the entrance. I love when he's a little rough with me. He doesn't treat me like a porcelain doll and I'm here for it.

He quickly retrieves some sort of key card from his wallet. As soon as he waves it in front of the sensor, the elevator doors open. We step in and I see only one button to the eighty-eighth floor, which illuminates when he runs his key card over it.

"I get such a kick out of the fact that even your apartment number has eight in it."

As he pins me to the side of the elevator, he says, "I couldn't pass up a building with the penthouse on double eights." He unbuttons and unzips my pants. "Now, where were we?"

"We were worrying about your Uber rating."

He shoves his hand down my pants and runs his fingers

225

through my wetness. "Now you can focus on the Layton rating."

"Maybe I'll post *#laidbylayton. Three stars. Too much of a tease. Do not recommend.*"

He slides his fingers inside me, but then remains still. "Okay. Then I won't move my fingers. I'll give you a three-star performance."

I wiggle my hips, but he's physically in control. "Fine. Four stars."

He pushes his fingers a drop deeper, but not to the spot he knows intimately. He stares at me in challenge.

"Okay, four-point-nine."

No movement.

"What? That's good enough for Uber."

The door pings our arrival. Without removing his fingers from my body, he uses his other arm to lift me through the door and into his foyer area, which is bigger than my entire apartment, and then eventually into a living room with windows overlooking the entire city. It's gorgeous.

"Okay, the view brings you to five stars."

He smiles as he sits on the couch and maneuvers my body so it's straddling his. All with his fingers still inside me.

"Good girl. Now, you told me you were going to fuck me tonight. Let's see what you've got. I hope it's worthy of five stars."

CHAPTER SEVENTEEN

ARIZONA

I slip out quietly early the next morning, as we have a game at noon, and I need to stop by my place to get some clothes.

I walk into my apartment and see my girls all sitting on our sofa hysterically laughing. "What's so funny?"

Ripley is grinning from ear to ear. "You missed the greatest thing that's ever happened in the history of the world."

"What? Tell me."

Trying to contain her laughter enough to speak, but failing miserably, she manages, "Kam and Cheetah broke the waterbed."

Bailey giggles. "Cheetah came running out of her bedroom buck naked. Let me tell you something, Santa isn't the only one with a big sack. That dude's balls must weigh him down. I don't know how he's so fast with those dangling between his legs."

Kam nods. "And they're crazy sensitive. I've never been

with a guy that has sensitive balls like that. I think he has a g-spot on his balls."

Ripley tilts her head to the side. "Is that a thing? Balls with g-spots?"

Kam shrugs. "I don't know. I never met a man with it until Cheetah."

I clear my throat. "His giant, sensitive, g-spot-bearing balls aside, how did the bed break?"

She smiles. "He was fucking me so damn fast and hard. We were in perfect unison with the motion of the bed...until we weren't. All I can say is that the wave was coming up while he was coming down and...*pop*! It practically exploded. I wish I had it on video."

I can't help but start laughing hysterically.

Kam is laughing too. "It was legit like surfing into our living room. Cheetah stood up and ran around like a mad man, looking for towels with his dick and balls flapping all over the place. As if towels would clean up the Hoover Dam breaking in my room. Bailey ran out of her room and started screaming."

Bailey nods. "Cheetah was going nuts. He was cursing in Spanish. The water was everywhere. *Everywhere*. You can't fathom how much water was in that thing. Her room, our living room, and the apartment below us are a mess. There goes our security deposit."

WE'RE in the huddle after the game. Coach Billie yells, "Way to spear them with your tongues, Anacondas!" She then hisses like a snake.

The whole team looks at each other in amused wonderment. Does Coach Billie realize what that sounds like?

We break apart and she places her hand on my shoulder. "Great game today, Arizona."

"Thanks, Coach Billie."

"Do you have a minute?"

"Sure. I need to shower and get to Layton's game, but I'll always make time for you."

We had an afternoon game today and Layton has an evening game. He couldn't come to ours because of his warm-ups, but we should have plenty of time to get there for the start of his game.

"I just wanted to wish you good luck at the *Sports Illustrated* event coming up. I know you had trepidation about a more provocative shoot, but you know it will help the team and the sport. Even with every team in the league on an upswing, we're still the most profitable. On behalf of all of us, thank you."

I smile. "Honestly, once I got comfortable, it wasn't so bad. It's no different than a bathing suit. Hopefully they got some good shots."

"I have no doubt they did. Good luck to the Cougars tonight."

"Thanks."

After I shower, I look at my phone, which has been in my locker since early this morning when I arrived at the ballpark for our warm-ups. There are several texts from Layton.

Layton: Just woke up. Why didn't you wake me before you left?

It was early. He was sleeping so peacefully. I didn't want to disturb him. We were up *very* late doing *very* naughty things.

An hour later, there's another text.

Layton: Shit. I wasn't thinking and took a shower. I need your scent on me. You know I play better with it.

I roll my eyes at his dramatics.

Layton: I know you just rolled your eyes. I'm superstitious. Your game should end in plenty of time for you to get your sweet pussy to the stadium to give me my magic potion refresher.

I squeeze my legs together at the thought. And then I wince. I'm sore as hell. He ended up giving me a five-star pounding all night long. It's not easy to catch an entire softball game with that situation happening.

Me: Just getting your messages and just getting out of the shower. I'll do what I can.

Layton: Are you naked?

Me: I don't shower with clothes on, do you?

Layton: Shit, I'm getting hard thinking about you showering.

Me: I'm shocked you're ever able to make it nine innings without a boner.

Layton: It's been a struggle since you came into my life, trust me. When you're in the stands in that tight jersey and short shorts, it's impossible. When you eat a hot dog, I just about lose my mind.

Huh? Me eating a hot dog makes him hard?

> Layton: Please hurry. I need my magic potion.

> Me: I said I'll do my best

Ripley, Bailey, Kamryn, and I head to the stadium. We walk in through the player family entrance, like always. An older man dressed as an usher greets us.

"Good afternoon, Ms. Abbott."

"Hi, Bernie." Layton often has him waiting for me to quickly escort me to the locker room area.

"Mr. Lancaster needs to have a word with you before the game. Please come with me."

I feign surprise. "Oh, okay. No problem." I turn to my friends. "I'll meet you guys out there."

Everyone else heads toward our seats, but I'm shown to the underground tunnel area where I see Layton waiting, already dressed in his uniform. My mouth physically waters. I do love seeing him in that uniform. He wears it so well.

He smiles and takes my hand as I approach. "Thanks, Bernie. I've got her from here."

"My pleasure, Mr. Lancaster."

As soon as Bernie is out of sight, Layton pulls me into an equipment closet and pushes me up against the wall. He kisses around my neck and moves his hands under my jersey, immediately pinching my nipples. "I missed you this morning...and all day. I watched your game on my phone. You were amazing. Your pop time on the pickoff play at first was almost inhuman."

"I love when you talk dirty to me in catcher language."

He smiles into my neck as his hands roam all over my body.

I run my fingers through his hair. "Squatting was no easy feat after our evening together."

He slides his hand down and rubs me between the legs on the outside of my shorts. "Is your pussy sore, sunshine?"

I nibble at his chin. "In the best way possible."

"Are you okay for me to get my refresher? You know I need it."

I nod and he immediately slips his fingers into my shorts and panties, running them through me over and over again before slipping them into me.

I can't begin to count the number of orgasms I've had in the past forty-eight hours, but somehow, I'm hungry for more. My need for him never wanes.

I see him wince.

"What's wrong?"

He adjusts himself with his other hand. "Being hard while wearing a cup isn't ideal. I might break this thing."

I can't help but let out a laugh. That doesn't sound pleasant. "How about I give you some relief? You know, just to make sure your cup is safely protecting you. We wouldn't want you breaking it or poking out from it. I now have a vested interest in its health and safety."

He gives me a sexy smile as he pulls his fingers out of me and rubs them all over the scruff on his face. I might have a spontaneous orgasm from watching him revel in covering himself in me.

Instead, I drop down to my knees and unfasten his baseball pants. I shimmy down his jockstrap and, sure enough, an extremely swollen, very large cock pops free. I'm not sure how he fit it in there in this condition. I'm not sure how that giant head fits in anything, including me.

I look up and am suddenly transported to over ten years ago when I used to lay in bed at night and look up at a poster of a slightly younger version of this handsome man, dressed in this very same pinstriped uniform. It feels surreal. Not even the hormonal eighteen-year-old version of me could have fantasized about this moment. I can't believe this is my reality.

I run my hands up his thick, muscular thighs as I lean forward. Dying to taste him, my tongue begins a long path at his balls and slowly licks all the way to and over his thick head. He circles that already oozing tip all around my lips, coating them in what he's offering. With labored breath, he says, "You're my every fantasy come to life."

I inwardly smile at him feeling the same way I am. The feelings between us are already so strong. I know I'm not alone in it. Everything he says and does tells me he's right there with me. Falling hard and fast.

He slides that big, beautiful cock of his as far into my mouth as I can take him. I open my throat so he can go deep.

His eyes darken, and his face is covered in ecstasy. He wraps his hand around my ponytail. "You should see what I'm looking at right now. You're wearing my jersey, in my stadium, kneeling in front of me, sucking my cock, taking it deep. So fucking perfect."

Sealing my lips and flicking my tongue along every engorged vein, I blow his fucking mind. It doesn't take long before he explodes into my mouth. I feel so satisfied giving this to him in his time of need. He spends countless hours giving my body pleasure I've never known possible. Over and over again. To be able to return the favor in some small way is extremely gratifying.

Still on my knees, I help him tuck himself back into his cup and lift his jockstrap back into place. He runs his thumb back and forth over my swollen lower lip as something special passes between us. I can't describe it, but I'm certain we're both feeling it. *I think it's love.*

I know he has to be on the field any minute now, but he's touching me in such a way that he doesn't seem like he's in any rush to end this powerful connection we're sharing.

After a few intense moments, he pulls his hand away to get himself put back together. As he's zipping his pants, the door to the equipment closet opens and we hear, "I'll be right there. I need to grab an extra rosin bag."

That's not any voice. That's my brother.

He takes one step in and stops short at the scene before him. I'm on my knees in front of Layton. Layton's belt and buttons are still unfastened. His hand is on his zipper. It looks like exactly what just happened in here. Not a scene any brother wants to walk in on, especially mine.

Through gritted teeth, he growls, "Arizona, get up off your knees. Now!"

Like a child caught misbehaving, I immediately stand.

He points at Layton. "I knew it. I warned you to stay away from her."

Layton blows out a breath and takes my hand in his. "I'm sorry, Q, but I couldn't. I tried. She's too special."

"I know. She's way too good for you."

"I agree."

"Stop this or I can't be held responsible for my actions. Am I making myself clear?" He toggles his finger between us. "This isn't happening. Whatever has started, it ends now. It's over."

Layton shakes his head. "We're not going to stop seeing each other. I don't care what you do to me. Hit me, hate me, whatever. She and I are the real deal. I'm not giving her up for you or anyone."

"You wouldn't know the real deal if it smacked you on the head. You're nothing but an overpaid has-been, trading his fading looks and former talent to sleep his way through Philadelphia and every other city we visit. You're a scumbag piece of shit, and you're going down, motherfucker. Right now."

Quincy takes an aggressive step toward Layton, but I move my body in front of Layton's and hold up my hand at Quincy. "Stop it! Both of you. First of all, I'm standing right here. Don't either of you dare talk about me like I'm not. Neither of you speak for me. Ever. Second of all, I'm not a fucking child, Quincy. Stop treating me like one. I'm twenty-eight years old. I know what I'm doing and who I'm doing it with. Don't you think I know a little bit about who I do and don't want in my life at this point? Regardless, it's none of your damn business. If I want to suck his dick on home plate in the middle of the afternoon in front of fifty-thousand fans, I will. It's *my* decision. Not yours."

Quincy looks at me with disgust. "You're playing right into his games. He's going to hurt you. Can't you see that? He's not capable of loving anyone but himself."

I feel Layton's arms wrap around my waist as he pulls me close to his body. "That's not true. Just because I haven't found the right person until now doesn't mean I'm incapable. You haven't either, Quincy."

My head is reeling with his comment, *until now*, but I don't have the mental energy to dive into that. I turn in his arms, pull his face down to mine, and softly kiss his lips. "Leave me alone with my brother. He and I need to talk. Have a good game. I'll be waiting for you afterward."

He whispers in my ear, "Is the dick sucking at home plate thing happening?"

I can't help but smile at his joke during this intense moment. I mouth, "Soon. I promise."

Quincy grits, "I heard that."

Layton lovingly rubs my face with the backs of his fingers before nodding, kissing me once more, and then walking toward the door. Quincy not so subtly elbows him on the way out.

Once we're alone, Quincy crosses his arms. "What are you doing, Arizona? It's going to be like Whitaker all over again. He'll toss you aside like yesterday's news. You're going to get your heart broken."

"It's different. Layton isn't Marc. You know it. You always hated Marc. Layton is your best friend. You must realize that he's a genuinely good person."

"You don't know shit about him."

"That's not true. This isn't just a physical relationship. We've spent countless hours talking. I know him better than I've ever known any man, even one I dated for several years and was prepared to marry. I can't help how I feel. I know it's the same for him. I'm...I'm falling for him, Q. I think I might be in love with him."

He briefly closes his eyes and takes a calming breath. "You can't be. This will destroy you. *He* will destroy you."

"Maybe. Maybe not. But I'm going to see it through. I know deep down that I'm feeling something I haven't ever felt before. I need to find out where this goes, and I need you to love and trust me enough to take a step back."

He moves forward and wraps me in his long arms. "I'm worried. I saw what your breakup with Whitaker did to you. I don't think you can go through that again. I can't bear to watch it."

"Haven't you seen the way I've been lately? It's like the fog of the past year has lifted."

He's still for a moment before eventually nodding. "Yes, I've noticed, and I don't want that fog happening again."

"It's because of him."

"You don't need a man to feel good about yourself. You're an amazing woman in your own right."

"It's not that. It's about finding the former me. The fun, confident me. The one who speaks her mind, *all* the time. He brings her out in me. I've missed her."

"I've missed her too.

"He makes me happy. He's not playing games with me in the slightest. I've never felt more supported and respected. Tell me, was he different on the road? You've been traveling with him for over six months. I know what normally goes on during those long trips. How was he acting this last time?"

He mumbles, "Like a married man."

I nod in satisfaction. "I know, because to my core, I believe he cares about me. I'm not in this alone. He's right there with me. It's my life. I need to live it. You need to let go."

"Maybe he was just playing it safe to secure his contract."

"No, he wasn't. You know that as well as I do. I care about his contract more than he does. When you were out doing God knows what, he was in his room on the phone with me. Every night. For hours, every night."

He squeezes me tight. "Just be careful. Please."

"I will."

"I love you, Z."

"I love you too." I release my hold on him. "And Q, don't talk to my man like that. The things you said to him are not okay. He's your best friend. Your past relationships with women aren't dissimilar. Don't be a hypocrite."

"You know nothing about me and my relationships."

"Why don't you tell me?"

His mouth opens and closes a few times, but he shuts down and eventually says, "I've got to get out there. I'll see you after the game."

I sigh. Why won't he talk to me? "Fine." I look him up and down. "Why are your arms so fucking long? You're like an ape. It's fucking weird."

He starts examining his arms and I giggle.

He narrows his eyes at me. "You're such a bitch."

I smile. "You're an easy target, Abbott."

He leaves and I make my way to our seats and join my friends. Kam looks me up and down. "You have something white and creamy dripping out of the corner of your mouth."

I quickly go to wipe it and she starts laughing hysterically. "Oh my god, I was totally kidding, but now you're busted, you ho."

I can't help the smile that creeps onto my lips. Now all three of them are laughing.

Just before the game starts, an adorable younger man with curly hair and a Lancaster jersey sits in the seat next to me. At this point, I think I know most people in the friends and family section, but I've never seen him before.

He turns to me. "You're Arizona, right?"

"I am. And you are?"

"Henry. I'm Layton's..."

I immediately throw my arms around him. "Oh my god, you're his little brother."

As I pull away, I notice him smile goofily. "That's what he called me?"

I nod. "Yes! He adores you. He talks about you all the time. I'm so excited to finally meet you."

"He talks about you too. I've seen a lot of pictures but you're even more beautiful in person."

Kam narrows her eyes at him. "Is Layton teaching you how to sweet talk women?"

He smiles. "He's the master. Just look at his girlfriend."

Kam nods. "Yep. She's a total hottie."

I roll my eyes at them. "How come you don't come to more games?"

He shrugs. "I guess I assume Layton is embarrassed by me. I'm kind of a fuck up. I don't want to cramp his style."

"He doesn't see you that way at all. He's proud to have you around. You should come more often. Have you ever gone with him to Linda's House?"

I see him stiffen a bit. "No, it's not my thing." He looks visibly uncomfortable. "My time with Layton's grandmother was the best part of my childhood. It went kind of downhill from there. I think walking into that place would dredge up some bad memories for me."

I nod. "I understand. If you ever change your mind, I can promise you that it's a wonderful place. I think it brings Layton a sense of peace just by hanging out with those amazing kids. Maybe it could do the same for you."

He pinches his lips together before giving me a small nod. "Maybe one day."

I loop my arm through his. "In the meantime, I want to know everything about you. Anything I can use against Layton is also welcome."

He laughs as we have a fun evening getting to know each other.

CHAPTER EIGHTEEN

ARIZONA

"You need to finesse my wood a little more gently, sunshine. He needs tender loving care to come to fruition."

I bite my lip. "It's just so big and hard. Besides, I like it a little rough."

"Be patient. Rub him evenly. Give him what he needs."

"It's taking so long."

He runs his hands over mine as we sand his new bat. "You said you were familiar with a woodshop."

"I never said I made a bat before. My family made furniture. It's different."

"I'm sure it still needed to be sanded."

"Hmm. I suppose I was never very good at that. I lack patience."

"Yes, I can tell." He squeezes my hip. "But you look sexy as fuck in those goggles."

We're both wearing safety goggles and I look anything but sexy in them.

I lift one of the bats he made yesterday. "Your bats are so much heavier than ours." I run my hand along it. "Why am I not shocked that yours has a big head?"

He lets out a laugh. "All baseball bats are like that. They're completely different from softball bats. Ours are tapered. Yours are more linear."

"I think the head of your bat is bigger than most."

He narrows his eyes at me. "I think you just like talking about my big head."

I lift my goggles and run my hand up his thigh. "I prefer feeling it."

He grabs my wrist before I reach my intended target. "You're a sex maniac."

I rub my nose along his neck. "I'm a Layton Lancaster maniac."

He sighs as he turns off the lathe, the spinning machine. "This is useless. Note to self, never attempt to make a bat with a sex-crazed lunatic."

I smile proudly.

He looks down at his watch. "We have an hour until lunch with your parents. Are you sure Quincy is picking them up at the airport? Maybe we should. What if they're stranded and they think it's my fault?"

He's adorably nervous about meeting my parents. They're flying in today and staying for Quincy's game tonight and mine tomorrow afternoon before flying out tomorrow night. That's how it always is with them, being terrified of leaving the store for too long. At least they're coming. I wasn't sure they would.

"Quincy can handle it. I love how nervous you are." I pinch his ass. "It's so cute."

He playfully swats me away and pouts. "I'm not nervous."

"Yes, you are." Running my hands up his chest, I breathe, "I think I know how to calm your nerves."

He has an appalled look on his face. "Are you crazy? We can't have sex while your parents are visiting."

"We're not sharing a room with them. They're not even staying with us."

"It just seems wrong."

"You let me suck your dick in a closet twenty feet from my brother, but my parents being in the same state is your hard moral line?"

He smiles at the absurdity. "Maybe you're right." He blows out a long breath. "I'm sorry that I'm so on edge. Your brother isn't talking to me, I'm meeting a girlfriend's parents for the first time in my life at thirty-four, we're about to start the playoffs, and all I really want is to fast forward a month to when you and I will be traveling together from exotic beach to exotic beach. Do you think it's messed up that I'm excited for the season to be over?"

This is the first time he's expressed any of this to me. "You're not excited about making the playoffs? It's a really big deal."

He rubs his hands up and down my arms. "I *am* excited, but honestly, I'm more excited for our trip and I'm *most* excited about us. Our schedules are crazy. I don't see you for days at a time. There are always other people, games, and practices getting in the way. I just want to be alone with you."

I want to be alone with him too, but I'm surprised he's not more enthusiastic about his team making it to the postseason. Most ballplayers live for that. Then it occurs to me. Does he still love his sport? "Layton, are you considering retiring after this year?"

He pauses for a moment as if in thought. "Frankly, the callous way in which the Greene family was willing to release me after all these years cut deep. I considered them family, especially Harold, and it's not like I have a backup family waiting in the wings. My knees are killing me, and, until you came into my life, I was playing like shit. But now I've had this resurgence. It's kind of hard to think about retiring when you're playing well."

"Have you mentioned any of this to Tanner?"

"He's floated retirement out to me a few times. He was hinting at it just before I met you and the ownership changed. You know they were planning to release me after the season. He asked me to consider retirement."

I place my hand on his chest. "Where's your heart in all this? What does it tell you?"

He tucks my hair behind my ear and rubs my face with his thumb. "That I want you naked on a beach under the stars in Thailand."

I throw my arms around his neck. "And you called me the sex maniac?"

He softly kisses my lips and smiles into them. "Maybe we both are."

Maybe it's time for Layton Lancaster to hang up his cleats.

He breaks away and begins to clean the mess we made. "Maybe you should check to see if their plane landed."

"Good idea. I left my phone in the bedroom. I'll grab it."

He nods his head toward the end of the table. "Mine is right there. You can check on that."

I grab his phone, but it needs a password to unlock it. I start to hand it to him. "Punch in your password."

He doesn't move. Simply looking over his shoulder, he says, "It's eight-eight-eight-eight."

He encouraged me to use his phone and he gave me the password without giving it a second thought. It feels like a lightbulb goes off over my head. I'm realizing what Layton and I have is already so much deeper than what I had with Marc.

This is special. We're special.

LAYTON

While the situation in which he found out wasn't ideal, I'm relieved that Quincy now knows about us. I was getting more than sick of hiding my feelings, though if I'm being honest, I was never any good at it. I can't keep my hands off her. She consumes my every thought.

I tried to sit down with him and tell him how much I genuinely care about her, but he's mostly been ignoring me. I suppose I need to give him more time to cool down. Maybe if he sees us together, how happy we are, he'll change his mind.

Arizona's parents are flying into town for two days. Apparently, they don't like to leave their store for longer than that. It works out for them to see both Arizona and Quincy play. I'm having lunch with them today and then I'll sit with them at Arizona's game tomorrow afternoon.

She and I are walking a few blocks to the chosen restaurant. I squeeze her hand. "Are you close with both of your parents?"

"Hmm. Obviously I love them, they're amazing people, but they missed so much of our lives for that damn store. Don't get me wrong, I appreciate the nice life we led, and we all get along really well, but they were slaves to that place. My father worked seven days a week, stopping only to eat and sleep. My mom was around in the evenings for us, but they never came to school plays or anything like that. She came to evening games, but he never could. It's not what I want when I have a family. I understand finances often dictate that, but I hope to be in a position where I can enjoy my children and my husband. Quincy has made substantial money for over a dozen years. He's offered to help them retire, which they declined. He even offered to simply pay for a store manager just so they could travel a bit and maybe even see their children play. How many parents have two kids who are professional athletes? But they won't take anything, and they won't take a step back. I've given up trying. I just appreciate them for who they are and try not to expect anything."

"I'm sure they care about you."

"They do. A lot. I never felt unloved, just...not prioritized. Aren't you supposed to enjoy your kids? It bothers Quincy more than it bothers me. We've talked a lot about it throughout the years. I think it's why he's fucked up about relationships, though he doesn't tell me anything. He's super secretive."

"I'm not sure he's fucked up. Maybe he just hasn't found the right person. It took me a long time too. It was worth the wait. You were worth the wait."

She leans her head onto my shoulder. "You're very sweet for someone with no boyfriend experience."

"You make it easy. You're a breath of fresh air in my life." I kiss her head. "Do you talk to your parents much?" I'm fascinated by their dynamic.

She nods. "I talk to my mother once or twice a week. There's no strain in our relationship. I didn't mean to make it seem that way. My father isn't really a telephone guy. Birthdays and anniversaries. That's about it. Though he's a bit of a sarcastic jokester so he may bust your balls. He'll definitely bust Quincy's. It's his favorite thing to do."

"How bad is today going to be with Quincy? He still hasn't spoken to me, and he throws elbows at me every time I pass by."

She has an unimpressed look on her face. "Quincy is a child. When he respects me as an adult, capable of making decisions, then I'll listen to what he has to say. Right now, I don't care if he doesn't like you. I do and it's my life to lead."

I need to make things right with Quincy. They're close and I don't want to come between them.

We arrive at the restaurant, and I take a deep breath. She grabs my face and brushes her lips over mine, whispering into them, "They're going to love you. I promise."

I nod and kiss her softly. She truly has a soothing presence over me. I don't know how I've made it this long without her.

We walk inside, hand in hand. I immediately notice Quincy glaring at me from the table and know he isn't going to make this easy.

I see an attractive, older couple sitting with him. They both look a little worn from the lifestyle they've led, but the family resemblance is there.

The man who I assume is her father stands and holds out his hand. He's very tall, which makes sense given Arizona and Quincy's height. He's a little round in the middle, but big and burly throughout.

Taking my hand in his very rough one, he shakes it

hard and sneers, "If it isn't the all-star playboy who's apparently using my daughter."

My eyes widen but Arizona starts laughing. "Cut it out, Dad."

His scowl morphs into a smile as he releases my hand and turns to give her a big, bear hug, lifting her off the ground. He spins her around.

The woman who I assume is her mother rolls her eyes at him the same way Arizona does at me as she reaches out to hug me. "Pay him no attention. I'm Pamela. That's Paul. He thinks he's a standup comedian." She squeezes me. "It's so wonderful to finally meet you. We see you on television all the time. And, of course, I hear about you from Arizona."

I smile at Quincy. "You don't call your mom and tell her about me too?"

He gives me the finger.

Pamela slaps his hand. "Stop being rude. No one is ever good enough for his baby sister in his eyes."

Quincy deadpans, "Layton is *definitely* not good enough for her. I promise you that. Not even close."

Arizona rolls her eyes, the same way her mother just did. I find myself wondering if I have any of my parents' mannerisms.

She crosses her arms. "Grumpy, if you have nothing nice to say, shut your big trap. You'd think, with your rapidly receding hairline, you'd learn to have a better personality."

Quincy doesn't have a receding hairline. She's messing with him, but he feels around his hair just to make sure.

Pamela shakes her head as she looks at me. "They've bickered since they were little kids. Arizona and her father love to push Quincy's buttons."

Paul lets out a deep laugh. "It's because Quincy was jealous that Arizona was faster than him, could hit a ball further than him, and was an all-around better athlete." He winks at me. "That's why he had to become a pitcher."

I can't help but start laughing at that. Their family banter is hysterical.

Quincy scowls. "That's not true. I became a pitcher because I throw a hundred miles per hour."

Paul rubs his back. "You certainly do, son. About five or ten miles faster, and you'll throw as hard as your little sister."

Arizona and Pamela giggle. I'm sensing that Quincy bashing is a family activity. Arizona mentioned a lot of ball busting. Once he and I are back on track, I'm going to have to figure out a way to join in the fun.

Quincy sighs. "I'm currently having one of the best seasons of my career and you're busting my chops?"

Paul nods. "Yes, you are. You should have been in the all-star game this year. That was bullshit. Don't be jealous that your sister is an all-star and is about to win the most valuable player award for her league." He smiles at Quincy and, in a condescending tone, says, "You're a very good player too, son."

I'm thinking that their parents pay a lot closer attention to them than they realize.

Paul grabs my shoulder. "And you. Look at what you've been doing the past few months. You're playing like you did years ago."

"Yes, sir. It's all thanks to your daughter."

He smiles. "Has she given you a few tips?"

"Something like that. She's my magic potion."

I wiggle my eyebrows at Arizona, and she narrows her eyes at me.

He nods with a tremendous amount of pride. "I'm glad to hear it. She knows her stuff."

"She's actually a very good teacher. We coach a baseball team of young kids together. She's taught them a lot. They adore her."

Quincy has a look of shock on his face. "You two coach a team together?"

Arizona nods. "Yes, it's a team of both boys and girls of mixed ages, but all under ten years old." She pretends to dust off her shoulders. "We're undefeated since I joined the coaching staff."

Quincy looks between the two of us. "I didn't know that. Why mixed ages? They should play with their own age group. Why don't the girls play softball?"

Arizona gives me an, *I told you so*, look before turning back to Quincy. "I agree, but it's a numbers game. The kids live in a group home. Layton and I discussed figuring something out in the off-season to help them find age, skill, and gender appropriate teams."

Quincy's face softens. "Group home? So they don't have parents?"

I nod. "Correct."

He pinches his lips together. "I'd be happy to help after our season is over."

I smile, filled with affection for my friend. "Thank you. That would be incredible. They would love to have a professional pitcher stop by."

Arizona lets out a laugh. "Randy will flip his shit if you show up, Q. He's a riot. He's our pitcher and is crazy competitive. The kid throws out old-school baseball terminology like it's his second language. I get the biggest kick out of him."

I look at Paul and Pamela. "We have a female catcher, Lucinda, on the team who idolizes your daughter. Arizona taught Lucinda how to throw from her knees and now she guns them down on the regular."

Paul smiles with pride. "Arizona has such a fantastic arm." He turns to her. "Though you need to tuck your glove when you throw. You're getting a little lazy with that."

Arizona pinches her eyebrows together. "Do you watch my games?"

Paul nods. "Of course we watch your games. I haven't missed one all season. We installed a big screen in the showroom so we can watch both of your games when they're on during the day."

Pamela smiles. "Dad started finishing up in the shop a little early so he can be home in time for us to watch your night games together at home."

Arizona and Quincy exchange bewildered glances. I'm not sure they realize how fortunate they are. Maybe their parents aren't physically around very much, but they clearly care. A lot. I would give anything to have that.

Pamela rubs Quincy's arm. "Are you dating at all?"

He smirks. "I see plenty of women."

"Anyone special?"

Arizona interrupts. "Nope. Since I arrived in town, he's been nothing but a watchdog for Ripley and me. Cockblocking is the only thing he does besides baseball and hair coiffing."

Pamela sighs. "Quincy, find yourself a nice girl and settle down."

Quincy frowns. "Not interested."

I turn to him. "Ever?"

He shrugs. "I don't see it happening for me. Drop it."

Recognizing a conversation topic change is needed, I ask, "Where did you all come up with the name Arizona? It's so unusual. I love it. I've never known anyone else with that name."

They smile at each other, and Pamela blushes a bit. "Paul and I were traveling to get some rare wood he wanted. We...well...we were in Arizona."

Arizona's eyes widen, and I let out a small laugh. It turns out I was right from the beginning.

I can't help myself. "And what about Quincy?"

They smile at each other again. "You remember that your father played a year of minor league baseball before deciding to take over grandpa's custom furniture business?"

Quincy nods. "Yes. In Florida, right?"

"Yes. It was a team out of *Quincy*, Florida. Things... happened there. We didn't want to name you Florida, so we went with Quincy."

Arizona and Quincy both sit there appearing disgusted and stunned. I'm grinning, doing my best to hold in the laughter.

ARIZONA

After the most disturbing lunch in the history of the world, I'm shopping with my mother and Ripley, who met us at a shoe store. We're searching for shoes to match our dresses for the upcoming *Sports Illustrated* reveal party. We've narrowed it down to a few pairs. The saleslady is in the back finding our sizes in all of them.

Quincy and Layton had to get to the stadium for warm-ups. Dad wanted to go with them and watch.

Mom squeezes my hand. "You seem very serious with Layton."

"We *are* serious."

"I'll admit that Quincy gave us an earful on the way from the airport to lunch today. He doesn't care for your relationship. He thinks Layton is a womanizer."

"I'm sick of..."

Before I can finish, she holds up her hand. "I'm not done. He had us concerned at first. You've had a difficult year. You've been incredibly fragile, and we've been so worried. But after spending time with you two, I don't see what Quincy sees. You're happy and lively in a way I haven't seen in nearly a year and a half. Your special Arizona sparkle and spunk is back. And the way Layton looks at you..." She clutches her heart. "I know what a man in love looks like, and that man is completely in love with you."

I can't help the smile on my face. "You think so?"

"I know so."

Ripley nods in agreement. "You'd have to be blind not to see that. He stares at you like he's going to tear your clothes off at any moment and..."

I cover her mouth and my mother giggles.

"Thank you, Ripley. I'll remind you that my mother is here, though she's done some oversharing of her own today."

I narrow my eyes at Mom, but she simply smiles. "Did you think you were conceived via immaculate conception?"

I sigh. "No, but our names are now officially tainted."

"Don't be silly. Let's get back to Layton. He didn't really

hide his feelings for you. What I want to know is how you feel about him."

I blow out a breath. "I think I might be in love with him. It's so different than it was with Marc. Everything about us feels good. Nothing is forced. It's open and honest. We truly enjoy being together. It's such an...adult relationship."

"Marc obviously wasn't the right man for you." She mumbles, "We all knew that even before the wedding."

I stand there in a bit of shock. "You never thought he was right for me? Even before the craziness of the wedding day?"

She exchanges glances with Ripley before looking back at me. "I didn't."

I turn to Ripley. "You too?"

She nods.

"Why didn't either of you say anything?"

Ripley shrugs. "I tried to push you a few times about what it was you loved about him. He wasn't attentive, he wasn't good to you, you fought all the time, you had nothing except ball in common, you were insecure, always thinking he was cheating, and he was kind of a dick to me. You were a little blind to it. I wasn't going to lay it out there and then have you marry him anyway, subjecting us to a lifetime of awkwardness. And...and you were pregnant. At some point, I let it go."

I suppose she's right. She did question me a few times about how he treated me. I always made excuses for him.

"What about you, Mom?"

"I felt the same. I wasn't going to risk you pushing me out of your life. I'm honestly not sad about what happened. It's for the best. I could have told you from the beginning that he wasn't good enough for you. He wasn't right for you."

"But you think Layton is?"

"I can't tell you that, only you can decide, but I can tell you that you are glowing in a way you never were with Marc."

Ripley nods. "She's right. You're so happy all the time again. I have the real you back." She pauses as if choosing her words carefully. "There's something more to it than what you had with Marc. Maybe it's friendship. You and Layton love spending time together and talking. You're best friends in addition to lovers. And with Marc, I always felt like you were walking on eggshells. You didn't enjoy each other. I'm not even sure if you liked each other. It's not like that at all with Layton. It's effortless. He's obsessed with you just as you are. Even in this relatively brief amount of time, he deeply cares about you in a way I never saw from Marc. Does that make sense?"

I nod, getting a little choked up. "I feel like my old self, and I feel very supported by Layton. He pushes to bring out the best in me and truly revels in my success. I think the right word is cherished. That's how I feel with him. I know his past, but, as he likes to say, it's simply because he never met the right person, *until now*. I don't even feel insecure around his groupies like I would have assumed. He pays them no attention and has never once disrespected me. I'm not sure I realized how much I needed that until I found a man that gives it to me in spades."

Ripley nods. "He only has eyes for you. That's more than clear. Even before you were...officially together, his attention never strayed. I think he was love bitten from the moment he met you. It just took you a little while to give in to what I know you were feeling."

"I agree, but everything has been perfect and easy with us. That's not real life. I tend to worry about what it will look like when things aren't perfect, but for now, we're happy."

Mom shrugs her shoulders in excitement. "Your trip with him sounds like it will be amazing."

"I'm so excited. Layton is busting at the seams for it."

"You're incredibly lucky to have the opportunity to travel. It's a dream come true. I would give anything to do that."

My heart breaks for her. "You could travel too, Mom. Hire a manager and see the world."

She gives me a small smile. "Baby steps. I've gotten him to stop working at a decent hour. We'll work our way up to a real vacation." She winks. "Maybe we'll go back to Arizona." She turns to Ripley. "What about you? Are you seeing anyone?"

"No..."

I interrupt, "Yes. She has a secret boyfriend that she won't tell me about."

Mom scrunches her nose. "Damn, I always held out hope that you'd end up with Quincy."

I make a gagging face. "Gross, Mom. They're like brother and sister. Right, Rip?"

"Umm...we're friends. And I'm not seeing anyone. There's no secret boyfriend."

"Why are you being elusive? I don't get it."

"I'm not. I'm simply not dating anyone."

I sigh in frustration, but the saleslady returns, and we both manage to find shoes that work. We're heading back to the apartment to grab our jerseys when we hear Kam and Bailey shouting in their apartment.

I let Mom into our apartment to use the restroom, and we head toward Kam and Bailey's to see what's going on. We walk in and I place my hands on my hips. "What are you two screaming about? We can hear you down the hallway."

Bailey rolls her eyes. "Kam would like to have a party tonight to celebrate it being two years since I lost my anal virginity."

Ripley and I start laughing. I shake my head. "I don't think people celebrate that, Kam."

She crosses her arm. "If that's true, how did I find this?"

She turns the mylar balloon she's holding to show us that it reads, "Happy Analversary."

Ripley falls on the ground laughing so hard. I can't help but join her. Bailey shakes her head. "Please don't encourage her."

Kam smiles. "Why are you embarrassed? Everyone does anal now."

I raise my hand. "Ripley and I don't."

Ripley bites her lip. "Actually, I have."

I gasp in shock. "What? When? With whom?"

"Years ago. After college, when I lived in Houston."

"Another secret?"

"Umm...I forgot to mention it."

"You forgot to mention that someone put their dick in your ass? It's kind of a big omission, pun intended." I sigh. "Shit, I guess I'm the only anal virgin left."

Kam pinches her lips together like a duck. "With the way you and Layton are together, I'm thinking in about a year, we'll be celebrating your analversary too."

MY PARENTS ENJOYED WATCHING Quincy pitch last night. He threw a shutout. My father was losing his shit the whole time, excited at the prospect of seeing him throw the shutout. I've never seen them this vested in either of us playing. It feels good.

Layton got over the whole not touching me with my parents in the state thing. He had me meet him just before the game to get his so-called *magic potion*.

Watching him smell his fingers before he steps into the batter's box is just about the most erotic, obscene thing I've ever witnessed. I'm appalled and turned on all at the same time. Maybe a little more turned on than appalled.

I had to sit there, next to my parents, and watch my boyfriend smell me on his fingers before every time he stepped into the batter's box.

Toward the end of the game, my mother placed her hand on my shoulder and asked, "Does Layton have a cold?"

"No, why?"

"He keeps wiping his nose."

I had to bite the inside of my cheek to stymie my smile. "Nope. He's healthy. *Very* healthy."

"I hope so. I don't want to get sick. We can't afford to miss any more work."

"He's fine, Mom."

"I'm glad to hear it." She mock shivered. "He's so handsome."

I stared at his ass in those baseball pants. "Yes, he is." And he's all mine.

TODAY IS MY GAME. Before it starts, I see Layton in his normal seat, flanked on either side by my parents, the three of them chatting away like old friends. I'm so happy that they're getting along.

"Arizona!"

I turn my head and see one of the owners, Beckett Windsor, shouting my name from the stands. I nod his way. He points down to his daughter, Andie, who I've met before. She likes to take pictures with me when she's here. She's adorable, asking about a thousand questions at a time.

I see Tanner's daughter, Harper, standing with her. There's also a third girl around the same age as them. I've never seen her before.

He waves me over and I head their way. The girls get excited as I approach. I love their enthusiasm.

I smile. "Andie, Harper, it's good to see you two. Who's your friend?"

Andie answers, "This is our friend, Dylan Knight."

"It's nice to meet you, Dylan."

"You too." She's a sassy-looking kid with darker hair and very light blue eyes. "Is it true that Layton Lancaster is your boyfriend?"

I let out a laugh and look at Beckett for some guidance. He simply shrugs in exasperation.

I point toward Layton in the stands. "Do you see him sitting over there? He's right behind our dugout."

Dylan turns her head and notices him for the first time. Her eyes light up. "I see him! Oh wow. He's even cuter in person."

Andie looks at her. "I told you he would be here. He always comes when they don't have games." She then turns to me. "She has a crush on him. She only came today because I said he'd likely be here. No offense, but I like Butch McVey. He's *super* cute."

Beckett practically growls. "Andie, Butch McVey is a grown man. You're seven years old."

She nods. "I know. He has tattoos like you, Daddy. Arizona, does Layton Lancaster have any tattoos? If so, where are they? What are they of?"

Before I can respond, Bailey walks over. Harper immediately jumps into her waiting arms as Bailey kisses her head. "Hi, sweet girl." She smiles at the other girls. "Andie, Dylan, are you ladies having fun?"

Dylan answers, "We are. We see Layton Lancaster sitting over there. Do you think he'd take a picture with us?"

I nod. "I know he would. Go over there and tell him that

sunshine said you need a picture with superstar. It's a special code. And Andie, Layton is *way* cuter than Butch McVey. I was only a little older than you when I had my first crush on a baseball player. Do you know who it was?"

The girls shake their heads.

I smile. "Layton Lancaster."

The girls all gasp. Andie looks at me wide-eyed. "Butch could be my boyfriend one day."

Beckett looks like he's about to vomit. Through gritted teeth, he suggests we all take a few photos so that Bailey and I can get back to our team.

When we're done, Dylan places her hand on my shoulder. "Don't worry. I won't ask Layton Lancaster on a date while he's your boyfriend. My mom told me it's always bitches before bros."

I can't help but let out a laugh. Are these girls seven or seventeen? "I really appreciate that, Dylan, and I totally agree with your mom."

We say goodbye and I see them walk over to Layton. They say something to him. He smiles as he finds me. I wink in return.

I watch him happily talk to the girls and take pictures with them for nearly fifteen minutes. I think I even see him record a video with them, which I assume is a TikTok. He's such a good man. If possible, I fall just a little harder watching him interact with them.

CHAPTER NINETEEN

LAYTON

"Should I throw the yakker or stick with the heat? This chump is a Punch and Judy hitter."

Arizona starts laughing. She loves Randy's deep knowledge and use of baseball slang. A yakker is a curveball, and a Punch and Judy hitter is one without power.

I pat his head. "Why don't you mix it up and work on a little bit of everything? We're up big and it's the last inning."

"Yes, sir, Coach Layton. This batter is about to enjoy a golden sombrero." A golden sombrero is when a player strikes out four times in a game.

He enthusiastically high-fives both Arizona and me and then runs out of the dugout onto the field to close out another victory for us.

Arizona shakes her head. "I freakin' love that kid."

"I know you do." I look out to adorable Perry in

rightfield. "I'm a little partial to Perry. He's the underdog. He hasn't made a catch all season."

"It's not for lack of your effort. You've hit him a million balls. He has a legitimate physical disability. He'd be great in a league specifically designed for kids with disabilities."

She lifts her eyebrows making sure I understand the implication. She's mentioned a few ideas about expanding league access for the kids on multiple occasions. It will be a big endeavor, but I'm thrilled that she seems passionate about it.

"I hear you. I asked my lawyer to start looking into creating a charity to help."

She has a huge smile as she wraps her arms around me. "Really?"

"Really. Don't get too excited. It's going to take a lot of hard work to get it up and running. And we'll need to raise funds to make sure it's sustainable. I don't want the kids to get something for a year only to have it taken away from them."

She kisses my cheek. "Can't wait to help."

I point to the field. "In the meantime, we need to close out this game. Cinderella needs to get ready for the ball."

Tonight is the big *Sports Illustrated* reveal party up in New York City. It worked out perfectly because neither of us have games so we can attend.

She narrows her eyes. "Are you calling me Cinderella?"

"No. I'm Cinderella." I daintily pretend to fix my hair. "I need to make myself pretty for you. I'm not sure it gets prettier than this, but I plan to try." I bat my eyelashes at her.

She snort-laughs. "I'm confident you'll be the belle of the ball."

"When they see your picture, sunshine, I'll be long forgotten. I promise."

She licks her luscious lips. "Are you trying to get lucky tonight?"

"I'm dating a sex maniac. I *know* I'm getting lucky tonight."

She smiles. Fuck, I love her smile.

We easily get the first two batters out. Randy was thrilled to achieve the elusive golden sombrero on the first batter. He cheered like he won the league championship. We're up by eight runs. I'm going to have to have a conversation with him about sportsmanship.

The third batter steps into the box. Randy winds up and throws the pitch. The batter connects and crushes the ball. It's a long flyball to rightfield. I mumble, "Shit." Perry gets so upset every time he misses a ball. It's heartbreaking.

I yell, "Perry, it's deep! Go back!"

He turns his little body and runs as fast and hard as his little legs are capable of taking him.

I yell again, "Stick out your glove! It's coming!"

I feel like the next five seconds happen in slow motion. He stumbles and starts to fall but manages to get his glove out. The ball comes down, and, by some miracle, it falls into his glove just as Perry's body hits the ground. He lays there, looking lifeless. I'm holding my breath.

After a few long beats, he holds up the ball. The umpire motions that it's the final out of the game.

The entire team is quiet and completely still. I think they're in shock. We're all in shock, including Perry.

And then all hell breaks loose. Every kid on the team

sprints out to rightfield and piles on top of Perry like he just made this catch to save game seven in the World Series.

Arizona is jumping up and down, screaming for him. She looks over at me. "He did it!" Her face falls a little as she places her hand on my back. "Are you crying?"

I wipe my eyes. "Maybe. Crying is a sign of emotional intelligence."

She laughs as she pulls my arm. "Come on, Coach Layton, let's go celebrate with your star pupil."

As soon as the kids' game was over, Arizona left to get her hair and makeup done with the girls. After a quick stop for celebratory ice cream, I dropped the kids back at Linda's House and now I'm knocking on a door.

It opens and Quincy's face immediately drops when he sees that it's me. "What do you want, Lancaster?"

"I want to talk to you."

He sighs as if I'm bothering him but opens the door wider in invitation. I walk through and toward his living room where I spent many days and evenings this past off-season watching football and basketball games. I sit on the couch.

He's silent, with a miserable, murderous look on his face as he sits across from me. He leans back with his legs wide open and his arm over the back of the chair, clearly trying to assert his dominance, but I'm not here to get into a pissing contest with him.

"I wanted to have this conversation with you weeks

ago. She asked me to hold off for the time being. I'm sorry you found out about us the way you did. Truly."

"With my sister on her knees in a fucking closet at the stadium? You can't treat her like a whore."

I squeeze the arm of the chair, trying to remain calm. "I don't treat her like a whore, Quincy. Not remotely. Do you really think your sister would stand for that? She doesn't do anything she doesn't want to do."

"So you're saying my sister has chosen to be a whore?"

I grit my teeth. "Don't fucking call her that again. I didn't come here to fight with you, but if you disrespect her again, the gloves come off." I blow out an exasperated breath as I run my fingers through my hair. "Look, I see no reason for you and me to ever discuss my sex life with Arizona. You know full well that your sister isn't a virginal nun. I'm not talking about this topic again. I'm here to talk about my relationship with her. Teammate to teammate. Friend to friend. Man to man."

He runs his tongue along his top teeth. "Say what you came to say, Lancaster, and then get the fuck out."

I nod. "I want you to know that my feelings for her are real. I've never in my life felt about a woman the way I do her."

"How long has it been going on? Since the beginning? Was everything you both told me bullshit?"

I shake my head. "No. It started just as we told you. With neither of us planning on it being anything but the PR relationship they wanted. I'm not going to lie to you and pretend like I haven't always been physically attracted to her. I have been since the second I met her, before I even knew she was your sister. But our plans for a platonic relationship were genuine."

He nods his head for me to continue.

"For several weeks, we spent a lot of time together and formed a genuine friendship. I truly like her. I like spending time with her, talking to her. Tension gradually built for both of us. The mutual attraction was there, and it wasn't going away. I'm not experienced in this department. All I know is that I couldn't help the way I felt."

He looks away for a moment and mutters, more to himself, "I understand. Believe me, I understand."

Choosing not to dive into his statement, I continue, "By the time the photo shoot rolled around, we both snapped. I'm not sharing any more details, but it's more than just physical."

I let out a deep breath, wanting to convey everything I'm feeling. "I love that we can talk ball all day long and never get tired of it. I love the way her mind works. I love her smile. I love her ridiculous laugh. I love how passionate and compassionate she is. I love how competitive she is. I love the way she cares about the people in her life. I love her personality. I love seeing her in my jersey in our stands. I love how much I miss her when I'm not with her. I love how excited I get just to catch a glimpse of her, even if it's on television while she's playing. It's everything. Every little thing about her."

He scratches the back of his neck as he considers my words. "You used the word *love* a lot in that little speech."

That's true. It wasn't even intentional. "I suppose you're right. I did. Admittedly, I haven't said those words to her. I need to wrap my mind around it. You know this is unchartered territory for me. But I know that I don't see my life moving forward without her in it." I shrug. "It could be worse. It could be Cheetah. Or Whitaker."

He lets a small smile crack through. "A friend of mine on Whitaker's team said he's still bruised and battered from the collision and brawl."

I can't help my own smile. "Serves him right. Too bad we don't play them again this season." I wink. "There's always next year. Let him piss his pants in anticipation of what we'll come up with for the next time."

Now his small smile turns into a big one. "Sounds good to me."

I hold out my hand. "I'm not promising forever, but I promise to always do right by her."

After a brief moment of hesitation, he shakes my hand in return, but squeezes it hard and pulls me close. "You'd better, or you'll be pissing blood just like Whitaker. For the rest of your life."

"Deal." I stand. "I'll see you tonight, right?"

"You bet." He sarcastically adds, "I've been counting the minutes to go to a party where they're going to unveil an oversized half-naked picture of you and my sister. It's the highlight of my year."

I let out a laugh. "She looked amazing. Soooo sexy."

His face drops. "Don't push it, Lancaster."

I smirk. "I would never." I'm totally going to fuck with him tonight.

CHAPTER TWENTY

LAYTON

I look in the mirror in my bathroom to put the final touches on my tuxedo as I get ready for the big reveal party. We haven't seen any of the photos yet. We're completely in the dark, along with every other attendee. I've been doing photo shoots for fifteen years, but I've never been more excited to see the results than I am tonight.

My mind keeps flashing back to that day. The one where everything changed for us. The first time we were skin to skin. The first time my hands and lips explored her body. The first time I truly saw her body. The look of bliss on her face every time I touched her. She's so damn beautiful.

We were both tentative at first. I wanted to be careful, knowing of her intimacy issues. But she never flinched at my touch, she welcomed it. I tried to be respectful but when she kissed me, my restraint went right out the door. I needed her in a way I've never needed anyone.

Every day since has been perfection. I never thought I could do this, be with one woman, but no one else matters anymore. Just her. How have I gone my whole life without Arizona Abbott?

I splash a little aftershave on my face when it really hits me. I'm in love with her. I'm head over heels in love with Arizona Abbott.

My daydreaming is broken up by my text tone ringing. I look down at my phone. It's Trey letting me know they're about to arrive to pick me up.

We've got a fun night planned. Our friends are all coming to support us. The Daultons generously provided us with a big party bus so we can travel to and from the party together as a group. It's a ninety-minute ride up to New York City from Philly.

My phone rings. I look at the caller ID and smile. "Hi, Frederick."

"Good evening, Master Lancaster. There's a rather large, rather gaudy, vehicle waiting for you. The inhabitants are loud and terribly uncouth."

I let out a laugh. "Thank you, Frederick. I'll be down in a minute."

"My most sincere pleasure, Master Lancaster."

I walk out of my building to the giant party bus where I can already hear loud music and even louder voices. I step on and see Ezra, Quincy, Trey, and Cheetah with drinks in hand, dressed in their tuxedos. I board to a sea of catcalls. I smile and do a little curtsy and ass shake for them all.

Trey pours me a glass of whiskey so I can catch up with them. We enjoy our drinks and conversation on the way to pick up the ladies. Arizona invited Gemma to get dressed with them, which I appreciated.

As we pull up to their apartment building, they all walk out of the front doors together. The second my eyes find Arizona, I think my heart skips a beat. She's in an elegant, strapless, long, form-fitting dress with a high slit. I'm not sure of the color. It's somewhere between pink and purple. She's in heels, which puts her over six feet tall, most of which is leg. Her hair is down with some sort of curls in the front. She looks like a movie star. And she's mine.

I practically jump out of the bus before it stops moving. I hear the boys laughing but I don't care. I grab her hand and kiss it. "You take my breath away. You're the most beautiful woman I've ever seen in my life."

She smiles softly as she straightens my bowtie. "And I'm thinking my teenage self had excellent taste in men. You look so handsome."

I suddenly hear a woman screech. "Eek. Trey, put me down."

I look over and see Trey carrying Gemma like a bride. "Umm...we'll be back in twenty minutes. My wife is hot."

She giggles as she playfully slaps his chest. "Put me down and get on the bus, crazy man."

He smiles down at her before carrying her up the steps onto the bus. The rest of the girls, who all look stunning, follow suit.

I whisper in Arizona's ear, "I'm going to rip this dress off you later."

"You'll probably want to wait until after we drop off Q."

"He and I had a good talk today."

Her eyes widen. "You did?"

"Yep. We're good. We came to an understanding."

"What was that?"

"That I'd treat you like a princess, or he'd remove my kidney...with a spoon."

She lets out a laugh. "That sounds fair."

I help her onto the bus and see that Ezra saved a seat next to him for Bailey. He has a crush on her, but she has never shown any interest in anything more than friendship. It hasn't stopped him from trying, in his own subtle, Ezra way. She sits next to him though.

Cheetah pulls Kamryn onto his lap as she walks by him. She shakes her head. "Nope. You had your shot, kitten. You blew it. Literally."

Trey gasps. "Did things end, *prematurely*? Shame on you, Cheetah."

Cheetah practically growls at him. "It ended because her bed exploded. *Literally*. Her waterbed burst. I had to surf out of her bedroom. Naked."

I turn to Arizona, and she nods her head in confirmation with an enormous grin on her gorgeous face. I definitely need to hear this story.

Quincy smiles at me. "Lancaster, you're now officially the last one on the bus. You know what that means."

I'm about to protest when Arizona places her hand on my chest and whispers, "I've got this one." She turns to our friends. "Technically, I was last since he was already on the bus. Here's a fun fact for you. Harry Styles has four nipples."

Kam's mouth drops. "No way."

Arizona nods. "Yep. Look it up."

Every single person pulls out their phones to google it. Sure enough, he does, in fact, have four nipples.

Trey peels himself away from his wife long enough to

open two bottles of champagne. "Let's put Harry and his four hairy nipples away for now to toast the man and woman of the hour." He pours everyone a glass and we all toast to our big night.

The entire ride to the party is spent drinking champagne and making fun of Cheetah. I almost feel bad for him, but he takes it all in stride.

We arrive at the party venue, which is a big, fancy hotel in Midtown Manhattan. There's a red carpet and several photographers. Everyone else gets out of the bus and walks the red carpet ahead of us, leaving Arizona and I alone for a few minutes before we make our grand entrance.

I thread my fingers through hers. "Are you ready to see our picture, sunshine?"

"You bet, superstar." She squeezes my hand. "It feels like that shoot was a lifetime ago."

I nod in agreement. "It does. It's been the best few months of my life." I kiss her neck. "I adore you."

"Hmm. I want to kiss you, but the makeup people will kick my ass."

I smile into her neck. "Later. And we'll more than kiss, I promise."

She bites her lip. "Will you judge me if I tell you that the day of the photo shoot has been running through my mind on a constant stream all day? It's the day that everything changed for us. I'm excited that it's memorialized. It was special to me."

I kiss her hand. "I feel the exact same."

She takes a deep breath. "Let's go before we don't make it out of this bus. You get out first and make sure I don't show my Britney."

I start to stand but she grabs me by the shirt and

pulls me back to her. She then licks my ear and whispers into it, "By the way, I'm not wearing any panties."

Oh hell.

ARIZONA

After an added minute or two to calm himself down, Layton steps off the bus and I see a million flashes go off. Unlike the first time, he doesn't pause to pose or wave. He immediately reaches for me. It warms my heart that he doesn't want to be in photos without me. For a guy who has no girlfriend experience, he certainly knows how to treat his woman and make her feel wanted. More than wanted. Treasured.

He helps me out of the bus, and we stand there, staring at each other. The flashes go off but we're in our own bubble. Sometimes I feel like I live in a fantasy. How many people get to be with the celebrity whose name they used to write in their high school textbooks with little heart doodles everywhere? The best part is that the real Layton Lancaster is even better than the fantasy.

Our bodies are pressed together, and our faces are only a hairsbreadth apart. He runs his hand up my arm, giving me goosebumps. *Flash flash flash.*

We stare into each other's eyes. *Flash flash flash.*

I'm choked up with a tidal wave of feelings as it finally truly hits me. I'm completely, undoubtedly in love with this man. *Flash flash flash.*

He leans his head down. *Flash flash flash.*

He reaches my ear and whispers, "I love you, Arizona Abbott." *Flash flash flash.*

My breath catches. *Flash flash flash.*

He kisses my neck. *Flash flash flash.*

I'm speechless. *Flash flash flash.*

He takes my hand in his. "Come on. Let's go inside and see our picture."

Wait, I want to say it back to him, but he's pushing us through the sea of photographers, protecting me from the onslaught.

I missed my opportunity. He told me he loved me, and I froze.

We start moving along the roped off portion of the red carpet, stopping every few feet to pose for pictures.

After smiling for what feels like a million photographs, we finally make our way inside. I'm still processing what he said. I was on autopilot through all those photos for the past fifteen minutes.

Before I can get out a word to him, the Daultons greet us. They're standing with an attractive couple, likely in their forties, both with dark hair and piercing green eyes.

Reagan flashes us her big smile. "You two look great. Are you ready for tonight?"

Layton kisses her cheek. "You look beautiful." He turns to me and smiles. "I think we're ready, right?"

I still haven't said a word since his L-bomb. I nod. "We are."

She points to the other couple. "Arizona, Layton, this is my mother, Darian Lawrence Knight, and my stepfather, Jackson Knight."

Darian excitedly holds out her hand for me to shake. "I'm thrilled to finally meet you, Arizona. It's so exciting to watch you ladies play. You're incredible. I played a bit in college myself."

Oh right. Reagan once mentioned that her mother played in college. "Thank you so much. Your daughter has done such a great job with the team."

She nods. "I'm excited that she brought you and the team to Philly. Good luck to you guys in the playoffs. Bring home the ship."

I let out a laugh. "We'll try."

Reagan winks. "Do more than try."

Just then, a man takes the podium and taps the microphone. "Good evening, everyone. I'm Daniel Nash, the editor-in-chief of *Sports Illustrated*. Thank you for being here tonight and thank you to all the participating athletes. We're thrilled with how the issue turned out. It's important to us to promote body positivity and to depict healthy, well-fed, well-cared for bodies. We'll show all the beautiful interior photos before revealing this year's cover couple. The decision was unanimous among the editorial staff."

The lights dim and the song, "Scars to Your Beautiful" by Alessia Cara begins to play. A huge screen illuminates and the photos begin to rotate, one at a time. The pictures of the other couples are gorgeous. Endless photos of some of the most famous athletes in the world and their partners.

Finally, they get to ours. We immediately smile at what we see. It's a great photo, where we're close but facing away from each other, each holding a bat with badass looks on our faces. Our jerseys are open, and our bodies are on full display. Admittedly, we look strong, athletic, and muscular. It's a nice photo and perfect for a body image issue.

Our whole crew starts hooting and hollering. They rush over to us with hugs and adulation.

Layton squeezes my hand. "I think I need a poster of that above my bed."

I giggle. "Me too."

The screen then scrolls to the cover, with the picture temporarily blurred. It gradually unblurs until it's revealed. There's a collective gasp in the crowd, though it may have been me. Nope, it was every single person here.

We're on the cover, but this photo is different from the interior photos. *Much* different. Layton has me pinned to a scoreboard. It's made to appear as though we're in the outfield. My legs, which have catcher's gear on them, are wrapped around his waist. He's got my hands restrained above my head with one hand and his face buried in my neck. My face is tilted up with my eyes closed and my lips parted in ecstasy. It looks like I'm mid-orgasm. Layton's leg and arm muscles are on full display. The photo is taken at an angle that, with my jersey wide open, you can see both my lace-bra-covered breasts as well as my stomach and upper thigh muscles. The subtitle reads *The Steamy Streets of Philadelphia*.

Ripley sucks in a breath. "Holy shit. I think I just came from that picture."

Layton's whispers, "Scratch what I just said, *that* one is going above my bed. Hell, I might wallpaper my entire bedroom in it. Maybe the whole penthouse."

I hear Quincy mumble in Layton's ear, "It's a good thing I know about you two, because I'd certainly know now."

Layton mumbles back, "We weren't even together yet when it was taken."

Kam throws her arm around me. "Well...that's one for the grandkids." She smiles. "You're a fucking queen. I worship at the altar of Arizona Abbott."

Reagan rubs my arm. "Congratulations. Being on the cover is a very big deal. You two did it. I had a feeling you would. You both have a certain quality that I knew would grab their attention. And now both the Cougars and Anacondas will reap the benefits. The upcoming playoff games for both teams are already completely sold out."

I simply nod. I can't take my eyes off the cover. Neither can Layton.

The other couples featured in the magazine all walk over to congratulate us. I don't think any of it has completely registered. The fact that we're on the cover of the number one sports magazine in the world, *or* the type of photo it is.

As we're shaking hands, Layton leans over and whispers, "Do you realize that you're on the cover of *Sports Illustrated* with my come rubbed all over your body? People may see your muscular abs, but all I see is them covered in me, marking you as mine. Our dirty little secret will now live on for eternity."

I swallow hard as I get wobbly on my feet. He has to steady me so I don't fall over. He does so with a big grin on his face. He winks. "Don't worry, even though you can't see my stomach, I know your come was on me too."

All of a sudden, everything starts spinning. I grab his arm, needing it for support. "Layton, I need some air."

His smile fades into a look of worry. He wraps his arms around my waist. "I've got you."

I don't know who we're talking to, but he says, "Excuse us for a minute. We're a little overwhelmed."

He immediately escorts me to an empty hallway and opens a door. We hear moans and see Reagan's stepfather with his hand up her mother's dress. Their lips are locked and he's really going to town on her.

Layton quickly closes the door, and we sprint around the corner. We turn and stare at each other, wide-eyed at what we just witnessed, but then we start hysterically laughing.

I have to hold my stomach. "Oh my god. I can't believe we just saw that."

Layton is leaning over, still laughing. "I think it's permanently burned into my brain."

As we start to calm down, he rubs my arm. "Are you okay?"

I take a huge breath. "It was just so intense. That picture. Holy shit."

"You look so beautiful in it."

"It's so sexual. So intimate. I can't believe they're putting it on the cover."

He smiles. "Every man in the world is going to be jealous that you're my girl."

I rub his face. "I *am* your girl. We didn't get to finish our conversation from earlier."

He nods in understanding.

"I love you too, Layton. So much. I was honestly thinking about it just before you said those words to me."

Our lips move toward each other, but just before they meet, we hear Tanner's voice. "There you two are. You're in high demand. You better get back out here."

Layton shouts back, "We'll be there in a minute."

He lifts my chin. "Tonight. You're mine."

I think I'm always going to be his.

CHAPTER TWENTY-ONE

ARIZONA

After hours of mingling and taking photos, we're finally on the bus on our way back to Philly. Our friends are all drinking and talking, but Layton and I are in our own little love bubble. I never want it to burst.

Everything is so perfect. We're in love, both our teams are about to start the playoffs, and in about a month, we'll be in Fiji, the first of four stops for the Fantasy Suits two-month shoot. Those are going to be the best two months of my life.

I'm sitting across his lap with him rubbing his hands all over me, uncaring that my brother or anyone else can see us. He's whispering in my ear about the things he wants to do to me tonight. It's driving me wild.

He nibbles on my ear. "Are you wet, sunshine?"

I squirm as I grab his shirt and practically pant, "So wet. I'm dying for you."

"I can't wait to smell you. To touch you. To taste you."

I breathe, "I want you to visit the pitcher's mound tonight."

He lifts an eyebrow. He doesn't know that one.

I bite my lip. "I want you everywhere." I wiggle my ass on him. "*Everywhere.*"

He sucks in a breath. I can physically see his dick growing in his pants. It's almost obscene. Thank god it's dark in the bus. There's no hiding that monster.

He squeezes my leg. "I need a taste. Just a little something to tide me over."

Still sitting across his lap, I subtly spread my legs just enough for him to slip his hand under my dress and between my thighs.

He does his best to be discreet though I notice Kam smirking at us.

His hand moves slowly. The closer he gets, the more I throb in anticipation. I want to grab his arm and push him in. He knows the slow seduction gets me worked up into a frenzy and takes full advantage of it.

His finger finally teases my entrance and then slips in. Just one finger, but he pushes it in deep, as far as he can go.

My eyelids flutter at the sensation. I have to squeeze his arm and clench my entire body just to try to maintain any composure.

I quickly look around. No one but Kam is staring at us.

After a few pumps, he pulls his finger out, runs it under his nose, and inhales deeply. His tongue then snakes out and licks across that finger.

I watch on with a slack jaw. If this man doesn't get inside me soon, I might actually pass out.

By unfortunate virtue of geography, we drop Ezra off first. Surprisingly, Bailey gets out of the bus with him. I didn't think she was interested, but I can't be bothered to focus on anything else besides Layton right now.

Gemma and Trey are dropped off next, and then we finally head to Layton's place. We pull around to his private elevator. He stands and grabs my hand as the bus comes to a stop.

When we're about to exit the bus, Quincy narrows his eyes at me. "Z, I can escort you home if you'd like."

Kam lets out a laugh. "Did you even see the cover photo? Did you pick up on any tension at the party or on this bus, or are you simply deaf, dumb, and blind? If you don't realize that they're about to go fuck their brains out all night, you're an idiot."

Cheetah starts laughing. "Kam bam, you're one of a kind. Q, have another drink. Say good night to Layton and your sister. She's *definitely* not staying on this bus with us."

I guess we weren't as discreet as I thought.

I do a little wave with my fingers and smile. "Have a good night. I know I will."

I hear Quincy snarl as we make our way off the bus and into the elevator where the last of my sanity snaps. Before the elevator doors even close behind us, I reach into Layton's shirt and rip it open, causing the buttons to spray all over the elevator.

As the doors close, I smash my mouth to his. Without breaking the kiss, he reaches down to the slit in my dress and tears the whole fucking thing from bottom to top without giving it a second thought, leaving me completely exposed.

He lifts me and I wrap my legs around him. Pushing me against the wall, he grinds himself on my bare pussy the entire ride up. I can feel the massive bump of his tip, even through his pants.

The doors ping our arrival at his penthouse, and he rushes us inside, his lips never leaving mine. Our lips and tongues duel like we can't get enough of each other. We can't.

Our mouths are fused together. His hands roam my body, anxious to touch every inch of me. Mine do the same to him. I'm so ravenous for this man.

When we reach his bedroom, he places my bare feet on the ground. I suppose I lost my shoes somewhere along the way. I don't even remember.

Breaking our lips apart, he pants, "Get on that bed completely naked. Spread your legs wide so I can see your pretty pussy drip for me. I'll be right back."

"You're leaving?"

He slaps my pussy so fucking hard. I think my eyes cross in pleasure. Why does that turn me on so much?

"Who's in charge, sunshine?"

I pant, "You are."

"Have I ever let you down?"

I shake my head. "No. Never." He always takes my body to places it's never been before.

"Lay down and do as you're told."

He walks out of the room. I quickly discard my shredded dress and lay down on the bed with my legs wide open, as instructed.

I'm there for several minutes. Where the hell is he? What is he doing?

My question is answered about a minute later when my every fantasy comes to life. I breathe, "Holy. Fucking. Shit."

Layton *fucking* Lancaster, the official king of the castle, walks back into the bedroom in a full Captain America costume. I almost come on the spot. I can feel my clit beating in rhythm with my heart. Pulsating. Throbbing. Dripping.

He went all in. It looks like it came from the movie set. Knowing him, it probably did.

It should be a crime how hot he looks. Incidentally, it should also be a crime to have the biggest, hardest dick on the planet while wearing those tights. They leave zero to the imagination. My mind is spinning. It's every fantasy I've ever had, all rolled into one. Captain America and Layton Lancaster. My mind is officially blown.

Through his mask, he runs his eyes up and down my body as he moves his tongue along his lower lip. "Is that as wide as you can go?"

I nod, though I push my legs just a bit wider.

"Good girl." He sniffs a few times. "I'd ask if you're turned on, but I can smell that you are."

Oh god. I know not to beg—he doesn't like it—but my sanity is barely holding on by a thread. I know I need to remain calm and let him control the pace. I'm secretly praying it's a fast one.

My prayers are answered when he throws a small bottle onto the bed before immediately sinking his face between my legs. I look down in awe. I have Captain America's tongue inside me right now. I might come in under ten seconds.

He sucks, licks, and nibbles me, eventually mumbling, "I can do this all day."

I giggle at the Captain America movie line before moaning as he latches onto my clit. My hips buck off the bed. I'm gripping the sheets for dear life.

He manages to both suck on my clit and flick it with his tongue at the same time. I feel his thumb tease my entrance. Slow circles until I can't take it anymore. He sticks it all of one inch inside me before I succumb to the all-night-long buildup and sensation of what he's doing to my body.

My world begins to tilt off its axis. I start to see red, white, and blue stars as I scream his name, feeling myself squirt. It's like I'm floating. Like my body rose above the bed, opened, and then a waterfall poured out of me.

My vision hasn't returned, but I hear him slurping. "You're so fucking hot when you come for me like that. I need to be inside you."

In barely recognizable English, I sputter, "Yes, get inside me."

With blurred vision, I see him lift his body and pull out his heavy cock from the confines of the tights. He immediately rubs the giant head through me a few times. It only serves to cause aftershock tremors to work their way through my body. He continues moving it through until his tip mercifully rests at my entrance. He pushes in about two inches before muttering, "Shit. I need to get a condom."

I wrap my legs around him as tight as I can. I must be out of my mind, given what I've been through in the past, but I respond, "Don't you dare pull out. I'm on the pill. Just get inside me."

Without another thought, he thrusts all the way forward until he's seated to the hilt. We both moan at the same time. Breathing heavily, he mutters, "I've never been inside a woman without a condom. Holy shit. You feel so good. So wet. So tight. So soft."

Despite my hazy state and overwhelming feeling of him being inside me, I have a moment of joy that he's experiencing a first with me like I'm about to with him.

I look up at him in his sexy Captain America mask. Our eyes meet as a moment of tenderness passes between us. It's the first time he's been inside me since we exchanged *I love yous*.

With pure lust in his eyes, he mouths, "I love you."

I mouth back, "I love you too."

I briefly think he might be gentle considering the

circumstances, but that passes quickly when he pulls nearly all the way out and then slams back into me.

I run my nails down his back as the onslaught begins. I never knew sex could be as good as it is with Layton. He takes my body to heights I've never bothered to contemplate. I think the emotional connection, along with the physical, makes it so good. Then again, it could simply be Layton Lancaster, my king.

He rides me hard until another earth-shattering orgasm finds me. My body feels limp. I hope I can walk tomorrow. It's unlikely given the pounding he just gave me.

He pulls out and flips me over, immediately burying his face in my ass. His tongue moves around my back entrance. Aside from a few of Layton's fingers now and then, I have no experience with any of this. I don't know what to expect. I only know that I want him to own every inch of me. I want to share this with him. I want to share everything with him.

He lifts his body off mine and pulls me up to my hands and knees. Grabbing the small bottle he threw on the bed, he opens the lid and squirts some of the cold liquid onto my ass.

I immediately feel his warm hands rubbing it all over and in my back entrance. Before I realize what's happening, two of his fingers are inside me. The further he pushes, the more intense the sensation. I feel pins and needles all over my body each time he moves them deep inside me.

His warm breath hits my ear. "I'll go slow. It's going to sting at first as you acclimate to me. As soon as I'm in, I'll be still as your body stretches for me. It's not going to last long. I'm so worked up and you're going to be so damn tight."

The warmth of his breath disappears as he pulls away and removes his fingers from my body. I marvel at the sudden sensation of emptiness.

As soon as I feel his tip at my back entrance, I start to panic. That tip is so damn wide. It might break me.

He must sense my fear, because he says, "Don't worry. There will be no backdoor slider. I'll get you nice and ready before visiting the pitcher's mound."

I giggle at his terminology as I look back and see him rubbing the oil all over his cock, adding a little extra to the head, a head which suddenly seems to have doubled in size. Or maybe it's just my imagination and fear.

He moves his tip to my entrance and begins to push in. Oh god. That's never fitting inside me. It's like shoving a grapefruit into a water bottle.

He spanks my ass and says, "That's America's ass."

I let out a laugh at another Captain America movie line reference, and I think it relaxes me a drop. At least enough for his tip to breach my entrance.

I collapse to my elbows, unable to manage the new sensation. "Go slow."

"I am. You feel incredible."

While continuously adding more oil, he gradually pushes in further and further. He's being so delicate with me. I desperately want this to be good for him.

I turn back. "Are you all the way in?" He must be.

He chuckles. "Almost halfway."

You must be kidding me. I blow out a breath. "Keep going."

Every little bit stings until I get used to it, and then I'm fine until the next bit moves deeper inside me.

Very slowly, he maneuvers inch by thick, long inch until I can feel his body meet mine. Without him even saying it, I know he's all the way in.

After just a minute or two, the last bit of pain subsides. I'm ready for him to take what he needs.

I look back again and smile at the absurdity of him being in my ass in a full Captain America costume. And then I start laughing. Hard.

He pinches his eyebrows together. "What's so funny?"

"Just a normal day, getting fucked in the ass by Captain America. I'm sure it happens to women all the time."

He narrows his eyes as he withdraws a bit but then slams back in. My smile quickly fades. It's not pain I'm feeling, it's pleasure. New and different pleasure. "Oh god, do it again."

And he does. In and out. Harder and harder. I thought this was going to be all about pleasing him. Turns out I'm into this. *Very* into this.

I'm barely able to hold my body up by my elbows. My face is planted into the pillow as I grip it and scream into it.

He reaches around and starts circling my clit with his fingers. Holy shit. The dual sensation is nirvana.

I feel my body tighten. "I'm coming."

"Do it. I can't last much longer. You feel too good. I've never felt anything better. I love you so fucking much."

And that does it for me. I have a warm sensation down the backs of my legs as I come in a different way to any other orgasm I've ever had. It feels like fingertips are pushing into my skin and dripping down my body.

"You're squeezing me. I need to let go."

"Let go." He pushes in deep and stills before grunting into his own orgasm.

We immediately collapse in a heap of oil, sweat, and our combined, excessive fluids.

Out of breath, we lay there silently as our heart rates begin to stabilize. He pulls me into his arms and peppers my back with kisses. "Thank you for giving me that."

I reach back and rub him. "Thank *you*, Captain America."

CHAPTER TWENTY-TWO

LAYTON

The playoffs have wreaked havoc on us seeing each other over the past few weeks. We're each on the road half the time and our home games don't always overlap days. It's a few stolen moments here and there and it's not enough. I want her with me every day, forever. I'm convinced of that.

The good news is that the end is almost here. Her final game is tonight in Miami. Their championship series is tied. It's a winner-take-all game for them.

We're in the World Series, but it's currently tied at two games apiece in the best-of-seven series. Our home game tonight is a pivotal one. The winner will only need one more game to take home the prize.

I know it's because of the desire to have maximum evening television viewership, but I hate that the Anacondas play at the same time as us. They keep updating their score on one of our scoreboards, but I wish I could at least watch their game considering I can't be there in person.

Despite concentrating on our own game, we're all monitoring the score closely. So many of the Cougars are now Anacondas fans. We see on the scoreboard that they're up by one run going into the bottom of the last inning.

At some point in the fifth inning of our game, while we're on defense, the broadcaster announces over the speakers in the stadium that the Anacondas only need one more out before the championship is theirs. They momentarily stop our game and play theirs on all our screens. All eyes in the stadium are on them.

Ripley is on the mound and the batter steps into the box. The first pitch comes in hard. The batter doesn't swing and Arizona frames it perfectly on the low, outside corner of the plate. It's a called strike and the crowd in our stadium starts cheering. I look around and smile, loving how vested our fans are in the Anacondas. I can't help but feel proud that I was able to contribute in some small part. I know it was all the girls and how they play, but I also know I helped a bit in getting people to come to see them play and fall for the sport and the players the way I have. Well, maybe not exactly like I have.

The second pitch of the at-bat is thrown. The batter, again, doesn't swing. It's a bit high and called a ball. Our crowd collectively boos.

The third pitch is high again, but the batter swings through it for strike two. One more strike and they win the championship. Our fans are standing, clapping in anticipation of the championship we can all almost taste.

The next pitch is thrown and the batter swings, making minimal contact. It's a little squib ball rolling toward Ripley. Shit. Ripley is slow as hell. She's never going to be able to make the play in time. All of a sudden, out of nowhere, Arizona pounces like an actual cheetah, scoops up the ball, turns her body, and fires a bullet to first base in the nick of time for the final out.

As soon as the ump gives the official signal of the out, our crowd goes wild. Arizona jumps into Ripley's waiting arms before the whole team piles on top of them in celebration. Without realizing it, I've got my hands in the air, jumping up and down. I look over at Quincy and he's doing the same, smiling at me.

I wish more than anything that I was at their game. I'm so happy they let us watch it live. I can't wait to talk to my girl and congratulate her. I've got tears in my eyes watching their celebration play out. The joy on their faces is everything.

They allow us a few more minutes to watch the girls enjoy the victory before they resume our game. I'm doing my best to stay focused on the task at hand.

An hour later, we're tied at the top of the last inning. We're in the field and they have a runner on second base with two outs. The pitch comes in and the batter hits a hard ground ball single up the middle.

Shit. The runner from second base will try to score. He's already rounding third base, barreling toward home. Cheetah got a good jump on the ball in center field. He charges it hard and comes up firing. Out of the corner of my eye, I notice the baserunner heading for me just as the ball comes in. He's sliding headfirst. I catch the ball and try to get my leg around but can't get it there in time. Though I get my glove down just before he reaches me and tag him just a hair ahead of his hand reaching the bag.

I hear a crunch as we collide and go down hard. I'm on my back on the ground but hold the ball up in the air so the ump knows I didn't drop it. He calls the runner out.

Yes! Now we can try to win the game in the bottom of the ninth inning.

It's so quiet in here. Why aren't the fans cheering like crazy? That was an awesome play.

I start to sit up, but the ump places his hand on my shoulder and gently pushes me back down. "Wait for the trainers, son."

"Why? I'm fine."

His face is solemn as he motions his head toward my leg. I just then look down and realize it's in a very unnatural position. I know immediately that it's broken.

The next ten minutes are fuzzy. The pain starts to settle in. It's unlike any injury I've ever experienced. I've suffered minor muscle pulls and tears, but nothing along these lines. The faces of the trainers are somber, but it's like being underwater. I hear people talking, but it's muffled, and I don't know what they're saying.

I'm eventually put on a stretcher. I look around and see Carter Daulton with a strained look on his face, standing behind the medical staff in his business suit. I make eye contact with him and shout, "Do *NOT* tell her. Let her celebrate their victory. Let her have her moment." I feel tears streaming down my cheek, not in pain, but at the thought of this ruining Arizona's moment. "I'm not fucking with you. Don't tell her tonight. Please."

With an expressionless face, he nods as I'm carried away and straight into an ambulance.

ARIZONA

The champagne celebration in the locker room has been the absolute best moment of my entire softball career. We all put on goggles to protect our eyes, sprayed each other with champagne, and danced like crazy for over an hour. The music was blaring, and the smiles were everywhere.

Winning the league with my best friends is everything. I wish it was a home game and we were in Philly celebrating with all our fans, and I *really* wish Layton and my brother were here, but I'll take it. Hopefully they can be at the celebratory parade planned for later this week. Life is good. It's great.

We're not flying home until tomorrow. After we get cleaned up, we're planning to party hard in Miami tonight. The South Beach nightlife is fun, and we intend to take full advantage of it. I can't wait.

I'm getting out of the shower when Reagan Daulton appears in the locker room. Her face doesn't look like she owns a team who just won the league. It looks the opposite, like we lost.

She motions her head for me to step into a private alcove area of the locker room. I tighten my towel under my armpits and follow her as uneasiness settles in. "What's up?"

"First of all, I'm so proud of you. You've done exactly what I brought you here to do. Our team is a success, the league's numbers are up, and we're already set to stay in business for another year. Make no mistake, you're a huge part of that, Arizona, and I appreciate you."

"It was your vision and your belief in us. Thank *you*."

She nods but looks hesitant for a moment. "I need to talk to you about something. He didn't want us to tell you, but you're going to see it on television or social media, and I'd rather you have the opportunity to fly home with me now rather than freak out all night and have to wait until tomorrow to fly with the team."

"Huh? What are you talking about?"

She places her hand on my shoulder. "It's Layton. He got hurt in the game tonight."

"Is he okay?"

She shakes her head. "No. His leg was practically snapped in half. He's already in surgery."

I suck in a breath as my head starts spinning. My hands start shaking and she takes them in hers.

"He specifically asked that you not be told so you could celebrate with your team. He knew you guys won before he got hurt. He wants you to stay and enjoy the moment with your teammates. My plane leaves in an hour. It's entirely up to you whether to stay the night or fly home with me."

"Of course I'm coming with you."

She nods. "I figured as much. Get dressed. I'll wait for you."

AN HOUR LATER, we're sitting on her private jet. I've scoured the internet. There's no additional information on Layton, but I've watched the collision at least fifty times. It was bad. He didn't have time to get his leg into position to absorb the hit properly. He was able to get his glove down into position and secure the out, but his leg took the hit at a bad angle and snapped. It's horrific to watch. My heart breaks for him.

Reagan interrupts my thoughts. "He's still in surgery. You won't find anything new. Trust me, I'm checking in."

I nod. "Thanks." I look down and then back up. "I guess you know we're in a real relationship?"

She lets out a laugh. "Umm, yes. I'm not an idiot."

"I know you're not. You're not going to void his contract, are you?"

She has a look of shock on her face. "Of course not. I'm not trying to screw him over on a technicality. He did what we asked of him. *More* than what we asked of him. There's no denying that he got the asses in seats at your games. You ladies put on a show that kept them there and got them vested in the team, but he got them there in the first place. I'm grateful to him. To both of you."

"When did you know?"

She smiles. "Francois sent me a few of the proofs right after the shoot." She fans herself. "They were hot as hell. I knew immediately it was no longer fake. You can't fake what I saw in those photos. The one they used for the cover wasn't even the hottest one. It's just the hottest one that wouldn't get censored."

I can't help but give a small smile at the memory of that day. "Do they look good?"

"They look fucking amazing. I immediately had our PR people pushing for the cover. They didn't need to push very hard. The chemistry you two share truly jumps off the page. Consider yourself lucky. I know plenty of people who wait a lifetime to share half of what I see between you and Layton."

I know she's right. I bite my lip. "Please know that I tried in vain to keep him at arm's length." I shrug. "He was my childhood crush. My fantasy man. I just couldn't help but be attracted to him."

She nods. "He's hot as hell. Of course you're attracted to him. Every woman in America is attracted to him."

My shoulders fall. She's right. Every woman wants him. "I suppose he can have anyone he wants."

"I saw those pictures. He wants you and only you. If I show you something, I need you to swear to keep it between you and me. I signed a non-disclosure."

"I promise."

She messes around on her cell phone screen for a few moments. When she gets to whatever it is she's looking for, she hands me her phone. "Tell me what you see in this."

I take her phone and my breath catches. It's one of the photos from the shoot. I'm standing in front of him, though slightly off to the side so you can see both of our bodies. Our shirts are open. His hand is on my stomach. I'm looking at the camera, playing the part, but he's looking at me. There's no mistaking the desire written all over his face. I've never in my life had a man look at me the way he is in this photo. Women dream of having a man look at them the way Layton is looking at me. It immediately gives me chills.

I breathe, "Wow."

"Yep. There's nothing fake about the way he's looking at you. The way he's touching you. The way he's *revering* you."

That's exactly what he does. He reveres me.

"You're right. Things are so good between us. It's almost like a fairytale. I just hate that it started with a lie. Let's hope strong relationships can come from less-than-ideal beginnings."

She's quiet for a moment before asking, "Can you keep another secret?"

I nod my head. "I can."

"Carter and I started off similarly. We staged a fake relationship for business purposes, and somewhere along the way, we fell in love. Hell, we went one step further. We faked an engagement. We weren't intimate or even remotely dating until after we were publicly engaged. Our real engagement came much later than people think."

"Holy shit. You would never know. You guys seem to have such a perfect marriage."

"No marriage is perfect, but I know I have a great one. I'm thankful every day of my life that he came to me with the fake relationship proposal. If he hadn't, I don't know that we would have found each other, though I feel like things happen for a reason. He's my soulmate in every way imaginable. He was in a bad motorcycle accident last year. When I didn't know if he'd make it, I couldn't even breathe. He's my everything. I know exactly how you're feeling right now, Arizona. His pain is your pain."

"I do feel pain." Tears sting my eyes. "This will probably end his career."

She shrugs. "Maybe yes, maybe no. But we'll honor his contract regardless. He'll get paid for the next three years whether or not he plays. Maybe he could do some coaching."

I nod. "He loves to coach. He coaches little kids in his free time."

She looks surprised. "I didn't know that."

"He doesn't like publicity for it. He doesn't want the press or any fans hanging around the kids."

"It sounds like there's more to Layton Lancaster than just being a baseball player."

I nod. "There is. So much more."

"You're in love with him." She says it as a statement, not a question.

"I am. I just worry that things have been too perfect. Life isn't perfect all the time."

"You're about to hit a less-than-perfect time. This injury will be hard for him. He's going to lean on you. The real relationships weather the storms. I truly hope it works out for you two."

A little while later, we land in Philly. As we're deboarding, she says, "Carter is picking me up, but I arranged for a car to take you straight to the hospital."

I hug her. "Thanks, Reagan. I appreciate everything you've done."

As we walk down the steps, I hear the roar of a motorcycle as it comes to a stop at the bottom of the stairs. The rider takes his helmet off and I see that it's Carter. He smiles at Reagan. It's not a sweet smile. It's an *I'm about to fuck your brains out* kind of smile.

Damn, he's hot.

She breathes, "I know."

"Did I say that out loud?"

Giggling, she says, "No, but I knew what you were thinking. I was thinking it too. I'm just happy he's all mine." She places her hand on my shoulder. "I hope our talk helped."

I nod. "It did. Thank you."

"Give Layton our best. We'll visit him tomorrow."

She walks over toward Carter, and he grabs her face and kisses her hard before they both put on their respective helmets. She climbs on the bike behind him, wraps her arms around him, and they drive away.

CHAPTER TWENTY-THREE

LAYTON

I blink my eyes open to fluorescent lights and hear the subtle beeping of machines. It takes a moment for me to absorb my surroundings, but I quickly remember what happened and that I'm in the hospital. Before I went under, they said it was roughly a four-hour surgery. It must be the middle of the night.

I can't move. Looking down, I see that my leg is in a giant Frankenstein-looking contraption from my ankle to the middle of my quad. My entire leg is lifted and immobilized in some type of sling device hanging from above. I couldn't move it an inch if I wanted to. It's swollen and bruised all over. It looks bad. *Really* bad.

I look around the room and see Tanner, Cheetah, Trey, Quincy, Ezra, and Arizona. They're all sitting in chairs. Quincy and Arizona are awake, huddled together, but the rest are sleeping in awkward, uncomfortable-looking positions.

And then it hits me. Arizona is here.

I slam my hand on the bed. "No! No! No!"

All six of them jump to their feet.

I look at Arizona and tears fill my eyes. I shout, "Why are you here? You should be celebrating with your team. This should be one of the best days of your life. I told them not to tell you." I toggle my eyes between all my friends. "Who told her, damn it? I want to know!"

She immediately takes my hand and kisses it. "It doesn't matter who told me. There's nowhere else I'd rather be."

I bang my head back repeatedly against the pillow. The machines start beeping loudly. Tears are running down my cheeks. "I didn't want you robbed of your moment. You've earned it."

Tears now pour out of her eyes as she kisses my hand again. "I'm exactly where I belong."

A man in a white coat, who looks vaguely familiar, rushes in and takes in my state of distress. "Layton, we need you to calm down. Your heart rate is spiking. Your body just went through surgery. That's a major trauma. It can't handle the added stress. It's not safe."

I'm so damn angry right now. Who told her? Who got her home so quickly? I can feel my face turning red as the machines beep in alarm with increased frequency.

The doctor places his hand on my shoulder. "If you don't calm down, I'm going to have to sedate you again."

"Don't you fucking dare! Someone take her back to Miami. Someone..." Before I finish my sentence, I feel Arizona's lips on mine. They're soft. They're uniquely her. They're my home. I immediately relax my shoulders and calm down. The machines gradually slow until the loud beeping noises come to an end.

She mumbles into my mouth, "If you don't shut up, the next thing I'm going to do is sit on your face."

Quincy moans. "Oh my god. I can't believe I just heard you say that."

Everyone else bursts out in laughter. Cheetah blurts out, "I'm totally staying for *that*."

She grabs my face and presses her forehead to mine. "Relax, superstar. Deep breaths. I'm not going anywhere."

I sigh in resignation. "But you should be celebrating with your team, not stuck in a hospital watching me sleep. Please. Go back. Be with them. Enjoy your moment in the sun."

"I did celebrate with them. And I'll celebrate more this week. They'll be home in a few hours. For now, I'm going to be here with you. If the situation was reversed, would you be out partying in South Beach or here with me?"

I don't answer.

"Exactly. Now shut up and listen to the doctor. If you get crazy and he has to sedate you, I'm going to let Cheetah shave your head."

I hear some of my friends snickering, but I don't care. Taking her hand in mine, I squeeze it in gratitude for her loving me the way she does. I can't believe she left her team's celebration to come and watch me sleep.

The doctor clears his throat. "Layton, I don't know how much you remember from when they brought you in. You were in and out of consciousness. We spoke just before you were sedated. My name is Dr. James Alexander. I'm the head of orthopedic surgery here at Pennsylvania Hospital. You suffered a tibia-fibula fracture in the area just below your knee. It was completely displaced. I know this is a bit graphic, but it was basically like a tree branch that snapped in half. We did our best to put your bones back into place, but we also had to insert pins to keep them together. When we went in, your knee was a bit of a mess, so we did some work on that too. You'll be immobilized completely in this device until the swelling goes down in a few days. You absolutely cannot move. If you do, you risk needing more surgery and prolonging your recovery period. Once the swelling subsides, you'll be fitted for a cast. It will be about three months before you're walking, and you won't be back to normal for a few months after that. The recovery timeline will depend on the extensive physical therapy you'll require to regain full motion. The more you put into it, the better the results."

"Will I ever be able to play ball again?"

He shrugs. "I can't make any promises. The position you play is demanding on your legs and knees. I'm not sure how you were playing with your knee as we found it. You must have been in substantial pain."

I subtly nod and see my teammates grimace, knowing I was hiding it.

He continues, "My best guess is that you're doubtful for next season, certainly the first half of the season, but perhaps with a lot of hard work, the season after is a possibility. You're going to lose a lot of muscle. It will take time to rebuild it. There are no guarantees."

It feels like all the oxygen has been sucked out of the room. You could cut the tension in here with a knife right now.

My career is over. I know it. Everyone in this room knows it. I'll never play baseball again. Just like that, the decision was taken away from me.

And the weird thing is, I'm not sure how I feel about it. A few months ago, this would have devastated me. But now, for the first time since I started this crazy baseball journey, I see a life after baseball.

There's a knock on the door and it opens. An exceedingly attractive woman in a white jacket walks in. If one of these fuckers ordered me a stripper nurse, I'm going to kick their ass.

Cheetah sucks in a loud breath. "Holy shit. That's the hottest nurse I've ever seen. I think I once saw a porn that started just like this."

Dr. Alexander throws an unimpressed look Cheetah's way. "This is *Doctor* Harley Lawrence Cooper. She's a heart surgeon. A *very* good one." He scowls at Cheetah.

She smiles in a way that tells me she gets this kind of reaction all the time. "I was paged, Dr. Alexander?"

He nods. "Yes. Thank you for coming, *Dr.* Cooper." Again, he scowls at Cheetah for a moment before turning back to her. "The patient was greatly agitated, and his heart rate was spiking to concerning levels. He seems to have calmed down now though."

She nods. "Why don't I just take a quick look to make sure everything is in working order?"

Cheetah interrupts, "He pulled his groin muscle. You should check there too."

Everyone collectively yells, "Cheetah!"

Dr. Cooper simply glances at Cheetah as she begins to look through a clipboard at the foot of my bed. "Hi, Layton. As Dr. Alexander mentioned, I'm Dr. Cooper. I believe you all know my sister."

Cheetah shakes his head. "I don't know anyone that looks like you, but I'd love an introduction."

Ezra smacks him in the arm. "Be quiet, dickhead."

Dr. Cooper does her best to hide her smile. "Reagan Lawrence Daulton. She's my sister."

I nod. "I met your mom a few weeks ago. Come to think of it, you look a lot like her. You don't look anything like Reagan though."

She sighs. "Yep, we get that a lot."

Cheetah asks, "Your mom looks like you? Is she available?"

Ezra hits him again.

Dr. Cooper lets out a small laugh. "Sorry, she's *very* taken."

Arizona and I exchange amused looks, both remembering when we saw them being completely taken in the closet at the *Sports Illustrated* party.

Cheetah lifts an eyebrow. "And you? Are you taken, Dr. Cooper?"

She holds up her left hand, wiggling her ring-covered finger. "Also *very* taken."

He mumbles, "Lucky fuckers."

After reviewing my file, she checks something on the machines and then pulls out her stethoscope and listens to my heart. "Layton, try to remain calm. Your body just endured a considerable trauma. If I see any more significant spikes, we're going to have to sedate you."

"I was upset about something. I'm okay now. It won't be a problem. I don't want to be sedated. Please."

Dr. Alexander thanks Dr. Cooper and she leaves. He then turns back to me. "I'll check on you in a couple of hours. In the meantime, Nurse Edna will stop by in a few moments to clean you up."

"Thanks, Dr. Alexander."

Dr. Alexander leaves the room and closes the door behind him.

Cheetah scrunches his face. "Nurse Edna? Are you getting a sponge bath from an eighty-year-old grandma? How about Dr. Cooper gives the sponge baths? I could use one from her."

Tanner rolls his eyes as he approaches the bed. He pinches his lips together, clearly trying to contain his emotions. Placing his hand on my shoulder, he says, "I'm so sorry this happened Layton, but you're strong. You'll bounce back better than ever."

We both know his words are hollow. I will definitely not be better than ever.

"Thanks."

"The play you made at the plate was incredible. Few athletes in the world could have made it. You're a legend in this sport, whether or not you pick up a bat again. Don't ever forget it."

"It wasn't enough." I saw just before I went into surgery that we lost the game. We're one game away from being eliminated.

Quincy pats my shoulder. "Don't worry, buddy. We'll come back."

Tanner nods. "Let's hope so. I'll call Fantasy Suits in the morning. Obviously you can't go on the trip." He turns to Arizona. "I don't know what it will mean for you. You should call Michael Longley and figure things out."

And then it hits me. Our trip. The one we've both been looking forward to. It's ruined. A sense of deep sadness rolls through my body. I've been dreaming of having my girl in all those places. Poof. It's gone.

Arizona shakes her head. "I'm certainly not going now, not without Layton."

Tanner shrugs. "Talk to Longley. You're under

contract and you're physically capable. Let's hope they'll agree to delay everything."

He turns back to me and squeezes my hand. "I'll check in tomorrow. You'll get through this. Love you, brother."

"Thanks, Tanner. I appreciate you being here."

He nods and then walks out just as an attractive young woman walks in the room holding sponges and a bucket. She has a huge smile on her face and a cheery demeanor. "Hi, Layton. I'm Nurse Edna. I'm going to get you cleaned up."

Frankly, she looks pretty happy about it. And she's not bothering to hide it.

She then turns to my friends. "I'll need everyone to leave the room and give us some privacy." She looks at Arizona. "You included."

My friends are all grinning like the dirty fuckers they are. Arizona most definitely is not. She walks over to Nurse Edna and practically rips the bucket from her hand. With an extreme amount of edge, she grits, "Thanks, Nurse Edna. I can take over from here. I'll get *my* boyfriend all clean for you. Every long inch." She gives Nurse Edna a not-so-sweet smile.

I can't help but let out a laugh. The first one I've had since this nightmare started.

Nurse Edna shakes her head. "I'm sorry, ma'am, but it's against hospital policy. Only trained personnel can give baths."

Arizona keeps her voice calm. She gets right into Nurse Edna's face, standing at least six inches taller, and looks down at her. "Nurse Edna, either you leave and let me take care of my man, or I'll shove this bucket up your ass. Either way, you're not touching him. Ever."

Nurse Edna's eyes widen as she hesitates for a

moment, but then hands the remaining items to Arizona and walks out the door.

We all burst out laughing as soon as the door closes behind her.

Quincy shakes his head. "Damn, Z, that was some territorial shit."

She points at them and narrows her eyes. "Get. Out. All of you."

Quincy's face drops realizing what's about to happen, but I'm grinning like a kid about to enter a candy store. Maybe this injury won't be so bad.

Ezra, Quincy, and Trey all start to leave. Cheetah sits in a chair. "I think I'll stay and watch. This is like real-life porn shit."

Arizona grabs his shirt and lifts him to a standing position. "Goodbye, Cheetah."

"Ugh, you're no fun."

They all leave, and she closes the door behind them. I'm still smiling as she walks toward the bathroom. "Aren't you going to lock the door, sunshine?"

She shakes her head. "Nope. I hope Nurse Edna walks in and sees what I'm about to do to you."

I chuckle as I hear her in the bathroom filling the bucket. If I was able to move enough to bounce in my seat, I'd be bouncing in it. Despite the horrific circumstances, I'm already hard thinking about what's to come.

She walks out of the bathroom and notices the new tent in my hospital gown. She lifts an eyebrow. "You're a dirty man."

"Yes. I'm *very* dirty. You should clean me. *Thoroughly*."

"Maybe I will." She presses a button above my head, and the back of my bed goes down until I'm lying flat.

She lovingly runs her fingers through my hair. "Tell me if I hurt you."

I turn my head to kiss her arm. "I will. Thanks for coming. I'm sorry you're missing the celebration."

She lifts my gown and stares at my cock lying hard and heavy on my stomach. She gives me a sexy smile. "I'm not. Frankly, I'm happy right where I am."

She lifts her sweatshirt up and over her head and tosses it on a nearby chair. "I wouldn't want it to get wet."

I nod. "Good thinking. Maybe you should lose the sweatpants too. There's nothing worse than having to sit around in wet pants. It's very uncomfortable."

"Good thinking." She bends at the waist and slowly removes them, tossing them next to the sweatshirt.

I slowly run my hand up her muscular, shapely leg. "You're so perfect."

She slaps it away. "And you're a bad patient. Stay still so I can properly clean you."

She dips a sponge in the soapy water, lifts it out of the bucket, wrings it a bit, and starts to softly clean my face. Even though the water is warm, I get chills, relishing her touch.

She meticulously cleans my face, neck, arms, and hands, and then works her way down. After moving my gown out of the way, she runs the sponge over my chest and abs. I see the pace of her breathing increase. Her nipples harden. She's turned on.

After she finishes each area, she peppers it with delicate kisses. It's sexy and sweet all at once.

She then runs the sponge up and down my good leg,

cleaning every last inch. She works her way higher up my thigh until she arrives at the area now standing at full attention for her.

Lifting my balls, she runs the sponge around in circles until she cleans them and then squeezes the soapy water onto my cock. She gives me long, slow strokes of the sponge over my length. She thoroughly cleans every crevice and vein, paying particular attention to the head.

"I think it's clean, sunshine."

She smiles. "It's a lot of territory to cover. You can never be too sure." In a mock, high-pitched voice, she says, "Hospital policy."

I chuckle. She's close enough now that I can reach out and touch her. I pull the cup of her bra down and run my thumb over her hardened pink nipple. "I missed you so much this week."

"I missed you too, but I don't want to hurt you." She looks down at my cock. "I want to sit on that, but I don't think it will work with your leg." She bends and gives my cock a long lick. "But I'm sure this can work. A little extra cleaning for the area. The patient has been a good boy and earned it."

A shot of pre-ejaculate oozes out of my tip. She kisses her way to it and laps it up with her sexy tongue.

"Sunshine, come sit on my face. I need to smell that pretty pink pussy of yours. To taste the sweetness too. That's the best medicine for me. You know it's my magic potion." I give her my best pleading expression, complete with a pouty lip.

I see her contemplate the logistics for a moment before removing her bra. I grab one of her breasts. "So fucking perfect. And mine. All mine."

She turns around and slides down her panties so

damn slow, putting on a show for me. I look at her ass, one that she now loves when I explore. She's driving me wild. My eyes flutter as soon as her curvy body is fully exposed to me.

I tug her arm, pulling her to me. "Time to give me my oxygen straight from the source."

She carefully climbs onto the bed. Facing her body down mine, she gently places both knees on either side of my head, giving me my favorite view.

I roughly grab her ass and pull her pussy straight to my mouth, immediately licking through her. "You taste so fucking good." I rub my whole face around, covering myself in her juices. "I missed your scent on me. I need it."

She leans down and grabs my cock, giving it a few long strokes before feeding it into her wet, warm mouth. I can feel the second my tip reaches the back of her throat. I moan into her pussy.

I plunge my tongue in and out of her opening. Her hips start to take on a life of their own, riding my face. She mumbles into my cock, "So good. Oh god, keep going."

I slide my fingers into her while my tongue finds her sensitive little button, rapidly flicking my tongue over and around it. She momentarily jerks but then grinds her hips in unison with my movements.

Meanwhile, her mouth and hand have my cock ready to take orbit, working together to give me the release she knows I need. It's only been a few days since we were together, but it feels like forever.

We both get into a rhythm, but the damn machine starts beeping again, indicating my heart rate is going up.

She immediately lifts her head. I thrust my hips as

best as I can, seeking the warm comfort of her heavenly mouth. "Baby, don't stop."

"You need to calm down."

"Your mouth is on my dick and your pussy is in my face. No chance of me calming down."

"Let's slow things down."

I latch onto her clit and suck hard.

"Oh fuck, Layton."

I push my fingers in deep where I know she loves it and then bite down on her clit. Her body starts to shake.

She grabs the base of my shaft and starts jerking hard as her tongue flicks all around the head. Her thighs squeeze my head as she moans into her orgasm. As soon as her delicious fluids squirt into my mouth, I lose control and shoot my load straight down her throat.

We're both lapping each other up when the door opens. I can't see anything, but I hear a female screech and then the door closes.

The beeping noise starts to subside. Arizona carefully maneuvers off me until her feet are back on the ground. She kisses my lips and then smiles. "Nurse Edna got the eyeful she deserved."

CHAPTER TWENTY-FOUR

ARIZONA

Layton has been relentlessly pushing the doctors to put him in his cast so he can attend my team's victory parade down Broad Street later this week. I know he'll be disappointed if he has to miss it, so I hope it happens for him.

I contacted Michael Longley from Fantasy Suits two days ago about delaying the photo shoot. He wasn't immediately agreeable and said he'd get back to me. I can't imagine what the holdup could be. It's supposed to be a love story, a sexy campaign. We can't do that without Layton.

I'm about to leave for the hospital when my phone rings. I see that it's Longley finally getting back to me, so I quickly answer. "Hi, Michael."

In his nasally voice, he responds, "Hello, Arizona."

"I'm glad you called. Are we set to delay everything until Layton is up and running again?"

"That's why I'm calling. We've discussed it internally and

feel your star power is particularly strong right now. Our window of opportunity is here and we're not willing to delay."

What? "But Layton can't travel in a full leg cast. I doubt you want him in bathing suit pictures with the cast on anyway." This makes no sense.

"Yes, dear, but *you* can travel. We've replaced Layton with Butch McVey. Frankly, we think you two make an even better couple with his star power being strong too. He's the *it man* of baseball. You're the *it woman* of softball. It's a perfect pairing. Frankly, we believe it to be a *more* perfect pairing."

"To be clear, I'm not going without Layton. I'm not doing a love campaign with another man. A stranger. I agreed to this because I wanted to do it with Layton specifically."

"To be clear, you signed a contract. There's no mention of Layton Lancaster in your contract. You should reread Paragraph Fifteen. Fantasy Suits has the authority to choose your partner. I encourage you to be mindful that you're obligated to make it seem as though he's your boyfriend throughout the shoot and the three months of promotion after the shoot. It's called the Boyfriend Clause, and we choose Butch McVey to be your boyfriend for the next five months."

What. The. Fuck?

I remember the boyfriend language pertaining to the promo period but wasn't worried because Layton and I are so solid. I never considered the fact that it could be someone else besides Layton.

"And if I refuse?"

"We'll sue you for breach of contract and go after you for our damages, which will be several millions of dollars. It took a lot of time, resources, and money to prepare these locations. We can't haphazardly change dates. The investment has been made and you'll be on the hook if you back out."

I don't bother to say goodbye as I end the call. I

immediately dial Tanner Montgomery's number. He answers after only one ring. "Hi. Is Layton okay?"

"He's fine. I'm not calling about his injury. I...umm...just got off the phone with Longley."

"And?"

"They want me to go with Butch McVey and threatened to sue me for millions if I back out."

"Shit. I was afraid of that. What about the promo period?"

"They said I'm obligated to pretend he's my boyfriend for the shoot and the promo period of three months." My voice cracks as tears break free. "That's a total of five months pretending that Butch is my boyfriend." I barely manage, "I can't do that."

He sighs. "I'm so sorry. This is why I told you to get a lawyer. That particular clause was concerning to me. I tried to tell you."

"I know you did, but I obviously thought it was Layton. I wasn't worried about the clause. He *is* my boyfriend. This was supposed to be a dream trip. Now it's a nightmare."

"I understand." He sighs. "Their contract with Layton has already been legally terminated due to the physically unable to perform his duties clause. I can represent you now. Do you want me to call on your behalf and see if we can work something out with them?"

All hope isn't lost. I'm sure Tanner can help. "Yes! Please. I'll do the shoot, but I want to do it next year when it can be with Layton, as we planned. I'll even take less money if they'll just wait. I won't do this without him."

"You may have to, but I'll see what I can do."

"Thanks, Tanner."

I hang up feeling sick to my stomach, but still hopeful that perhaps Tanner can make this go away.

LAYTON

"Doc, you gotta let me out of here."

Dr. Alexander pushes my chest back down toward the bed as he carefully examines my leg. "Stop moving. You're the worst patient ever. I've seen a lot of bad ones, but you take the cake."

I blow out a breath. "I'm not missing that parade. I want to celebrate my girl and her teammates. I'll go in this fucking Frankenstein device if I have to."

"No, you won't." He gently examines my leg. "The swelling seems to be mostly gone. I think we're okay to get you into casting tomorrow, but you *must* remain still today. The slightest agitation could reignite the swelling, in which case, I will not cast it." He points his finger at me. "If you go to that parade, which is probably a mistake given how many bodies can bump into you while there, you need to be in a wheelchair and somewhere that people *can't* bump into you. I want a bubble around you."

"Yeah, yeah. The Daultons said they'd take care of it if you give the green light. I'll march down Broad Street in a tank if I have to, but I'm going."

He rolls his eyes. "Fine, but I'm warning you. Stay off your leg. You're still healing from the surgery."

"I got it."

Just then the door opens and Arizona walks in. My whole agitated mood lifts from simply seeing her face. She's been incredible. She sits with me all day and most of the night until they kick her out, she brings me good food, and, the best part, she gives me my daily sponge bath. We might need to continue that routine once I go home, especially the bathing.

The public outpouring of love has been amazing. I've received countless cards, flowers, and various get-well gifts. There's even a nightly vigil with hundreds of people outside my hospital window. I'm so thankful to my loyal Philly fans.

With Tanner's permission, I released a video on social media thanking the fans and giving them a status update. I let them know exactly who's been taking care of me. It's practically played on a loop on every television station and across all of social media.

There's already speculation as to whether I'll play again. I decided not to address that in my video. My future in baseball is unknown. As for the present, I'm getting antsy. I need to get out of this bed and out of this hospital.

Dr. Alexander smiles at Arizona. "I have some good news. My favorite pain in the ass patient is getting casted tomorrow so we can send him on his merry way."

She giggles. "You just want to get rid of him, right?"

Dr. Alexander lets out a laugh. "You bet we do." He moves toward the door to my room. "I'll leave you two alone." He points at me. "Don't move. Remember, any increase in swelling and the cast isn't happening tomorrow."

I salute him. "Yes, sir."

He leaves, and after a nice long, soothing kiss, Arizona pulls a chair up next to my bed. "I'm happy you'll be at the parade. I know how much you want to go."

"Of course I want to go and celebrate the team. You ladies are getting so much press right now. It's great. This town needs it after the disappointing end to our season."

The Cougars were eliminated from the World Series last night. It was an away game, so I haven't seen the guys yet. I'm sure they're bummed. We thought we had a chance to win it this year, but we ran out of gas.

She scrunches her face. "I spoke with Quincy this morning. He's blaming himself for the loss."

I shake my head. "He pitched a great game last night. Good enough for us to win. Our bats simply weren't there."

"That's exactly what I told him, but you know how he is. He's shouldering the blame."

"That's ridiculous."

She takes my hand. "There's something I need to tell you. I spoke with..."

Before she can finish, her cell phone rings. She looks down at it. "It's Tanner. I was just about to tell you this. Fantasy Suits isn't letting me out of my contract. Now that yours is canceled, he can represent me. He said he'd call and try to work something out."

Shit. I was afraid of this.

She accepts the call. "Hey, Tanner. You're on speaker with Layton and me."

"Are you okay with me talking about your business in front of Layton?"

She rolls her eyes as if the answer is obvious. "Of course."

"It's not good, Arizona. I made very little headway. They want you to go shoot as previously scheduled, and they want it to be with Butch McVey. They've already come to terms with him."

My eyes widen. "What?"

She nods. "Longley mentioned Butch when I spoke with him earlier today. They not only want me to shoot with him, but they also want me to pretend like we're together. Obviously, I told them no. They threatened to sue me for breach of contract."

My head starts spinning.

She looks down at the phone. "What else did they say? Is there any good news?"

"As a show of good faith, they'll reduce the promo period from three to two months after the shoot, but that's it, Arizona. The contract is iron clad. You're going to have to go, and you're going to have to act like you're dating Butch McVey for the full term. You can't be seen publicly with Layton once you step on that plane. That's a breach of the terms of your contract."

Tears fill her eyes. She croaks out, "That's a total of four months. I won't see him for two and then what are we supposed to do, date in secret for the next two months? This is ridiculous."

Tanner is quiet for a few moments. "I'm so sorry. Once shooting begins, you and Layton will only be able to see each other behind closed doors. It's crystal clear in the contract that you can't have another boyfriend. They were very adamant about the wording of the *Boyfriend Clause*. Your boyfriend is whoever they choose, and they're choosing Butch."

I don't need to add to her pain right now, but I'm internally freaking out. Visions of her on a beach, half-naked, with Butch McVey's hands all over her body immediately stream in my mind.

I grab her phone. "Thanks, Tanner. Let us go. We'll talk to you later."

"Sorry, buddy."

I end the call, and she begins sobbing into her hands. Heavily. I've never seen her like this.

I tug her hand. "Get into bed with me."

"I don't want to hurt you."

I open the blanket, unwilling to take no for an answer. She gingerly slides in on my good side and buries her head in my chest.

I simply hold her while the only sounds in the room for a long time are those of her crying. I'm trying to be strong for her, but it's not easy.

I rub her back. "It will be okay. *We'll* be okay. We've got the secret relationship thing down cold."

She sniffles and lets out a laugh. "We sucked at loving each other in secret. We fooled no one."

I smile. "That's true. But it's because our feelings are so strong. Strong enough to overcome this speedbump." I caress her hair. "I'm going to be immobile for the next few weeks anyway. You'll be back before we know it. And then we can simply hide in bed until the contract is over. I wouldn't mind being stuck in bed with you for two months. In fact, I prefer it."

I do my best to give her a reassuring look, but she still looks pained.

"Four months is basically as long as we've known each other. I barely remember life without you anymore."

I wipe the tears from her face. "What's four months when we have a lifetime together?"

Her eyes swim with love. I hope mine don't swim with the deep fear I'm currently feeling.

CHAPTER TWENTY-FIVE

TWO WEEKS LATER

LAYTON

I wake up as I have every morning for the past two weeks, with Arizona's mouth around my cock. I think she's trying to get in two months of sex in two weeks. My dick might fall off from overuse, but I want to be as close to her as I can before she boards the airplane. Today. In less than two hours. My heart hurts at the thought. The impending feeling of emptiness consumes me, but I'm trying to shower her with as much love as I can while I still have her.

I lift her chin and look at her gorgeous face, one that I'm going to miss so damn much. "Climb aboard, sunshine."

She smiles as she crawls her deliciously naked body up

mine to her knees, positions them on either side of my hips, and grabs my cock.

I place my hand over hers and look her in the eyes. "Do you trust me with your pleasure?"

She breathes, "Always."

Together, we run my tip through her wetness and her eyes flutter. "I want you inside me."

I slap her pussy with my dick, and she gasps before her eyes roll back in her head. "Oh god."

"I might be on the bottom, but I'm still in control. Do you understand that?"

She nods as I bring my tip to her clit and start circling it. "You're going to get off on my cock before he even enters you, and then you're going to get off again with him deep inside you."

She nods again, panting like she's about to lose control.

Together, we continue to move my tip around her clit. Her juices are dripping down onto me. The whole scene is erotic. I'll think of it every day while she's gone.

Within only a minute or two she comes all over me, covering my bare cock. We haven't bothered with a condom since Captain America night.

"Good girl. Now put my cock in *my* pussy and take him how you need it."

She breathes, "I need you deep. So deep."

"I know you do. It's yours. I love giving it to you."

She licks her lips, brings my cock to her entrance, and begins to wiggle her way down onto me. Because of my leg, this is the only position we've been able to do. I feel like less of a man not being able to fuck my girl properly, but she doesn't seem to mind taking the reins for a bit.

After some maneuvering, she's fully situated with me

inside her. She rubs her hands up my chest and bites her luscious lip. "I'm going to miss your giant head."

I chuckle. "Which one?"

"Both."

She takes my hands and places them on her breasts. "I want to commit your touch to memory. Even when we're apart, I want to feel you inside me. I need to feel your hands on my body. All the time."

I want that too. Especially when Butch McVey's hands are on my property. I lift my upper body and wrap her in my arms, so our chests are flush together. I kiss up her neck. "Don't forget what we have. Don't forget that you're mine."

She tilts her head back and moans, "Never. I love you."

"I love you too." So much so that I'm doing my best to mask the devastation I'm currently feeling. Fear *and* devastation.

After we make love for what we both know will be the last time for two months, we sit there and hold each other, neither wanting to let go. I manage to touch and worship every inch of her body, knowing it will have to sustain us both for two months. I inhale and taste her. I never want to let go.

Eventually she pulls away and runs her fingertips lovingly over my chin. "I need to shower before we go. Do you want me to help you shower?"

I shake my head. "No. I want your scent on me as long as I can get it to last. I might not shower for two months."

She scrunches her face. "Eww. That's gross."

"Nothing gross about your fluids, sunshine."

An hour later we're in a limo sent by Fantasy Suits, on

the way to the airport, making out like teenagers desperate for every last second of contact.

As we pull into the private airstrip, we see a small corporate jet with Butch McVey standing at the bottom of the stairs. He's got a fucking smug look on his face. I dislike him immediately.

I haven't had a ton of contact with Butch McVey. I've met him a small handful of times at various events and, of course, have played against him. He has the whole bad boy image going for him and he seems to play it up. Where I'm old-school baseball, he's the new kid on the block and everyone wants a piece of him.

She brings her face to mine. Our blue-green eyes meet. "I'll video call you every night. It will be just like when one of us had road games. It's basically an extra-long road trip."

Except with the time difference, I know it's not feasible, but I'm not saying that. I simply nod my head and swallow down the giant lump in my throat. "I left a gift for you in your suitcase. Open it when you arrive."

She softly kisses my lips. "Thank you. I left one for you too." She gives me her sexy, mischievous smile. "It's on the ceiling of your bedroom."

My spirits lift, if only for a moment, knowing what it is. "I can't wait to see it...and then jerk off to it for the next two months."

She giggles. "Call me if you need a little audio to go with that."

"I will. Did you pack Captain America?"

"I did. I'll miss my real Captain America though." She closes her eyes and smiles. "You fulfilled every fantasy of mine that night. It plays on a loop in my mind. I'll be thinking of it and you every night when I go to bed."

I kiss her again. "Every minute with you is my fantasy. Hurry home, sunshine."

With lumps in our throats, we step out of the limo, her on two feet and me with crutches and a mammoth cast on my left leg. Butch immediately walks over, holds out his hand, and smiles. "Hi, Arizona. I'm Butch. It's nice to finally meet you. Congrats on your recent championship."

She takes his hand as I watch on. I hate them touching. And then I start imagining how much more of her he's going to be touching over the next two months. Despite the frigid cold temperature, I can feel sweat dripping down my back.

"Thank you. It's nice to meet you as well. Do you know Layton?"

He nods as his eyes meet mine. "I think we've met a few times throughout the years, right?"

He holds out his hand while looking so fucking pompous. I want to punch him in the face.

I shake his hand hard, very hard, in return. "I think so. Here and there. Maybe when you were still making a name for yourself." I stare at him, conveying my best, *stay the fuck away from my girl*, face.

He gives me a fake smile. "You're showing your old age. Perhaps you have some memory issues. I've been a name since my rookie year when I led the league in hitting."

Arizona turns to the man carrying her luggage onto the plane and then back to me. "I'm going to make sure my bags get onto the plane. I'll be right back to say goodbye."

I nod as she grabs her smaller carry-on bag and makes her way to the stairs leading up to the plane.

As soon as she's out of earshot, he says, "She's even hotter in person. Enjoy your last moments with her. She's all mine for the next few months. I would have done this trip for free. She and I with our hands all over each other all day, every day."

"Enjoy your *fake* PR relationship while it lasts."

He smiles. It's a fucking self-satisfied smile. "Who says it will be fake, Lancaster? I'm going to be spending every day and *every night* with her. It's only a matter of time. I hear she likes ballplayers. She'll no doubt have interest in the best one in the sport, not a gimp who will never play again."

He tilts his head and makes it obvious that he's staring at her ass as she ascends the staircase. I grit out, "Keep your fucking eyes off my girl."

He lets out a laugh. "We're going to be practically naked, all over each other for the next two months. My hands will be on that ass and everywhere else on her sexy body. You just remember that when you go to bed with your dick in your hand every night."

"Keep it professional, McVey."

"Like you did?" He turns and looks me in the eyes. "You're a sinking ship, Lancaster. You're a washed-up has-been. Your career is over, and your stock is plummeting. I'm the star of baseball now. She's the star of softball. We're the natural pairing, not you two. You're only holding her back. You must realize that. Don't be so fucking selfish. Just let her go."

I have to sit there and listen to him articulate things that admittedly have gone through my head lately. "She's too good for you, McVey."

He lets out another deep laugh. "She's probably too good for both of us. Nonetheless, the cream always rises to the top. And guess who's on top right now? Guess who will be on top of her?"

I'm about to punch him in the face when Arizona walks back out of the plane. She looks at me from the top and the stairs and smiles. Arizona Abbott smiles are the kind that can start wars just to catch a glimpse of them. I feel them in every inch of my body.

He mumbles, "She'll be smiling at me like that soon enough."

I want to shove this crutch up his ass but I'm trying to play it cool in front of Arizona. I don't want to make our last moments together about him. They're about us.

Arizona walks down the stairs and wraps her arms around my neck. "I'll call you when I land."

I nod as her lips meet mine. I know she only intends for it to be a peck with Butch standing right next to us, but I deepen it. I feel her stiffen when my tongue slides into her mouth but then she gives in and does the same to me.

Our lips move over each other's. Our tongues swirl together, and I try to convey my feelings as best I can with that kiss. The one that will have to last us the next few months.

I pull her body as close to mine as I can. I can't believe I have to live without this for two months.

When it ends, she runs her nose along my neck and whispers in my ear, "Have you sufficiently pissed around your territory?"

Not even close.

ARIZONA

I watch Layton through the window as the plane taxis away from him. He just stares at it, looking so sad and lost. I can't believe that I won't see him for two long months.

I know why he kissed me the way he did in front of Butch and I don't blame him. I'd feel the same way if the situation was reversed. I've spent the past two weeks reassuring him, doing everything I could to show him nothing but love. How committed I am to our relationship. But I'm sure putting me on a plane with Butch wasn't easy.

I'm not a fool. I know the next two months are going to put a strain on our relationship. I simply hope we can weather this storm. It's our first true test as a couple.

A deep voice breaks my train of thought. "He's a big boy. He'll manage."

I turn away from the window and toward Butch, who is sitting across from me. I suppose I understand the appeal of Butch McVey. He's an attractive man in a completely different way from Layton. He's tall and well-built like Layton, but where Layton is clean-cut, Butch isn't. His arms are covered in tattoos, his dark hair is shaved very short on the sides and is much longer with a small man bun on top. He's got big, light brown eyes with thick, dark eyelashes. I imagine all of that coupled with his puffy lips makes him an appealing package, just not to me. I only have eyes for one man.

"I know. I'll just miss him. Road games aside, we don't spend much time apart. It will take a little time to get used to it."

He lifts an eyebrow. "You've only been together for a few months. It can't be that serious."

"I know it hasn't been long, but we're very much together,

and the next few months aren't going to be easy. To be clear, we're *very* serious."

The stewardess comes by and offers champagne. I initially decline, but Butch insists. "We've got a very long plane ride ahead of us and four months of being seen as boyfriend and girlfriend. Perhaps we should get to know each other."

This feels a bit like déjà vu, having gone through a similar conversation with Layton months ago. I can't believe it's come to this.

As we sip champagne, Butch and I spend the next few hours getting to know one another. He's not so bad. He was raised by a single mother in a small town. She now battles dementia, so he moved her into his house with a full-time nurse.

He's a little flirty, but I think that's his nature. I doubt he means anything by it. He knows I'm with Layton.

ABOUT SIXTEEN HOURS LATER, we land in Fiji. It's the most exotic, beautiful place I've ever imagined. I have a moment of sadness that I'm not experiencing this with Layton. I desperately wanted to have this adventure with him, not a stranger.

We're going to be here for two weeks before we move on to Thailand for two more weeks. The next two weeks will be in Bora Bora, with the last two being in Hawaii.

The way our schedule is set up is that we get a day off every three days to sightsee and relax. With the exception of one or two twilight shoots per location, our evenings are mostly free. Butch said he's scouted several restaurants for us to go to. Apparently, Michael Longley has also made reservations for us at restaurants that are sure to get us a good amount of press attention. I'm dreading those nights.

We arrive at our villa, which is beyond luxurious. I'm surprised that Butch and I are sharing a place, but I suppose it's like having two separate bedrooms in the same house. And we're technically supposed to be a couple, so I guess we need to be seen coming and going from the same place. I can't imagine people will believe I've simply moved on from Layton to Butch in a matter of days, but that's not my problem. I frankly don't care if they buy it or not. In four months, they'll know my so-called relationship with Butch was bullshit.

I've studied the contract a thousand times, both trying to find a loophole and making sure I know exactly what's expected of me when it comes to my interactions with Butch. I need to outwardly act like Butch is my boyfriend and I'm not allowed to outwardly act like I have another boyfriend. That's it. I'm not doing anything beyond the bare minimum. I'll have dinners with him and let the press take their photos of us, but nothing more than that.

As soon as I get to my room, I rip through my suitcase to find the gift Layton mentioned, dying to know what he left for me. I quickly find something wrapped in a side pocket.

Tearing it open, I start crying at what I find. It's his jersey, almost the exact same as the one LeRond had made for me, but this one has a different name on the back. It reads, *#lovedbylayton*. I can smell his cologne on it too. He sprayed it. I inhale deeply, already missing him.

I then look over to the dresser. In a large vase sits what must be ten posters rolled up. Without even opening them, I know what they are. I notice that there's a large envelope next to it. I walk over and open it. It's our *Sports Illustrated* issue. Fuck, this cover is so hot. Our passion radiates from it.

Layton has signed the bottom, *Best day of my life.* I already miss him.

My emotional moment is broken by a knock at my door.

I wipe my eyes clean of the tears. "Come in."

Butch walks through. "Do you want to do a little exploring, so we don't fall asleep? We need to try to stay up so our bodies adjust to the time difference."

"I think I'm just going to unpack and call Layton. I'm exhausted."

"It's the middle of the night there. Call him in a few hours when he's awake. We're in freakin' Fiji. Come on. Let's get out of the villa."

I sigh. He's right. "Okay. Give me five minutes."

"I'll be waiting out front. It looks like we can walk to the local village."

As soon as he leaves, I FaceTime Layton. I know it's the middle of the night for him, but I said I'd call.

He doesn't answer. It goes to voicemail. I have a pang of disappointment. I thought he'd wait up for me.

Butch and I head out to the small town nearby. It's unique looking. It's not very modern, but incredibly charming, littered with small shops and cobblestone streets.

We're walking around the shops when my FaceTime rings. I look down and see that it's Layton.

Before I know what's happening, Butch grabs my phone. "Let me say hello." He accepts the call with a big smile. "Hey, buddy. Did you call to make sure I landed safely? You're so sweet."

I playfully swat his arm. "Give me the phone." I see Layton's handsome face, but he doesn't look happy. He looks furious.

"Why is he answering your phone? Where are you?"

"We're walking around the village, attempting to stay awake. Are you in bed?"

"Yes, I tried to stay up for your call. I must have dozed off. You landed safely?"

"Yep." I look around. "It's so beautiful here. I wish you were with me."

Butch motions that he's running into a store. I nod that I'll wait for him.

I look down at my phone. "What are you up to today?"

He looks so sad. "I'm interviewing a few physical therapists via Zoom." He knocks on his cast. "When this comes off, I want to hit the ground running. How was the plane ride?"

"It was fine. We got to know each other and then I slept for a bit."

"Did you get my gift?"

I smile. "Yes. I love it. I *really* love that it smells like you. Thank you. And love my *bouquet*."

He grins as his eyes move up toward his ceiling. "Thanks for my poster. You look gorgeous in it. I'm going to have a permanent boner waking up to this every day."

It's one of me alone from the *Sports Illustrated* shoot. It's revealing and sensual. I knew he'd like it.

I giggle.

His face turns serious. "Arizona?"

"Yes?"

"He's going to try to sleep with you."

"No, he's not. He's been a gentleman so far."

"It's bullshit. He's a scumbag."

"He knows I'm with you."

"He doesn't care."

"It doesn't matter what he wants. It's not happening. I'm in love with someone else."

He scratches his sexy chin. "If things...feelings change for you, you can tell me. I don't want to hold you back."

"Where is this coming from?" I knew this was going to be hard, but it's day one. Are we already feeling insecure?

He sighs. "I'm sorry. I just miss you already. It was hard to put you on that plane with him."

"I know. I miss..." Before I can finish, Butch knocks into me with some big fruity drink in hand. Some of it spills over onto my phone.

"Crap. Butch just spilled a drink on the phone. I need to clean it. I'll call you tomorrow. Love you."

I end the call and Butch gives me a sheepish look as I clean my phone. "Sorry." He holds out a drink. "This is for you."

I see he has one for himself in his other hand. I take it. "Thank you."

He clinks our plastic cups together. "To beginnings."

"To beginnings."

CHAPTER TWENTY-SIX

LAYTON

"He wants to fuck her."

Cheetah rolls his eyes. "Every man in this country wants to fuck her, me included. It doesn't mean they can or will."

Cheetah and I lounge on my sofa. I think my friends are taking turns babysitting me. They've each individually given me a time slot this week that they want to hang out. I know they're just trying to keep my mind off Arizona half-naked on the other side of the world with Butch McVey draped all over her, having dinners with her, and buying her drinks that I know he purposefully spilled on her phone so she'd have to end the call with me.

"What if she drinks too much? Or what if she decides she wants to be with him? He's the big swinging dick of baseball now, not me. I'm just a regular guy who might never walk straight again."

He sighs. "Layton, look at me." I do. "You two are the real deal. I would give anything to have what you share with her. She's as into you as you are her. I'm certain of that."

"What if..."

Before I can finish my sentence, my phone rings. I look down and smile. "It's her."

"Answer it, Romeo."

I accept the FaceTime call and see her face. She's sitting in a very tiny, string bikini with a woman brushing her hair for her. It looks like she's on the beach but in a shaded area. She breathes, "Hey, superstar."

Before I can answer, I hear Butch's voice. "Yes, dear."

Cheetah's eyes widen.

She giggles. "I wasn't talking to you, dope."

He's in a fucking bathing suit too. He places his hands on her bare shoulders, leans over her, and smiles into the camera on her phone. "I want to see Layton too."

I hate his face. I hate that his bare body is touching hers. He's covered in tats. He looks like he belongs in a motorcycle bar, not on a beach with my gorgeous girl.

I notice her squirm out of his touch. That makes me smile.

I ask, "Where are you?"

"In the production tent on the beach. It's the only place I can get reception besides the villa. We're about to shoot. I'm in hair and makeup. I figured it was the best time to call. You'll be asleep by the time we're done, and I didn't want to go the day without talking to you."

"You don't need any makeup. You're naturally beautiful."

Her face softens before dickhead interrupts again.

"That's what I told them too. She doesn't need anything. My girlfriend is sexy as hell."

She turns her head and warns, "Watch it, Butch. Go put on your makeup. I think you need it more than me."

Cheetah and I smile at each other.

She looks back at the phone. "What are you up to today?"

I move the phone so she can see Cheetah. He wiggles his eyebrows. "Move that top down a drop so I can see your pink nipples. I dream of them every night." He flicks his tongue suggestively.

She smiles and shakes her head at him. "That was a one-time show. I was desperate for my sexy man. It had been too long."

"Do you want me to scratch his chest for you? It was so hot when you did that. I think I have a new fetish from watching it."

She bites her lip. "I think I left deep enough marks on him that they should still be there."

I smirk as I lift my shirt and show them both the evidence of her statement. "I wear them proudly. I can't wait for a refresher. From you, not Cheetah."

We all laugh.

We chat for a bit before she's called to go shoot. We hang up and Cheetah has a pained look on his face. "Yep, he definitely wants to fuck her."

I blow out a breath. "I know. And right now, they're shooting with his hands all over her body." I tug on my hair. "The thought is driving me insane."

"Sorry, man. It sucks."

"How did I become this person? Maybe this is why I've never had a girlfriend before now."

He gives me a compassionate look. "You never had a

girlfriend because you never met the right one. Now you have. We both know that. Don't deny it."

I blow out a long breath. "I won't deny it. You're right. I just hate our circumstances at the moment. I'm miserable."

He gives me a hopeful look. "The gang is going out this weekend. You should come with us."

"I don't know..."

"You're coming. It will be good for you. You can't sit here and pine after her for two months. A distraction will be good for you. Sitting here thinking of him touching her isn't healthy. Try to stay busy. Time goes by faster when you're busy. Find a new hobby other than jerking off to her picture."

I give him the finger. "Do you think she's better off with him?"

He rolls his eyes. "Fuck no. He's a douche. Stop letting him mess with your head. You two are the real deal. Even a blind man can see that. I meant what I said. I would give anything to have what you have with her."

"Really? You seem to like the bachelor life."

"It's getting a little old. My mother is driving me nuts about not being married and giving her more grandkids. I'm going home for the holidays, and I know it's going to be nothing but a verbal attack from everyone about me still being a bachelor. My six siblings have produced seventeen grandkids. I'm the black sheep of the family. I'm half tempted to hire someone to pretend to be my girlfriend for the holidays just to keep them all off my back."

"You should take Kam home with you. You guys have become friends, and you have a good time together."

He lets out a laugh. "Kam and my family? Umm...no.

Bailey would be perfect though. My mother would love her. Not a bad idea, Lancaster."

ARIZONA

I can't help but start laughing. "Oh my god, stop tickling me."

Butch chuckles. "It helps you relax. Stop being so uptight. Have fun with this. There are worse things we could be doing to earn a buck."

He's standing behind me on the beach, his front pressed against my back. We've been taking photos for hours. It's been a long day, our third in a row of shooting. I more than welcome the day off tomorrow.

The photographer instructs, "Butch, put your thumbs in the sides of her bikini bottoms. Like you're about to pull them down."

He immediately obliges, always anxious to touch me. If he pulls them down too far, I will turn around and punch him in the face.

The difference between him and Layton is remarkable. Butch takes advantage of every opportunity to have his hands on my body, without ever seeking permission from me. Even the first night Layton and I went to that party, he asked permission to touch my back. He asked permission to hold my hand. At our photo shoot, he always sought my agreement before taking things up a notch. That's how a man is supposed to treat a woman. Not like Butch who gropes me whenever he can without giving it a second thought.

He's so self-absorbed that he doesn't even pick up on my

overt cues that I don't like it. How did I get myself involved in this?

I can't wait for a day off tomorrow. I need a break from him.

He pulls me close to his body. I can feel his erection. Ugh.

I wiggle away, creating distance between us, but he simply steps forward and does it all over again.

He whispers in my ear, "Want to go for a hike tomorrow? There's a volcano nearby."

"I'm exhausted. I might just relax tomorrow and do some reading by the pool. If I'm up for it, I'll get in a workout."

"Cool. I'll do it with you."

Fucking great.

CHAPTER TWENTY-SEVEN

LAYTON

I t's Saturday night and I just ordered an Uber to take me to meet my friends at Screwballs. It's twenty minutes out.

Arizona has FaceTimed me the past three days at the same time, while she's in hair and makeup. Butch is always hanging around. She flinched at his touch the first day. She didn't the next two. She's getting used to him touching her. Comfortable with it.

There's already been a photo of them on location and speculation has begun about us breaking up and them now dating. I knew this was coming, but it doesn't make it hurt any less. I'm sure Longley will gradually roll out their relationship until it's a frenzy just as their promotional tour begins.

I wobble through my lobby. Frederick rushes to help me. "It's splendid to see you out and about, Master Lancaster."

"Thanks, Frederick. I'm meeting some friends."

"For cigars and brandy, sir?"

"Umm, sure." More like beer and peanuts.

Frederick kindly helps me into my Uber, which I take to Screwballs. I smile when I maneuver my way inside and see all my friends sitting in our booth. I'm glad I came. I desperately needed this.

Using my crutches, I slowly make my way to the table. I knew Trey and Gemma weren't coming, but I also don't see Bailey. I look at Kam. "Where's your sister?"

"She's babysitting Harper tonight."

"Oh, I didn't realize Tanner was out tonight." I thought he mentioned that he was staying in. I must be mistaken.

I notice a new girl sitting with Ezra. She's adorable. I hold out my hand. "Hi, I'm Layton."

"Hi, Layton. I met you a few years ago. I'm Daisy, Ezra's childhood friend."

That sort of rings a bell, but I play it off as best I can. "Oh right. I didn't recognize you. Umm, your hair is different."

She nods. "Yes, it's shorter."

"Are you in town visiting?" Ezra is from a small town in the Midwest.

She nods. "I am."

"What was little Ezra like as a kid?"

She smiles at him. "The same as he is now. Sweet, talented, and handsome."

Ezra has his arm around her and squeezes her close. "Aw, stop it. You're making me blush. I'm telling Steve you said that."

I pinch my eyebrows together. "Steve?"

Ezra nods. "Her fiancé."

Fiancé? Ezra and Daisy look very comfortable together. It's weird. Whatever. Not my business.

Cheetah winks at me. "You're last to arrive, buddy. Pay the piper."

"Seriously? Have you seen how slow I am these days? I'll be last to everything."

Cheetah shrugs. "Sorry, man. You know the rules."

I sigh as I sit with my giant cast hanging out of the booth like a robot. "It's a proven fact that cuddling can relieve physical pain."

Cheetah starts laughing. "Do you want me to come home with you tonight to cuddle? You can be the big spoon if you want."

I roll my eyes.

Ripley gives me a soft smile. "I like that one. It's sweet. Have you spoken with Arizona today?"

"Yep. I got to watch Butch grope her via FaceTime for my benefit for what feels like the hundredth day in a row."

She takes my hand and squeezes it. "It's not like she's enjoying it. She loves you. She misses you."

I let out a breath. "I hope so. This whole thing is fucked. I should have paid her way out of the contract."

I tried but Tanner wouldn't let me.

My train of thought is broken by a sultry, female voice. "Hey, Layton."

I look up and see Delta standing next to me in barely there clothing. "Hi, Delta. Long time, no see. How are you?"

She tucks her dark hair behind her ear. "I'm well. I hear you're on the market again. We should hang out."

"You heard wrong."

She pulls out her phone. After fiddling with it for a

minute, she hands it to me, pointing to the screen. It's a photo of Arizona and Butch at one of their shoots. She looks so beautiful. Her long, blonde hair is messed to perfection. Her eyes are sparkling. She's already tan. Butch has his hands on her hips and they're both laughing.

I feel like my heart is being ripped out. She's smiling at him. She should be smiling at me.

I toss it back at her. "It's just a photo shoot. They're playing it up for the cameras. It's their job."

Her eyes widen. "It doesn't look like an act to me. There have been photos of them on dates too."

Ripley practically snarls. "He's not interested. Hit the road. No skanks welcome here."

Delta narrows her eyes at Ripley. "What are you going to do, fat ass? Sit on m..."

Before the sentence is even finished, Quincy pops out of his seat with speed I didn't know he was capable of and gets right in Delta's face. "If you ever talk to her like that again, it will be the last words you utter."

Delta's eyes widen in fear while the rest of us look at each other in shock. We've never seen this side of Quincy. Yes, he threw shade at me for a while, but not like this.

He motions for the attention of the owner and gives a mock slice across the neck while pointing to Delta. Within seconds, the owner walks over and escorts her out with Quincy crossing his arms, glaring at her the entire way.

Ezra pulls Quincy's shirt. "Have a seat, Q. Relax, big bear."

He ignores Ezra and sits next to Ripley. "Are you okay?"

She gives a small smile. "I'm fine. It doesn't bother

me. I've had comments like that my whole life. I'm used to it."

He rubs her face. "It's not fine. No one should talk to you like that. You're beautiful. You're perfect."

She mumbles something we can't hear which only serves to enrage him further. He stands and pulls her arm. "I need to talk to you. Now!"

They walk away and disappear behind the corner.

I shake my head in disbelief. "What just happened? Is something going on with them?"

Kam leans back in her seat with a self-satisfied smile. "I've been saying for months that I think they're fucking in secret. At a minimum, she has a crush on him and hasn't done anything about it because of Arizona. But tonight, I'm realizing it's definitely not a one-sided thing."

I nod. "I think you're right. I've never seen him territorial about a woman like that. I've never even seen him give a shit about a woman, besides Arizona, before tonight."

They all start speculating about Quincy and Ripley while I pull out my phone and scroll through the newly leaked beach photos. They're not nearly as sexy as our photos, but she looks happy. I don't want her to be sad, but I want to be the one making her smile. I should stop looking at these photos. It's not healthy, but I can't seem to help myself. Every morning I wake up to a new wave of them.

Cheetah throws his arm around Kam. "I think you need to give me a second chance." He rubs her arm. "You have to admit, before the Hoover Dam broke, it was going well. Our bodies worked together like a well-oiled machine."

She removes his arm. "Sorry, kitten. Like a porn star, you blew it."

He groans. "That's such bullshit. It's not my fault the waterbed popped. Can we at least make another bet? One that gives me a fighting chance." He looks around. "Pick any girl."

Kam sighs in frustration before her face turns uncharacteristically serious. "I've got one for you, big mouth. Tell me two authentic things about me that have nothing to do with sex, my body, or my current softball team. If you actually know anything substantive about me, I'm yours for the night to do with as you please." She crosses her arms and tilts her head to the side, assuming she's busted him.

Cheetah smiles, intertwines his fingers, and stretches them out while cracking his knuckles. He literally hands Ezra his beer and says, "Hold my beer."

Turning back to Kam, he leans toward her, almost in challenge. "Kamryn Sarah Hart, age twenty-eight, is the younger of identical twins by nine minutes. Incidentally, that's also your number, but we're not talking about the Anacondas. Your parents are Beverly and Chris. They still live in the same Southern Florida house that you grew up in. You have no other siblings. You were the Gatorade Player of the Year in the state of Florida during your senior year of high school. You had your choice of full athletic scholarships to any college in the country. You chose UCLA because they were willing to take Bailey, who, at the time, wasn't considered as strong of a player as you. You like dark chocolate, not milk chocolate. It's your comfort food. Milk chocolate makes you gassy. You love dogs but realize you can't have one right now because of your life on the road. When you retire, which you plan to do after the twenty-eight Olympics, your first order of business will be to adopt a dog. You smell like peaches, and I know firsthand that you taste like them too, but I'm not allowed to talk about your body. You don't like Doublemint Gum. You and Bailey were in a commercial for it when you were little kids, and they made you chew it for days until it started to physically make you sick. You refused to ever chew it again. You chew grape bubblegum on the field and blow giant bubbles that make my dick hard because I've never been more jealous of a piece of gum in my life. You hate it when..."

Before he finishes, Kam's lips smash with his. He immediately pulls her onto his lap. As though no one else is around, they grind and go at it for a solid five minutes until he slides out of the booth, with her still attached to him, and walks out the front door.

Ezra's eyes look like they're about to bug out of his head. "What the hell was that? How did he know all those things?"

I shake my head. "I have no idea."

ARIZONA

We finished our first full week of shooting. Honestly, I thought it would be easy to pose for a few pictures. I didn't realize how exhausting it is. It's not only the long days of shooting, but it's also doing it without the man whose hands I want on my body. Feeling like I'm on guard at all times makes it more stressful and tiring.

I want to crawl into bed and call Layton, but I'm having dinner with Butch tonight. It's one of the pre-arranged reservations made by Michael Longley, who checks in daily to remind me of my obligation to make it look like Butch and I are dating. He also told me that he doesn't care for me wearing sweatpants and oversized T-shirts when Butch and I go to nice restaurants. He sent a dress for me to wear tonight. A tight, revealing dress.

Butch knocks on my door at the allotted time. His eyes widen when I open it. "Wow. You look beautiful."

"Thank you. You clean up nicely too."

He offers me his arm as we make the short walk into the village.

The restaurant is actually on a beautiful beach setting with music playing. The moon is illuminating the water. The ocean looks majestic. I take a quick picture of it and text it to Layton.

> Me: Promise me we'll come back here one day so you can make love to me on this beach at night.

I get no response until I see that the text bounced back as unsent. The reception here sucks. We only get it in our villa and on the beach because the production company paid for Wi-Fi at the shoot. Otherwise it would just be the villa.

I sigh in frustration. I guess I'll send it later.

We sit at the table and Butch orders us a bottle of wine. He doesn't bother to ask if I want wine. I rarely ever drink it. If I were here with Layton, I'd already have my favorite beer waiting for me. That, or a tequila shot.

I start to wonder if I've taken for granted the way my boyfriend treats me. He always has my beer of choice waiting when I arrive somewhere. We never mention it. He just does it for me. He does a lot of things for me without me asking. He oils my glove, cleans my hairbrush, always has the food I like in his refrigerator, has made space for me in his bathroom, always compliments me, and treats my friends well. Layton Lancaster is a unicorn.

"Are you texting him?"

I realize my head has been buried in the phone as I think about my man. I miss him so much.

Knowing I'm being kind of rude, I place my phone on the table. "Sorry. Yes, but there's no reception here."

We chat for a bit. I slowly sip the wine, not caring for it. He still manages to fill my glass every few minutes.

He smiles. "Is it true that you and Layton started as a PR relationship?"

"Where did you hear that?"

"Around town. A few people have mentioned it."

I don't feel like he needs to know the whole story. "We were asked to make a few appearances together. Things quickly took off from there. There's absolutely nothing fake about us."

He nods. "I see. You know, he'll probably never play ball again."

"Layton is strong. He can accomplish whatever he sets his mind to. He's overcome a lot in his life. If he wants to play again, he'll play. If he doesn't, he won't. Frankly, I just want him to be happy."

"For your career, you might be better off on a different arm. One who's a bright star, not a fading one."

"I have a good career because I've worked my ass off and I'm a great softball player. My love life has nothing to do with it. Back off, Butch."

Realizing a change of topic is needed, he challenges, "Tell me a secret. Something no one else knows about you."

Not interested in having a bad relationship with him, given the amount of time we have to spend together, I decide to play his little game. "Hmm. When I was in Little League, like five or six years old, I was afraid to miss a minute of the games. If I had to pee during a game, I'd just go in my softball pants." I smile. "It happened at least a dozen times."

He lets out a deep laugh. "That's priceless. Kind of gross and endearing all at the same time."

I nod as I sip my wine. "Definitely gross. I'm not sure about it being endearing. And you? Tell me something no one else knows."

"It's hard to think of something that no one knows. I'm a pretty open guy. Oh, I've got something. I was a competitive ballroom dancer as a young kid."

"Is that a thing young kids do?"

"It is. My mother made me take lessons as soon as I could walk. She was a dancer back in the day. I was one of those kids with slicked-back hair and tight clothes, dancing the mamba at eight years old." He mock-dances in his seat as he says it.

I can't help but laugh at the image. "Can you still dance?"

"I can." He motions his head toward the orchestra playing lyric-less music. "I'd love to show you."

I nod. "You're on. I need to see this."

He stands and holds out his hand. "Join me."

I shake my head. "No, I don't dance well. I just want to watch you."

"I don't dance alone. Ballroom dancing is meant to be with a partner."

I sigh, dropping my napkin on the table. "Fine. Just so I can see it with my own eyes."

He smiles as he takes my hand, and we make our way to the dance floor. He whispers something to one of the orchestra members and then slips him some money.

Suddenly they start playing an upbeat Latin-sounding

tune. I don't know the difference between a tango, a samba, and a mamba, but it's along those lines.

He grabs my hips and brings them flush to his. I gasp at the unexpected contact.

"Relax. It's part of the dance. It's all in the hip movements. Follow my lead."

He begins moving his hips to the beat and forcing mine to move with him, giving me instructions the whole time.

He's genuinely a great teacher and an incredible dancer. I learn a few moves and we end up dancing to several songs. I'm having fun for the first time since we've been here.

I eventually notice that our food has arrived, and I motion toward the table. We sit and have an enjoyable meal together.

CHAPTER TWENTY-EIGHT

ARIZONA

Last night wasn't terrible. We had a good time. He was funny. We did a lot of laughing. It was nice to finally feel a little relaxed.

My phone rings and I see that it's Ripley FaceTiming me. I miss her so much. "Hey, Rip."

"Hey, girlie. How's it going?"

"I miss home, but I'm trying to make the best of it."

"Glad to hear it. Is it as beautiful as it looks in the pictures?"

"Even more beautiful. It's a part of Earth that's hard to imagine exists in real life."

"And Butch? How's he?"

"He's fine. A little flirty and handsy, but he knows I'm with Layton. We get along."

"Have you spoken with Layton?"

"Of course. Every day."

She bites her lip.

"Why the look? What's happening?"

She shrugs. "He's not doing well."

"Is it his leg?"

"No, babe. It's you. He said Butch's hands are always on you when you two FaceTime. Have you seen all the photos that Fantasy Suits has been leaking?"

"No. The internet is crazy restricted in this country. I haven't seen anything."

"Every single day, they're leaking new, provocative shots of you and Butch."

"We're shooting bathing suit ads. I'm not sure what I'm supposed to do to prevent that from happening."

"It's not just those—though they're hot too—it's you two hanging out. Did you go dancing with him last night?"

I sigh. "We were having dinner. We danced for a few songs. It wasn't intimate or anything. We're just friends."

"That's not how it looked. I saw Layton before that photo leaked and he was a mess about you and Butch. The guys said he wouldn't get out of bed after the dancing photos and videos came out."

"There are photos and videos of us dancing?"

"Yes."

I blow out a breath. "Shit. Why is he being so insecure? I've never given him a reason to not trust me."

"If the situation was reversed, how would you feel? Seeing Layton half-naked with another woman. Seeing him dancing and laughing with her."

I sigh. "Yeah, I get it. I didn't see any photographers at our dinner. Can you take a few screenshots of the photos online and send them to me? Maybe screen record the videos."

"Sure. I'll do it right now. Give me two minutes."

After a bit of silence, she sends them over and I'm in shock at what I see. They're professional shots. The videos too. I know immediately that it was arranged beforehand, which means Butch and Michael planned the whole thing. His whole ballroom dancer bit was a gimmick to catch us in provocative photos outside of the beach shots. I'm such an idiot.

"Shit. These look way worse than it was. I swear."

"I know, babe. There's probably someone else that needs to hear that."

"I'll call him. How are things otherwise?"

"Good. It's so nice to make money with all these sponsorships. This is the first off-season I don't have to work a nine-to-five job to pay the bills. I see Kam a lot. We don't see Bailey much. She's busy at the Montgomery house. Kam thinks she's banging Tanner."

"Really?"

"Yep. She's convinced of it."

"Wow. Has Bailey said anything?"

"She's denying it."

"What about Ezra?"

"I don't know. Like I said, we barely see her. He did bring a woman with him when we went out. Apparently, she's engaged and they're just old friends, but they were all over each other."

"What about the guys? It sounds like you've seen them."

"We've seen them. We went to Screwballs. That's where I saw Layton."

"I'm glad he's getting out."

"Some of the skanks at Screwballs are smelling blood in the water with you and Layton. They're hitting on him and showing him pictures of you and Butch."

"Seriously?"

"Yes." She raises an eyebrow. "How does that make you feel?"

"Of course I'm upset. Who wouldn't be?"

"So imagine how much worse it is for him to have to see

pictures of you and Butch every day. In *very* compromising positions."

"I get it. I'm calling him now.

"Arizona?"

"Yes?"

"You've come back to life over the past few months. Don't risk anything changing that. Layton loves you and treats you the way you deserve. Marc never loved you like that."

"I know. You're right. Thanks. Love you."

"Love you too."

We hang up and I feel like shit. Layton deserves more than me talking to him when I'm surrounded by Butch and other people. I've been ignoring his needs. We need to be playful like we've always been. Our calls are always rushed.

I smile, knowing exactly what we need.

Five minutes later, the FaceTime is ringing. He answers sitting on his couch in his boxers. His hair is a mess and there are food containers everywhere. I didn't realize how bad it had gotten.

I breathe, "Hey, superstar."

He doesn't even look at the phone. Without any expression on his face, he mumbles, "Is that for me or Butch?"

Oh no, he's really hurting.

"Why don't you look into the phone and find out?"

He looks down and his eyes widen. I'm lying naked on my bed with my legs slightly open.

He sucks in a breath. "Holy fuck." He squeezes his eyes shut for a moment. "I miss you."

I run my hands over my breasts. "I miss your hands on my body. I miss you making me moan. It's been so long." I pull out my vibrator and run it around my nipples. "Let's go to the bullpen together. Talk me through it. I need you to get me off." I lick my lips suggestively. "Are you ready to play ball?"

His jaw slackens as he slips his hand into his boxer shorts and begins stroking himself. Eyeing my toy, he asks, "Is that Captain America?"

I nod. "It's a poor substitute for my real Captain America."

He smiles. "He's Captain America Junior." After rubbing himself for a moment, he abruptly stands. "Wait one second. I have an idea."

He quickly moves off camera and then returns moments later with his Captain America mask on and his boxers nowhere to be found. I giggle. "I think you with nothing on but that mask just moved to the top of my wet dreams."

I hear him chuckle. It's music to my ears. This is exactly what we needed. Fun, intimate time together.

"Sunshine, spread your legs wide. Move the camera and let me see your pink pussy."

I do, giving him an extremely up-close view of what he wants.

"Now run Captain America Junior gently through your pussy until it's nice and wet."

"I've been wet since the second your face came on camera. I miss you." I run it through me. "I wish this was you. When you run your giant tip through me, I can barely control myself."

"Me too, sunshine." He's pumping that gorgeous cock of his. "Are you nice and wet? Wet enough to handle my cock?"

I bring the camera close so he can see. "Yes. Can you see what you do to me?"

"Keep the camera right where it is and slide Captain America Junior in. I want to see the moment it enters you."

I do and let out a moan. "His head isn't as big as yours. Do you have any idea how good it feels the exact moment your tip pushes inside me? I feel it in my whole body. I have to hold back so I don't come on the spot. There's nothing better."

I see him smile. I'm just now realizing how many days it's been since I've seen him smile. Too long. I've been selfish.

"Turn it on." I do. "Slide it deep, where we know you like it. I love how deep you need it. I love that I can give it to you there."

I push it in as deep as it will go. "Oh god, Layton. You know my body so well. I ache for you. No one has ever known my body like you. No one has ever made me come like you. *Ever.*"

He takes a deep inhale with his nose. "I can almost smell you, sunshine. You have no idea what your scent does to me." His cock is oozing, hard as a missile.

"I know, superstar. That's why I rush to the stadium to give you pre-game reminders. I love it when you smell your fingers before each at-bat. Our dirty secret for no one else in the world to know."

"You're my muse. Your scent is my fuel, and your taste..." He squeezes his eyes shut and smiles. "It's a pussy power bar."

I giggle. "I've never seen that in stores."

"Because your pussy power bars are for *me* only. I played so well the last half of the season because of you. Because I love you so fucking much."

My back arches as I move the vibrator in and out as fast as I can. "Ahh. I need you. I need to feel your hands. Your cock. All of it. I love you too."

"Slap your pussy the way you like it."

I try to slap my pussy the way he does it but it's definitely not the same. "I need it to be you. I love it when you slap me. It drives me wild."

"Next time I see you, I'm going to slap your pussy so fucking hard. You'll come before my cock even touches your body."

"Oh god. I want that. I can almost feel it. I'm coming, come with me."

I scream out into my orgasm just as he grunts into his.

I look into the camera and see his come-covered stomach. I breathlessly whimper, "I wish I was there to lick that off or, better yet, rub it into my body."

His cock jerks at my words and another squirt exits his tip. He's so fucking sexy.

Just then, there's a loud knock at my door. I hear Butch's voice shout, "Zona, let's go get a drink."

I look at the phone and see Layton's smile completely drop. Ugh. Why did Butch need to pick this moment to knock on my door? We were making progress and he ruined it.

I shout back. "I'm tired. Go without me."

He attempts to open my door, but it's locked. "Why is your door locked?"

"Because I don't want to be disturbed. Just go."

"I'll wait to see if you change your mind. We can go to that seafood place you like."

The one he likes, not me.

"I won't change my mind. I want to talk to my *real* boyfriend. Goodbye, Butch."

I look back down at my phone to Layton's defeated face. "You should go if you want."

"I'd rather talk to you." I sigh. "I know this is difficult for you. It's difficult for me too."

His face hardens. It's unlike him. "I don't go out and dance with women though. You don't have to wake up every morning to photos and videos of me with another woman's hands all over me. One that told you point blank that she's going to steal me away from you."

"He said that to you?"

He nods.

"I'm sorry about the dancing. I was duped. It was totally innocent, but I promise I won't make that mistake again."

He's silent.

"Layton, I know this is less than ideal. Work with me. I want us to be okay. Why don't you tell me about your day?"

He knocks on his cast. "It's hard to do anything with this fucking thing, plus it's been cold outside. It's easier to just stay home."

"You should go visit the kids. Even though the season is over, I know they'd love to see you. You mentioned teaching the older kids how to make bats. You can still do that with your cast."

His face softens. "That's not a bad idea. I'm having Thanksgiving food delivered there in two weeks. I usually see them then."

"What are you doing for Thanksgiving?"

"I just told you. I'll stop by there in the afternoon to make sure they received everything."

"What about Henry?"

"He's weird around the holidays. He and I will probably meet up for dinner once I'm done at Linda's." He mumbles, "Hopefully."

My heart breaks a little for both of them. I need to talk to my parents and Quincy about it. Maybe our friends too.

CHAPTER TWENTY-NINE

LAYTON

Every day. Every damn day there are new photos of Butch with his hands all over my girl. I know Michael Longley is doing this to drive a wedge between Arizona and me, but it doesn't make it any easier. At least the photos of them in public have been minimal. Nothing as bad as the morning two weeks ago when I woke up to a million photos and videos of her dancing and smiling in his arms, but I'm still having trouble seeing her with him.

Like an immature child, I ignored her most recent call, knowing what I had originally planned for this specific day before my injury. She didn't know about it, and it's not her fault, but I just can't talk to her right now. I want to wallow in my misery.

I'm lying in my bed, like I do most of the time, when the lights in my bedroom flick on. I rub my eyes. "What the fuck?" I see Quincy at the door. "Why are you here in the middle of the night?"

"It's noon, Lancaster." He sniffs a few times and then has a look of disgust on his face. "Why does it smell so bad in here?"

I point to my cast and mumble, "It's hard for me to shower with this thing. It's a whole fucking production."

"I'm not sponge bathing you like my sister does, but I'll help you into the shower."

I can't help but smile thinking about her sponge baths. "Hmm. She gives the *best* sponge baths."

He narrows his eyes. "Not a word about it."

I chuckle "How did you get up here?"

"Even your fucking doorman is worried about you. He called up here twice and then just let me up when you didn't answer. I think he thought you were dead. He also thinks it's eighteenth-century England. What's wrong with that dude?"

"He must have been a butler in a previous life. I get a kick out of it." I cover my eyes. "Can you turn off the lights? I have a headache."

"No. You're being pathetic. If you have a headache, take some Advil like a normal person. I'll get you some."

He opens the drawer in my night table and sucks in a breath. He points into the drawer. "What the fuck is that? Is it what I think it is?"

He pulls out a velvet ring box and I nod.

"May I?"

I nod again.

He opens it. "Wow. It's beautiful. Is this for my sister?"

I lay my head back on my pillow and blow out a breath. "It was. I bought it before my injury."

"Isn't it a little soon for this? You haven't been together that long."

"It doesn't matter. She's in Thailand with Butch fucking McVey. I had the most perfect spot picked out there. Today was the day it was going to happen. If she couldn't be with her family for Thanksgiving, I wanted it to still be special for her. They're not shooting. She told me yesterday that she and Butch are going to the very spot I had picked out to propose. Obviously she didn't know what I was planning, but it still fucking hurts. It should be me there with her. Me proposing to her. Instead, he's with her." I pull my hair. "I can't get the image of them there out of my head."

His face falls. "I'm sorry. That sucks, but you can't sit here and wallow in your misery."

"Do you think there's anything going on between them?"

Without missing a beat, he says, "No. Absolutely not. Maybe my sister isn't perfect, but she's loyal. She wouldn't cheat on you or anyone. It's not who she is. And despite my protests, she's in love with you."

"Do you think she's just staying with me out of pity?"

"No. Fortunately for you, she's not seeing how pathetic you are right now. Where's arrogant Layton Lancaster? The one who thought he was god's gift to women. What the fuck happened to you?"

I knock on my cast. "This happened?"

"Snap out of it. It's a temporary setback. Shit happens."

My body deflates. "I want to snap out of it. Fuck, Q, I've never felt like I had this much to lose. Maybe this is why I never let anyone get close. I lost my parents. I lost my grandmother. Even the Greenes tossed me to the side of the road like I meant nothing. And then I find this amazing, perfect woman. One that I genuinely see myself spending the rest of my life with. I don't know if I can bear to lose her too. I'm...I'm terrified."

He sits on the edge of my bed. His shoulders sink. "I'm sorry for everything you've been through. I never thought about it like that. We complain that our parents aren't involved enough in our lives, but I know we're lucky to have parents that love us." He places his hand on my shoulder. "She loves you. Trust me, she does. And Arizona Abbott loves with her whole heart."

"Will you call me a pussy if I tell you I miss her? That it's like I can't breathe without her?"

He looks up at my ceiling. "You're a pussy for having a poster of my sister on your ceiling, not for missing your girlfriend." He shrugs. "I miss her too. She's a bright light in all of our lives, not just yours."

"The brightest. It's like I finally knew where I belonged. She feels like home. And Butch is a huge star trying to steal her any chance he gets. I'm a sinking ship. He's the *it guy*. How can I compete?"

"I don't think that's how she sees it, but you should talk to her, not me. She's worried about you. She asked me to come see you."

"She did?" At least I know she cares.

"Yes. You're coming to Thanksgiving tonight, right?"

"Are you sure your family wants Henry and me?" For the past few years I've done afternoon Thanksgivings at Linda's House and then usually would have a quiet meal with Henry. When Quincy invited me to Thanksgiving with the Abbotts, I asked about Henry, and they were more than welcoming.

He sighs. "I'm only telling you this because I think you need to hear it. I was supposed to go to California for Thanksgiving. Arizona called my parents and begged them to come here so that you and Henry could have a nice family holiday. You know what a big deal it is for them to travel. She's paying for them to come. All to make sure you'd have a happy Thanksgiving."

I run my hands through my hair. "Fuck. I ignored her call earlier. I'm such an asshole."

"I knew that all along." He scrunches his nose. "Butch McVey is a dweeb. There's no way my sister ends up with someone who has a man bun."

I smile. "You have longer hair."

"And yet do you ever see it in a man bun?"

I let out a laugh. "Not once."

"Right." He stands and sighs. "Come on. I'll help you shower. I can't live with your stink anymore. I won't subject my parents to it. Is there something to cover the cast?"

I nod toward the big plastic wrap in the corner of my room. He grabs it and returns. "I'm about to say something I never thought I'd say. Lancaster, drop your drawers."

I slide off the bed, stand as best as I can, and drop my boxers to the ground.

He scrunches his face. "Why is the head of your dick so fucking big?"

I smile. "Your sister doesn't mind. In fact, she loves it."

His face falls. "You want me to break your other leg?"

I laugh and it feels good. "She especially likes it when I..." I purposefully don't finish that sentence. I simply wink at him.

He allows a small smile to break free. "I'm going to let it slide just this once because I'm happy to see a smile on your face. Just once, Lancaster. You keep that shit between you and her."

I nod. With a straight face, I say, "We should *head* to the shower."

He narrows his eyes at me.

"Do you need a *head* start?"

"Lancaster."

"No worries. I'll *head* that way and you can follow when you're ready."

He growls. "You're a dead man."

AFTER MY SHOWER, we stop by Linda's House. The kids all run to me when I walk in the door, not having seen them since my injury. I should be spending more time here instead of wallowing in self-pity. I decide at that moment that I need to get my act together and stop hiding from the world. Stop being depressed about my injury. Stop being depressed about Arizona and the entire Fantasy Suits situation. These kids need me. I think I need them too.

Randy sucks in a breath when he notices Quincy. "Quincy 'The Ace' Abbott?"

Quincy smiles. "That's me. Are you Randy 'The Rocket' Richards?"

Randy's eyes widen. "You've heard of me?"

Quincy shrugs. "According to my sister, you're the best nine-year-old pitcher in the country. Is that true?"

"Coach Z said that?"

Quincy nods. "She did. She told me that I need to

work with you over the winter to help you develop a change-up. Are you interested?"

"You want to teach me the Cookie?" A Cookie is an easily hittable pitch. Even though a change of speed is necessary at higher levels, younger kids don't like to throw it, preferring to show off the faster pitches.

Quincy lets out a laugh. "Yep. I'm told my *Cookie* is pretty good. You need to have a solid change-up if you want to take things to the next level." He holds up a big bag I hadn't noticed and looks around at all the kids. "Can I interest you all in signed balls? I have enough for everyone."

The kids all explode in happiness. I mouth to him, "Thank you."

He smiles in return.

I get to enjoy watching them eat the food I had sent for their Thanksgiving feast. While they're eating dessert, I pull Perry aside.

"Buddy, you know I have to do a lot of physical therapy to get my leg back into shape, right?"

He nods, rarely choosing to speak.

"I was talking to my physical therapist about you. His name is Nick, and he helps people build muscles after injuries. Nick wants to help you build muscles in your arm. I checked with Linda to make sure it's okay, and it is."

Perry looks down. He's frightened.

"Honestly, I'm a little scared to go to physical therapy by myself. I haven't used my leg in a long time. I need a friend to come with me to work on muscle-building. Will you be that friend? We can build our muscles together."

Perry looks up and smiles as he nods his head.

"Phew. I was nervous, but now that I know you'll be with me, I feel better."

Just then, the doorbell rings. I see Linda make her way toward the front door. A minute later, she walks back in and looks at me. "There's someone at the door for you."

"For me?"

"Yes, you."

I slowly walk to and open the front door, completely shocked to see Henry standing there, looking nervous. If there's one place Henry is unlikely to be seen, it's at any group home. "Henry? Is everything okay? I thought we were meeting at Quincy's place."

He looks around and takes a few deep breaths as if he's trying to calm himself. "Can we talk?"

"Of course. Are you okay?"

"I think so." He holds out a cup with a lid. "Here, I brought you some homemade hot chocolate. I thought you could use it right now."

I take it and smile at the gesture. "Thank you. What's going on?"

"Arizona called me."

"She did. What for?"

"She said you weren't doing well and that you might need to talk to me."

I'm such a dick. She's over there away from her family and friends, worrying about me, making sure I'm taken care of, and I can't be bothered to take her call. I don't deserve this woman, but I'm not letting her go.

"I was planning to see you in a few hours at Q's. You're still coming, right?"

"Yes. I just thought it might mean more to you if I

363

came here. I...I know how much this place and these kids mean to you. I want to try to understand it."

I hug him. I know this is a big deal for him. "It *does* mean a lot to me that you're here. I think it's a great first step for you."

"It is. But I realized that our relationship has always been about you taking care of me. You're clearly hurting right now. I want to be here for you too."

"I'm okay."

"You're not okay, and I want you to know that you can talk to me just like I sometimes need to talk to you. You don't have to pretend everything is perfect in front of me. That's how it's supposed to work for family, right?"

I nod. "You're right."

"And I want to give you the advice you've often given me. Sometimes life doesn't go as planned. You can't let it get you down. You can't let it push you into a black hole of despair."

I smile. "You *do* listen."

"Sometimes. But I'm being serious. I know what it's like to feel lonely, like the cards are stacked against you."

I nod. "I think that's how I feel. In some way, I've always felt it. I've been holding onto the Cougars because it was my family. Then this warm, kind, wonderful..."

"Hot."

I let out a laugh. "Hot woman came into my life. She filled it with everything I could ever want. And then I broke my leg and felt like I could lose her. It gutted me. I haven't handled myself well."

He takes in what I'm saying. "I clearly don't know dick about women, but I'm pretty sure this one isn't going anywhere."

"I hope you're right."

"Layton, I appreciate everything you've done for me. I'm not sure I've ever truly thanked you."

I place my hand on his shoulder. "It's been my pleasure. Can I introduce you to everyone? Can I give them a little background?"

He tentatively nods so I grab his arm, we walk inside, and we sit on the sofa together.

"Can you all gather around? I want to introduce you to my special friend."

They sit on the ground in front of us and I begin. "I think most of you know that, like you guys, my parents couldn't raise me. I lived with my grandmother throughout almost all of my childhood until I moved to Philadelphia to play for the Cougars."

Randy gives the Cougars claw and growls.

Henry laughs.

I continue. "My grandmother..."

Henry interrupts, "We called her Gammie."

I nod. "Yes, Gammie. Like Linda, she loved to take care of special children like you and me. Henry was also one of those special children. Yes, he's a little younger than me..."

Henry interrupts, "A lot younger," and all the kids giggle.

I smile. "Yes, he's *a lot* younger than me, but he and I became really good friends. When I was able to, I moved Henry to Philadelphia so he could be near me. Because even though we're not related by blood, Henry is like a brother to me."

Henry's eyes start to tear.

I continue, "You guys are forever linked by your time here. You're brothers and sisters in all the ways that

365

matter. So if you're having a day where you're feeling lonely or sad, remember all your brothers and sisters around you. That's what Henry and I do for each other. This way, we're never lonely or sad."

They all smile as they look around at one another.

Henry clears his throat. "If it's okay with Layton and Linda, I'd like to come hang out with you guys. Some people in our hometown thought I might be a better ballplayer than Layton. Maybe I can teach you a few tricks he doesn't know."

I can't help but laugh at that. The kids all join in.

The doorbell rings again and Linda gets up to answer it. About thirty seconds later, mine and Arizona's friends walk in.

I look at them all. "What are you doing here?" I turn to Cheetah. "I thought you were going home for the holiday?" I thought they all were going to their respective homes.

He shrugs. "Arizona called us all. She invited us to Quincy's feast with you. We decided to stick around."

I look up and down the line of people, including Ezra, Trey, Cheetah, Bailey, Kamryn, and Ripley. "All of you?"

They nod. Trey turns to the kids. "And we brought you guys lots of goodies."

The kids are all in awe as they receive gifts from their idols. I'm choked up with emotion over my friends' selflessness.

We sit around for a bit, hanging out with the kids. It snowed last night, so the kids ask to go out back and play, which Linda allows.

We're all standing at the window watching them when Kam looks at Linda. "Do you date?"

Linda lets out a laugh. "No, not in over a decade. Come to think of it, two decades."

Kam pulls out her phone. "We should make you a Tinder account. You're a hottie, Linda. What kind of men do you like? Or women? Or both?"

Linda lets out a laugh. "I'm seventy-two. My general preference is for *men* who are simply alive."

Kam smiles. "I've got this. We're going to find you someone."

I warn, "Kam. Leave it alone."

Cheetah shakes his head. "I agree with Kam. Linda should go on Tinder."

Linda pinches her eyebrows together. "What's Tinder?"

Ripley smiles. "It's a dating app."

I shake my head. "It's a hook-up app, not dating. It's not appropriate for her."

Linda appears confused. "What's the difference?"

I'm about to say it in benign words when Kam interrupts, "Tinder is basically for fucking. You see someone cute, meet up, and have sex. You can date if you want, but that's not the purpose of the app."

Linda thinks for a moment. I assume she's going to be disgusted, but she pulls out her phone and shrugs. "Maybe I should download the app and check it out."

I'm in shock.

She shows her phone screen to Kam. "Did I download the right app?"

Kam starts laughing hysterically. "Umm, that's Grindr, not Tinder."

Cheetah practically falls on the floor in laughter.

Linda's head toggles between the two of them. "What's that?"

Kam smirks. "Tinder for gay men."

Linda's eyes widen as she fumbles with her phone, pressing all kinds of buttons. "Oh no, I think I just committed to a year subscription to Grindr."

What the hell is happening right now? Less than an hour with Kam and she's committed to a year of Grindr.

Kam reaches for her phone. "Give it to me."

In the thirty minutes the kids are outside, Kam removes Grindr, installs Tinder, and they set up Linda's Tinder account, complete with a picture of her. I think they put Linda's face on Kam's body.

As they're discussing her answers to questions on Tinder, I hear another knock on the door.

I hold my hand up to Linda, who takes a step toward the door. "I've got it. I wouldn't want to pull you away from Tinder."

I slowly manage my way to the front door and open it, surprised to see Reagan standing there. There's an attractive blonde woman about her age standing with her. "Reagan? What are you doing here?"

She smiles. "Hey, Layton. This is my sister, Skylar."

Good lord. The knockout tree didn't miss anyone in this family. Skylar is stunning and looks more like Reagan than their other sister, Dr. Cooper. Unlike Reagan, Skylar has a sweet, shy appearance.

I hold out my hand. "Hi, I'm Layton Lancaster."

She smiles as she shakes it in return. "I know. It's nice to meet you. I'm Skylar Remington."

I look back at Reagan, wondering why they're here.

"Arizona mentioned this place and how much it means to you. I wanted to show you a little support." She and Skylar both lift big bags from the ground next to them. "Here are a few dozen Cougars and Anacondas jerseys along with a few other goodies. I thought you could distribute them to the kids." She hands me a large, bulky envelope. "And here are season ticket passes for next season for all of the kids as well. You can save them for Christmas if you want."

I take it in my hand, words momentarily escaping me. "This is really generous of you. Thank you."

"Our pleasure."

"Do you want to come in?"

"We're on our way to our mom's house for the holiday. All of our kids are in the car." I look at the street and notice a big car full of kids. There seems to be a lot.

Reagan must notice my look of surprise. "My sister is a breeding machine." Skylar playfully narrows her eyes at Reagan, but Reagan continues, "We just wanted to drop off everything. Have a happy Thanksgiving."

"Thank you. You too."

To say the kids flip out at the jerseys is a complete understatement. I'll save the season passes for Christmas when both Arizona and I can give them to the kids together.

I'm moved by everyone's actions, especially Arizona's in reaching out to so many people on my behalf.

ARIZONA

It's my first Thanksgiving away from my family. It would have been my first celebrating with Layton. This has been the longest month of my life. I'm so homesick. I want this photo shoot to be over.

Butch and I hiked today at a beautiful park today. I would have given anything to be there with Layton. It would have been so romantic.

He didn't take my call this morning. It hurt, but I know he's struggling with everything right now. I hope a nice Thanksgiving helps him manage the depression he seems to be suffering. I did my best to give him a happy day.

He and I have been up and down over the past few weeks. I don't know what else I can do. I'm trying, but he's being so insecure.

I need to be ready for dinner in five minutes, but I have time for a quick call to my mother to wish her a happy Thanksgiving.

I dial her number and she answers. "Arizona! How's my sweet girl?"

Hearing her voice makes me realize just how sad I am to not be with my family. My voice immediately breaks. "Not great, Mom."

"Oh no. What's wrong?"

"I'm homesick. I've never been without you guys for Thanksgiving. And I miss Layton so much. He's upset with me. I know how much seeing photos of me with Butch is hurting him. I hate it, but I don't know what else I'm supposed to do. It's out of my control. If I could get out of my contract, I would. He knows this."

"We'll see him tonight. I'll talk to him about it. I'm sure he knows how much you care for him. He misses you."

"Thank you for flying in. I want him to have a special day."

"It wasn't easy to get away again, but you ask for so little, we couldn't deny you this."

"Do you think I'm crazy for missing him so much? It's not

like we've been together that long. Did we get too intense, too fast?"

"Time doesn't matter. You're in love. You don't like to be away from him. That's normal. Why do you think I work with your father?"

"I guess I've never asked why you work with him. It's all I've ever known."

"I didn't at first. As you know, I was a teacher for many years. Your father was married to his job. I rarely saw him. I made the decision that if I couldn't beat him, I'd join him. Now we get to spend our days together."

I never thought of it that way. She works with him so she can be with him. It's kind of sweet.

"That's why you work all those crazy hours? Because you want to be with Dad?"

"It is."

"You missed so much for Quincy and me growing up. All to be with him?"

"Yes, I missed a few daytime activities here and there, which killed me. But he needed me at the store. I ran the business for him. I never missed anything of yours in the evenings. That was my hard line with him. We had dinner together every single night. I was a working woman, Arizona. I'd think you of all people would respect that. If I remained a teacher, I wouldn't have had my days off either."

"I suppose I never looked at it that way. I thought you simply chose the store over us."

I hear her sniffle. "I'm sorry you felt that way. I hope you know how much I love you and your brother. You two and your father are my world."

Butch knocks on my door and shouts, "Are you ready, Zona?"

I fucking hate that nickname. At this point, all things

Butch McVey annoy me. From his overly friendly touches to his over-confident demeanor. Layton has always been sexy and playfully confident. This guy is just asshole-arrogant confident. It's not attractive.

I'm on edge, but I know I have three more months, so I'm trying to keep it amicable. I'm one more misstep away from snapping though.

I pull the phone away from my head and yell back, "In a minute."

I bring the phone back to my ear. "I'm sorry if I upset you. I didn't mean to. You were an amazing mother. I'm sorry if I made you feel otherwise. I need to run. Unfortunately I have dinner with Butch. Give everyone my love. Tell Layton I miss him."

"I will, sweetie. Happy Thanksgiving."

"You too."

I head to dinner with Butch and we have an amiable meal. That's about all I'm capable of tonight.

He tries to grab my hand on the way out of the restaurant, but I pull away and he sighs. "We're supposed to be boyfriend and girlfriend."

"Butch, I have dinner with you almost every night. I'm living up to my end of the bargain. I know you have to touch me during the photo shoots, but outside of that, it makes me uncomfortable. It makes my boyfriend uncomfortable. You and I are fake. We're a boardroom creation with an expiration date. Layton is my real boyfriend. I need you to understand the difference. You seem to be struggling with reality."

"Why are you so loyal to him? He's probably banging half of Philadelphia while you're here keeping me at arm's length."

I narrow my eyes at him. "No, he's not. Clearly you don't understand the word commitment."

"He's yesterday's news. His career is over. Don't you see

how much sense you and I make? We're appealing both physically and on paper. You and Layton simply don't make sense anymore."

I'm so sick of this guy bashing Layton. "I'm not discussing Layton with you again. Frankly, my relationship with him is none of your business." I sigh in frustration. "Have you ever considered the fact that I'm simply not attracted to you? Even if I was single, which I'm not, you aren't my type. There are no circumstances in which you and I would ever be together."

He gives a cocky smile. "I'm everyone's type, sweetheart. And you clearly have a thing for ballplayers. I'm the best one around."

What is wrong with this guy? I think he has a screw loose. I point my finger in his face and raise my voice. "I find myself wondering if you have a hearing issue, so let me say this loud and clear. I'm not interested. You and I are *never* happening. I need you to respect my boundaries and keep your hands the fuck off me."

He rolls his eyes. Has this guy ever heard the word *no* in his life?

He pushes his big body against mine, pinning me to the building. He grabs my chin. "I think if you'd just..."

I snap. I've now asked him multiple times to stop touching me. He's not getting it, so I knee him in the balls. Hard. He goes down like a pile of bricks. "This is the last time I'll say this. Don't touch me. Stay the fuck away from me."

He grumbles, "You bitch."

"That's Mrs. Bitch to you. Actually, I'm Layton's bitch. By the way, he's a thousand times the man you are. When we're shooting, and you have to touch me, it makes me sick to my stomach. I have to pretend it's him just to get through every day with you."

I'm done with this guy. I walk away and leave him on the

ground in front of the restaurant. I don't give a shit that he's hurt, and I most definitely don't give a shit that we could have been photographed fighting.

I walk along the beach and think. I can't take another three months of pretending to be Butch McVey's girlfriend. I didn't mind him as a friend at first, but now he makes my skin crawl.

I'm not far from the production tent. As soon as I get close, my phone pings with all the texts and emails I missed for the two hours we were at dinner and didn't have cell service.

First, I see a text from my mother.

> Mom: No need to worry. That man of yours is so madly in love with you. It seems like he had a nice day with your brother.

I smile. I had asked Quincy to go over and talk to Layton and to go with him to Linda's House.

There's also a text from Layton.

> Layton: I'm sorry I've been an asshole. Thank you for everything you did for me today. You're the most amazing woman. I'm lucky you're mine. I love you. I miss you. Four weeks, one day, and seven hours until the real Captain America is with you again. The things I want to do to your body are probably illegal in Thailand anyway. Happy Thanksgiving. It's the last one we'll ever spend apart.

Tears roll down my cheeks. He has no idea how much I needed to hear this from him tonight.

I don't want to wait another month to be with him and then see him only in secret for two months after that. I wipe my tears and pull up the contract on my phone. I've reread the

Boyfriend Clause over and over again. There has to be a way around this. Maybe I need to come at it from a different angle.

And then it hits me. Holy shit. I can't believe this never occurred to me before. I've been looking at this all wrong.

I quickly find Tanner's number and hit dial, praying the call goes through. He answers immediately. "Arizona? Is everything okay?"

"Everything is great. Do you have a minute?"

CHAPTER THIRTY

TWO WEEKS LATER

LAYTON

The past few weeks have been tough but at least there's some light at the end of the tunnel. Arizona is on her way from Bora Bora to Hawaii now for the last leg of her trip. Two more weeks, and then she'll be home. We'll have to be together in secret for another two months, but at least we'll be together.

While photos from their beach shoots leak daily, there have been very few of them out socially. I know my girl enough to know her smiles are fake. Sometimes Butch is touching her back when they're out for dinner, but her shoulders are always turned from him. I know what her face looks like when it's filled with love and affection, and I don't see it in any photo. I was a fool to think otherwise.

She's clearly doing the bare minimum required by her under her contract. She calls me every moment she can, sometimes three or four times a day. I think she's going out of her way to keep my mind at ease. I love her even more for that.

Thanksgiving with the Abbotts and all my friends was a fun, family day that I can only hope to have more of in the future. I sat down with both Quincy and Arizona's father and told them I plan to ask her to marry me after her contract with Fantasy Suits expires. They gave me their blessing. I've been brainstorming ideas, trying to come up with something more romantic than what I had planned for Thailand.

I've spent nearly every day since Thanksgiving at Linda's House. It's lifted me out of this depression I've been in since Arizona left and I broke my leg. My passion for spending time with those kids grows every time I'm there. It's made me think about what I want for my future. What my true calling might be.

When Henry isn't working, he comes with me. As it turns out, he's amazing with the kids. He's kind of a goofball himself, and they eat it up. I have a few ideas about getting him even more involved, but I want to talk to Arizona about it when she gets back. I want her as my partner in everything.

I hate how I acted those first few weeks after she left, letting my fear of abandonment rear its ugly head. I hate that I took it out on her. Never again. She's my angel.

I've done my best in the past two weeks to be nothing but supportive, trying to make it easy for her. I'm not the only one struggling with the separation. Missing Thanksgiving with her family and being away from home isn't easy. There's no need for me to add to her stress. I want to be strong for her.

I make myself dinner and get ready for Arizona's call when she lands in Hawaii. Her time zones are getting closer and closer. The end is near.

My phone rings and I see that it's Frederick from the front desk. "Hi, Frederick."

"Splendid evening, Master Lancaster. I hope I'm not disturbing your peaceful slumber. There's a Tanner Montgomery who wishes to have a visit with you. I suggested it was a late hour for a house call, but he insisted I ring you promptly."

I can't help but smile at his formality. "Thanks, Frederick. Send him up."

This is unexpected. I wonder why he's here. It's not that late, but it's also not normal for Tanner to come by at nine in the evening.

A few minutes later, he walks in and smiles. "Glad to see you dressed and showered. That's progress." He looks around. "And no smelly old takeout boxes. Even better."

I roll my eyes. "I had a pity party for a month. I'm getting it together now. Arizona will be home in two weeks." I point to my cast. "This monstrosity comes off two weeks later. I'm counting the seconds until both happen."

"You start physical therapy right away, right?"

"As long as the x-rays show that I'm healed, yes."

"Great. Are you going to try to get back into game shape?"

I shrug. "I'm not sure what I want. I held on tight to the Cougars for so long because it was the only family I had. I'm starting to see things a little differently now. Maybe there will be life for me after baseball."

He smiles. "I couldn't agree more." He grabs my jacket off the coat rack and throws it at me. "Put this on. We're going on a little field trip."

"Where to? It's late."

"What are you, eighty years old? You sound like Mr. Pole In My Ass Frederick. It's just after nine. You're fine. I have a surprise for you."

"A good surprise?"

He smirks. "I'm more than confident that you'll like it."

He mentions that he's parked out front, so we head out through the lobby. I notice Frederick's back to us, and he's on the phone. In the heaviest South Philly accent I've ever heard, he says, "Yas, ma. I heard yous. Drink a little wooder and eat a begel. Yous feels better. I'll stop by after dis fuckin' stoopid ass job."

Tanner and I look at each other in astonishment. Is that Frederick's normal voice? What the fuck?

We both start laughing hysterically. Frederick turns around and looks at us wide-eyed. He knows he's been busted.

He straightens his back and speaks into his phone. "Good day, Mother."

He lifts his head. "Pleasant evening, Master Lancaster."

I smile as I shake my head. "You're so busted, Frederick. Are you from South Philly?"

His face and shoulders drop. "Yas. No ones wood hire me wit my accent, so I created a new persons."

I nod in understanding. "It's cool. Please be yourself around me. I'll miss the stuffy Mr. Carson though. Maybe bring him back now and then, but moving forward, I want the real Frederick."

He slowly nods. "It's...umm...it's Freddie. Yous can call me Freddie."

I smile. "Will do."

We make our way out to Tanner's car and start driving. At some point, it's apparent that we're heading toward the stadium. "Are you making me clear out my locker already? I haven't officially decided that I'm retiring."

He lets out a laugh. "Not quite yet."

He pulls up to the executive entrance. I see a small light on in the lobby. The entire stadium is otherwise dark. He grabs my crutches for me and helps me out of the car. "Head on in. There's someone waiting for you."

"Are you going to stay out here and wait for me?"

"Just go, man."

With my crutches in toe, I make my way inside. The door to the building closes behind me. It's completely quiet and looks empty. I shout, "Hello? Is anyone here?"

As if in a dream, Arizona appears from around the corner. She's wearing jeans and her *#lovedbylayton* jersey. I suck in air before breathing, "Arizona?" Blinking a few times, I ask, "Is this real? Am I hallucinating?"

She smiles. Her unique, larger-than-life Arizona smile. My whole fucking heart practically explodes in happiness.

She starts running toward me. I want her to jump into my arms, but I know she won't because of my leg. She stops just as our bodies touch for the first time in six weeks. I immediately feel mine come back to life at the simple physical contact with her.

Her hands move up my chest as she looks up at me with tears in her blue-green eyes. "I've missed you."

Before I can answer, her lips meet mine in the

sweetest, most perfect kiss that has ever been. I drop my crutches and take her into my arms.

Her soft lips are on mine. I inhale her. My body's reaction is involuntary. I feel it in every nerve ending. I need her scent like I need oxygen.

Our tongues meet and I get to taste her for the first time in what feels like forever. It's everything.

We kiss and kiss and kiss. Time goes by and neither of us stops. We just keep kissing like the starved lovers we've been. Her fingers run through my hair, mine up and down her body, touching everywhere I can reach.

When the time comes to break apart, we don't go far. Our foreheads remain together. The wetness I thought was her tears is a mixture of both of our tears.

"How are you here? I'm still worried that this is a dream." I look around and yell, "Cheetah, are you here pranking me? Did you drug my dinner to make me hallucinate this?"

She lets out a small giggle. "I promise it's really me. They gave us forty-eight hours off. Some kind of equipment issue. We got the extra day while they wait for the replacement to be delivered so I jumped on the first plane available."

"It's a fifteen-hour flight."

"I'd gladly fly thirty hours to spend eighteen with you."

I pull her body as close to mine as I can. "I'd do it to spend one minute with you. I missed you so fucking much."

"I missed you too."

"It was like missing a part of my body that I need to survive."

She nods in understanding as she looks me up and

down. "You know, gray sweatpants are the Achilles heel of every woman on this planet. It's an unwritten, secret law."

The corners of my mouth raise as I make a mental note to order more gray sweatpants. "Is it *your* Achilles heel?"

"Every inch of you is my Achilles heel."

I run my hands under the back of her shirt. "Why are we here at the stadium and not home in my bed? I need your skin on mine."

She pulls her head away slightly and gives me her sexy smile. The one where I know that my dirty girl is here and that I'm about to experience unimaginable levels of pleasure. "Follow me, superstar."

"I'd follow you anywhere." I pick up my crutches and we make our way through the stadium and onto the field. I see a pile of blankets and pillows by home plate. I look at her in bemusement.

She bites her lip. "I think we have a little fantasy we'd both like to see play out at home plate. A certain promise I made a few months ago."

My cock practically pokes a hole in my sweatpants. She takes immediate notice. "I thought you'd like that."

"I like anything with you."

When we get to home plate, she turns to me. "Dance with me, superstar. Just one dance."

I nod as she presses a button on her phone. "Until I Found You" immediately starts playing. Knowing she had this planned brings more tears to my eyes. I'm such a mush for this woman.

I drop my crutches again and take my girl into my arms as we sway to the beat of the song we danced to on the night we met.

With her arms around my neck and our bodies moving in sync, she looks up at me. "I hate that you've doubted my love for you over the past six weeks. It hurt me."

I'm suddenly filled with so much shame. "I'm sorry. I've been a mess. I know I'm on my way down and out. He's on his way up. I started to wonder if he wasn't the better choice for you, but..."

"It's not your choice to make. It's mine. I didn't fall for Layton Lancaster the baseball player. Yes, maybe that was part of the initial attraction, but that's not love. Us playing and talking ball is something we have in common, like any other couple who has common interests. But we're so much more than that. I fell in love with Layton Eugene Lancaster, the man with a heart of gold. The man who makes me smile. The man who supports me, respects me, and treats me like a queen. The man who gives of himself, not for the accolades, but because he's filled with compassion and generosity. The man who makes me feel things I've never imagined feeling, who lights me on fire with a simple touch. The man who I not only see in my future but as my future."

She grabs my face. "I know you long for family and a sense of belonging. I'm your family now, Layton. My family is your family. One day in the future, when we're ready, we'll expand our family. Together. That's what I want. Is it what you want?"

I nod as tears fill my eyes. "It is. More than anything"

"I'm secure in our relationship. I wasn't in my past relationship, but I think it's because on some level I knew he wasn't the right one for me. Even though I probably should be a little insecure given the attention you garner, I simply don't feel that way with you. I know women throw themselves at you, but I trust you and I trust the depths of what we share. Moving forward, can you be secure in our love too? Can you trust me and what we have? Nothing and no one, especially a douchebag like Butch McVey, will *ever* cause me to stray from our path. *Our* path. Together. You and me."

"I promise."

We keep moving to the slow beat of the music as she continues, "Sometimes life throws you curveballs. But I believe everything happens for a reason. I thought my world was ending a year and a half ago, but now I wholeheartedly believe it was for the best. If things didn't happen as they did, you wouldn't have come into my life. Life threw us both a curveball two months ago, but I believe that someday we'll realize there was a reason for it. Things were so perfect for us. Too perfect. Maybe we needed to weather a storm to make sure our foundation is solid."

I nod. I'm so filled with emotion for this woman. I'm in awe of her strength. "You're right. I guess I was the last to arrive at that conclusion."

Her face lights up as we continue dancing to the music. "You know what happens when you're the last to arrive. Let's have it, superstar. Give me an obscure fact."

I rub her gorgeous face with the backs of my fingers. "You can fall in love in as little as four minutes. I think I fell for you that first night we met, within minutes." I wish I had the ring with me right now. I'd propose to her right here at home plate. "I love you so much."

"I love you too."

Without a word, she moves her lips to mine again, but this time it's not sweet. It's full of passion and need.

Six weeks of passion and need. A lifetime of passion and need.

She claws at my shirt as I move my tongue around her mouth and taste every inch of her sweetness. She gives it back to me in spades.

She bites down on my lower lip as her hands move to my sweatpants and pulls them down. My cock bounces free, impossibly hard and already visibly leaking for her. Desperate for her long-absent touch.

She looks down at it and licks her lips. "I've missed the sight of that perfection."

I can't help but grin widely. "Your brother was appalled by the size of my head."

She giggles. "Why was my brother looking at your dick?"

"He had to help me shower one day."

Her face turns serious. "That's my job, and can we not talk about him right now? I've been dreaming of buffing your helmet on home plate since the second I mentioned it months ago."

I chuckle at her expression as she drops to her knees and grips my cock. Her tongue makes a slow, sensual path from my balls to my tip. She worships every inch of me on the way up.

I love how fascinated she is with the head of my cock. She closes her eyes and licks around it several times like it's her favorite ice cream cone before I finally see it disappear between her lush lips.

My tip drags along the roof of her mouth as she gradually takes me deep. I can feel the moment her throat squeezes around me.

I grab onto her hair and begin to slowly thrust my

hips. "Six weeks of missing this perfect mouth. The way it takes my cock. No one does this better than you, sunshine."

She traces her tongue along every engorged vein as my cock slides in and out. She's taking me so fucking deep down her throat, her eyes are watering. I've never seen anything more beautiful.

She momentarily pulls away and mumbles, "Fuck my mouth. Give it to me. Deep," before taking me back inside.

I grab a fistful of her hair, much harder this time, and thrust my hips with fervor as I shove my cock deep down her throat until she gags on me.

She not only takes it but manages to apply suction. Her cheeks are hollow and she's moaning like I'm her favorite dessert.

I've been so starved for the touch of the love of my life. In a matter of minutes, I tell her I'm coming.

She doesn't release her grip as I shoot a hot, long load down her throat. It feels like it's unending. I can hear her choking on the volume, but she never pulls away.

I don't think I've ever felt more satisfied. It's like I expunged my body of all the sadness I've felt.

I rub her soft face with my hand as she pulls away and licks her lips. "I missed your taste."

"Not as much as I missed yours." I shove her to the ground, on top of the blankets.

I manage to maneuver myself down with my cast and quickly claw away all her clothing, desperate to get to her body. I remove mine as well. It's cold out, but my body is on fire for her.

Her legs spread in invitation, but I spread them

wider, as wide as they can go, wanting to see everything. I slowly run my fingers and eyes from her toes to her head. Her pink nipples are hard and taut. "All mine. Every inch of you. Mine to please. Mine to love."

She nods. "All yours. Always. Never doubt it again."

I position myself between her legs, feeling her wetness all over my stomach. My mouth and hands worship her full tits with the attention they deserve. Licking, sucking, nibbling. Those pink nipples that play on repeat in my dreams are finally back in front of me. She's so damn perfect.

My hand trembles as it trickles down her body. I think I'm still finding it hard to believe she's really home. That we're really here in the stadium doing this.

I run my fingers through her pussy and then immediately bring them to my nose for a deep inhale. My eyes roll back. "So fucking good."

As soon as I lick my fingers, I become ravenous to taste more of her. I slide down her body and bury my face in her pussy. I rub it around, covering myself in as much of her as I can. I know I don't have long with my girl. The need to be lathered in her when she leaves again is overwhelming.

I lick through her tasty essence. Despite coming moments ago, I immediately harden again. My need for her never wanes, not for a second. I'm addicted.

She pulls my hair and writhes beneath me. "Oh god, Layton, I've missed this. I've missed your mouth. Your tongue. Don't stop."

If she's feeling like I felt moments ago, she doesn't need any teasing. She undoubtedly wants to get right to the main act.

While sucking her clit into my mouth, I slide three fingers deep inside her and she lets out a loud moan. I can already feel her tightening around me. She's so worked up. I love it.

I know what my girl needs and where she needs it.

With my fingers still knuckle-deep, I pull my mouth off her. As soon as she lifts her head to protest, I slap her pussy. Hard.

Her back arches and she yells out as she comes so fucking strong and long. I curl my fingers to drag it out for her. If anyone is in or near this stadium, they heard her scream. She's going off like a fire hydrant. I'm covered in her juices. I revel in it.

She eventually collapses back down, completely spent. With heavy breaths, she mumbles, "I think I just floated."

I smile as I kiss my way up her body and nudge my tip at her entrance. "Are you ready for me, sunshine? It's been six weeks, one day, and thirteen hours."

She smiles at my precision and answers by wrapping her legs around me and lifting her hips. Her eyes widen. "What about your leg? Do you need me to be on top?"

"I'll be fucking my girl properly tonight. So hard that you'll be feeling it for the next two weeks until you come back home to me."

I wiggle until the head of my cock eventually breaks through. Getting it in is always the hardest part. Her eyes flutter. "I think I could come from just the h..."

I immediately push all the way in. She sucks in a breath, and rasps, "Nope, this is even better."

I bring my mouth to hers and lick around her lips, tasting her sweetness. I want to savor every second we have together on this short visit.

I begin my strokes in and out of her. We stare at each

other as our connection becomes so damn intense, I don't know if I can control myself. There's nothing better than the feeling of her under my body, wrapped around me again. Our two bodies becoming one.

We make love in a way we never have before. In a way that tells me something I already knew. That I'll never want to do this with anyone else for the rest of my life. It's more than just physical between us. I've had plenty of sex in my life, but nothing compares to what she and I share. A connection that shatters all preconceived notions of mine. It was always meant to be her, my soulmate.

In the glowing aftermath, we lay silent, with her in my arms. She looks up at me. "I bet you never thought I'd make good on my promise to buff your helmet at home plate."

I let out a laugh. "I can't say that I did, but I can say that I've imagined it more than a few times since you mentioned it. The real thing was even better than the fantasy."

She turns her head, taking in our surroundings. "You know what I've always wanted to do?"

"What?"

"Run the bases in this stadium. This place is practically a landmark."

"Well, Cinderella, here's your chance."

"Now?"

"Why not?"

"It's freezing cold and I'm naked."

"Live for the now, you never know what tomorrow will bring. Trust me, I would give anything to be able to run these bases right now." I sit up and grab her shoes. "Put these on and go. I'll be here under the blankets, ready to warm you when you get back. I know you'll get around very quickly."

She bites her lip as she contemplates it before nodding. "Fuck it. I'm doing it."

She slips into her shoes, stands completely naked, and starts sprinting toward first base.

I'm laughing as I yell out, "That looks faster than Cheetah. Keep going!"

She turns toward second base and grabs her tits so they stop bouncing. I'm hysterically laughing at the vision of her running the bases naked with her hands supporting her breasts. She's grinning from ear to ear, looking so carefree and happy.

In no time, she makes it back to me, quickly removes her shoes, and slips back into my arms under the blanket all while snort-laughing, my favorite sound in the world. She's shivering, but I immediately engulf her with my warm body and rub my hands all over her.

"Feel good, sunshine?"

Her smile is larger than life and lifts me into the clouds. "It felt amazing."

"I'll never see anyone running these bases again without the vision of you running naked in my mind."

"I'll never look at home plate the same again."

"That too."

She runs her fingers through my hair. "Can I admit something to you?"

"Always."

"I picked number eight because of you, not Yogi Berra."

I grin. "I knew it! Can I admit something to you?"

"Always."

"I started reading Cheetah's romance novels while you were gone. And I like them."

She giggles and I kiss her just because I can.

We go at it several times throughout the night. Neither of us want to sleep, knowing time is limited, but eventually sleep finds us.

CHAPTER THIRTY-ONE

ARIZONA

I'm awakened by a female voice cooing, "Ooh, he's even hotter in person."

I blink my eyes open as my face is hit with a rush of cold air. I immediately remember that I'm sleeping on home plate in the Cougars' stadium, unable to contain the feeling of contentment that I'm back in Layton's arms. What I don't understand is why I'm seeing double of Reagan Daulton standing over us.

I tap Layton, who's wrapped around me like a blanket. I croak out, "Wake up, superstar."

In his sexy, gravely morning voice, he manages, "No. If I wake up, you'll have to leave again." He squeezes me tight. "I'm never letting go."

"We have company."

He lifts his head off me, opens his eyes, and pinches his eyebrows together. "Do you see two of Reagan Daulton, or is it just me?"

There are legitimately two of her. One is wearing a blue pantsuit and the other pink.

Both Reagans laugh. The one in pink says, "I was right. Definitely hotter in person."

Blue Reagan elbows her in a teasing fashion. "Don't harass my employees."

I shake my head. "What is happening? Are you twins? Reagan, you have a twin?"

Blue Reagan smiles. "We get that a lot. This is my cousin, Jade." She points to pink Reagan, who apparently is named Jade. She's holding a can of something. I try to make out what it is.

My vision must be blurry. It can't be what it looks like. "What are you drinking, pink Reagan...err Jade?"

She holds up the can. "Pussy Juice. It's an *all-natural* energy drink. I love Pussy Juice in the morning. Layton, how about you? Do you drink Pussy Juice in the morning?"

I feel him smile into my neck before crooning, "Only if it's manufactured in Arizona."

Both Reagans start laughing. I can't help but join in.

Real Reagan pulls fake Reagan's arm. "Let them get dressed. Arizona, we'll meet you both in my office in ten minutes. Everyone is already there waiting for you."

I nod. "Thanks."

When they disappear, Layton sighs. "Shit. Are we in trouble for being here? Is this trespassing?"

I shake my head. "No. I arranged it with Reagan ahead of time. I scheduled a meeting with her and a few others for this morning."

"Who else is coming?"

"Tanner and Reagan's mom, Darian. She's a corporate attorney."

"What's the meeting about?"

I smile, excited to finally tell him what I've been working on. "I've spent two months staring at that damn contract with Fantasy Suits, trying to find a loophole. Two weeks ago, one occurred to me. I ran it by Tanner, and he loved it. He set a few things in motion for me. Reagan's mom specializes in these kinds of contracts. I should have hired her in the first place. I won't make that mistake again. We're going to discuss it with her, and if you're game, the days of Michael Longley and Butch McVey pulling our strings are quickly coming to an end. And we get to burn Fantasy Suits for being assholes on the way out."

His face lights up like it's Christmas morning. "Whatever it is, I'm game."

Thirty minutes later, Layton is grinning like a Cheshire Cat. His reaction far exceeded my expectations, in the best way possible.

Reagan's mom, Darian, shakes her head in disbelief. "I can't say this would have ever occurred to me. It's brilliant. Maybe you should go to law school, Arizona."

I can't help but smile. "Maybe I will."

"It's a little risky, but in my opinion, you're legally correct. If they go after you, I think you'll prevail, but that won't prevent them from possibly suing you. I just want you to be aware of the risks."

I've considered it over the past two weeks. I'm confident in this course of action, willing to move forward and let the chips fall where they may.

Reagan leans back in her chair and steeples her fingers. I can see her deep in thought for a few moments. "We'll back you, Arizona. We owe you that much for everything you've done for this team. If they come after you, we'll underwrite your losses. You have my word."

My eyes widen. "Wow. That's very generous. It could be a lot of money."

She shrugs. "I'm pretty sure I'll benefit greatly from your plan. There's no reward without a little risk. I'll roll the dice with you." She winks. "We're in this together."

THREE WEEKS LATER

Tonight is the first big promotional event for Fantasy Suits. We're in Los Angeles. They're going over the top with a huge party to celebrate the first few ads, which dropped this week. They look good, but not as good as the *Sports Illustrated* cover of Layton and me. Butch and I simply don't have the chemistry that Layton and I share. There are certain things you just can't fake.

On some level, Fantasy Suits must now realize that they should have waited a few months for Layton to heal. The ads would have been so much hotter. Layton and I sizzle on and off the pages. We always have. There's no denying that.

Layton begged the doctors to take his cast off a few days early, wanting to be at his best for tonight. The doctors acquiesced on the condition that if the x-ray didn't show complete healing, they'd get to put a new cast back on.

He agreed, and fortunately, the x-ray showed that he was completely healed. He's walking with a cane now, which should only last a few weeks as he regains muscle and agility in the leg.

At the allotted time, Butch knocks on my hotel door. I stand to answer it, but Layton holds up his hand. "Allow me."

I blow him a kiss, knowing how much he's been anticipating this moment. Maybe even more than I have. "Go right ahead."

Layton opens the door, looking ridiculously handsome in his tuxedo, with a huge smile on his face. "Hey, Butch. We'll be ready in a moment."

The look on Butch's face is priceless. Shock isn't a big enough word.

"Umm, I don't think you should come, Lancaster. I wouldn't want Arizona to have issues with her contract."

Layton winks. "You let us worry about that." He turns back to me. "Sunshine? You ready?"

"I am, superstar."

I stand in my long, revealing red gown, picked by the executives at Fantasy Suits. It's not as special as a Bouvier design, but I don't mind it too much. It's very flattering and Layton seems to be enjoying it. He can tear it off my body later if he wants. I don't care if it gets ruined.

He takes my hand in his and kisses it. "You look radiant. Edible." I see pure hunger in his eyes. Yep, this dress is getting torn off me later. I have butterflies in my stomach just thinking about it, but that's nothing new for me when I'm around Layton. He always gives me butterflies in my stomach.

I flash Layton a playful smile, and then purposefully give Butch a fake one. "Butch. Let's get this over with. Layton wants to devour me. I don't like to keep him waiting."

Layton loudly whispers so Butch can hear, "I'm definitely ripping this off you later."

I giggle as we head down the elevator and out of our hotel.

The three of us sit in the limo on the way to the venue. Butch is deliciously, awkwardly silent, typing away on his phone. Layton and I make googly eyes at each other, whispering and laughing the whole time. His hands haven't left my body. Hands that have the green light to do as they please to me. I catch Butch glancing at Layton's hands on me a few times. Yep, buddy, this is what it looks like when a woman wants to be touched by a man. Take note.

The limo arrives at the site of the event. I see Michael Longley standing there, impatiently waiting. He's pacing with a worried look on his face. A frantic look. Butch must have given him the heads-up that Layton is here. We couldn't have scripted this any better.

The limo door is opened before the vehicle even stops. Michael practically dives in. Pointing at Layton but looking at me, he shouts, "He can't be here! This is a breach of your contract. We'll sue you for every penny you have and every penny you'll ever earn."

I maintain a calm demeanor, having played this moment over and over in my mind for more than a month. I want to word it perfectly. "Can you tell me *exactly* what the breach is?"

His eyes widen in frustration. "You know damn well it's the Boyfriend Clause. *We* choose your boyfriend. You can't appear in public with any other boyfriends for two more months and you know it!"

"I'm well aware of that. I'm here with Butch, your chosen boyfriend. I'm happy to attend anything you'd like me to attend with him. I haven't gone back on that in the slightest."

"Layton can't be here as your boyfriend!"

I deadpan, "He's not."

Michael sighs in annoyance. "He's right here. I'm not blind."

"I'm sorry. You misunderstood me. He's not my *boyfriend*. He's my *husband*. I've run your wording by several attorneys. It's clear that I can't publicly have another *boyfriend*, you were *very* specific about that language in the contract, maybe a little *too* specific. Michael, you know as well as I do that there's no language about a *husband*. Oh, and can you please change my name on all the promotional materials? I now go by Arizona Abbott Lancaster. Or Mrs. Layton Lancaster. Whichever you prefer is fine with me."

I give him a huge smile. One I've been sitting on for weeks as this plan and this precise moment took shape in my mind.

Michael's face drops. He knows we've got him. There's nothing he can do. His look of defeat tells me that no lawsuit is coming my way. He poorly worded the contract and now he'll have to live with the ramifications.

Layton takes my hand and kisses my rings, making them obvious to both Michael and Butch. "Mrs. Lancaster, shall we?" He turns to Butch. "You can take her right arm. That's for the boyfriend. The left is all mine. The husband."

I was nervous to suggest marriage that day in Reagan's office. I wasn't sure if Layton was ready for it. I was wrong. *Very* wrong. He was more than ready. He agreed in under two seconds and then immediately took me to his apartment, where a ring was already waiting. He got down on one knee to officially propose. Well, he got down as best he could with his cast. It was kind of adorable watching his determination to get down on his knee. The fact that he had already purchased the ring set my mind at immediate ease. The fact that he had already asked for blessings from both Quincy and my father was everything.

He told me of his original plan to propose in Thailand. I'm sad we didn't have our special moment there, but we've got a lifetime of memories to make.

Per my instructions, Tanner filed the necessary marriage license paperwork before my short visit to Philly three weeks ago. Reagan was able to marry us right away. Apparently, she's an ordained minister, having married a few members of her family over the years. We quietly got married before I boarded the plane back to Hawaii to finish out the shooting portion of the contract.

It was an easy two weeks for Layton and me, as we spoke constantly, planning the big reveal.

We've kept it a secret from everyone, which was hard, but Tanner is issuing a press release as soon as we text him, which I plan to do right now. We'll celebrate with our friends and family when this stupid contract is over and we have nothing hanging over our heads. Layton also wants to walk down the aisle without a cane, which should be about that same timeframe.

He's still uncertain of his future in baseball, but the one thing we *do* know about our future is that it's together. My fantasy man is now forever my reality.

EPILOGUE

THREE AND A HALF YEARS LATER

LAYTON

"Wave to Momma, angel."

In Ryan's sweet little voice, she yells, "Hi, Momma," as she waves her hand enthusiastically.

Despite our little girl and me being in the stands, Arizona hears us, turns around, and waves back with a huge smile on her face. The smile that still makes me weak in the knees. It's so big we can see it through her catcher's mask.

I look down at our two-year-old daughter, who's the spitting image of her mother, as she sits on my lap and takes in her surroundings. How many little girls get to watch their mother play in a gold medal game at the Olympics? Not many. I hope Ryan always remembers this.

I've taken about a thousand pictures to make sure she does.

I have a small moment of sadness knowing this is Arizona's last game ever. She had already planned to retire after the Olympics, but her being pregnant right now only solidified that for her. We intended to begin trying after the games, but life happens, and she's a few weeks along. I'm a nervous wreck watching her out there, praying she doesn't have any big collisions behind the plate, but it was her decision to play while pregnant, and I support her wholeheartedly.

I never played baseball again after my leg injury. While I don't think I could have ever played catcher considering the damage to my leg, I probably could have batted and played first base. I simply lost the desire. The Cougars and my teammates were my family for so many years, I was terrified of letting go. Of being alone. But once Arizona Abbott Lancaster came into my life, the need to desperately cling on to baseball dissipated. I played so well the last few months of my career, and the team made it to the World Series. I wanted those to be my final playing moments. I got to go out on top.

I also truly love to watch Arizona play. Retiring enabled me to be at every game of hers. I haven't missed a single game since the day of my injury. Even when Ryan was an infant, I watched with her strapped to my chest, sleeping soundly.

I spent the past few years on the coaching staff of the Anacondas. We've won the championship all five years the Anacondas have been in existence. The team and the league are now thriving. I love that I played some small part in its success.

They moved this past season up a few months to

accommodate the players in the league competing in the Olympics. It was that or lose them come time for the Olympics. It was a smart decision.

Arizona and I also founded a charity that helps kids in both group homes and foster homes join baseball *and* softball leagues. All are age and skill-level appropriate. It assists them with costs and transportation. We run several tournaments throughout the year as fundraisers, attracting huge crowds because of our famous friends helping out. It keeps us busy in the off-season, and Henry busy every day. We made him the director of the charity, and he's thrived in that role, finally finding his true calling. He's never been more stable, and my days of worrying about him are behind me.

Besides our charity, we constantly field offers for us to model all types of clothing together, especially bathing suits and lingerie. Our issue of *Sports Illustrated* became their all-time best-selling issue. The demand for us to model as a couple skyrocketed and has never waned. We accept a handful of offers each year, usually those being shot in exotic locations. Our heat and chemistry always leap off the page. I suppose there's just something special about watching two people with storybook passion. Advertisers more than recognize it. It never fails to excite me to see what others see when they look at us. Even when Arizona was pregnant, the demand was there for her to model maternity clothing. No woman has ever looked more beautiful than my wife while pregnant with Ryan.

Quincy plops down next to me looking exhausted. His daughter is already squirming in his lap. "This kid is going to be the fucking death of me."

Ryan gasps and places her little hands on her hips.

"Uncle Q, you said a bad word."

"Shit."

"Another. That's two funny facts you have to tell me."

"Hmm. Let me think. One, there's nothing soft about softball. It's only called softball because it started as an indoor sport with a softer ball. Once it moved outdoors, the ball was hard, but they never changed the name."

Ryan turns back to me. "Is that true, Daddy?"

"Yep. If you think about it, it's kind of a silly name for the sport."

She turns back to Q. "What else? You owe me two."

"Aunt Ripley was a baby in her mommy's belly the first time softball was a sport in the Olympics."

"Like my mommy has a baby in her belly now?"

I have no idea how Ryan knows that. We didn't tell her. She must have overheard us talking about it.

Quincy snaps his head to me. I smile while holding my index finger to my lips letting him know that it's a secret.

He looks down at Kaya. "You've had it easy with Ryan. I hope you get a red-headed devil child like mine."

I let out a laugh. It's true. Ryan is the easiest child ever. She's spent most of her first two years either on a softball field or at some beach location watching us have our pictures taken, with her even being included in an ad campaign or two. I think it tires her out. Or maybe she's just mild-mannered. She's curious though, absorbing everything around her. I suppose it's not shocking that she knows we're having another baby. She misses nothing.

Kaya, on the other hand, is a raging lunatic of a kid. She's been causing trouble since the very beginning, but that's a story for another day.

My in-laws sit down on the other side of me. Ryan leans over to hug and kiss them both.

A few years ago, they hired someone to manage the store. They began to travel and visit more often. Arizona and Quincy both love having them around. They've even mentioned moving to the East Coast a few times.

When he visits, Paul works with the kids at Linda's House, teaching them carpentry. He's mentioned wanting to do more of that in the future.

We all enjoy the exciting, back-and-forth game. Well, Paul, Pamela, Ryan, and I do as we watch on. Ryan is mesmerized seeing her mom out there. Almost as much as I am. She can't wait until she's old enough to be on a team. Of no surprise, she wants to be a catcher. She already has a good arm for her age.

Quincy has to chase Kaya up and down the stands throughout most of the game. He hasn't been able to watch very much. I catch the ladies on the field laughing at it a handful of times.

I feel my phone buzz and look down at the incoming text.

> Cheetah: What's happening? There's a fucking reception issue at our game. I'm going nuts. I'm gonna get my ass kicked for texting in the dugout, but this is bullshit. They promised us updates.

Cheetah still plays baseball for the Cougars. They're mid-season, so he couldn't be here.

> Me: We're up by one run going into the last inning.

Cheetah: Sweet.

Cheetah: Yes! It just went live on our
screen. Watching now.

There are two outs. The batter from Japan steps into
the batter's box. Ripley is on the mound. The pitch
comes in and the batter swings. It's a hard-hit ball on the
ground. Kam dives toward third base to stop it from
rolling into the outfield, gets up on her knees, and fires it
to first base for the final out.

The crowd goes nuts, yelling and clapping. Arizona
runs out to Ripley with her hands raised, as does the rest
of the team. Ryan is jumping up and down with
excitement.

I hear my phone pinging and look down.

Cheetah: Tell Kam no one is better on their
knees than her. She can get back on her
knees again when she gets home next
week.

I laugh as I shake my head. Cheetah never changes,
not that I'd want him to.

As soon as the pile of players clears off Arizona, she
jogs toward us with that big smile of hers. I think my
heart skips a beat. This woman has done it to me since
the day we met.

She leans over the front partition and kisses me.

I touch her face with one free hand, the other holding
Ryan, and mumble into her mouth, "I'm so proud of you,
sunshine."

She mumbles back, "Thank you, superstar."

She pulls away, takes Ryan into her arms, and walks

back out toward the celebration. Ryan is giggling like crazy, thrilled to be joining the fun with the team. What a special moment for them both.

I snap photos of the celebration, looking on at my beautiful family with tears in my eyes. I'm a lucky man.

A few hours later, Ryan and I watch as the team receives their gold medals. Seeing the person you love achieve their lifetime goal is just about the most rewarding thing you can imagine.

I look at Ryan in my arms, watching her mother with awe. "Ryan, your mommy worked her whole life for this. Winning an Olympic gold medal was her dream since she was your age."

Ryan nods in understanding. "What was your dream, Daddy?"

I toggle my eyes between her and Arizona. "I'm looking at it."

THE END

WANT a glimpse into Arizona and Layton's future? Check out the extended epilogue.

ACKNOWLEDGMENTS

To Arizona and Layton: Thank you for allowing me to dive into sports romances. Baseball and softball are near and dear to me. Arizona, you are a trailblazer as the first softball playing FMC in a romance novel. Way to slay!

To the Queen, TL Swan: This amazing journey would never have begun if not for you and your selfless decision to help hundreds of women. You are a shining example of the girl power quotes I place in each dedication. This crazy and unexpected new path in my life has brought me so much happiness. I owe it all to you. Please know that I try every single day to pay it forward.

To Lakshmi, Thorunn, Mindy, and Brittany: You're my daily sounding boards. You are my beta bitches and "porn friends." Your constant advice, counsel, guidance, and therapy keep me sane. Thank you for being such *good girls* and supporting me.

To Jade Dollston, Carolina Jax, and L.A. Ferro: You are my bookish besties. Our daily texts are my lifeline. I love the support we have for each other. I REALLY love that we are doing a project together. Book Boyfriend Builders for life!

To My OG Beta Readers Stacey and Fun Sherry: Thank you for being there for me since day one. You've been my biggest and hottest cheerleaders every single step of the way.

To The B!tch Squad Members: Thank you for flooding my phone with notifications and making me smile every single day. I continue to marvel at your support and appreciate every ounce of it. Please keep loving my books.

To Chrisandra and K.B. Designs: **Chrisandra**: Thank you for making me feel illiterate. That's what makes you such a great editor. Thank you for GIFs indicating that you want to unalive me for using italics on song names. **Kristin**: Thank you for helping this artistically challenged woman. I love that I popped your cherry on this book with the illustrated cover. You hit it out of the park!

To My Family: I truly feel bad for you. An immature mother and wife can't be easy. To my daughters, thank you for tolerating me (ish). Thank you for telling everyone you know that your mom writes sex books. I appreciate that by the time you were each six, you were more mature than me. To my handsome husband, thank you for your blind support. You never question my sanity, which can't be easy. But let's face it, you do reap the benefits of the fact that I write sex scenes all day long. There's a lot of you in Layton Lancaster (the good stuff, not the bad).

ABOUT THE AUTHOR

AK Landow lives in the USA with her husband, three daughters, one dog, and one cat (who was chosen because his name is Trevor). She enjoys reading, now writing, drinking copious amounts of vodka, and laughing. She's thrilled to have this new avenue to channel her perverted sense of humor. She is also of the belief that Beth Dutton is the greatest fictional character ever created.

AKLandowAuthor.com

ALSO BY AK LANDOW

Signed Books: aklandowauthor.com

Made in United States
North Haven, CT
04 July 2024

54389270R10252